atmospheric masterpiece, blending together a quest for a missing manuscript and a missing mother with the bond two sisters have with each other. Chilling, addicting, haunting, and truly marvelous, *White Fox* is the kind of mystery that brilliantly mixes multiple forms of writing: news stories; beautiful prose; and an engaging final film script of a woman who has been lost for ten years. Sometimes the greatest monsters hide right in front of you, and Manon and Thaïs are just discovering this as they hunt to find their mother. Written beautifully and intricately spun, *White Fox* is sure to be beloved by all who get their hands on this golden work."

—CODY ROECKER, bookseller at The Novel Neighbor

"This book is addicting. Every page, each new word, made me want to read that much faster. Reading it felt like tumbling down the best kind of rabbit hole. Manon and Thaïs are such beautiful literary foils, and such realistic teen sisters. It was beautiful and ominous and awe-inspiring all at once. Faring is incredibly gifted, and the world will be that much richer when it gets this book."

—CASS MOSKOWITZ, bookseller at Books of Wonder

"Sara Faring's second novel somehow manages to top her first! *White Fox* is a combination of *Revenge* and *Night Film*, with the added bonus of that mysterious Hollywood glamour we all love so much."

—ISABELLA OGBOLUMANI, bookseller at Buffalo Street Books

"Atmospheric and thrilling in the vein of Marisha Pessl's terrifying *Night Film*, Sara Faring's *White Fox* weaves an eerie, mesmerizing spell as sisters Manon and Thaïs, haunted by their mother's long-ago disappearance and their business magnate father's emotional abandonment and subsequent death, return to their isolated Mediterranean home to find the truth of what happened to their family. Their digging into the past, guided in part by clues in their mother's last screenplay, uncovers scandals and mysteries and dark secrets that will keep you turning pages madly in this twisting tale of a family that is not at all what it seems."

—JOY PREBLE, bookseller at Brazos Books

WHITE FOX

SARA FARING

【Imprint】
MAKE YOUR MARK

NEW YORK

[Imprint]
MAKE YOUR MARK

A part of Macmillan Publishing Group, LLC
120 Broadway, New York, NY 10271

Library of Congress Cataloging-in-Publication Data is available.

ISBN 978-1-250-30452-0 (hardcover) / ISBN 978-1-250-30453-7 (ebook)

Our books may be purchased in bulk for promotional, educational, or business use.
Please contact your local bookseller or the Macmillan Corporate and Premium Sales Department
at (800) 221-7945 ext. 5442 or by email at MacmillanSpecialMarkets@macmillan.com.

Book design by Carolyn Bull

Imprint logo designed by Amanda Spielman

First edition, 2020

1   3   5   7   9   10   8   6   4   2

fiercereads.com

Steal this prize and doom yourself to a life as rhubarb, rhubarb, rhubarb,
reeking of the foulest forgotten honey wagon all the while.

For my favorite human,
C, with the crushed-ice eyes
and the laugh like a song
I want to play on repeat

BOY

CLIP FROM *NOT ANOTHER GIRL OF ICE* (1978)

Mireille Foix, age sixteen, winner of the Best Actress Award at the 1978 Cannes Film Festival

[Film rolls]

> *The scene opens in a midnight wood, dense and tangled, its rotting breath palpable. The locals call it Delirium Forest, and it's famous for devouring people whole, for reshaping the most solid of realities. A figure is visible inside, the moss-choked air around it glowing like an aura. The figure seems to float above the forest's gnarled roots, impervious to its thorns, its nettles, its spines and raking branches. As the figure moves deeper inside, its luminescence fades, and a deep, guttural buzzing builds.*

At the fringe of the forest, a scummy parking lot, tongued by sagging bags of trash. And there, beside them: a broken form, lying in a growing pool of his own blood, thick as ink. A black cat edges around the mess, sniffing.

"Leave it," a woman's voice hisses, a static burst, and the cat skitters away.

The woman's wearing a ripped white camisole and fuchsia hotpants; she's gripping a tire iron, white-knuckled and red-eyed. Platinum hair. Chapped, bitten lips. Without even seeing her whole face, we know she is beautiful and that her beauty is like a fishhook: delicate, sharp, designed with ancient wisdom to hurt, to trap. She rests the tire iron on her shoulder, and its rusted edge drips fresh crimson freckles on her and the torn camisole strap.

The woman: She's no more than sixteen, all bruised skin and bird bones, the icy-blond wig on her head askew. Shivering in muddy boots.

She doesn't notice us.

She's staring into the woods. Faintly luminous, still. The humming grows louder, more ominous, and the woman leaves the safety of the bloodied asphalt to meet it. Her eyes never stray from the wild deep as she is guided away from us. Away from us, and into the carnivorous dark beyond. The droning intensifies, into its cracking and fizzing crescendo, until the woman finally—disappears.

[Film stops]

Mireille Foix possesses Grace Kelly's elegance crossed with Audrey Hepburn's mischievousness, Katharine Hepburn's wit, and Marilyn Monroe's pure, languid sex. She was born and raised on the mysterious Mediterranean island of Viloxin, and her idyllic childhood—spent free-diving for scallops with her fisherman father (now deceased) in a whitewashed cottage on the forested fringes of a minuscule seaside town—is nothing short of mythical. Today, she is her country's greatest cultural export and patron, thanks to her Foix Institute. She is also the last Star with a capital S, deemed the most beautiful, charismatic, and intuitive woman living today by a swath of Tinseltown A-listers. Mireille Foix is a goddess, come to Hollywood on her golden Viloki scallop shell.

—Vogue magazine, 1996

To most, the name Henry Hammick still conjures an image of a shadow in a lab coat: mysterious, bizarre, impenetrable. What were we to make of this monolith of a man who left behind his family, his career, and his home country to start over on an isolated, volcanic Mediterranean island half a world away? He moved to Viloxin in the 1970s at the age of thirty and never looked back. Since launching his groundbreaking pharmaceutical company, Hero Pharmaceuticals, Hammick's team has single-handedly introduced several history-changing medications and medical devices, most notably Ladyx, a treatment that slows the growth of many cancers.

Hammick has immersed himself in everything Viloki, from studying the largely unknown island history and social practices to Viloxin's poignant poetry and burial customs. His command of the local language, Vilosh, has awed scholars. And now, after earning Viloki citizenship for himself, Henry Hammick has taken a traditional Viloki name for legal reasons: Hëró. Yes, it's pronounced *Hero*, just like the name of his company. But don't hold it against him: Hëró

Hammick, founder of Hero Pharmaceuticals—now worth billions of newly minted euros—is this decade's God among men.

—*Time* magazine, 1997

The Foix-Hammicks believe Viloxin is their Camelot. Their Eden. Do I find this realistic? No. I certainly do not. They know nothing of this island, nor even of themselves. My family has been here hundreds of years, documenting its darkest nooks and its myriad depths, and I can assure you: The Foix-Hammick family does not venture below the surface in any of its endeavors—*especially* Mireille Foix Hammick's so-called *White Fox* film script. It is no Holy Grail. And no script—no family—concerns me. Despite their best efforts, they too shall disappear from our city, from our volcanic hills, from our lavender-scented meadows—in due time.

—Antella Arnoix, March 2009

RUNAWAY FOIX ON VILOXIN!
POLICE COMMISSIONER CONCLUDES
THAT MIREILLE ABANDONED HER CUBS.
—*The Viloki Sun*, July 2009

One year ago today, beloved film star Mireille Foix disappeared from her grand country home, Stökéwood, taking with her a crocodile purse, an Hermès scarf, one pair of calfskin gloves—and the only known copy of her secret film script, *White Fox*. The *Viloki Sun* gained exclusive access to a segment of this script, photographed by Foix's former manager, Daria Grendl, in the months preceding Foix's disappearance. It is speculated by some that *White Fox* possesses clues to Mireille Foix's current whereabouts—or to a shocking discovery she made before she vanished—as it eerily references the very items that went missing with her. Some call it the Viloki Holy Grail, claiming that Mireille Foix hid the secrets to building the ideal society inside.

Read on to discover for yourself a chilling excerpt, transcribed here from Grendl's photo. The world may never have the chance to see what might be this legend's greatest work.

Captor opens White Fox's red purse and looks through the contents.

> CAPTOR (V.O.)
> You say you are strong, but I know you cannot stomach the polluted mess in the mirror. Cannot reconcile it with the beautiful fantasy world you created around yourself.

Captor examines a pair of calfskin gloves, a wallet. Captor finds photographs.

> CAPTOR (V.O.) (CONT'D)
> A world of unbridled hope, of answered prayers, of selfless goodness, of smiling children—

Captor flips through photographs, finding one of smiling children. Two girls, beautiful girls, their identities unknown.

                    CAPTOR (V.O.)
          How sweet the photograph was, inside
          your ruined red purse.

Captor reenters chamber with clients inside and
watches White Fox, now stone-faced.

                    CAPTOR (V.O.)
          Evolve or die, White Fox, dear. Evolve
          or die.

Who is this captor? Grendl is staying mum.

"I simply thought it would be edifying for investigators
and those who loved Mireille alike to understand her mindset
prior to her departure," Grendl explains. "It should be plain to
readers that a troubled Mireille felt trapped and ran off."

Read on for Grendl's exclusive list of Mireille's Viloxin
haunts—ideal for those seeking a warm weather escape!
                              —*The Viloki Sun*, May 24, 2010

HERO TO HERMIT! "HE'S SICK, PARANOID,
IRRESPONSIBLE—AND HE REFUSES TO LEAVE
HIS STÖKÉWOOD HOME," SAYS HERO PHARM
BOARD MEMBER.

                              —*The Viloki Sun*, January 2014

NONI
NEW YORK, 2014

Two blocks from our home, an underground psychic was waiting for us with a secret message. Her basement shop blends into the row of dirt-encrusted town houses on West Tenth Street during the day, but at night the shop's magical features come alive: carefully painted wood paneling; a neat row of budding, overgrown plants; and a buzzing neon sign of a purple crystal ball.

"You have the money, right?" Tai whispers to me, between blowing on her hands, that shock of cherry hair in her face.

It's been five years since Mama disappeared, but strangers still notice us on the street sometimes, whispering "Is that . . . ?" to their friends with that sideways-sneak look, so we had decided to wear plain brown wigs tonight to stay incognito. But then Tai wanted to use the red one from her devil costume, and Tai gets what she wants. *You're only thirteen*, Aunt Marion cried, when she saw the crop top and

7

leather miniskirt my sister was wearing. *Mama wore a thong swimsuit in a movie when she was thirteen*, Tai snapped back.

I hike up my loose jeans and pull the envelope out of my fleece sweatshirt's kangaroo pocket. "Two hundred big ones," I whisper back. We had been saving for months.

Tai grabs my shoulders and squeals, this infectious grin spreading from one bubble gum–pink cheek to the other. There's so much innocent hope in her lined-and-mascaraed blue eyes, so much it makes me quiver, but of course I'm smiling back before I know it. Tonight could give us clues, if not answers. My stomach hasn't felt settled in days.

Tai follows me down the steps, and we push inside the storefront—a bell jingles. The entry room is dark: patchy red velvet seating and finger-thick vines crawling everywhere. The smell of patchouli mixed with something heady and sweet, like cloves in hot wine. A stained, paisley curtain fringed in golden thread blocks our view into the back. A lone television on the wall plays a grainy video of spooky nature scenes on silent loop: a duck moving across a shadowy pond, wet red leaves falling from a tree, a lush forest that looks familiar.

"Hello?" Tai calls, scratching at her wig's netting.

Wind chimes tinkle in the back. I pull Tai onto the lumpy love seat up front just as a black cat pushes through the curtain—a furry lump in its mouth—and bounds up onto its window seat in between two ferns. It drops its catch and paws at it.

"Ew," Tai whispers, before rubbing at her bare legs. "What time is it?"

"It's eight-oh-one," I whisper back, just as *she* walks through the curtain, short and squat and dressed in black silk from head to toe: the imposing Madame Morency.

"Carmela!" She claps at the cat. "You promised your days hunting young and delicate creatures were over."

8

The cat yowls, and Madame Morency notices the two of us, clutching hands on the love seat, our hearts beating too fast in the small room.

"You're my eight o'clock, ladies?" she says in her deep rasp, head tipping to the side. "Sisters. You're very young. What loss could you have possibly suffered?"

Tai's purple nails dig into my skin.

"How old are you, exactly?"

"Aren't you a psychic?" Tai says, before I even open my mouth. "We're eighteen," she adds, with that confidence of hers that springs up from nowhere.

Madame Morency's lip quirks. "I will not begin any session without honesty and an open mind. It's best you see yourselves out."

"There's no legal age requirement to visit a fortune-teller in New York State," I reply, sweating hands squirrelling into my sweatshirt pocket. My lips snag on my braces. "Telling fortunes in general is a class B misdemeanor, anyway, though, and—"

"Fine," Tai interrupts, just as Madame Morency crosses her arms at me. "We're just kids. But we did lose someone important when we were really young. And we made this appointment because we need your help to reach her." She holds out the envelope of money. "Won't you help us?"

Madame Morency inhales and exhales, and as she does, something behind her eyes softens. I know it's not just pity. Everyone softens when they look at Tai: Her daintiness, her toughness, and her beauty combine to make her special. Mireille Foix Hammick–special.

"Follow me," Madame Morency says, taking the envelope and stuffing it into her waistband before shuffling back through the curtain.

Tai grabs my wrists and squeals again, eyes flashing brighter than neon.

9

The cramped back room is lit by dozens of candles. Two book-shelves overflow with rotten-smelling books and strange artifacts borrowed from a nightmare: a set of golden teeth, vials of amber liq-uid swirling with many-legged creatures, and a tiny, misshapen skull (the cat's victim comes to mind). We settle at a rickety, black cloth–covered table, across from Madame Morency, who peers at us with the heavy-lidded yet sharp eyes of someone who sees too much every day.

"Where are your cards?" Tai asks, examining the empty table before us, like something will push through the cloth at any moment. "Or, like, your crystal ball?"

"I do things differently." Madame Morency extends her veined, wrinkled hands across the table. "I don't even need my eyes to have the sight. Now, give me your hands. One each. Don't be afraid."

Without hesitation, Tai gives her one, while I wipe the sweat off my left palm onto my jeans and reach out. Her skin is smooth and soft and fine, like a child's.

Madame Morency shuts her eyes, humming to herself, and a breeze picks up, blowing through the curtain, flickering the candles, and bringing to life the blackened wind chime in the corner. I feel a chill; *wasn't the door closed?* Tai looks at me, her eyes wide with the thrill of it.

"Silence," Madame Morency snaps, and even the wind chime goes quiet. A minute ticks past, the kind that feels as gluey long as an hour. The air is thick with lost memories, with that decayed scent of crum-bling brick walls.

When Madame Morency speaks again, her voice is a curious, rasping thing coming from the deepest part of her. "Why did you tell me your mother was dead, girls?"

The hair on the back of my neck pricks up.

"We didn't say that," Tai whispers back.

We didn't say anything about mothers at all.

"The message I am receiving is not coming from the other side," Madame Morency continues, her hand cooling in mine. "It's coming from the film between our worlds, the pond scum separating us from them. It says she is not gone."

I can feel Tai swallow next to me, see the goose bumps colonizing every inch of bare flesh. Her fingers are pale in Madame Morency's grip, and I can't feel my own. My eyes are glued to the woman in front of us, with her tightly shut eyes and her craggy face. Looking for signs of mystical truth, of anything at all I can cling to hard.

It says she is not gone.

"Her energy is mirrored across the globe," she continues. "So strong in places that a lesser psychic would mistake it for the true source. When and where did you last see her?" Madame Morency asks in this wheedling, odd voice. "Be precise."

I know we both remember: Mama tucked us into bed, wet-eyed, that night at Stökéwood, five years ago. Tears from a migraine, she'd said, shrugging on her favorite gray cashmere housecoat, petal-pink gloves in hand. I didn't know if she was telling the truth then, and I still don't. But I never saw her again, so I couldn't ask.

Tai opens her mouth to answer, but I stiffly shake my head. Dad told us never to share details with strangers. Aunt Marion and Uncle Teddy, too.

"I see her clearest in a hidden tower, extending into the sky," Madame Morency rasps, when we don't reply, and even though this means nothing to me, Tai stifles a squeak. She reaches for my free hand with hers, and her bones crunch into mine as Madame Morency speaks. "Otherwise, so many men contaminate her space. How is one supposed to keep a clear head with so many men and their opinions?"

She exhales slowly. "Does a red handbag mean anything to you? Cut from the skin of a creature that crawls?"

My stomach falls, but I feel weightless and chilled. I hear the news report in my head: *She took with her a red crocodile handbag with a pearl clasp—*

But anyone could know that.

"I need as much information as you can provide," Madame Morency continues in a strange purr. "Don't be afraid, girls. This is all part of the process."

Tai's eyes beg me to let her spill the truth. But I'm already wrenching my hand from the psychic and standing up. In my mind, halfway out the door. This woman is a trickster, a liar, a fraud. My blood rings in my ears. I'm the big sister, and I should've known better. I'm trembling with barely contained hurt, tears bubbling into my eyes. I take Tai's wrist, and she gapes at me.

"Where are you going in your brown wig, little one?" Madame Morency says, a wicked smile coming to her face, eyes still closed. "You can't hide the truth from me."

"We're going." I pull Tai toward the curtain. "You don't know what you're talking about."

"Fine. Run off. But you will find no answers until you go back there," Madame Morency calls after us. "To the place where you both saw her last."

But we're already disappearing down the street, both of us crying for different reasons, Tai ripping the wig off her head with starry-hot eyes and whispering, *She's alive, I knew she's alive; she's alive, I knew she's alive*, and my throat burning with fury that I could be so foolish, that I could think anyone would give us answers without trying to use us, that I could be so desperate to believe any voice but the one that feels like it comes from my gut, the frightened one repeating over and over, *She's dead, she's dead, she's dead*.

I will avoid the block with that psychic's shop, taking meandering detours that add minutes to my walk, for the next four years.

But as it turns out, the psychic was right.

∞ ∞ ∞

My little sister Tai and I will find our mama, the woman once known as Mireille Foix Hammick, a decade after she disappeared. After ten years—ten long years spent wandering that purgatory of uncertain loss—it will take only one week to solve our mystery. One week of madness, brilliance, deception, trust, weakness, strength, abandonment, love, and sacrifice in the belly of our birth town, Limatra, and the fringing forest of delirium to its west.

Not everyone will survive this week.

But just as every story comes to an end, it must also start at the beginning. . . .

NONI
NEW YORK, 2018

"But I'm Mireille Foix's daughter," I speak into the cold air, watching my breath cloud and vanish.

My cheeks flush as the words stick in my throat. This is the worst kind of introduction. I can count on one hand the number of times I've used this excuse—*but I'm her daughter*—to get my way. I'm not Tai. My sister breathes *I'm her daughter.* Not me.

The hulking god of a man—bare forearms rivered with veins, even in the cold—stares down at me, shivering in my too-small leather jacket and Mama's old patched Jordache jeans. We're standing in front of a bar; specifically, its ivy-draped underground entrance in a West Village town house, blocks from where I've lived with Tai and Aunt Marion since I was eight years old. Right next to the psychic's shop, her storefront even more run-down and overgrown than before.

The bouncer shakes his bald head, egg-shiny in the amber streetlamp light. "And I'm telling you right now, you're not Mireille Foix's daughter."

I'm not going to say it doesn't hurt, being told I'm not her daughter, but I deserve it. I deserve to feel uncomfortable for trying so hard to fit in with the too-cool girls at my school for the first time, months before graduation. *You're seriously coming out with us?* they said, smiling with matte maroon lips, slinging their moms' beat-up black Hermès Kelly bags over their own forearms, snappable freckled twigs.

I finger my real ID in my pocket. *Manon Foix Hammick*, it reads. Five foot five—maybe not the aesthetic opposite of Tai's lithe five foot seven, but it feels that way. Brown eyes that could've been pulled from Dad's skull, nothing like my mother's and Tai's blue ones.

Age eighteen.

I deserve to feel uncomfortable for trying so hard to sneak into this stupid bar.

My phone buzzes in my pocket, and I rummage for it, sweaty-palmed. The bouncer snaps his fingers. "Hey," he says, shooing me down the garbage-filled street with a gesture. "Move along, superstar. No ID, no entry."

Are you still coming, M? We just ordered a pitcher of elderflower sangria, reads the message from Kelly.

Kell, not Kelly, she said to me, green eyes narrowing when we were making these plans the last day of fall semester. *Seriously, Manon? We've gone to school together for ten years. You know it's Kell.*

My cheeks burn again thinking about it. It's impossible to forget how she and her friends treated me when I had just arrived at their fancy prep school. The brightness in their eyes dimmed when they realized I wasn't exceptional in the flesh, like my parents, like Tai. That I had no more juicy stories about Mama and Dad than the tabloids did. *Okay, but what about Viloxin? What's it like?* they would ask. And even though Viloxin—this Eden so closely tied to my parents' legacy, this foggy island that radiated mystery—was the closest thing I had to an identity . . . I didn't remember it. Not well. My Viloki childhood was just a collection of genuine yet elusive feelings, tied to bursts of colors and smells, borrowed from photographs and stories later seen and heard.

So I avoided everyone by hiding in the library during schooldays, and I spent weekends thrift-shopping and visiting botanical gardens with Aunt Marion, my father's spinster sister and the closest thing to a parent. I trawled the internet and made friends there, anonymously, while Tai thrived in the richly colored limelight of the real world. I hid from the city's overwhelming stimulation in the church garden twenty steps from this bar, reading book after book (high fantasy, gothic romance, you name it), while everyone else . . . *lived*, in this sprawling city that contains millions of lives.

I was afraid of that reality. I'll admit it now.

But this is the second-to-last semester of senior year. It feels like my last chance to really *live*, to make up for lost time, to figure out what the cool kids know about the glitzy underbelly of this city loved the world over.

Almost there, I type back, all chapped knuckles and numb fingers.

My phone buzzes immediately. But it's not a reply from Kell; it's my sister, calling me for the first time in months.

"Where are you?" Tai says, and she sounds out of breath but still sparkly, always like a song you want to play on repeat. "Something huge happened."

"Meeting some friends at a bar," I reply.

"Oh, fuck off." She laughs shakily. She's walking somewhere—I hear the clacking of her heels. Tai is always in heels, dagger-sharp. "You're watching a movie at the IFC alone—don't lie."

My jaw would set if I let it, but we've played too many rounds of this game for that. "Aren't you supposed to be in Paris, influencing?"

Tai is the one with beautiful gemstones of stories that she's sharpened to points, to use on people like weapons, to convince them of her specialness in jabs and prickling scores. I've seen them all on her social media accounts: how Scorsese pulled her knotty hair into pigtails on the forest patio; how Tilda Swinton wrapped her in a towel and told her, between bloody plates of barbecued beets, that she detested the Harry Potter films (the ones Tai wasn't allowed to watch, at age six) because they romanticized the cruel, lonely setting of boarding school.

But Tai doesn't need our parents' shine or those old stories to convince people she's special anymore. Everyone just sees her precious gleam for what it is: something you brush up against once in a lifetime, something you want to bottle up and keep close.

"I leave tomorrow," she says. "I told Marion I left tonight so she would get off my case. Listen, where are you?"

When the Kells asked me to come, they also asked if Tai was free. I said she was gone.

"Come on. Tell me. It's important," Tai adds, as if I'm the younger sibling, stubborn and silly.

"Corner of Hudson and Tenth." I lower my voice, with a sidelong glance at the bouncer, rubbing his hands together. "I'm, uh, I'm in line at the door."

"See you soon," she says, hanging up before I can wonder why she didn't snipe back, *In line?* Something really huge must have happened.

I settle on a stoop down the block, the December chill nipping at me, burrowing under my clothes. Trembling a little—from nerves or embarrassment or what, I don't know. The bouncer has forgotten about me. He welcomes in a leggy couple—in softly rumpled leather and denim—like royalty. And less than three minutes later, Tai clacks toward me, creepy-shadow tall, in a floor-skimming midnight sleeveless coat, her arms covered in whisper-thin cashmere, her hair a signature curtain of jet black.

Her blue eyes sparkle like crushed ice when she smiles.

I stand and brush the stoop dirt off my jeans, but she strides past me, swooping into the arms of the bouncer, who beams at her and laughs disarmingly.

"My baby girl!" he says, hugging her hard. "Happy birthday month, my love. I didn't know you were coming tonight."

"Dom," she says, turning around to face me, "how did I never tell you I have a sister?"

"She's with you?" he asks, half frowning. The *she* sounds like an *it*.

"That she is," she says, patting me on the cheek with faux tenderness. "She even blew off a movie at the IFC for me."

∞ ∞ ∞

The bar's interior is warm and perfumed, and so is Tai. We don't spend much time together anymore—even though she's a year younger, she runs with a crowd a decade older—but being with Tai is like magic. Everyone stares at her when she arrives, then softens into the space around them, like watching her hasn't made them jealous, competitive, or wary. Watching her has taken them out of themselves for a minute, transported them into *her* world, where she pads around, full of verve and viv and utterly carefree.

It's a lie, but it's more beautiful than many truths.

"Sit," she says, pulling me down next to her into a very private nook, before I can even look for Kell and crew. A waiter in a white tuxedo jacket appears, blocking our view into the rest of the bar, with two coupes of pink champagne on a silver tray.

One glass has *TFH* etched on it. I kid you not. That's the one she plucks from him, with the most gracious, appreciative smile.

"Thaïs Foix Hammick," I say aloud, just as the model-beautiful waiter clears his throat so that I'll take the other glass. I grab it, but before I can crane my neck for Kell, much less clink glasses with Tai, she's setting hers down and pulling her phone out of her pocket.

TFH, reads the monogram on its custom leather case. It has our mother's Viloki crest painted on it, too. A white fox curled beneath the blood moon.

"Look at this," she says, music swelling just as I notice her midnight-manicured hand shaking, phone extended toward me.

Dearest Tai, an e-mail reads, from a French name I don't recognize. *The editor in chief and I would like to be the first to invite you and your sister to be the guests of honor at a black-tie retrospective of your mother's work, sponsored by Dior and held at the Foix Institute in Limatra, on May 24, 2019—*

Bile burbles up the back of my throat. "That's the day she disappeared."

"Ten years ago to the day," Tai whispers back, eyes navy-rimmed saucers.

"That's . . . inappropriate." What I mean is *grotesque, obscene, cruel*. But I don't think Tai would take kindly to my bashing Dior, her future "employer" when she drops out of high school after this year. She's their "fresh Viloki face," and she won't let anyone forget it. Even though all it means is that they miss cashing in on Mama.

"It's an honor!" She plucks the phone from my hand and points at the message. "Guests of honor!"

"Has deciding to drop out of high school killed off your last two brain cells?" I ask, before I can stop myself.

"We have to go," she whispers back, ignoring me. "We have to. It's our heritage, and our country, and we belong there."

I've never heard a worse canned speech, but I still can't tear my eyes away from hers.

"I called Teddy—"

I pull back. She already called our beloved uncle Teddy, our father and Marion's little brother, tech billionaire and world traveler. Mama was close with him, too, ever since she saved his life in Palm Springs when he was young. He was chatting obliviously on his satellite phone, developing the product that led to his first million, and Mama crept up behind him, hooking the rattlesnake at his feet around a bent branch and flinging it into the desert. That first product, Pocket Girlfriend, is used by a massive number of men and women on Viloxin and abroad—it's essentially a sophisticated Tamagotchi. A girlfriend you can keep in your pocket, I guess. He dedicated it to Mama.

But now his company has more products and takes up *twenty-five hours a day*, as he likes to say. He has far less time for two orphaned misfits. "He said he'd get Stökéwood and the Limatra apartment set up for us."

I try not to feel the sting of being left out of this phone call, and consider her glassy, pleading eyes again. "Why do I feel like you need something from me?"

She licks her lips like a cat, and I realize: She needs *me* to clear the trip with Aunt Marion. My closest confidant. Tai calls us "two peas in a puke-green knitted pod." Aunt Marion saw how destructive the media attention in Viloxin was after Mama disappeared. She's let us spend only a handful of weeks in our birth country in the past decade.

Viloxin is a fourteen-hundred-square-mile lush volcanic rock the size of Long Island, vaguely shaped like a heart. Its people, my mother's people, fiercely love their own. When Mama, Tai, and I walked around Limatra—the largest (and only) city on the heart's bay, crafted from black basalt and sole-worn cobblestones—people would stop and kiss her hand and cheeks, stroke our black hair, run out from shops and homes to feed us chestnut-flavored sweets.

They paled and shook in front of our father, praising him in low tones.

They mobbed Tai and me, sobbing and supplicating at our pre-pubescent feet as we entered and exited friends' homes and therapists' offices, hollowed out, in the weeks after Mama disappeared.

"Aunt Marion only let us spend *three days in Limatra* for Dad's funeral, Manon," Tai says, reading my mind. She slurps down champagne to stem the tears lacquering her eyes. "Dad's fucking funeral."

Three days was more than enough last summer, in the place where Mama disappeared, where Dad became sick and paranoid, dying very much alone. Three days was all that was *safe*. If we went back for longer, it would mean facing too much pain at every turn. But Tai doesn't get that, because I'm the one who always shields her from it.

I pluck the phone from her hand and keep reading the invitation. "'Cochaired by Antella Arnoix'"—my blood runs cold, and she glares at me—"'and Tiro *Nítuchí*?'"

Nítuchí. Our father's right hand, once upon a time. Evil in human form, the bogeyman in our most vivid nightmares. I will never forget Nítuchí's first visit to Stökéwood after Mama disappeared.

The company offers its condolences, he'd said in Vilosh, standing at the threshold of her library and casting a long shadow.

My stomach slowly roiled with hot glue; Tai whimpered beside me. I refused to answer, choosing instead to stare at him and scowl. The little man had blinked at me and paused for several seconds. I felt better, for a moment. But then I detected the smallest smug smile growing on his face, a tumor of a thing. It wasn't just telling me he had suspected she would abandon us—so many of our father's colleagues had wondered aloud if dedicating herself to motherhood and her Foix Institute would be too banal and dry a life for her. Taking a flighty actress for a wife was an imprudent risk our father had been warned about, I'd come to learn from gossip rags years later.

No—on Nítuchí's smirking face I saw pure, unadulterated satisfaction that Mama was gone. She was a problem, neatly solved. A mistake, corrected. His malevolence was as easy to detect as Mama's presence in her lavender smell.

You should learn how to speak Vilosh and English in the presence of your father's colleagues. Your mother was not sufficiently concerned with your education. But you are, after all, only female.

The thought of him filled me with a sense of doom.

Now he's the acting CEO of Hero Pharmaceuticals, ever since he forced Dad to step down. And apparently the cochair of this retrospective, for reasons I don't want to think about.

"Forget about them," Tai says. "We're not kids anymore."

But seeing him and his cronies wouldn't be the worst part of returning to Viloxin. No.

Going back would mean seeing all the places where our mother loved us *so much* that I still remember to this day how safe and content I felt, something I have yet to feel again.

Going back would mean seeing where she left us for good because that love wasn't enough for her. Seeing the place where I know, in the deepest, darkest sticky pit of my soul, that she killed herself.

I guzzle down some champagne, setting the glass on the mirrored table before us, and Tai's petal-pink lip juts.

"C'mon, you know it's bullshit that Marion is keeping us from Viloxin, Manon."

"Are you seriously pouting?" I cross my arms and shiver, even though the bar is too warm now and sweat's slicking my neck. Because I have a secret I haven't told Tai.

I kind of, sort of, want an excuse to go back to Viloxin, too. Not to be the toast of the town, the cultural princess of Viloxin back on home turf, like I'm sure Tai wants to be. But to get to know Mama and our homeland again, on my own terms. Not the shiny, flat versions everyone thinks they know.

I'll write her truest story into a book, so everyone can understand just how deep her magic ran, how we'll never find anything like it again.

I sigh and uncross my arms. I pick up my coupe of champagne and extend it toward my sister, ready to clink.

Her face spreads into a wide, easy smile. "You'll do it? You'll help me convince her?"

My lips quaver into a small grin, and for the first time in years, we are smiling at each other. We clink glasses, the deal sealed.

That's when the music shifts up-tempo and sparklers burn into the frame of my vision. Three waiters in tuxes, Dom the bouncer, and a posse of effortlessly cool people approach our corner, holding the fizzing fireworks with toothy smiles and bearing a frosted cake full of burning candles.

"What is happening?" I hiss at Tai.

But she's already hopping onto her heels and clapping her hands, cheek-kissing everyone and anyone, by the looks of it. Even strangers are turning and breaking into grins. "I didn't even *dress*," she says, in between smooches and squeals, and I'm left alone at knee level with the cake. The hastily applied icing on it reads: *A very, very special happy birthday to our favorite Foix Hammick!*

Her birthday isn't even for another two weeks.

I wonder if ulcers can instantaneously crop up and burn your stomach lining.

"We know it's only a matter of time until everyone in the world knows you're just as special as your mom and, you know, breathes this collective sigh of *relief* that the Foix Hammick magic isn't gone forever," an older woman in black leather and gold cuffs says in a low rasp, rubbing Tai's back with her skeletal fingers. "Just you wait."

And Tai's smile doesn't even waver as she replies, "Oh my gosh, no, stop; she may be back some day; I know my mama better than anyone, just you wait—"

That's when I smell Kell's perfume, and I see my classmates approaching my sister like they're worshipping at the altar of her.

Tai kisses them before gesturing to me and saying, "Kell, you know Manon, right? You're her year!"

Then all three swivel and blink at me in tandem, their faces little perfect pored games of shadow and light in the presence of Tai's shine, and I wish I could melt into the cushions below me like the stubby candles on the very, very special cake.

Not a day goes by that I forget just how different Tai and I are, because every time I look at her, I know.

THE ETHER
TAI

thais: Who's the fo(i)x on viloxin now—cc: mama's outrageous spring
   '92 oscar de la renta outfit
1 hour ago
3,893 likes
241 comments
botbabe123: Pretty! <3 <3
kellyinnyc: Enjoy x
linos.is.bae: Is Linos with you?
basickitty123: I mean I DIE for that skirt
saxim: I can't wait to see you, Basil!
thais @saxim see you soon Monty :*
manonymous: This was clearly taken at JFK
troll123: Lol idiot
troll456: F*cking airhead

linos.is.bae: I will kill u if ur Linos's gf

themeatmandeli: You look just like your mom! #Mireille4Ever #FindBF2Day #BestJellyDonut4Ever

teddyclaus: Qt π

Instagram Live Transcript

Tai: Hi, friends! Guess who I'm video chatting with today?

Live comment: *Is it Linos Arnoix?*

Live comment: *Linos ? <3 <3*

Live comment: *U and linos are soooo cute I die. Prince & princess of Viloxin*

Live comment: *When's the royal wedding? #TaiHimUp*

[Tai laughs]

Tai: No! It's not Linos Arnoix. We're just friends. [Tai blushes] I *can* be just platonic friends with the most breathtakingly beautiful and deeply eligible bachelor in Viloxin. I'm seventeen, y'all. No, no—I've got an even better surprise. Here's a hint.

[Cheery text notification sound BLINGS]

Live comment: *MONTY!!! biffle goals*

[Tai beckons off-screen]

[Screen splits, and on a second screen, Saxim waves]

Tai: It's Saxim, aka Monty! My forever best friend. Monty, do you remember how we made friends?

Saxim: Of course. Because we would both lay down our lives for an admission letter to Hogwarts. Can you imagine studying there? Just the smell of the books—

Tai: Monty's a Ravenclaw!

Saxim: And Basil's a Hufflepuff dressed in Slytherin skin.

[Tai laughs]

Tai: We used to play this game—a total Potter rip-off—called the Miraculous Adventures of Basil and Monty.

Saxim: We thought Basil and Monty were fine British names.

Tai: They are! [Tai shakes head] Wow. Am I a little too proud of our spin-off? Maybe. But it tied us to each other forever. Good thing my parents finally let me read the books, right?

Saxim: You mean, good thing you snuck into the school library and stole a copy. I'll never forget casting fake spells with you in the Stökéwood gardens.

Tai: Real spells, Mont. Always real. But wait, before we put people to sleep with our prepubescent inside jokes, can you please tell me about the delicious video you discovered? You promised you'd tell me. [Tai looks at camera] She's been keeping it a secret from me. I wish I could squeeze it out of her through the screens.

[Saxim grins]

Saxim: Did you all know Tai and her sister were child actors? No? Okay, good, because they weren't.

Tai: True, true. The family business was a no-go. That's why I also failed chem, right, Monty?

Saxim: They weren't *officially* child actors, but they *were* forced to film a promo video for the Viloki tourism bureau when they were respectively six and seven.

[Zooming in on Tai's eyes popping]

[Tai bursts out into laughter]

Tai: Oh no.

Saxim: Oh yes. It's a cult classic.

Tai: Monty. Monty! Mont—

[Film rolls]

It's grainy, and as it opens, one sees two narrow backs on a stone wall covered in vines. Manon sits on the left, wearing the black turtleneck she insisted on wearing at all times, and Tai is on the right, wearing the mandated Viloki-green tank dress, with one

26

of her mother's Hermès scarves tied around her neck for modesty. The production team curled the girls' black hair and pinned each lock, in what they said was an angelic fashion. But the girls really look like two ninety-year-old widows with bad dye jobs and perms.

Manon turns to face the camera. She has stripes of rouge on her cheeks and, if you look carefully, on her fingers, from where she tried to paw the gunk off.

"Fítsím," Noni says, her brown eyes suspicious and forest-deep, the traditional hello less a greeting than a warning she had one take left in her.

"Fítsím!" Tai calls over her shoulder simultaneously, smiling wide.

"Welcome to Viloxin," they say in unison, when a uniquely dated drumbeat begins and those words, Welcome to Viloxin, appear in acid-green script across the screen. Behind it, Tai cocks her hip while Noni tugs at the hair spray—stiff curls in her hair, and then they cancan out of sync.

"Viloxin is a very special place," says an unknown voice-over actor, inexplicably imitating Sean Connery. We fade into a helicopter shot, panning over the furious riptides of the deep sea circling the island.

"Miraculously settled by a shipwrecked group of heretical artists fleeing the Crusades, Viloxin was difficult to access for generations," he continues, as we move toward the Viloki coast, ravenous, foaming waves smashing its razor-sharp basalt rock cliffs.

"But those fleeing other countries knew they had a safe haven there," he notes, as the camera approaches the small basalt houses that form much of Limatra. "Transportation advances breathed new life into the country in the twentieth century, and Hero Pharmaceuticals was born, alongside the Foix Institute," *he says, as we cross the sparkling skyscraper that is the Hero Pharmaceuticals headquarters—so large, in that small-city footprint, in the path of dormant Mount Vilox.*

The camera roams past the Foix Institute and toward the dark, lush forests at the base of the volcano, where Stökéwood lies.

"The island of Viloxin will be the first place on Earth where good health and rich culture are a certainty, where self-actualization is within reach for all—"

Smash-cut to Noni and Tai in a field of foxgloves, waving at a camera far above. A group of smiling people in white lab coats and green Viloki robes join them, walking stiffly.

Tai and Noni squint into the sun, and then, singing the unofficial Viloki anthem off-key, they spin around and around until they drop into the undergrowth, breathing hard.

"Viloxin," the voice-over booms as the camera zooms into their faces, both girls collapsed on the grass. "Where dreams live."

The lighting warps and the frame freezes, turning the faces greenish-brown and paralyzing them: Tai's in a childish grimace-pout, and Noni's in a serene, wide-eyed stare, inside a circle of clapping scientists.

[Tai is speechless]

Tai: Oh my gosh. Look at my baby resting bitch face.

Saxim: I've never seen anything creepier. Did David Lynch film this? I love it so much.

Tai: You would! [Tai wipes brow] I'm sweating. Talk about a blast from the past. I'm going to be honest, Monty, I still don't really know what *self-actualization* means.

Saxim: What were you looking at, at the end?

Tai: You mean, why did I look constipated? I think we were

staring at my mama, actually. She was off-screen, dangling chocolates to get us to behave.

Saxim: That makes infinite sense.

Tai: This might be an overshare, but she was working on a secret project in the library—like, seriously, every day—and I was so happy when she took a break for this. Seriously, I remember being overwhelmed with joy.

Saxim: . . . Secret project?

Tai: I mean, let's be real. I'm pretty sure it was *White Fox*.

[Tai looks at camera]

Tai: Hey, if any of you film buffs who are good at the internet find a copy of the script anywhere, slide into my DMs, okay? That includes you, Mama, if you're watching.

[Tai winks, as Saxim's smile freezes]

Tai: Okay, bye, y'all. Monty, I'll call you back in a sec!

[Saxim ends video]

[Tai clicks the wrong button to end video]

[Tai sighs, and her face wobbles]

Tai: Oh my freaking freakity freak, what was *that*, Thaïs Foix Hammick?

Live comment: *T are you ok?!*

Live comment: *She looks so young & scared rn what is wrong w our Viloki queen*

[Tai startles and grins big, then waves]

[End of video]

VILOXIN
NONI

The road splits at Viloxin airport: one path shoots you toward the tiny, glittering jewel of Limatra city, nestled at the sea's edge, and the other weaves you deeper into the lush, hilly terrain at the base of Mount Vilox. To reach Stökéwood, people take the latter, past the affluent neighborhood of Mitella, where the upper crust of Viloki society lives, and through a wooded area known to locals and foreigners alike as Delirium Forest.

In the old Viloki legends, one ventured inside to see vivid glimpses of the future, or treasured glimpses of the past, long thought lost. Inside the forest of delirium, the present melts away to nothing at all. That's why they find bodies inside, lost to dehydration, smiles stretched across the corpses' lips. That's why my classmates' nightmares lived inside this forest. Inside this brain-tingling, dark beauty.

On this stretch of forest road far west of the city, we've hardly seen a building for half an hour, much less a single soul. The dancing green foliage outside threatens to burst through the car's windows at every turn. This surreal green is home, in a way that sends a chill up my spine. It smells of moss, thyme, and earth, intermingled.

But I can't shake this feeling we're being watched, by someone quiet, someone careful. I've felt that way ever since we landed—I froze at baggage claim, where a group of elderly locals followed us like ghosts, whispering with half smiles and gesturing with wrinkled hands. When I told Tai, she replied casually, "Of course people are watching us. We're practically royalty." A stranger with gnarled, arthritic fingers helped her lift her luggage off the carousel.

Now, Tai reaches her phone across my body, toward the window on my sunnier side.

"Must you?" I ask, swatting her hand away.

"I'm just sending Linos a photo so he knows I'm here," she explains, as if Linos Arnoix, Viloxin's resident Narcissus, has ever noticed anything beyond his own aristocratic reflection.

She won't even tell me if they're dating. If pressed, she says they're *just friends*. Tai taps away, the volume on her phone excruciatingly turned up all the way. "And yes, I can hear you judging me and shitting on him inside your brain, by the way," she adds, eyes and fingertips glued to her screen. "Your skull's not that thick."

I would open my mouth to tell her I don't think she meant to say that, but it's not worth the oxygen.

When we reach Stökéwood's gate—a movable, massive iron fence straight out of a Gothic novel—the driver buzzes the house via the intercom about a dozen times, to no avail. When I punch in the gate code I remember, nothing happens, either. Only then does my heart start to falter, like it's missing a beat in my chest. Random childhood memories stab me—Tai skinning her knees on the gravel a few feet off; Mama tying red balloons to the fence before a birthday party. *I know this gate. But where is everyone?* We knew Teddy wouldn't be here—he sent the car to pick us up—but we didn't expect to arrive at an empty house that wouldn't let us in.

Now that seems naive.

Tai, the driver, and I heave ourselves against the prickly iron gate until it scrapes against stone and opens enough to let the car through. As we drive up the winding, forest-lined path, I look ahead for any sign of our home itself, but the trees are overgrown, shadowing the gravel.

"What the hell is that?" Tai asks, clutching her phone to her chest. Outside the car window, a large, bearded man in gray runs out of the woods and toward us, another six-foot figure in a neon vest and beanie stock-still behind him.

"Misses Hammick! *Fitsím!*" the running man shouts at the car window. He stops running, his hands falling to his knees as he catches his breath.

Tai shrinks back, but I see it now: the security guard uniform, complete with badge and radio. He looks like he's fiftysomething— and local, on account of his Viloki greeting.

"Misses Hammick, your uncle sent me to man the gate. I'm Tomí," he says, extending a machine-oil-coated hand through the open window, which I take in mine, relieved.

His skin is warm and rough and greasy to the touch. He looks tired, and the reddish blooms by his nose make me think he's a heavy drinker. I wonder how long he's been here.

"I'm sorry I wasn't by the gate when you arrived—the security system was acting up," he says, pointing at the man in the beanie behind him.

My stomach lurches as I realize—

The figure is stiff. And when I squint, I see it has no nose or mouth: just a flesh-colored plastic mask. Its eyes dilate strangely, zooming in and out, as I stare back at it.

"It's . . . a mannequin?" I ask.

"It's state of the art," Tomí corrects. "One of Clouded Cage's new surveillance machines that uses facial recognition technology. You girls can rest easy, Misses Hammick, with the two of us here, and Mina inside," he adds, pulling up his sagging pants. I smell sweat and cigarettes and stale booze. Dad couldn't stand drinkers: He even frowned and batted Mama away when she'd had too much wine.

"Is Mina your wife? Do you both live around here?" I ask, as Tai sighs quietly next to me—frustrated, I guess, that I'm prolonging the chat with our sole living security guard.

But Tomí chuckles. "No, no. You haven't met Mina? I thought she'd been here for years. You'll see—she's gone to great pains to get the house ready for you." He leans closer and waves at Tai to catch her attention. "Hi, Miss Hammick Number Two. I hope you had a good journey?"

She looks up from her phone and smiles after a beat. It reads genuine, even though I'm sure it's not. Tai has never been referred to as Number Two in her life.

"A long one," she replies. "Thank you for the good wishes."

Tomí's cheeks burn. He nods awkwardly and pats the car door, as if urging us along. "Sorry to keep you!" And he hustles back into the forest dark, where the motionless robot watches and waits.

"Don't be rude," I whisper to Tai under my breath, as the car rolls forward.

"I'm so tired and hungry I could cry," Tai says. "We can suck his dick later, okay? Just let me unpack and take a bath."

"*Thaïs Hammick*," I hiss back, with a look at the driver.

But he and Tai are already staring straight ahead, where Stökéwood's peaks have appeared. Its silhouette grows from a jagged yet familiar mound into its full over-the-top glory, throwing my heart into its first backflip. My childhood home, Stökéwood. A several-centuries-old basalt castle, built in an H shape (*Fit for a*

Hammick, they said), with four dangerous towers accessible only by rusty ladders, with double-height ceilings made for a place of worship, with underground tunnels and mazelike corridors leading to so many rooms lost to the light. The hypermodern extension is visible too—built in an H shape (*For Hëró*, they said) by our father forty years ago. Dozens of filthy twelve-foot windows of glass wink at us ominously, the cataract-filmed eyes of an elderly grande dame lost to madness.

Once built to look imposing, now Stökéwood looks like an abandoned castle from a postapocalyptic movie, well past the cusp of dereliction: It looks like a place where good goes to die.

The car stops short of the rotunda near the front door, and while Tai wrestles with her explosion of monogrammed leather bags, I slip the driver a few extra bills to linger outside the front gate. There's no chance I'm staying the night here, what with the family apartment in Limatra—I have an appointment in town this afternoon to do research for my book, anyway. He refuses all of my cash politely, explaining he will simply wait outside the gate until I return. I watch him discreetly crane his neck to try to spy inside the house, but the overgrown five-foot spears of green foxglove planted in abundance block any view through the windows. Stökéwood sentinels, those *foxít*.

How is it that all of this still exists? Dried-out stone marlins wait in the rotunda's fountain longing for some liquid to spit into the sky. Viney weeds sprout from between unkempt stretches of gravel and stone tile. The adjacent forest has eaten into the once well-manicured gardens around Stökéwood, seizing back its territory. Soon, the tangled roots of the chestnut trees will spread outward in the shallow soil like desperate fingers, buckling the stone that supports the house.

I'm afraid. Anxious, really. I can feel the coppery anxiety bubbling up from my gut and into the back of my throat, and I instantly feel a crawling urge to whip out my notebook and write through my thoughts until they subside. I couldn't relax on the flight, much less write or read a single page. I spent the whole time thumbing through the lavender notebook Aunt Marion gave me, where I'd scrawled a list of all the places I remember from childhood in Limatra and Noxim, the town by Stökéwood. To write my book about Mama—the book that will snap back at the world's view that she was just some dressed-up, made-up *doll*, the book that will show she ached and raged and loved—I need to visit these places again and log every memory of her. That's how I'll get to know my mother again: not by wallowing in the soul-sucking mystery of her disappearance, but by carefully exploring the many sides of her *life*.

Tai doesn't know.

We find the spare set of keys behind the withered, potted gardenia plants by the front, as promised by Uncle Teddy's assistant. The lock on the smaller wooden side door by the kitchen doesn't seem to match any of the heavy iron keys, so we try the massive, intricate wrought iron front door (modeled after Rodin's *The Gates of Hell*), which opens after much fumbling and a heavy-handed push. Tai switches into dusty sheepskin slippers in the shallow entrance, padding forward, and I follow suit, shivering as my feet slick in the dust.

"Hello?" she calls.

My eyes adjust to the dark. The entryway feels like an otherworldly cathedral, but it looks almost as I imagined it: walls of costly, imported marble reaching as high as the eye can see, studded with sconces, long-gone dark; the grand wooden staircase that once led up to our bedrooms but leads nowhere now, on account of the moth-eaten velvet rope threaded across its mouth; a heavy oak table, where Mama once placed five-foot-tall arrangements of flowering branches, lavender, and other wildflowers, bare now.

What's most different is that the house beyond it . . . looks like a maze.

Its vaulted, awe-inspiring vastness is punctuated by gargantuan stacks of old paperwork on the ground—uneven paper stalagmites, blocking the way in and out.

I don't dare to pick them up and read them.

In the year before Mama disappeared, I spied on my parents in this very hall from the top of the stairs. *What am I to make of this?* Mama asked him, holding up a tabloid I couldn't read—recognizable only from its flashy, bright colors, and its big font. Mama always told us tabloids were rubbish when we passed them at newsstands.

It's nonsense, Mireille, and you should know better than to believe it, Dad replied, moving to leave, and I thought the matter settled.

But she stopped him, latching a hand on his forearm. *Don't treat me like a child.* And the way she said it, tremulous and soft, made me scared for her.

He just scoffed. *If only you were as easy to manage as a child. If only you didn't encourage the damned obsessives to pine after you. Did you think it wise to involve yourself with that bigoted snake Daria Grendl again? All she and her kind do is stir up trouble for us.*

Trouble for us? she said, dropping his arm. *You mean for Hero Pharm. You sound like Nítuchí's puppet.*

I crept into Mama's bathroom later and found her crouching around a smashed bottle of perfume, her face swollen. I couldn't find the nerve, the words to ask her what had happened. I only asked if she and Dad were okay, and she replied by urging me onto her lap with a sigh and telling me a story about a fox who becomes a man's wife, a story I found incomprehensible and unsettling.

So I found the tabloid later that night, in the kitchen trash can: HERO A MURDERER? KILLER RUMORS SPREAD ABOUT HERO PHARM AND ECCENTRIC FOUNDER HENRY "HËRÓ" HAMMICK.

I would find other tabloids like it, over the years, and eventually I would understand what they meant. The rumors were that the

God among men's desperation to boost Hero Pharm corporate profits resulted in the hasty formulation of faulty medicines that caused thousands of deaths, many of them on Viloxin.

But those rumors, swirling for more than a decade, only hit mainstream papers two years ago when the Hero Pharm board refused to answer fresh inquiries and in a written statement pointed to our reclusive, eccentric dad as the responsible party for *any and all formerly suboptimal testing procedures.* Dad was forced to step down as CEO of his brainchild, and he locked himself into Stökéwood for good.

He wouldn't even explain what happened; just like he did after Mama disappeared, he told me *not to worry about matters outside my control,* and to *focus on my studies.*

It was Aunt Marion who filled me in. She told me his first love was his work, even when Mama was around. She told me that a colleague of his deposited me and Tai on her doorstep with a huge check, some months after Mama left (I remember that much). Dad visited once, very early on, and the visit was so deeply uncomfortable—the three of us silently eating curried lentils at Aunt Marion's cramped kitchen table, Dad quietly criticizing us for watching endless TV instead of studying—that both Tai and I were plagued with nightmares of Mama and pitched into despair for a month afterward. Aunt Marion had words with him then, and the visits ended before they could truly begin.

Sometimes the press would ask her about the Hero Pharm rumors coming out of Europe—or about us, the supposed heirs to Dad's pharmaceutical company. But she never answered, and eventually they stopped.

She informed me, in a solemn tone, that Tai and I would have to participate in Hero Pharm corporate dealings one day, but she could offer no more information; Dad might not lie to anyone's face, but he was, as always, extremely secretive.

Dad died without even telling us he was sick.

Tai steps forward and lifts a plate of withered fruit rotting atop one of the boxes of paperwork, left by God knows who and untouched for days or months. She grimaces at me, silent for once.

A voice echoes from the depths. I follow Tai down the vaulted stone hallway with its antique *machíkíl* cleavers pinned to the walls and its sagging Biedermeier chests—once prized but now riddled with termite holes—past the dining room with its twenty-foot-long dining table made from a single petrified tree and its three whimsical Murano glass chandeliers—handmade to depict the Greek Fates—past the oak-paneled library, its ladders ringed with fewer cobwebs than expected, and into a small, plain ground floor area I've never seen.

The door is open. The room's walls are white-painted drywall, undecorated, and the furniture—chairs, low tables, a bed—is made of plastic or metal and easily folded away. There is one small window. The room is impeccably clean, despite being filled with machinery and paperwork—he was never one to remain idle, even when ill. At least here it smells brightly of peppermint salve and lemon-scented cleaner, not of decay and death. A machine in the corner beeps as Tai approaches the bed, with me just behind her.

Dad must have converted part of the old house into a treatment room. The sight is enough to make me bite my lip so hard it might fall off.

The bed is empty, of course. But his clothes are stacked on top of the clean sheets, and I spot the Mickey Mouse T-shirt Tai insisted on buying at Disney World and mailing to him when she was twelve years old. There's the cozy waffle-weave shirt he used to wear while reading the science journals out in the garden. At the bottom of the pile are the matching flannel pajamas Mama got all of us for Víxmís one year, stained by the juices of platter after platter of roasted scallops and chestnuts.

It's impossible not to imagine him here, alone. So small in the bed, smaller than ever before, but deeply familiar, with the cloud of white hair that replaced the jet black and a peaceful, blank expression. A plain white shirt buttoned simply down the front, loose around his concave chest.

When the tears come, hot and fast and unexpected, it's easy, somehow, to forget that we decided to stop protecting each other, that Dad and I were never close at all.

Mama was the one I loved—the one who loved me—and—

Mama killed herself.

I'm sure; I'm sure, even though there's never been any official evidence. She was a complex prism of a woman working her whole life to crush this paper doll vision people had of her. And she mostly failed. This harsh reality, plus chemical imbalances, stressors, genetic vulnerability, and so, so much more—they are just some of the billions of facets of my mother they never saw. That's what my Stökéwood memories imply—that's what I had to convince myself, in order to move on.

The machine in the corner moves then—rattles forward—and I jump away, tasting blood. It's more than a machine. It's got legs, two jointed hunks of plastic. It's got a light panel for a face, and two eyes shaped in the emoji-approximation of a friendly smile. It's . . . a Clouded Cage–branded robot. One of those boxy things I've seen on the internet, produced by an arm of Teddy's sprawling tech company. A cousin of the security mannequin in the yard.

"Jesus H. Christ on a bicycle," Tai says under her breath, as the robot's legs grind and stomp toward us, and I wipe my wet face, hard, before Tai can see.

It takes me a minute to notice that the robot holds an origami box made of notepaper in its hands.

"For you," the robot says, bowing.

Its voice is honeyed and familiar somehow, not the expected graveled electronica. *Feminine. So it's a she*, I think, a cold finger tracing my spine.

"Mina?" I ask.

Hearts fly across her panel in greeting as I take the box from her. The paper feels familiar between my fingers. It's grained with nubby flecks of real lavender, the same kind Mama used to use.

"Should I . . . open it?" I ask, stunned into speaking my thoughts.

"Holy fuck," Tai whispers, dropping onto the bed. "Isn't that Mama's favorite paper? What if it's from her? What if——?"

"It's not," I reply curtly, bitter metal on my tongue.

I sit on the edge of the bed, next to Tai, and carefully undo the folds in the paper, remembering how to refold them as best I can. My fingertips leave imprints on the tissue-thin sheet. My breath catches when I see Dad's spidery script—

And the July date, the week before his death in August.

To my daughters:

It pains me that you should return to your childhood home on so unhappy an occasion. I hope you can forgive me for delaying news of my illness and deterioration; I have followed along with great pride as you excelled in America, and I did not wish to disrupt your progress. Life is to be spent creating something greater than oneself—it is not to be spent bemoaning the inevitable passing of an old man whose best days are long behind him. I differ from many of those my age in this belief, but I believe your mother would have agreed.

It is she who also provides me with the reason for this letter today—it is she who requires that I ask a favor of you in this delicate moment.

I carry with me a few sources of great shame in life. One is that I lacked the courage, or the wisdom, to share the truth about her with you. Your mother was not who she said she was. She bore secrets that no child should hear about a parent who has left this

40

*world—not, at the very least, until they become adults. Or so I
believe. In fact, some of these secrets are still not mine to share—
and I imagine there are others still unknown to me.*

My voice wavers and breaks. The words are unlike Dad in their sheer
quantity and in their melodrama. "Should I . . . keep reading?" I ask. A
futile question, meant only to provide a couple of moments to help quiet
the panic building in my skull. Because it would be impossible for me to
leave this unread, if it truly holds secrets about Mama, good or bad.

Tai nods, riveted, tears already staining her pink cheeks. I turn my
eyes back to the page.

*Your mother was a mystery to me in many ways. In her
final months with us, I believe she discovered something dark in
Viloxin, perhaps at my own company, that she would not reveal
to me. She would not speak to me in those final months, and she
refused to explain why. And so, my daughters, that leads me to
another great source of shame: I returned to my work, out of frustration and foolishness, for this was my custom at the time, and
she in turn devoted herself to a new and final project at her institute. A project by the name of* White Fox.

A tremor zips from my fingers to my shoulders. We'd always
been told growing up that her final project did not actually exist—that
those long nights she spent working were imagined. I never believed
it in full. We simply believed it as much as we needed to, so that in
our memories, our hours together remained her most precious ones.
"So *White Fox* was real," I whisper.

Yes, White Fox. *I very much appreciate that this script has
wreaked havoc on our lives since portions were leaked to the media*

41

those years ago, while you were in America. As the script was lost with your mother, I thought it was best to tell you, as children, that it never existed. That the document leaked to the media was false. Why sully the memory of your mother by speaking about a lost and incomplete nightmare of a text? But the situation has changed, and I now believe every fragment of White Fox *held clues only you two can decode. She once mentioned to me that the script was, at least partially, "a map for my two girls to better understand me, once they are grown."*

This brings me back to the beginning: What exactly is this favor that I ask of you now, my daughters?

I ask that you find your mother.

I pause, fingers trembling too hard to read on.

"Manon!" Tai tears the pages from my grip as spots sparkle and fade in my vision. She reads on as I focus on my breath.

She is living on Viloxin, though she is drastically changed from the woman we knew.

Tai's voice shakes. "What the fuck?" She looks at me, eyelashes fawn-wet. "She's alive? I knew it. I fu—"

"Keep reading," I urge.

Here is my truth: I saw her with my own two eyes in this very forest, one month before writing this letter. I think she wishes to contact us but cannot find the right way. I am certain she does not live on the property, for I and my team have searched every inch of this place since, and we would have found her. Unless, of course, she does not wish to be found by me.

I hope you can find her, and I hope you can accomplish what I could not, in these past nine years. I hope you can determine what happened to your beloved mother on and after that fateful night of her disappearance. What she discovered, where she went, and why. I cannot, with any certainty, tell you if she ran away or was kidnapped. I have myself cycled through those and far more punishing possibilities over the years.

But I know now she did not want to leave us forever.

Tai pauses, eyes refilling with tears, and looks at me.
I encourage her with a nod, a painful lump caught in my throat.

Asking you to look into her disappearance—and to look for her now—is a decision I will struggle with forever more. Alas, that decision has now been made, as I put pen to paper, and there is no going back.

I understand that this is no easy task. I hope that the two of you might work hand in hand to indulge this final wish of mine. No private detective has succeeded. No avid fan of hers, no colleague. Not even myself. I can only hope that her own daughters—who possess pieces of her—might better understand my precious fox.

She lives on Viloxin, my daughters. Find her.

I hope that you will forgive me one day for asking this of you, and for allowing you to remain ignorant of her true nature. My aim was to protect you from our humanity. I only realize now, as my body fails me, that we are all only human, that there is a beauty in this, and that parents must, in the end, have faith in their children to cultivate and manage their own humanity as adults.

I will warn you, whether or not you choose to take on this task: Viloxin and Hero Pharmaceuticals itself are much changed since you lived here. Take care in choosing whom to trust. I have not barricaded myself inside of Stökéwood simply because of ill health: There are those who wish our downfall, all of us. I leave this note with Mina now, because it is the only way I know it will be secure, and I only hope you meet her before too long. She's been my most loyal companion for these past eight years.

From a man to his daughters: I have loved you both, I love you both, and I will love you both, as long as a single spark of consciousness allows. I know that your mother felt the same, for as long as I knew her.

Tai folds the note in half, ignoring the careful creases, and I sit in silence, lost for words.

"We love you too, Dad," Tai says into the empty air, breaking into a sob and rubbing her nose on her shirtsleeve.

But I am not Tai.

It is impossible, at first, for me to think about the actual specifics of the letter. His proclamations of love. His confession that Mama wasn't who she said she was—and that not only did *White Fox* exist, but she wrote it for *us*. His assertion that—my God—he saw Mama and thinks she's *living* on Viloxin.

That's all overshadowed by a storm cloud electric with rage—full of confusion, of all-consuming fear, of the nagging suspicion that there's so much more we don't know. Why leave this letter upending our understanding of Mama with this . . . thing, when he could have called us and told us himself? If he privately entertained the idea she might be alive, why say nothing when I claimed she was gone for good?

Who is this man who claims to love us as long as a single spark of consciousness allows?

All I know is I wish he were here now so I could scream these questions at him, though I know I would break down in tears the moment I smelled his papery skin.

"This is ridiculous," I whisper to myself, head throbbing, hands blue with cold, as I lead my sister into the hallway and shut the door. As if not to disturb him. "We tell no one about this, Tai. Not a soul."

Tai swirls to face me, blue eyes charged. "I need to tell Saxim. And Teddy and Marion, at least——"

I grip her by the arm. "No one, Tai. He gave us nothing real to go off of, no one to trust but *Mina*——"

"He's gone, Manon. Cut him some slack. And you're missing the point. He said she's *living on Viloxin*. She's out there."

"And gave us what proof?"

Her hands clench into fists. "He saw her. And Dad never lied."

I scoff. He could have been hallucinating on meds when he saw her. He could have been *dreaming*. She saw the tabloid headlines just like me: *Sick, Paranoid, and Irresponsible*. That's why we can't tell a soul. No matter that he sounded sharp as ever in his letter. I'm picking at my hangnail—a bad habit, like the lip biting. But it reminds me I'm in control. Besides writing, it's the little things like this that keep the fizzy pennies of anxiety at bay.

"Read between the lines, Tai. It was one last-ditch effort by a guilty old man to make us feel like Mama didn't kill herself and abandon us, since he *did* ditch us," I blurt. My thumb bleeds as Tai stares at me with barefaced shock. Another memory reaches me with a searing flash: Mama quaking with fury in this very hall, jabbing a ringed pointer finger into Dad's lab-coated chest, telling him, *If it was up to you, I would remain trapped at Stökéwood forever, an empty-headed Marie Antoinette playing in her Petit Trianon. Only I will die here.* Mama tried her hardest to convince us of her brightness, but it was there, the shadow side, strengthened by the disappointment of motherhood and the murmurs about Dad. "She didn't want us more than her career, than the rest of her life. Neither of them did. It's best we come to terms with that and move on."

It takes her another moment to digest my words. My mouth tastes sour. I feel cut open, my fears exposed. But a part of me knows I've also said the words to hurt her, because I need her to be as hurt as I am; I need her to understand that no matter what Dad saw, Mama

45

can't be alive, *she can't, she can't,* but I regret that when Tai's face wobbles and she hides it by rubbing her cheeks with her hands.

"Fuck. I can't believe the way your brain works," Tai says, dropping to the floor, her back against the wall. "That's the first conclusion you jump to." She's trembling, even though her jaw is set.

"You're wrong," she says. "They both loved us more than anything."

And it burns to watch, to listen as she convinces herself of a truth she felt so assured of as a child.

I cross my arms so they won't betray me by shaking.

"Stop looking at me like that. Please stop." Tai wraps her arms around her knees and squeezes tight. "If she's on Viloxin, hiding . . ." She wipes her face. "We'll find her and hear the truth from her," she finishes, looking up at me with sweet, drooping eyes designed to skewer hearts. "I know we haven't exactly been on the best terms. But we need to at least try to do this together. How is that not the most obvious thing in the world to you?"

"Try? Try how? What can we do that the actual police can't? If she's here, she's hidden herself from them for the past decade. Our mother is dead, and we're here for the retrospective. Well, I am," I snap. My arms won't stop vibrating, loose in their sockets, and my teeth are chattering, too. *This house.*

"Don't talk down to me. I know all of that. I know." She releases her knees and presses clenched fists to her eyelids before looking up at me, her whole face brimming with that secret hope that's so tender and naive it makes me sick. "Stop staring at me."

"I'm not." But of course I am. She's beautiful even when she's upset—with her feline, heart-shaped face, her baby-pink cheeks with their cherubic gleam, her puffy lips, and her oversize eyes— and that irritates me. Sometimes pain just shouldn't be beautiful. But it's more than that, of course: Everything about Tai annoys me now. Her hundreds of thousands of followers, and the fact she's almost always putting on a show for them. It makes me half expect that she's livestreaming this moment right now. I remain on edge with her—on the offensive, as always. "I'm leaving Stökéwood, and I'm not coming back," I decide. "And you're coming with me. We're staying at the apartment in Limatra. I already made sure it's habitable. This is done."

I open my eyes, finding her blue ones set on me, sparkling with a sharpness I haven't seen in months: She has an idea, and that idea is all that matters.

I know it's the idea that our father just planted in her head, ready to sprout and grow thorns.

"This is bigger than you and me," she says, staring me down. "Even if she isn't alive, he believed someone might be responsible for what happened."

And that thought sickens me. Of course it does. It took years of excruciating work to sit with my belief that she killed herself. And now, because of one letter, I can't tear the image of Mama, bruised and battered, from my mind. It's an amalgamation of her own movie clips, lines pulled from the tabloid report on *White Fox*, and my own imagination overheating. My pulse has run off; my skin is feverish. Of course someone malicious could have forced her to disappear, could have locked her up for ten long years, could have led Dad to believe she might still be out there, eager to return. It's horrible, it's nonsensical, and it's all I want to believe.

"We can't be here right now," I whisper. I wanted to feel close to Mama again, but I wanted to do it on my terms.

"What if she found something out about Hero Pharm and they fucked her up?" Tai says, talking over me. "Imagine what she might have uncovered. Imagine what she might have left as clues in *White Fox*."

My eyes flick to hers, then away. Tai, the expert manipulator. I know some of the men at Hero Pharm are bastards. But Dad was their leader. He was meant to know everything—to be responsible.

I thrust my bloodied hand into my pocket. "Why aren't you listening to me? *White Fox* disappeared with her. And to look for her, we don't have to stay here. You can be so thickheaded—"

"This is my *home*, Manon. I've only been on the grounds for ten minutes in the past decade, and pretty soon it's going to be sold off. If Aunt Marion hadn't refused to let us come to Stökéwood for Dad's funeral, we would've gotten this note sooner. But now it's been ten months since he left that note for us, even longer since he saw her, and every day that passes takes us further from her. Makes it more difficult for us to . . ." She rubs her eyes. "Sense her."

I stare at her in front of me, sparrow small with her plane-matted black hair, and the edges of my coldness melt. I'm unable or unwilling to tell her that's not how time and space work.

Because I get it: When a mother supposedly reappears, after ten long years away, surely her children should feel her warm presence, no matter how near or far, pulsing like a newly born star.

I don't feel that.

"I'm not leaving," she says abruptly, eyes ablaze, "and you can't make me change my mind. I'm going to spend the night in this very, very special place where we made so many happy memories. I'm going to find *White Fox*." She rises with a crack of her knees and storms toward the bathroom. "And tomorrow, I'm going to find Mama, because I know she's still here."

As if it's as easy as that. As if we're not going to find so much pain in our search, too much to bear.

Mama.

I walk the hall I walked countless times as a child, and I'm flooded by images of her, my chest filling with a choking glue.

Tai's right: The Mama I knew *is* here, in a way, trapped in every stone of this place where good goes to die.

Coocoo! she croons, crouching to tickle me under the chin and read alongside me after she catches me poring over D'Aulaires' Greek myths, pressed up against those very stones—even if it means less time at cocktails with the adults, even if it means smudging her lipstick and mussing the hem of her silk dress. *Better to look lived-in*, she says when Dad tuts at her.

The long meals in the dining room, just down there, where we sit in matching silk pajamas to learn to enjoy smoked Viloki sheep cheese and scallops and rock snails, where a shell slips the grasp of my tongs, flying straight at Dad's face, and we all howl and double over with laughter, even him.

Skipping down the hall with her, hand in hand, my head still warm from where her fingers wove a French braid into my scalp. Napping together in the library—running my finger over the seam on her face made by the blanket we shared.

Mama, swiftly layering cream-colored makeup that smells of paint onto the fine, freckled skin of her chest with a blank stare into the mirror, until she glimpses me rounding the bend and drops the tube on the counter, her face cracking into a toothy, grateful smile, swirling around to hug me, kiss me, wrap me in her small arms in such a way that they felt more welcoming and generous than a cocoon.

And waking up that second morning after her disappearance, only to crumple by this very door in my sweated-through striped pajamas, hit by flashes of understanding all of that might just be gone forever.

I knock over one stack of paperwork, scattering the top sheets, and I pick them up with unsteady hands, squinting at the photocopied text. Old documents eaten around the edges, section titles in bold beneath the retired Hero Pharm logo.

MEDICATION NAME

TRIAL #

DATE

RESULTS

I drop it like it's singed me. I don't need to be Dad to understand what he was collecting.

It's a paper cemetery for the victims of his experiments over a multi-decade career. Tests gone wrong, side effects found too late. The man who told me to spend my life *creating something greater than myself* was living inside a cemetery of his mistakes.

Maybe neither of my parents were who I thought they were.

I find my way through the maze and to the front door before Tai can intercept me, heart pumping the blackest blood, and I break into a run to meet the car that dropped us off. It's still waiting outside the front gates, as promised, to take me to the city apartment in Limatra.

Tai can enjoy her reunion with this broken place, with her so-called happy memories, barbed things doomed to hurt us. She'll manage, by texting Saxim and Linos and the hundreds of vapid people in her orbit.

Tomí salutes me from the window of the guardhouse. I swallow hard, desperate to ignore the regret building in my chest—*you shouldn't leave Tai alone, don't leave Tai alone*—but . . . she thinks she's an adult, right?

And she knows where to find me.

As the fields and forests outside grow sparser and interspersed with more neon-lit buildings and parking lots, the buzzing in my skull subsides, and I let my shoulders fall and my eyelids droop.

I have secrets, too, Mama. I know how they nourish and how they nip. Help me understand yours.

Just don't make me go back there.

BOY

Live Video—THAÏS 12 months ago—Oh My G*d I Found a Stökéwood Home Video!!!
[Video starts]

Mireille and the girls are running, running, running through the moss garden, past the spitting carp, around the two giant hunchbacked chestnut trees, down the gravel road, and into the forest, painted emerald and gold by the afternoon sun.

They run over a moldy log, under a broken branch, through a spiderweb thin as a ghost bride's veil. In the distance, the corner of the cabin's roof appears. The chimney spits out thin whorls of smoke.

Tai takes a leap, landing on a rotted mess of roots, and her foot slips through.

She shrieks and falls to her knees. The camera rushes toward her, while still capturing another figure in the distance, reaching the cabin: Manon. She swirls around to track the shriek and doesn't slap her hand against the splintery wooden exterior wall.

"Hello?" Manon calls into the woods.

"OW OW OW OW," Tai shouts, still flopped on the ground with her foot trapped.

"Tai?" Manon says, squinting through the branches. "Is that you?" She steps away from the cabin, but in the wrong direction.

"Mama, help meeeeee," Tai shouts, even though the cameraman is right next to her. "Mama! Help!"

The normal chatter quiets as a cloud passes overhead, darkening the leaves. Somewhere a dove calls—its cooing low and mournful.

There is rustling in the branches. The camera spins around, ragged breathing audible.

"Mama?" Tai calls, hesitant.

The rustling continues. "It's probably just one of those mangy foxes that scampers across the lawn," the cameraman says. His voice is low, but he sounds like just a boy.

That's when Mireille runs out of the darkness, dropping to her knees. "Shut that off," she snaps at the camera, but he doesn't. She loosens Tai's foot with a surgeon's precision, frowning at the weakened roots, and kisses her ankle all over, until Tai breaks out in giggles.

"My poor lamb!" she says, kissing Tai across the forehead, the cheeks, and the shoulders as Tai squirms.

Tai smears the lipstick off, still laughing.

Manon comes trudging up behind them. They exchange a look. Mireille reaches for one of her hands, which she grants her, tentatively—then the other. She pulls Manon into her arms, too.

"My girls." She leads them toward the cabin, and Tai makes a point of slapping the outside wall hard, with a minxish grin at Manon.

Inside, a small stove burns. Somebody has laid out little painted cakes and miniature cups of tea.

Mireille pours tea into bone cups, so fragile.

"Chípí chípí," they say, clinking.

"What about my prize?" Tai says, without looking at Manon.

Mireille smiles and pulls a wrapped package from her pocket. "For you, Thaïs. An incredible display of agility," she says, bestowing it upon Tai with both hands.

Tai gives it a shake; it sounds full.

But then Mireille pulls out a second box and extends it to Manon. "And for Manon, whose caution in the forest—whose effort to protect us all—never goes unnoticed."

Manon smiles with tight lips and cuddles the box in her lap.

"But that's not fair," Tai says. "Only the winner should get the prize."

"My little one." Mireille ruffles Tai's hair. "Just as your sister looks to you for your great sense of adventure, for your open delight in the world, so must you look to her for her caution and awareness," she says, placing a hand on Tai's shoulder. Her eyes are dark. "These woods can be treacherous. You never know which trees will curl their roots around your ankles, which foxes will prance right down a foxhole with you in tow," she whispers. Her voice takes on a goofy pitch as she reaches for their necks with little fingers. "And which forest vines will grasp for your necks!"

The girls burst out into laughter, clutching their necks, contorting themselves to escape her tickles. The chocolates fall to the floor, and the camera takes a step back.

"We give up!" Tai shouts. "Leave us alone! We give up!"

They fall onto her in a pile, hysterical. Smiling.

Mireille, stroking their black hair, stiffens.

Mireille goes still then, her arms holding the girls close. "Let's be quiet, my loves," she says, looking out the scratched window *into the thick black-green tangle of the woods. "Your father's friends won't like that we're here."*

She watches the shadows outside as they thicken and multiply. As they turn the forest into something ominous and lush—dusky and replete with melancholy.

"But the forest is so lovely, isn't it?" Mireille continues. "Beauty isn't that which is beautiful, it is that which pleases us."

The cameraman steps back, then turns, the camera zooming into the meaty dark of the woods. He softly clears his throat.

"Your mother is so special," he whispers. "Are you special, too, girls?"

[Video ends]

TAI

This won't be super bubbly and fresh like I want it to be, but life's only like champagne in that it can be not-so-easy to digest sometimes, right?

Here's the truth: My parents each gave me a secret from the world, one beautiful egg of a secret each that I've carried with me since I was a snot-nosed kid, very, very carefully, so they would never crack.

Dad told me I was born with the mark of luck on me. It came in the form of this gross little fatty deposit at my temple—Mama had it removed by a plastic surgeon when I was a year old so I wouldn't be teased, thank God—but Dad told me the luck itself would never leave me, and . . . it hasn't.

And Mama: She used to take me up the ladder to the tower hidden in her bathroom, to the nest with the view of the forest that was only ours.

I was her special baby girl, and this was our special place.

She would wrap me in a cozy blanket, and cuddle me, and read to me from books like *The Twenty-One Balloons*, which she stored in a metal box, covered in foil animal stickers I had insisted we buy from this airport kiosk in Frankfurt.

The secret grew when she left. I knew she might have left a message for me there, but the room was locked and closed so that no one could enter. I couldn't tell Dad or Nons, because it was *our* secret place. Ours alone, and telling them would ruin it.

And I wanted to be the one who found her message, anyway.

I planned a lot in secret, in the days after she left. I was so goddamn industrious. I planned how to break into her bathroom (a set of master keys from Dad's Stökéwood office, where he slept most nights). I planned how to reach the rope coiling down from the ceiling (a step stool), and I planned how to pull and hold the attached ladder down (a hand weight from the creepy old home gym).

I put my plan into action, one rainy night, when Noni was curled on her side in bed, refusing to speak to me, and Dad was talking to Uncle Teddy downstairs.

Reaching the magazine box at last, I shut my eyes as I placed my fingers around the rusted latch.

It opened easily.

But it was . . . empty.

I scrabbled around the bottom, sure I was missing a compartment, and I knocked the flashlight off the ledge with my elbow. The jolt of it hitting the marble floor below broke me into sobs, thick, hot, wet tears that streamed out of me because I no longer cared if I was found. My hunch, the one I had so carefully tended, was wrong.

Mama had left me nothing.

It was one of the students from the institute—a part-time assistant to the family—who found me crying up there. In those days, they helped Dad with us, with everything, and he called them all Boy, which I recognize now was colossally fucked. This young guy helped me down, and I made him swear on his life he wouldn't tell anyone about the secret tower. He shrugged, probably thinking I was just some silly kid, and ruffled my hair before helping me off to bed.

The whole experience rattled me. I never snuck back into her bathroom again, at least not before we were shipped off to the States.

But if Dad did see Mama, and she had been back to Stökéwood since . . .

She might have left a message there for me. Where she knew only I—not Dad, not Manon—could find it.

So, as soon as Manon ditches me—as I suspected she would—I blast disco music saved on my phone and I slink around the stacks of moldy paperwork and make my way up the creaking grand staircase, past the moth-eaten velvet rope used to keep visitors away. It's actually cleaner than I thought, besides the nasty plate of withered fruit in the hallway and an actual shag carpet's worth of dust. The electricity works, even if some of the bulbs flicker. What's spookier is that the upstairs furniture has been sold off, but you can see the stained divots in the carpet, where the legs stood. My empty bedroom has been repainted asylum white, and everything in Noni's bedroom has been replaced with just two crisp white cots that could probably only fit me with my arms folded over my chest like a mummy. I find an old *Spirited Away* poster of Noni's rolled up in her closet, next to a useless, yellowed wall calendar with horrible, off-kilter drawings of old Viloki castles from 1988. Stökéwood is Miss December. Blasting ABBA, I prop both against the wall for pizazz, before edging toward Mama and Dad's bedroom.

The door is stuck—not locked, I don't think, but jammed—which sends a shivery ache through me. It also smells like a small animal died from starvation in the vents while watching endless seasons of *Love Island*. I raise the music's volume to keep the wrong kind of ghosts away.

The good news is, I can still access Mama's closet because it has a separate entrance on the floor. That's how big-ass it was. Most of its once-sparkling contents have been stripped away and auctioned off, but I can actually smell lavender in the cedar corners if I close my eyes. I find the secret cabinet that seamlessly blends into the wood, and it clicks open softly, revealing a couple of halfway-decent vintage pieces, forgotten for all these years. They probably need major dry cleaning, but I still spend too long running my fingers over their intricate beading and imagining that maybe she was the last person to touch one of them.

Then, with the feel of those nubs still imprinted on my hands, I push through to her private bathroom for the first time in a decade.

Her personal effects are gone—some went to me and Nons, like the glass bottles and gilded jewelry bowls and luxurious signature cosmetics, for us to spritz and spread onto our prepubescent bodies, to feel her close for just a minute even though that was probably a giant waste of La Mer—and others were just disposed of, I guess. The green-veined marble, which always looked like frog skin to me, is so cool to the touch. I turn the golden fleur-de-lis-shaped sink handle with a rusty squeak: The water spatters amber for a minute, then runs clean.

With my fingers, I work my way under the sink, toward the latch behind the false panel.

It's still there.

My nerves are the size of elephants in my stomach. I could vomit, but I don't want to clean, so I swallow five times, then take a quick yogic breath of fire and press down on it. And wait.

I hear a clunk overhead, and the panel in her ceiling exhales and cracks open half an inch.

Jammed.

When I was young, the panel would drop open like an unhinged jaw, and a woven rope would fall through the air, tonguing at the top of Mama's head. *A sick monster is licking you!* I would squeal. *No, I'm climbing up Rapunzel's marvelously thick yellow braid*, Mama replied, tugging on its greasy length to bring down the ladder.

I run for a broom, for a stick, anything to help me smack at the panel. I find an old chair in the hall. Straining on my tippy toes, I *just* make it, and with a *shooooomf*, years' worth of dust swirls through the space and blankets me, transforming the bathroom into a disgusting and magical space in the low light. Coughing, pulsing with adrenaline, I yank down the rope and ladder, which now seem small— as if made for children.

I feel disembodied as my palms and fingers close around the first rung. The flaking metal stings the skin on my palms. I don't know if it'll hold my weight. But it held hers, so I begin to climb, limbs shaking.

The windows in the tower above my head are dark with grime, so it's impossible to see out as I pull myself up, up, up. I feel, by memory, the first ledge by the window. That's where she sometimes lay down the blanket for us both to relax on.

"Our tree house," she whispered to me, and then she would find one of the books we stashed in the black metal magazine storage box, so they wouldn't get wet if the windows broke when a storm rolled through.

I step onto the ledge, feeling my way around the dark, and that's when my foot hits something with a clang.

The magazine box.

I feel faint.

Leaning toward it, I fall into a sneezing fit and almost tumble through the hole, down to the marble. I steady myself, head swimming.

The box is too heavy for me to carry. I take a breath, wondering if I can steel myself and manage anyway, like how moms stop cars barreling toward their children on TV. I peek down at the marble floor of her bathroom, and my nerves make a choice for me, shoving the magazine box straight through the opening.

It lands with a clattering banging *BOOM* that would wake the dead, and I scramble back down the ladder, knees wobbling.

The magazine box hasn't cracked the marble, but the marble has cracked *it* open. Spilling out are blackened pages, bound together.

My vision fizzes out as I fall to my hands and knees and start crying.

Because I see it.

Two words on the cover page:

White Fox.

"You fucking did it, bitch," I sob, clutching the script to my chest. Never in my life have I been more elated and frightened and buzzing full of these conflicting feelings, buzzing full enough to burst open wide, guts and heart pouring onto the filthy marble floor.

I win. I did it. I knew her. I found it.

The girl with the mark of luck does it again.

NONI

As soon as I arrive at the Limatra apartment, I take a searing-hot bath, hot enough to peel the skin right off me, turning the rest as satiny pink as a newborn's. I do this sometimes—usually after I binge-watch Mama's early movies for hours on end, after the banshee in my head starts to wail, *See this fresh young thing? She's dead; she's gone; she's dust.* I dunk my head under the water, sweating and burning, and give myself permission to cry, since Tai isn't around and doesn't seem to be coming anytime soon.

How could it even be possible Mama's still alive? How could my instincts be so wrong? Does this mean I gave up on her?

No tears come, and no answers come, only that filthy feeling of guilt, which I try to wash clean with more dunks in the hellish soapy soup.

I can't accept she might be alive, not intellectually. But the idea tunnels its way to the forefront of my thoughts anyway, leaking its toxic sweetness like the perfect drug.

I leave the bath when I start to feel faint and pad around the apartment barefoot. It's as gray and soulless as concrete every time I see it. There is no trace of Mama here, even though she chose this place because she wanted a cozy nook near the institute. The living room is bare except for uncomfortable black leather furniture (the modern kind missing real cushions, backs, and arms), and I gag every time I smell the wood-polish scent. The only two bits of decor—above a fake fireplace I can't turn on—are a *machíkíl* cleaver and a dreary Viloki painting of the original settlers playing cards at a tavern. The kitchen cabinets are empty, and the expensive coconut water in the fridge—I glug down two, pink sluicing down my chin—screams *Teddy's assistant was here.*

Dad didn't stay here at all the past few years, but he never sold it. I wonder if he was keeping it for me and Tai, or if he thought Mama might return.

I change into a fresh pair of jeans, clean skin still raw, before hitting the streets alone. *The book, don't forget the book you need to write.* I'm late for my afternoon appointment: a meeting scheduled weeks ago at the store Mama took me to once a week as a child—our little secret.

The street is quiet in May, the afternoon light streaming through the tree branches so that the sidewalk looks paved with scales of gold. I walk past finely dressed young women, pale-faced and light-footed, filtering out of the glass palaces of Dior, Chanel, Hermès as they close for the day. This neighborhood is known for its luxury boutiques and upscale tea parlors, where the Viloki mulberry tea is priced like the rarest threads of saffron, even though it tastes the same as everywhere else. Soon, the city will swell with summertime visitors, who buy luxury goods like they're convenience store trinkets.

But Limatra isn't homogenous, like other Mediterranean hot spots—because its founders were Norman, Arab, Byzantine-Greek, Lombard, Swabian, Albanian, Aragonese, Jewish. None of the people I pass on the street share Mama's bronze skin and reddish-brown hair. A hundred unique sets of wrinkled eyes watch me from every row of a passing silver Hero Pharm bus, which transports people from the factory near the airport to stops throughout the city.

The only common characteristic of these faces is their glum, bored expression. Tired and closed off, like the commuters I see on the subway back home.

I wonder if it was like this ten years ago. I wonder what Mama and Dad hoped it would be like today.

Some institute students pass me then, whispering, their bags stuffed with bundles of clean-bristled paintbrushes and plastic-wrapped sketchbooks for summer session. They wear rainbow-colored leather loafers and cashmere sweaters, one with this distinctive curling script on it reading *I'm a boss* that reminds me of something I saw Tai wearing once. "I'm finally ready to focus on my art," one says, and they don't notice me in my old baseball cap, my run-down sneakers, my untrendy jeans. And that's fine: I aimed to disappear. Only a solitary man reading on a bench lets his newspaper dip for a moment to eye me as I approach the shop: Katox Floral.

I bite my lip to keep from crying: It looks exactly the same.

Same telltale green sloped roof, same carved wooden door—out of place and quaint here, where most buildings are slick and composed of glass and basalt.

For fifty years, Katox has been known far and wide as one of the most esteemed practitioners of the school of Viloki floristry. Mama ordered an arrangement from him once a week in the early years, coming in from Stökéwood to pick it up herself and nestling it in her library office. Those days, she'd ask me to meet her by her desk—

Shh, she'd said, *it's our secret; don't tell Tai*—where she shared old Viloki stories and taught me how to write my own. One morning, she brought *me* to Katox for the first time. My face hurt from smiling while she showed off just how much I knew, to this diminutive older man with chunky glasses who looked like a wise old owl. She took me the next week, then the next. It was our day.

When I was fifteen, I read an old interview where Mama said she considered her florist to be a "close friend and spiritual guide," and I knew she meant Katox. I knew how much those visits meant to her—to us. When I emailed his store weeks ago to schedule an appointment, his assistant—an accommodating, if curt, Foix Institute alum—told me a short afternoon session would have to suffice, because now Katox works only two hours a day, two days a week, certain seasons.

I hold my breath, feet tingling as I step inside. The shop is freezing—and empty. I glance back outside, wondering if the curious man reading the newspaper was Katox, but he's disappeared.

I look around: the showroom is crafted entirely of chestnut wood, like I remember, its beams of light showcasing minimalist arrangements spaced along the thin tables, and an emerald-green silk curtain separates this showroom from the back of the shop.

And even though the store feels like a museum, all the arrangements seem very much *alive*, each bud breathing in its place like a proud performer, which isn't something I've ever felt about flower bouquets in the States—those manage to look both stiff and wilted. Granted, my experience with them is limited to grocery store bouquets and online snapshots. But there's magic in these arrangements that wouldn't translate into a photo. The branches reach out toward me like fairy fingers. If I focus, I can remember standing with Mama, running my hands over the nodes of the spindly, berried limbs of an arrangement resembling these.

Lílium, she whispered, kissing my forehead and pointing to the prickly-looking red spider lily beside us, with its reaching tentacles.

Swípí, she said, circling delicate pink closed buds.

Sweet . . . pea? I asked, and she laughed.

Yes. Viloki name taken from the English. I promise I'm not inventing anything.

If she's still alive somewhere, would she have walked by Katox's store just once in the past decade, if only to peek through the glass and steal a glimpse of this sublime beauty?

If only to remember those days with me?

I'm staring at an alien-looking, sparse bundle of spiky flowers when someone whispers something in Vilosh behind me, tickling the back of my neck. I jump; it's a squirrelly young man in a marled sweater and an apron, his brown hair tied into a bun on top of his head in a fashion suspiciously reminiscent of Tai.

"Manon Hammick?" he asks, though I know we both know he knows. His hands are wet with flecks of green. "I'm Malto." He wipes his fingers on his apron as he sneaks a look at the curtain concealing the back of the store. "Are you ready?"

Before I can nod, a bell rings in the far room, and Malto spins away from me on his heel before hissing, over his shoulder: "Katox only has six minutes. Don't make eye contact. Don't mention what day it is, or, God forbid, what year: He doesn't think linearly." He sniffs the air. "He doesn't like perfume, so it's good you didn't wear any. Oh, and he speaks in riddles. But don't tell him that, because he might stop talking completely." He hesitates by the curtain, as if he deals with that silence often, before more or less pushing me into its silken embrace.

I stumble through, and there he is: the wizened old man, shorter than I am, with a wispy white beard and a chunky pair of black glasses. Katox. I recognize him, and a warm smile spreads across my face. He's wearing a pressed, moss-green smock and clogs, hunched over a sink exploding with barbed sprigs of luscious blossoms.

I stop and stare, waiting for him to acknowledge my presence in any small way.

"Though this flower blooms only one week a year, I do not believe it is any more precious for it," he says at last, in formal, old-fashioned Vilosh, handling the stems. My mouth opens and closes as he sighs. "But I do adore it, and I miss it when it's gone. I am nothing but a soft overripe fruit myself, now, all pulp and old bruising."

We stand in silence, his eyes still trained on the flowers.

I'm not entirely sure he knows I'm here.

"Mr. Katox," I say. "I'm . . . Man—"

"Fruit never drops far from the tree," he interrupts. He still won't look at me, but his expression softens from one of reserve into something gentler yet unreadable. "She moves with such muted yet contagious delight around my shop."

I wonder if he's talking about me—if he was watching me through the curtain. I'd been tiptoeing with awe.

"Mr. Katox," I say quietly, "I—" I clear the wobble in my throat. Is he saying he's seen her? He's seen Mama? "Mr. Katox, I don't know if you remember me. Are you saying you've seen or spoken to my mother, Mireille Foix Hammick . . . recently?"

He smiles with only his eyes. Wandering toward another sink, he passes a hanging scape of lilies and outlines their arc of movement with one hand. In that single motion I see a lifetime of reverence for nature.

"I see her everywhere," he says, and a shiver runs through me, as he plucks a flower from a bundle in the second sink by the throat. "Painted, florid, on signs meant to be grazed by as many eyes as possible. But we haven't spoken afresh since the day she went silent, like a dormant bulb beneath the dirt, protecting her bloom until spring." He smells the flower's freshness and checks the sharpness of the tool in hand. Then he slices cleanly through the base of its neck. It's violent work, and it sends a chill through me. *A dormant bulb beneath the dirt.*

"Mr. Katox," I say, stepping closer to try to catch his eyes. "Wait. You mean you spoke to her the day she disappeared?"

He pauses over the arrangement. I can't see his pupils behind the thick lenses, but I watch him blink. "A dormant bulb beneath the dirt, protecting her bloom until spring," he repeats, impenetrably.

Goose bumps bubble up under my shirt, tender to the touch. Katox says the words like they mean everything, but they mean nothing at all. I bite my lip hard to stop the hope from draining out of me.

But if he knew anything, someone—the police, a fan, my father— would've learned it before me. A cruel voice whispers in my head: *There is nothing you can learn about Mama that someone else doesn't already know.*

"Are you . . . *crying?*" Katox asks, turning to look at me for the first time. His eyes are clear and dark behind the thick lenses, something coldly similar to bemused disdain inside of them.

"Mr. Katox," I say, wiping away the moisture that came from nowhere. I feel like I'm seven years old, red-cheeked and mushy. "Did she say anything to you that day? I need to know."

He considers me head-on. Then he glances at his little golden bell, as if about to ring it, before crossing his arms.

"She will never leave you, not unless it's absolutely crucial to your survival," he says, with the utmost seriousness. *She will never leave you.* As if she's not already gone.

I can't help but wonder why he says this in the future tense. Is it like his assistant said—he doesn't think linearly? Or is he just a callous old man? Because it's painful to imagine Mama abandoned me for my own good. Especially now, when she might be . . .

I banish the thought.

Before I can respond, he slides the vase over the chestnut countertop toward me.

"For you and your sister," he says. "The bloom."

The flowers are a gorgeously empty gesture: graceful expressions of nothing more than this man's pride in his lifelong rapport with nature. *For your sister, the bloom.*

It hits me then—this memory of Tai crying, her face this hot, red, wet, yowling thing, on one of the last days Mama and I came back from our Katox outing.

Why did you leave me? she screamed in between sobs, a pint-size storm in the foyer. She'd been fighting a fever the night before. *Why did you leave me?*

Mama dropped the arrangement in my arms and ran to her.

For your sister, the bloom.

I want to shove the flowers right back at Katox, splashing his green smock and his prim expression.

He barely acknowledged my existence. I know I shouldn't care, but somehow . . . this visit cheapened all my good memories here.

He turns back to clean the countertops, contented, and rings a golden bell with one hand. Malto darts out from the front of the store, shepherding me away from his teacher and out of the shop before I can gather my thoughts.

I stand on the front doormat, hands locked around the oversize arrangement.

This was useless.

There's nothing here for me to collect, to pad and soothe my rough and scraped-raw psyche, my bottomless pit of *need* for her love.

But where will there be something?

I walk away, glancing through the luxury-store windows and debating walking inside, but I can't imagine finding anything of value in any of them. This is Tai's domain, not mine.

"Wait!" someone shouts behind me.

I stop in the middle of the street and see Malto, jogging toward me with his apron balled up in his hands. He looks healthier and more alive out here, in view of the sun.

"I heard you asking questions about your mom," he whispers, with a sidelong glance at a shopgirl passing us on clacking heels. "You should talk to the assistant who I replaced. His name is Yuki. I don't know anything else about him because Katox keeps no records, but he worked here while your mom was a customer, and I'm sure they spoke. Katox refuses to talk about him—I think he left on bad terms—but he once accused me of chattering endlessly like him." He stares at me, and I can glimpse a different person inside him, someone who isn't afraid of his domineering boss. "I'm sorry if he offended you. He's—he can be an asshole."

"Why do you stay with him?" I ask, before I can stop myself. The whole point of the Foix Institute's programs—of Hero Pharm's programs—was that smart, motivated young people could get the education they needed to work anywhere.

His eyes narrow. "Where else am I supposed to get work? This isn't exactly New York," he says pointedly, and I feel my innards shrivel.

Catching me wince, he softens. "This is the cream of the crop on Viloxin. I went to your mom's institute for interior design, and this is who they paired me with. It's a small island." He wrings his apron in his hands. "Working with one spoiled old man who makes bank is better than catering to boatloads of tourists."

I open my mouth to reply when a distant bell rings, and Malto pales.

"That bell haunts my goddamn dreams," he says, before sprinting back the way he came.

I pass a small bakery that smells of vanilla and fresh brioche, and I buy some snacks, hoping it'll help my blood sugar. Too many coins drop from my fingers, and my nails are blue when I collect the change.

Yuki. It's not a common name, but it's not uncommon, either. He could be anywhere right now, just like Mama. But at least it's a clue.

I walk down a smaller side street, carrying the flower arrangement and the snacks, passing a wall of intricate graffiti as well as what look like very secure, upscale apartment structures. There are video cameras visible on every building, but no pedestrians at all. Clouds pass overhead, turning the alley gray. A melancholy quiet settles over me that makes me feel isolated and heartsore. Hooking the snack bag onto my arm, I check my phone with a free hand, and that's when I see them:

Dozens of missed calls from Tai. Text after text, reading: *CALL ME THE F BACK*.

I curse and fumble with everything in my arms, dialing her back and getting her voice mail, again and again.

Only then do I hear the irregular footsteps over my nervous heartbeat, over that ominous buzzing that starts somewhere between my ears.

I sneak a look back at the main street. An unfamiliar man in jeans and a military jacket lopes toward me, his bearded face half-covered by a hat. Newspaper in hand.

It's the man from before. Reading, on the bench outside Katox's shop.

"We need to talk," he calls down the alley. Something about his tone, his gait sends a prickling warning up my neck. There's something wrong with him. He reminds me of the fans, of the obsessives who sometimes approached Mama, who sometimes find Tai, even me. The ones who reached for Mama's hair, who got close enough to smell her because they felt entitled to it.

He saw me, before. He recognized me. I don't answer, increasing my pace instead. We're alone on the side street, and the road only becomes quieter from here. Emptier. His footsteps don't quicken behind me, but I hear them, his shoe soles scraping against the sidewalk. The flower arrangement feels so heavy in my arms, and even though it's wrapped at the base, I hear water sloshing inside.

"Did you hear me, Manon?" he says, the mockery in his voice not cold enough to conceal his hunger. "Stop."

But when I hear my name, the buzzing overwhelms me, and I run, weighed down by the arrangement I cling to still. As I turn right on the next street, a Mercedes-Benz sedan emerges from a garage, engine purring like velvet, blocking me. I hurry toward its front windows, but the car roars away, its driver still faceless.

And I am alone once more, except for the crackling static in my head, except for the coppery tang of those fizzy pennies, except for—

I hear the man repeating my name, like it's a warped nursery rhyme, like he needs me, gaining on me with each rasp of his feet.

I consider dropping the arrangement and bag of snacks and running. I consider turning and shouting, *What do you want? Leave me alone.* I consider surprising him and throwing the bundle at his face. How far would it go? It's so heavy.

And I'm not so strong.

I look up at the cameras watching from every building facade. But what good would they do, those unfeeling sentinels? Always reporting, never acting.

"Jesus Christ," he says, almost amused, as if I've made him work for it, as if my terror is both thrilling and inconvenient, and the footsteps behind me quicken, quicken impossibly, and before I know it, the buzzing reaches its brutal peak and hot panic floods me as I smell *him*, his foul onion stench, and when I turn to face him, he is tipping back his hat. He has white, raking lines on his left cheek, like a fox scratched him long ago. His furred cheeks rise, and he smiles at me with glittering fury. The smile says: *You should be afraid of me.*

And my body obeys, that smile stealing my breath away.

As I open my mouth to scream, to try to make a sound, his free fingers brush the ends of my hair, and with that sickeningly gentle touch my humming arms and legs are awakened, and I throw the flower arrangement into him with all my might—*Why was I still holding it? Why?*—and the vase crashes into his gut, then shatters into glass shards at his feet, and I do not see his eyes, but in that moment I know that I can—

Run.

I sprint, surprised my bakery bag is still hooked on my arm, jostling, and as my feet pound the concrete, my fizzing brain replays that tortured split second in which I braced for him to take my hair in hand and drag me to the floor. I can almost feel the sting of my scalp and the scraping of my knees, and my eyes burn with tears as I round the corner, pushing deep into one crowd, then another. Ramming past an old woman and her rolling shopping cart, past a group of schoolgirls sporting striped school bags, past two young women chatting brightly in slacks and sensible heels. Hoping to dissolve into the infernal humming in my head, to dissolve into nothing, so no one can grab me ever again.

BOY
The Viloki Sun—
January 15, 2010

The Viloki Sun can exclusively report that an ex-employee of
Hero Pharm has come forward with new information about
the "myriad stalkers" who harassed the Foix Hammick family
in the years prior to Mireille Foix's disappearance.

"It was hell to be that family—you never knew if a stranger
on the street was unnaturally obsessed with Mireille or Hëró
or, worse . . . their little girls," he notes. "I'm not surprised
Hëró sent the girls away and isolated himself completely.
There were always whisperings that something was wrong
with him. Hëró refused to be disturbed while working, so his
team of advisers frequently kept important information from
him. He wasn't quite right in the head; he couldn't handle
reality."

Who are these mysterious advisers? All we can surmise is

that Tiro Nítuchí, Hëró's right-hand man, who now jockeys for the CEO role, was surely among them.

But does this employee have any theories as to why Mireille Foix disappeared? Readers will remember that the *Sun* exclusively printed excerpts of the report in which the police commissioner concluded she left her family—and the spotlight—of her own accord.

"Why do I think Mireille left? I think she got tired of all the negative attention from Hero Pharm's issues, which sullied her brand as 'nouveau queen of Viloxin,'" our source says. "Maybe she even killed herself."

We approached Antella Arnoix, Hero Pharm board member and matriarch of the Arnoix family—the oldest known family on Viloxin—for comment. It is speculated that Antella Arnoix and Mireille Foix Hammick were very close. However, her representative informed the *Sun* that "the Arnoix family doesn't discuss the Foix Hammick family anymore."

It seems the "nouveau queen of Viloxin" has lost her reputation among the aristocratic Viloki set. And what about Arnoix's new neighbor in the posh suburb of Mitella—Mireille Foix Hammick's brother-in-law, Teddy Hammick? On that subject, Arnoix did *not* remain mum.

"Clouded Cage is eroding the moral fabric of Viloki society with its toxic inventions," conveyed her rep. Is the Arnoix family furious, perhaps, that Clouded Cage founder, Teddy Hammick, recently expanded his Mitella mansion, absorbing the meadow plot next to their centuries-old castle? Or perhaps they're miffed because they were granted an ownership interest in Hero Pharm by Hëró Hammick in the 1970s, but there's been no such luck with Hëró's brother and his prize monolith, Clouded Cage?

TAI

I read every single page of *White Fox*. Every page of the three parts in my hands. I try to dial Noni, I do, but I can't resist what's in those pages. When I finish, I manage one solitary mind-muddling half hour of unrestrained sobbing on the cold green marble floor before running down the drive to the edge of the woods for a single bar of cell service and desperately calling my sister, who—shocker—doesn't answer. I feel weird spilling the exact nature of the news to a voice mail box, so eventually I just beg her to call me. And then, of course, I call Saxim.

When my childhood best friend hears that I've discovered three parts of *White Fox*, she tells me to give her ten minutes to persuade her mother to let her borrow the car on a school night—otherwise, she'll hitchhike. This from a person who bites her nails to the quick watching characters break rules in movies.

"Bless you," I whisper, my voice still tear-cracked and oddly Maggie Smith–ish, and I hang up and walk along the woods back to the house, remembering, in this pungent flash, the jag of fear in Saxim's beautiful moon eyes when I tried to drag her into its depths to play a "spooky" version of the Miraculous Adventures of Basil & Monty. Stökéwood is so much quieter now, its true nature hidden under overgrown roots and a crust of moss. Lost to the forest of delirium, forgotten by most of those around it.

But not forgotten by Mama and me.

Vibrating with adrenaline, I change into Dad's Mickey Mouse T-shirt and drop to the floor in his sickroom, clutching the script. I shiver with a cup of dirty-tasting tea, ruminating over its contents. I don't know what to make of the script; it was too much, so much.

And I'm also afraid. Afraid I'll start to dig into every single dark detail, only to discover that *White Fox* is another empty magazine box, telling me she didn't love me—didn't care as much as I think she did. I already know, from a single read, that it contains many baited traps.

I turn up that 1970s playlist on my phone until it's loud enough to burst eardrums.

"I promise to take care of your family," interrupts the robo-nurse from her perch in the corner, in her honeyed, calm voice, and I almost leap out of my skin.

Her name, she reminds me—blinking her long-ass lash pixels—is *Mina*.

"Don't forget the retrospective tomorrow night, Thaïs," she says, her eyes curving into cheerful n's. "It should be a marvelous night."

I choke on my tea, spluttering and splashing it on Mickey's red hotpants. "Excuse me?"

"Oh, my dear," she says, electronic eyebrows drooping at the ends with concern. "Do drink more slowly."

"Who programmed you to be such a mom, Mina?" I ask. I can . . . almost trick myself into believing she's a friend.

"It is most important to be courageous and kind," Mina replies inexplicably, something wise and mystical to her flat-paneled face.

"I mean, sure."

I forage for dinner, which is a cold packaged deal, found in multi-colored stacks in the otherwise empty fridge and ordered by Mina from some sadistic cafeteria. I sit eating on the same floor of the sick-room, back against the wall, eyeballs zooming from the empty space on Dad's bed to the side table where I've set down *White Fox*.

"Hi, parents," I say to the empty room. The Bee Gees croon, as I pick through a lump of what might be salt cod and imagine having dinner here with him, blurring time so it's one year ago.

"My compliments to your chef, Dad," I say aloud. "These salt cod strips are both soggy and jerky-tough."

He would smile, lips pale, and shake his head. Maybe I would try a sip of Dad's dinner, some green goo fashioned by Mina, too, only to realize that it's definitely a controlled substance and entirely magical. Mina's panel would darken with concern as waves of pleasant heat roll through to my toes, and I would start telling Dad horrible, outdated, your-mama jokes. Dad and I would laugh with each other like we haven't in a while, at—really—nothing at all, and he would become, for a moment, the softer, more tender version of the Dad I knew. I would take his hand, smaller than ever, but lily-white and perfect, the nails shaped recently by someone, someone meticulous. *Thaïs*, he would say. *I'm so glad you're here.*

And that's when "Rocket Man" by Elton John starts on my play-list, like Dad's summoned it.

And I remember.

Remember when I was six years old and Dad was working late in his office downstairs. I had a habit of sneaking down in my pajamas when everyone else had gone to sleep and peering around the corner. Sometimes, very late at night, Dad would play music on his record player. He loved David Bowie and Elton John, and night after night, I would watch him, pencil in his mouth, hunched over his desk with a single light on, working after everyone else had gone to sleep. Sometimes he would catch a glimpse of me down the hall and beckon, and I would sit on his lap, listening to the music while he worked, until he told me it was time to go to back to bed.

But one night.

One night, I peeked around the corner, and "Rocket Man" was playing: a song I loved, because sometimes he tapped his pencil and hummed and smiled when it played. A song I'd memorized, to keep its magic close.

When he caught my eye, I hid back. But then, I poked my head out and mouthed the words, each and every one perfect. At first, Dad just blinked, but after a minute, his mouth wobbled, like he was fighting a smile, and then he broke out into a closed-mouth grin.

Floating on air, I darted out into the open and mouthed the words and danced, the little six-year-old doing karaoke in a darkened hallway at night, the lamp on her dad's desk her only sun, moon, star.

And Dad began to laugh, and Dad stood, and I ran for him, and he took my hands, and . . .

How we danced, spinning in our socks and dipping and howling at—

"Your friend is coming up the drive, Thaïs," Mina says gently, dissolving the memory. I would be crying if my tear ducts could manage. They ache from earlier, and my skin feels tight to the touch.

The headlights of Saxim's mom's car shine through a grimy Stökéwood window before I hear its engine. I bound through the house, bubbling over with fresh energy, itching to show someone my discovery, and by the time I reach the front door, the car's headlights have gone dark and the doors are closed. The woman with her back to me is tall, lithe, and elegant, her black hair tied up into a French twist, and if it weren't for her school uniform and the fact I know Saxim's mom is so petite, I would think it's her mother. Saxim turns to face me, slipping her cell phone in her pocket, and her eyes are exactly the same as always: dark and wet and long-lashed and gleaming, the kind of eyes you could fall into if your feet aren't firmly planted on the ground. It's disorienting to see her: this girl, this woman who has been my lifeline for years, a relationship only deepened by the special-edition pink clamshell keychain Pocket Best Friends Uncle Teddy gifted us after I left Viloxin to live with Aunt Marion. Besides cultivating our Best Friends (which involved loads of faux electronic hairstyling), we communicated every day, and I woke tingling to see the neat bubbles of her therapeutic replies, painstakingly typed after she finished her homework. No one else used the custom application in the entire world, so I was Basil, and she was—

"MONTY!" I shout, launching myself at her. She startles as I wrap myself around her, but her giggle is the exact same, too: unapologetically joyful, infectious, life-affirming. She smells the same: like heady gardenia.

She's stiff under my arms until she replies, in bad British English: "By Jove, Basil, you haven't changed a spot." She holds me extra-long, feeding me her Saxim strength and love like only she could when we were younger and life was difficult in those small ways that felt impossibly large.

When I pull away, she looks as shiny-eyed and tight-cheeked from smiling as I feel, and I take her supple hands and remember them tenderly braiding my hair, and pulling mine, dripping, out of the pool.

"Aren't you going to invite me into the manor and offer me a spot of tea?" She squeezes my palms.

"Quit saying *spot*, you nerd, or you're going to make me break out before the retrospective," I say, leading her into the house. "God, I've missed you. We need to talk."

∞ ∞ ∞

We're cozied up on the sofa in the library, under two moth-eaten baby alpaca blankets (Basil always chose green, and Monty always chose petal pink), with cups of tea (made with ancient, dusty, possibly bio-hazardous tea bags), when unfailingly polite and kind Saxim finally alludes to the reason I called her here.

I've been avoiding the topic of the script, which winks at us both from a side table, choosing instead to fill her in on the sanitized, sit-com version of my life in America: how it took forever to wrangle the handle *Thaïs*, how I'm on my way to becoming a boss, how radically joyful romantic comedies are all I want to watch, how it's not so much about curating a genuine feed as it is distilling your You-ness down into something super flavorful and digestible, how I want to hate Aunt Marion for being crotchety and judgmental and, yeah, secretly blowing money Dad left us on crystals and hypnosis classes, but so much of the hippie bullshit she says comes true (like celery being a power vegetable), and . . .

She sets her mug down on a side table, and a dust bunny launches itself onto her pristine white blouse. I swipe at it uselessly while she flinches it off. "I still can't believe you found it in a single afternoon," she whispers, tugging the fabric smooth. "It's as if you called it into existence. Are you and Manon managing?" She turns toward the hall. "Where is she? I wouldn't be able to let it out of my sight. What a shock—"

"It's a goddamn miracle, Saxim. Mama left it for me." I smile to myself, jaw aching.

Saxim watches me. "So, reading between the lines here . . . Manon hasn't seen it."

I meet her eyes and bark out a sparkling laugh. "I tried to contact her! She wouldn't answer my calls! How was I supposed to stop myself from reading this?"

Her mouth wrinkles.

"It was Manon's choice to abandon me here. I think I deserve a victory lap, don't you?"

"A victory lap?" Saxim's eyes darken.

Sometimes I choose the wrong words. But how could anyone understand, even if I chose the right ones? I am the only person who connected with Mama in this way. I am the only person who found her secret message to us, after a decade apart. I am the only person who can reclaim the joy we felt here.

I am the only one who knows for certain that Mama is alive and on Viloxin at this very moment. But I remember my promise to Noni after reading Dad's letter: *Tell no one.*

"Enough about *White Fox* for now, okay?" I say, sounding and feeling like a faux-jolly talk show host. "Let's just remember the good times, all right? I refuse to remember this place as anything but happy, Saxim. Because I loved growing up here. On Viloxin, and at Stökéwood. Remember the pool games we used to play? And the treasure hunts Mama would set up? Remember grade school, with the set lunches and the uniform with the hood, and learning the alphabet with the calligraphy brush? I mean, it was . . . pure life, in a way you just don't get now. I wouldn't trade those days for the world."

I stop speaking—*pure life? Am I high?*—but I'm breathing hard, and the air looks speckled and strange around Saxim, who is silently watching me. When I stare back, she averts her eyes and looks out the window, scratching at her sleeve.

"What?" I ask. My hands are shaking again, and I don't know if it's the radioactive tea, jet lag, or nerves. I need Saxim to be normal, even as I acknowledge I don't know what that means. Bright? Happy? Reassuring? Responsive? "You need to tell me what you're thinking, Saxim. Please."

It takes another full minute of silence before she opens her mouth. "What is with this American obsession with being happy all the time? We're not filming for an audience, Tai."

I swallow hard and feel tears prickle my sockets. "What? What do you mean?"

She says nothing. Her eyes could swallow lakes, could swallow entire underwater worlds.

"Please, say something."

She smooths one eyebrow carefully, slowly. "I love you, Tai—I always will, but I won't watch you act when it's just the two of us," she says.

My breath stops. For one sticky moment, I feel caught, exposed, wounded.

"If you want honesty and company, I will always give it," she adds, pushing her hair behind her ears. "But I won't help you delude yourself."

My lips are dry.

"Do you want to know what I remember from our childhood?" she says. "What I really, truly remember?"

I don't want to know. I want her to let me be an animatronic theme park host, smiling and delighting with my falseness until my battery pack powers down. But it's Saxim, who loves me, and I love her, so I bite my tongue. We stare at each other until she speaks.

"We were strange and lonely kids," she starts. "You and Manon rarely left Stökéwood, and you always kept to yourselves at school. We became friends because I was a loner, too, and you needed someone else to play one of your invented schoolyard games when Manon didn't overlap with you during breaks. Your mother had you homeschooled for a bit, don't you remember? I guess we spoke to that genius intern your dad kept around, some. What was his name? He must have been in his twenties, though."

I shiver and drink down the grassy dregs in my cup of tea to keep myself from looking at her. "I mean, there were obviously speed bumps when it came to integrating, but Dad and Mama were good at handling them. You have to remember that. They made me feel special and loved, and I think every child needs that," I say, the words spilling out like sparkling tangled balls of thread that blacken as soon as they fall. "And I'm sorry if Manon never felt that way, you know? But I felt it. That's why I am who I am today. That's why I found *White Fox*."

The air between us, thick with upset dust, wavers in my vision. And Saxim says nothing, because she knows I'm full of shit. I sip at my teacup again, and a shred of loose tea lumps into my mouth. It's sour. I spit it out, pawing at my tongue like a cat, and Saxim watches me still.

"Tai," she says calmly, doing and undoing her cuff button with her fingers.

"Yeah," I say hastily, knowing full well I'm doing it again. Rationalizing. Lying. "Okay. I'm sorry." I've begun to sweat through the cotton T-shirt. It feels as if Stökéwood is expanding and contracting around us in the library, like a heart.

"They were kind, but they were very busy, Tai. I remember your mother working on that project, I suppose, in the library, and kissing us on the head and shooing us away when we interrupted her. Your father, I . . ." She stops, watching for pain in my eyes. "There were a few different nannies, though, and the intern, and your uncle, too, of course, who took us to polo games."

I swallow, the lump in my throat dry as a hairball. "Uncle Teddy is the best." I sound far away—like I'm hearing my own voice spoken back to me, down a tunnel. "He's all I have now. Him, Aunt Marion, Manon, you." *Until Mama is back*, I think. Saxim watches me with a tender mix of pity, horror, and love. I shouldn't be able to stand it. But it's so honest, it just makes me want to cry some more.

I wish she wouldn't look at me that way.

When I start to cry this time, wiping my nose on Mickey's ear, she wraps me in a hug. "I'm sorry about your dad," she whispers in my hair, tugging the T-shirt straight. "I know how much you loved him."

And I wasn't thinking about him before, but now I am—thinking about him and the fact that how much you love someone doesn't matter if you're too late to tell them properly. Like, I always shouted *weloveyadad* every time we hung up the phone, but I just can't stop thinking about how he lived in that drab and lifeless sickroom alone, for who knows how long, hiding out from the men who turned on him, calling him sick, paranoid, irresponsible (I read the articles—I read all of them) and pushed him out of his own company, giving him an honorary title that meant nothing.

The same men who did something to Mama, to make her hide herself away.

Dad knew it, and he tried to root out the evil. That must have been why everything soured for him at Hero Pharm. It must have been.

Not because he was sick. But because when he lost his trust in Hero Pharm, they turned on him, the *paranoid hermit founder*, leaving him to rot here, in the dark.

But I say none of this aloud. Because I know a part of myself would love to stop in self-pity city all night long and just feed off of Saxim's sympathy—if she'd give me any. So instead, I bring my hands to my wet eyes, letting the tears soak into my skin like some kind of janky serum, and melt away.

"Can you tell me about your life, Monty? I've been so rude. And I've missed you so much," I say, as soon as I find my voice. I sound crystalline and breakable.

She watches me carefully, and her shoulders soften. When she speaks, I don't say anything for a while. I only listen and absorb, aware it's something I don't do often enough. As she talks, I settle back onto the cushions, and she reaches out and smooths my hairline.

And even though part of me wants to hate her: for her version of the truth; her mentions of her vacation to the Greek islands with her parents; her tidy adolescence spent winning scholarships, playing harp like a freaking angel; and becoming best friends with an effervescent dynamo who dresses exclusively in latex on weekends . . . I can't help but love having Saxim next to me, slowly, carefully drawing circles in the dust with her foot.

It isn't until later, when we've drained and refilled our cups of tea at least half a dozen times, that I ask her if she'll read it with me. *White Fox*.

"Without Manon?" she asks.

"You're my real sister, Saxim," I say. "You know that." And even though her mouth wrinkles, I mean it, I do.

PART ONE

CAPTOR (V.O.)
This is the story of a woman with a
secret.

EXT. DELIRIUM FOREST—NIGHT

Wet leaves flashing past, branches whipping at the
face and bare arms of someone running. Someone
whose face is unseen. BREATHING and FOOTSTEPS.

WHITE FOX (V.O.)
In the beginning, she ran.

There's a SHADOW in the dark, approaching. Many
SMALL SHADOWS, multiplying and turning the forest

blacker than night. The breathing quickens, the footsteps accelerate.

                    WHITE FOX (V.O.)
        But she didn't run fast enough.

SHADOW passes over and fills screen.

EXT. STREET—NIGHT

Bombed-out Limatra, late 1945. Streets filled with rubble. An air of misery. But the small red-light street remains desperately alive. Painted signs flash luridly, and drunks stumble past, singing to themselves. There's a torn poster among the rubble advertising a performance by a famous dancer named White Fox.

Bicycle bells and the sound of distant engines intermingle with shouts of manic mirth and fear. A man is ejected from a bar for unruliness. A glimpse of a scantily clad woman in the window above, before the blinds are shut.

INT. GENTLEMAN'S CLUB / CELL—NIGHT

A dark cell, with a SINGLE, PENETRATING SPOTLIGHT.

WHITE FOX, with tear-streaked cheeks in a stained dress. Elegant, despite the circumstances.

Her hair, once pinned, is falling: It would be pure

white, but it is stained dark with charcoal or some
other powdery substance.

                    WHITE FOX
               (speaking into the dark)
          Let. Me. Go.

Unseen CAPTOR, androgynous yet cheeky voice,
clicks on the LOUDSPEAKER, visible above White
Fox.

                    CAPTOR (O.C.)
          No.

White Fox screams.

                    CAPTOR (O.C.)
          The room is soundproofed, dear. It's just
          you and me. It's always just you and me.

White Fox stops, shell-shocked.

                    WHITE FOX
               (speaking into the dark)
          Let. Me. Go!

Unseen Captor sighs.

                    CAPTOR (O.C.)
          This is growing tiresome, my dear White
          Fox. It's auction time, soon. Time to

turn on your famous charm. You won't
like the men who want you when you're
despondent and hopeless.

                    WHITE FOX
I'm not . . . You can't just kidnap
people off the street like this. My
friends will find me. I'm not some . . .
sack of meat . . .

                    CAPTOR (O.C.)
Who will find you, darling?

White Fox feels along the walls for a seam.

                    WHITE FOX
You can't just dress me up and subject
me to this. You're evil.

                    CAPTOR (O.C.)
Am *not*. I'm neither bad nor good. I
ride the changing tides. As should
you.

A CRACKLE over the intercom.

                    CAPTOR (O.C.) (CONT'D)
They are here.

LOUDSPEAKER clicks off.

A hidden door CREAKS open. White Fox glances up.

INT. GENTLEMAN'S CLUB / AUCTION ROOM—NIGHT

Captor, androgynous, manicured hands folded, speaking to swarthy men in the shadows: CLIENTS who have come to bid on the latest prize, White Fox. She is visible through dark glass, seated on a chair. Heavily made up and clearly sedated.

                    CLIENT 1
          You were right. She's quite special.
          Looking a bit worse for the wear, though.

                    CAPTOR
          I assure you she still tells the most
          charming stories.

Clients confer. Grumbles of disagreement.

                    CLIENT 1
          Is she not . . . too well-known, in our
          former circles?

                    CAPTOR
          She is forgotten by everyone who
          matters. Forgotten, yet still biting,
          as her name suggests.

White Fox blinks slowly behind the glass.

                    CAPTOR
          I'll take first bids in five minutes.

Clients confer among themselves, watching White Fox through the glass beside them as she groggily adjusts her hair.

> CAPTOR (V.O.)
> Oh, what will become of you, dear White Fox?

Captor exits into the hall.

Captor opens WHITE FOX's red purse and looks through the contents.

> CAPTOR (V.O.)
> You say you are strong, but I know you cannot stomach the polluted mess in the mirror. Cannot reconcile it with the beautiful fantasy world you created around yourself.

Captor examines a pair of calfskin gloves, a wallet. Captor finds photographs.

> CAPTOR (V.O.) (CONT'D)
> A world of unbridled hope, of answered prayers, of selfless goodness, of smiling children—

Captor flips through photographs, finding one of smiling children. Two girls, beautiful girls, their identities unknown.

                    CAPTOR (V.O.)
        How sweet the photograph was, inside
        your ruined red purse.

Captor reenters chamber with clients inside and
watches White Fox, now stone-faced.

                    CAPTOR (V.O.)
        Evolve or die, White Fox, dear. Evolve
        or die.

INT. GENTLEMAN'S CLUB / AUCTION ROOM—LATER

Clients and Captor sitting in darkness, during the
auction. Plumes of cigar smoke.

                    CLIENT 2
                    (to CAPTOR)
        I'll take her, I said. No matter the
        cost.

INT. GENTLEMAN'S CLUB / CELL—LATER

After the auction. White Fox is alone. She screams.
She beats on the ground, on the walls, on her own
flesh.

She looks once more at her ruined reflection on
the mirrored walls.

                        WHITE FOX
                     (to reflection)
            I suppose I'll have to save myself.

INT. GRAND OLD HOME / BEDROOM—NIGHT

A clean and minimalist room with many bookshelves,
a moon-shaped sconce on the wall, and a window
overlooking a green yard.

White Fox, bare-faced, clothed in a clean dress,
is seated on a green cushion. She combs her clean,
long, white hair.

White Fox stares out at the green yard. Foxgloves
outside her window. She hears muted chattering
from an unknown source. She rises, attempts to
open the frame, and finds it locked.

She is a prisoner of this beautiful place.

She COUGHS BLOOD into her palm and wipes it on a
cloth calmly. She's clearly ill, and it's serious.

INT. GRAND OLD HOME / LIVING ROOM—NIGHT

Lavish furnishings; high, vaulted ceilings; priceless
art.

CLIENT 2 is the lonely man who claimed White Fox
by purchasing her at auction.

He sits in another room, observing photos of himself, his lost wife, and his children, from many years ago. His wife resembles White Fox without her makeup.

Client 2 enters White Fox's bedroom. She is seated on the cushion, and she quickly conceals her bleeding mouth. He stands by the door, looking down at her.

                    CLIENT 2
        I'm sorry to disturb. But I gave you a
        week to get settled, and you have yet
        to say a word to me.

White Fox looks away in silence and tightens her dress.

                    CLIENT 2
                  (frustrated)
        You have no right to treat me so.

White Fox recrosses her legs and looks at him coldly.

                    WHITE FOX
        You have trapped me inside this room.

                    CLIENT 2
        That isn't true. I told you: Should you
        want to go outside, you must only ask

the moon and the stars. They're waiting
for you.

Client 2 points toward the window. As if that helps.

> WHITE FOX
> Crazy old man, speaking in cruel riddles.
> Is that all that remains of you now? What
> *is* it that you truly want from me?

> CLIENT 2
> I found you, and I saved you.

> WHITE FOX
> So it's *company* you want?

Client 2 and White Fox stare at each other.

> WHITE FOX
> What's wrong with you? You could have
> bought a book. Or a cat.

White Fox COUGHS into her hand and sees speckles
of blood, unseen to Client 2.

> WHITE FOX (CONT'D)
> I'm sure I'm going to die soon, anyway.
> What a waste of your money.

Client 2, confused, hands her a handkerchief, which
she refuses. He looks concerned.

                    CLIENT 2
     I want to know what made you this way.
     I want to help you.

                    WHITE FOX
     Why? Why won't you just let me go?

                    CLIENT 2
     Where would you go?

Client 2 rubs the skin on the bridge of his nose.

                 CLIENT 2 (CONT'D)
     I am all that you have.

White Fox turns away and stares dead-eyed at the
wall.

Client 2 watches her in silence with a growing
sadness. Eventually he slides open the door.

                    WHITE FOX
       Wait.

Client 2 stops. CLOSE IN on his elegant, sunspotted
hand.

                    WHITE FOX
     I can tell you my stories. But only if
     you'll really listen.

Client 2's hand pauses on the screen door.

                    WHITE FOX (CONT'D)
          You must sit over there, in the far
          corner of the room.

After a moment of reflection, Client 2 nods and
walks over to the far corner, where he sits with a
few creaks of his old bones.

White Fox sits up, her eyes scrolling back to a
different time and place.

                    WHITE FOX
          Where should I start? You know parts of
          my story already.

                    CLIENT 2
          Start at the very beginning, please,
          so that I might understand. Before you
          landed in that unsavory hovel I plucked
          you from.

                                        DISSOLVE TO:

EXT. OLD-FASHIONED HOME - DAY

The home is on cobblestone streets in front of a
canal. Industrious people mill about the street in
conservative dress.

                    WHITE FOX (V.O.)
          This is the story of my first home as
          White Fox, in the home of the gray-
          haired woman who paints herself young.

A YOUNG WHITE FOX with pure black hair and delicate features appears lugging a bag. She approaches the home and knocks hesitantly. She cannot be more than eight years old.

>   WHITE FOX (V.O.)
>   I was an innocent then, or so I like to
>   think.

GRAY-HAIRED WOMAN opens the door. Her face appears beautiful and ageless, if heavily made-up. Only her signature gray hair reveals her age.

>   GRAY-HAIRED WOMAN
>   (beckoning White Fox inside)
>   Ah, the child. Come in, come in.

>   WHITE FOX
>   I'm M—

Gray-haired Woman shushes her and looks behind her at those milling about the neighborhood.

>   GRAY-HAIRED WOMAN
>   Don't mention them. Your family is gone
>   now.
>
>   My, pretty as a fox you are. No, child,
>   from now on, you are to be called FOX.

Gray-haired Woman turns her back and reenters the home. White Fox follows her inside, lugging her bag.

INT. OLD-FASHIONED HOME / LIVING QUARTERS - DAY

A messy, if traditional home.

Several young women flurry about moving pots of
strange liquids and creams. The smell is foul, and
White Fox wrinkles her nose.

Gray-haired Woman leads her toward a long hallway
and points to a door.

                    GRAY-HAIRED WOMAN
          This will be your room. I expect it to
          be tidy at all times.

INT. OLD-FASHIONED HOME / LIVING QUARTERS - DAY

WHITE FOX sweeping floors as other girls get
dressed in green robes and thick makeup—some even
blackening a coin shape on their eyelids so they
would appear to be attentive even when their eyes
were closed for a blink.

INT. OLD-FASHIONED HOME / KITCHEN

                    WHITE FOX (V.O.)
          She was a fair guardian if not a sen-
          timental one.

White Fox eating a meal of plain broth and rice
with the Gray-haired Woman as other girls leave
the house elegantly dressed.

                    WHITE FOX
          Madame, how old are you?

Gray-haired Woman tuts.

                 GRAY-HAIRED WOMAN
          How very rude. Ladies do not speak of
          their age.

                    WHITE FOX
          I only ask because you look so young,
          and yet you have gray hair.

                 GRAY-HAIRED WOMAN
                     (aghast)
          Really, Fox!

INT. OLD-FASHIONED HOME / BATHROOM - LATER

White Fox peeking in on Gray-haired Woman applying
a dark salve to the inside of her mouth before
dipping a toe into a large bath of milk.

White Fox GASPS.

                 GRAY-HAIRED WOMAN
                   (frustrated)
          Come in then, you little fox.

White Fox guiltily edges into the room.

GRAY-HAIRED WOMAN

    Closer.

White Fox nears the edge of the bath and looks into the liquid.

It turns out it isn't milk but rather something gummy and shining.

White Fox tries to dip her finger into the liquid, and the Gray-haired Woman tries to stop her, nudging her in accidentally.

WHITE FOX falls and grabs for the Gray-haired Woman's dressing gown before dunking into the bath with a SPLASH, clothes and all.

CLOSE IN on White Fox's surprised face emerging from the viscous goop.

WHITE FOX (V.O.)
    I felt that I was drowning: This liquid
    filled my nose, my mouth, my eyes. It
    tasted sweet, like mulberries, and
    poisonous.

INT. OLD-FASHIONED HOME / BEDROOM - NIGHT

White Fox examines the roots of her hair, which have begun to grow in white. OLDER GIRL sees her and whispers to FRIEND. White Fox turns to them both, and they silently leave her.

White Fox finds Gray-haired Woman and cries to her.

                    WHITE FOX
                 (clutching hair)
          What have you done to me?

              GRAY-HAIRED WOMAN
                  (angrily)
          Like giving good dreams to a pig.

Gray-haired Woman's expression is one of contempt.

                  WHITE FOX (V.O.)
          Giving good dreams to a pig. I had not
          heard this expression before. And I would
          not realize what had happened until years
          later. For the next few months, my hair
          would grow in white, but nothing else
          would change. They would begin to call
          me White Fox, and still Madame would not
          explain what I had done.

INT. OLD-FASHIONED HOME / LIVING QUARTERS - DAY

OLDER GIRLS packing up and leaving the house to
much fanfare.

                  WHITE FOX (V.O.)
          As the other girls completed their train-
          ing, they began to leave. I alone was
          left, and I began my training in earnest.

INT. OLD-FASHIONED HOME / BEDROOM - DAY

White Fox learning appropriate harp techniques.

White Fox learning how to move elegantly.

White Fox staining her hair with a mix of charcoal
and mulberries.

                    WHITE FOX (V.O.)
          As the years passed, I remained petite
          and young as ever. Some of my features
          blossomed, but were it not for my way of
          speaking and acting and my white hair,
          I imagine I could have passed for a
          teenager my entire life. But one day
          everything changed.

INT. OLD-FASHIONED HOME / LIVING QUARTERS - DAY

White Fox coughs during a practice performance and
sees a stain of shining blood in her hand.

                    WHITE FOX (V.O.)
          I told Madame, of course.

INT. OLD-FASHIONED HOME / BATHROOM - NIGHT

WHITE FOX receiving a small tub of dark paste from
Gray-haired Woman.

GRAY-HAIRED WOMAN
It keeps you young outside forever. But
inside, you will begin to rot. If you
do not scrape the insides of your mouth
and rub this paste inside it with every
new moon, you will deteriorate and feel
much pain.

White Fox cries silently.

WHITE FOX
How could you do this to me?

GRAY-HAIRED WOMAN
(tsking her)
The other girls would kill for this
curse of yours.

INT. PERFORMANCE HALL - DAY

WHITE FOX performing and receiving greater and
greater acclaim.

WHITE FOX (V.O.)
But the first rumblings of a war could
be felt, and I knew this moment of
prosperity would not last forever. I
explained to Madame that I wished to
educate myself.

INT. OLD-FASHIONED HOME / LIVING QUARTERS - DAY

White Fox crying on her knees before Gray-haired Woman, and Gray-haired Woman pulling her to her feet to slap her.

                    WHITE FOX (V.O.)
          She insisted that I needed her paste,
          and if I stopped performing, she would
          keep it from me.

          She controlled me in this way. I feared
          bleeding out, and so I used her paste.
          I felt that I'd become a demon. Good
          for nothing but that creamy inch-deep
          of flesh.

INT. OLD-FASHIONED HOME / BATHROOM - DAY

White Fox stripping her mouth of its membranelike skin and rubbing it raw with paste.

                    WHITE FOX (V.O.)
          I couldn't bear it anymore. Working for
          her, *needing* this evil woman who used me.

INT. OLD-FASHIONED HOME / LIVING QUARTERS - NIGHT

White Fox slips into the hallway and sneaks into the Gray-haired Woman's room.

She is sleeping on a cushion with a blanket.

White Fox creeps past her and removes a large tub of paste from beside her. Gray-haired Woman stirs, and White Fox turns.

CLOSE IN on White Fox's face, cold as it has ever looked.

A shadow falls over the Gray-haired Woman.

>   WHITE FOX (V.O.)
>   And so I stole the magic she had on her
>   and escaped.

EXT. OLD-FASHIONED HOME — NIGHT

White Fox entering a car outside the house with several bundles in tow.

INT. GRAND OLD HOME — NIGHT

Client 2 sits in the same corner of the bedroom, watching White Fox.

>   CLIENT 2
>   You stole from the woman who raised you?

White Fox seethes.

>   WHITE FOX
>   She mistreated me.

White Fox's hands curl into fists.

WHITE FOX
You said you would *listen*.

Client 2 looks pensive.

CLIENT 2
This bleeding of the mouth—this continues
to afflict you now?

WHITE FOX
Yes.

CLIENT 2
Is there no other way to help you,
besides finding you that cream?

WHITE FOX
Of course there is. There are three
other ways that I have been taught. But
I can't make any of them work anymore.

∞ ∞ ∞

We stop at the end of Part One, and I feel disembodied.

"I know her," Saxim says, breathless. "Oh my gosh, I know her."

"*What?*" I shoot up onto my bare feet, yanking her up with me. We're bouncing on our toes.

"Tai, she's Daria Grendl. She has to be."

I freeze. I haven't heard the name said in years, and hearing it now sends prickling needles up my spine. Daria, who leaked those bits of *White Fox*. Daria, who swore Mama ran away from us.

"Saxim," I say patiently. "There was no shortage of bitches who controlled and used Mama. And Daria's a lifelong redhead." When I

107

was twelve, I crafted a sad excuse for a voodoo doll with red hair just like hers, using a disgusting holiday sweater I found in Noni's closet.

"Box redhead," she says, rummaging for her phone. "She was just on local news talking up an article she's writing for the retrospective and ranting about refugees using up Viloki resources. The station showed an ancient clip of her with your mom, where she had premature gray hair. I swear."

I must look distant, because she rattles my hands in hers, as if to wake me up. "I actually taped it and was going to show you, because she teased some kind of big announcement. Nonsense, I'm sure, but I thought you should know. Since Daria always claimed to have insider knowledge."

"Show me the clip." I tie my greasy hair into a rapid-fire bun. "I'm going to find her."

BOY

Transcript of *Viloki News* Video Interview with Daria Grendl
May 7, 2019

Interviewer: You've been the hottest source for details about Mireille Foix's life ever since she disappeared. Mount Vilox-hot. And rumor has it, you're putting together an anniversary piece for the magazine hosting the event—with a secret inside.

Daria Grendl: An explosive secret. I won't say anything more. Not yet.

Interviewer: Do you stand by your assertion that Mireille ran away?

[Daria pauses, smiles]

Daria: Who am I to disagree with the police commissioner of our fair island? [mumbling] Now if only he'd focus on deporting the rabble polluting Limatra.

Interviewer: What makes you believe with such certainty that
    Mireille ran away?

[Daria lights a cigarette, inhales, and blows a smoke ring]

Daria: She's Mrs. Foix Hammick to you. And *I* know Mireille
    better than anyone roaming the surface of this godforsaken
    planet.

Interviewer: And yet you divulge secrets about her to the public?

Daria: I do this all for Mireille. She would never want people to
    stop talking about her; to stop thinking about her.

Interviewer: Do you have anything to say about this week's news
    that the director who worked on Mireille's first feature film
    has died by suicide?

Daria: He should've held out a little longer.

Interviewer: What exactly are you suggesting?

[Daria blows smoke at the camera and shrugs, a smile spreading
    across her face]

Daria: She'll be back.

NONI

Did you hear me, Manon? The stalker's voice worms its way deep into my brain, mining through its tender folds until it snags on the sharp ruffle of my spine. Before I'm even at the Limatra apartment, I call a taxi to spirit me back to Tai and Stökéwood.

I slide across the cab's cracked leather seats, my skin still slick with sweat, and speed into the twilight haze of the mountains. It was a mistake to come to the city alone, and it was a mistake to leave Tai in the country. She won't answer any of my calls, so I'm left looping her frantic messages again—not explaining, never explaining. *It's about Mama,* she says, her voice tinny and tremulous, seven years old again.

I debate calling the police, too, after my encounter this afternoon. But what did the man accomplish, besides scaring me a little? I log what happened into my notebook, and I manage to sketch the man, poorly, with his three scars—clichéd, like he's a haunted-house actor, really—and a slow warmth and strength begin to steady me.

When I arrive at Stökéwood, Tomí lets me in, bleary-eyed and reeking of booze, and I run until I find Tai, curled up asleep on the sofa in the library, a note beside her in Saxim's neat script explaining she left to get some rest before summer school the next day. Tai looks so small and pale and unformed, like she's a sapling that could blow away in a strong wind.

I decide not to wake her and tell her about the man: I'm the big sister, the protector, and I wouldn't even know where to start. The encounter warps in my memory, and what I remember most is the shattering of the vase, and that smile. That smile that terrified me, like he *knew* me, knew my filthiest secrets, when he does not.

I turn to grab another blanket, and I see something there that sends a painful beat of blood through my heart. There, on the table beside her, the cover font big, the paper crumpled.

There it is.

White Fox, the title reads.

Before I can process it, I'm convulsing, my world dissolving into a frothy, metallic din.

This is what she found. This is why she called. I wait for the clamor to stop, those building, fizzing coins. But they don't.

I run for my bag and reach for my anxiety pills inside, the ones I'm meant to take in emergencies, and I down two before I sit back down.

Is it real?

How on earth did she find it?

The magnitude of my mistake—leaving Tai here today, to be the one who found this—guts me so hard and fast again that I taste metal. I am furious with myself, so angry that all I can do is count my breaths and wait for the medicine to kick in.

But I can't resist the frantic pull to read, to discover Mama afresh, and so I pick it up with hot-cold hands, and can't breathe until I reach the very last page.

∞ ∞ ∞

It's incomplete.

It's incomplete; it's incomplete; it's incomplete, I repeat to myself, flipping through the pages of those three horrifying parts again and again, fingers itching for more. *It has to be incomplete.*

But I know these words are hers.

I know Mama wrote this; I know it like I know her smell, like I know the feel of her hands on my cheeks, even though they're only fragments of memories now. It's in the expressions, in the rhythm of her voice, in the images only she would commit to the page. She told me a fairy tale, growing up, a story about a wild fox who becomes a man's wife, only for their relationship to sour.

I never understood what she meant. But I know now that she meant to burn it into my memory, so I would understand this was her work in this moment.

The three pieces of *White Fox* in my hands weave a brutal tale of men owning her, of men passing her along like a beautiful trinket, like a fragile doll. Of White Fox never gaining her independence.

I know, when she was a young actress, Mama thought of herself this way: as nothing more than a commodity. It's what so much of the world thinks of her—the world that *doesn't* know how hard my mother worked to open and run the Foix Institute, a place born from a desire for future Viloki generations to escape limiting circumstances, just like she left behind her quiet life with a difficult father on the shore.

I reject most of the world's version of Mireille Foix Hammick: that pretty, painted shell.

But then why do the three pieces of *White Fox* in my hands show only her disillusionment, her depression, her fear, and her fury?

If she could be alive—if she left this for us—why not show White Fox overcoming it all?

It makes me sick.

I let my beating head fall into my hands; I try to scrape the opening image from my mind: of a woman running, running from shadows that multiply, and her captor looking through the same red purse she disappeared with. *Red purse. Calfskin gloves.*

It can't be a coincidence.

Mama was telling us something.

"Nons?" Tai asks, stirring on the sofa. "What time is it?" She blinks up at me, clearing gunk from her eyes with a closed fist. She sees me, script in hand, and shudders. "Shit. You found it."

"You mean *you* found it."

She clears her throat. "Mama had a secret tower in her bathroom—"

"I know," I snap, and her blue eyes sharpen. "You're telling me no one checked it?"

"Of course they did," she whispers, as if we're not in a giant, forgotten house all alone. As if the ghosts can hear. "She must have placed it there after that." She swallows hard, her throat rippling under a choker necklace with a hanging sun charm. The skin beneath its rays is rubbed raw, like she scrubbed at it in her sleep. "She must have come back to leave it for us." She stops, stares at me, and we both feel the weight of what she's said. "You're shaking."

"Of course I'm shaking," I reply, stiffening up. "Did you read it?"

"Listen," she says, coming to her elbows. "Saxim recognized someone in it."

"So you and Saxim both read it?" Bubbling fury ripples down my arms. And something hot and thick and poisonous like jealousy, too. *Such a mistake.*

"You weren't answering my calls. You would've done the same."

I feel that flaring at the back of my throat. We can't fall back into those old patterns. I made that mistake before, and it meant I left this place when I shouldn't have. It meant Tai was the one to find *White Fox*. The one to find her. I take a breath.

"So, what? Who did she recognize?"

She tells me that the gray-haired woman is Daria—that bigoted snake Daria—and how she contacted her through her website, on a lark.

I cross my arms. "As if contact pages really work."

"They work if you're a Foix Hammick, and the page owner is a leech who loves the sweet taste of our blood," she says, holding out her phone with a limp wiggle.

And there it is. A time already set in black pixels, for tomorrow morning in Limatra.

∞ ∞ ∞

I follow Tai up the creaking wooden stairs to our makeshift shared bedroom, with its spartan twin cots. I refuse to let go of the script, so she pushes her cot toward mine so we can reread *White Fox* together. I stop only when Tai's gasps and murmurs of shock go silent, and I turn to find her face shining wet.

I wipe her tears away with my sleeve, their familiar, humid salt hitting my nose, and then—I remember Tai crying while I picked through our father's brittle bones last summer. I guess grief is like that: the banshee patiently waiting in the many-halled house of your mind, so quiet in certain moments, until you turn a corner and see how it takes up rooms and rooms, cracking their floors and windows with its volume, its weight.

At the private family ceremony, Tai sobbed in thick, heaving sighs, for once in her life giving herself up to being unappealing, with her nose running, her eyes running, and her mouth running: "I'm so sorry. I promise this is my last night of crying," she said each night, in between blowing her nose on a rough paper napkin she found in her purse. "No one wants to be around a sobber."

"No one's watching us, Tai," I replied, even though my head felt heavy and swollen, and even touching the fringes of reality in my thoughts was painful.

When the crematorium expert spoke, Tai listened, heaving with uneven breaths in the forest-green robe-dress that belonged to Mama. It was that humid kind of August heat that makes even existing tiring, but the crematorium was frigid. We passed each delicate fragment of Dad between us with our fingers until each one—some small as a man's thumbnail—reached its final resting place inside a cinerary urn he had chosen himself. She held my sweating left hand so tight the whole time that I got bruises on the edges of my fingers. But I didn't notice until later, because all I wanted to do was help her stop shaking: I could feel it, down to her very core, this recognition that her dad was gone, as I handed the bones with my right hand to Teddy and Marion.

It helps me, and it has always helped me, to pretend she needs help only I can give.

At the funeral feast, we stared at the platters of smoked scallops and seared lamb, too heavy and rich for my grief-weak stomach, and I cut up piles and piles of scallops for her to eat. But back at the hotel, Tai plopped herself in front of the smart TV to watch endless episodes of *The Office* with Viloki mulberry twists dropped into ice cream and a virtual IV of meme accounts on Instagram. So I just drifted, taking hot bath after hot bath, then staring at the faded gray wood of the hotel desk and its comically tiny hydroponic herb garden for hours in my hotel robe.

That was when it hit me, that I had lost a biological parent beyond a shadow of a doubt. The certainty was somehow both cruel and just.

"At least we still have Mama," Tai whispered to me that night, loose-mouthed on the verge of sleep.

I blinked up at the ceiling, silent. My little sister would always feel that precious agony that lay on the cusp of the painful and the pleasurable: Would Mama reappear one morning and we'd pretend the past decade hadn't happened at all? Would the decade, in fact, melt into nothing, like so many nightmares had? Or would Tai glimpse her on the street in the night and run and run to pin her down? Would she save Mama herself from the clutches of darkness that had taken her from us, and would Mama cry with relief?

I was sad for my sister then—and so jealous of her. Tai's brain didn't betray her by coaxing her into the darker reunion possibilities: Mama scraped empty by difficult years we would never know about; Mama revealing, stone-faced, that her departure had been for the best; Mama coming back only to leave us again. These were the possibilities that fractured my heart—the same ones Katox alluded to today.

I'd told myself Mama killed herself so that she could be in control of her own story. So that *I* could control her story, and my own feelings of grief.

But today I realized that until Mama is found, I'll always possess the same kernel Tai did—that warped, proud privilege of believing Mama could be alive. A privilege I buried deep (so deep Tai could not see it) but held so close without thinking about it. A thorned privilege blooming and unfurling now, with the suggestion she might be within reach.

If she left *White Fox* for us, maybe she wants us to find her.

Or she wants Tai to find her, a small voice whispers back, in my head.

But Tai needs *me*.

I look at the clock on my phone, as Tai drifts to sleep on my shoulder: Less than twelve hours of sleeplessness to go.

It's only when I map Daria's address again and cross-reference it with my notes that I realize: Daria Grendl has arranged to meet us on Limatra's old red-light street, the same stretch where White Fox is held captive, in that foul fairy tale of a script.

∞ ∞ ∞

The old-fashioned row houses of the red-light street look like wax cottages left in the sun too long. They are made of painted wood, but on this foggy morning, they look especially soft and rotted. They must have once been quaint businesses, ten or more years ago—I remember this being called the "French quarter"—but everything is shuttered and dust-ridden now. Only a couple of buildings wink at us from the road, low lamplight inside their windows. Even *Tai* feels no urge to drape herself over the bannister of the adjacent canal for pictures—her nose just wrinkles at the faint smell of old fish, while I check the addresses of each house.

I do a double take when we reach the correct number. The house in front of us is painted crisp white, with too-sweet seashells and miniature anchors adorning it: a beach cottage plucked from a movie, or—

"What the *fuck*, she stole Mama's childhood home," Tai whispers to me, shivering in the clouded patch of shade that has drifted over us. We've never visited the seaside house where Mama grew up—it was destroyed in a storm when she was in her twenties, and the "dangerous" nearby seaside town famously ceased to exist in the seventies, when Hero Pharm bought up the land to turn it into a nature preserve—but we saw Mama's watercolor painting of it, the one that hung in her office, and the single grainy photo of her next to the cottage in a bikini.

Daria Grendl must have seen it, too.

I cough to try to clear the unease bobbing in my throat. It's too late to retreat. I ring the doorbell.

An eerily familiar red-haired woman in a silk robe-dress opens the door. She processes us with a left-right flicker of her large wide-set eyes, and my hands curl into fists before I can stop myself. It's her: Daria Grendl, the villainess, the woman we loved to hate as children, because she took any opportunity to flash the precious nuggets she'd stolen from her time with Mama.

Daria tucks the pen in her right hand behind her ear, then she ever so slowly places said hand on her cheek and shakes her head in faux admiration. That's when I notice her skin's not quite right— because she's wearing pale pink gloves, so similar to the ones Mama took with her.

I don't dare look at Tai, whose blue eyes are probably burning through my skull. *What the fuck?* I can almost hear her hiss, over the thrumming in my head that *this was a mistake, a mistake, a—*

"Look at this. Two of you . . . Aren't I lucky?" Daria's mouth curls into a broad yet off-kilter smile. She doesn't move to open the door for us. I hear grainy voices talking over each other on a television inside. "I'm Daria, of course. You both would've been so little when your mother and I were working together in our prime. Or maybe you weren't even born? Come in, come in," she says, only drawing the door open enough for us to squeeze past her, her gaze still hot on us like she's a furrier and we're rare lynxes at the zoo. "Do you like my home?"

Her home, then. I wonder, with a shiver, if I should expect a faithful re-creation of the interior of Mama's childhood home—not that I would know what that means. She never told us stories about it herself—*the past was past for a reason*. At first, in the darkness, I only smell stale tobacco, spilled coffee, and, faintly, sewage. Mothballs, too. But my eyes adjust: The whitewashed house's dark interior is no dream—it redefines filth. The front room's packed with ruined wooden furniture and filled to bursting with wet-looking books—

drawers sag with them; shelves overflow. Stained fabric lies in a pile in the corner, reeking of sick. Tiny fruit flies speckle old, crusty containers of lemon yogurt—above them, a display of rusted-over *machíkíl* cleavers on the wall. Tai hovers on the doormat behind me, lips pinched.

"Shoes off," Daria snaps, pointing at a few soiled, mismatched shearling slippers next to where I stand. Something dark and many-legged scuttles past me and out the door, desperate for fresh air, maybe, and Tai flinches into the cracked doorframe, before shooting me a look.

"It's such a nice day outside," Tai says brightly, course-correcting, even though it's plainly overcast. "Why don't we find a café? My treat." Her eyes hold on mine. "Come on, Manon."

As if I'm the one who lured us here. As if we could have any kind of private conversation of substance with Daria out *there*.

She bounces on the toes of her heeled shoes, so ready to retreat, and my mind could shove her right off her spindly stilts with its frustration. We came here with a purpose. She made the appointment. But the second it upsets her delicate sensibilities—

"I'm agoraphobic," Daria replies flatly. "I don't go outside." She looks Tai up and down with amused slowness. "Now. I gather you're here because you saw my interview—or perhaps, to talk about my upcoming article. If that's the case, kindly remove your mother's 2007 Prada shoes and come inside. Before I change my mind." She disappears into the room beyond.

I'm the first to obey. My toes crunch on something inside the slipper, but I don't say a word. My eyes flick to Tai's, which are flaming. She keeps almost falling while easing off her heels, until I try to steady her.

We find Daria in the second room, a dining room–cum kitchen, where we're surrounded by scummy, food-encrusted appliances and posters from all of Mama's movies, adorning the soot-stained, mold-fringed walls in lacquered golden frames. I hear what's playing on the television in another room now: Mama and a man. An old interview, her voice so carefree and young. *It's true; it's true; I promise you*, she says, with that sparkling shot of a laugh, the one that makes me think of Tai's life now. I try to swallow that dry knot of resentment, tasting stale smoke.

Daria sits at a small square table, one of its legs propped up by a book titled *The Prince*, and motions for us to sit across from her. A black notebook, wrinkled around the edges, sits on her edge of the table beside an overflowing ashtray, where she's perched a lit cigarette, sizzling down to its filter.

"I was surprised that you emailed," she says, picking the cigarette up for a drag. "I thought you two fell off the face of the earth after Mireille's . . ." Her gloved hands draw lazy circles in space.

"Almost," Tai says, grinning big and fake. "America. Land of the free."

The same slow smile stretches across Daria's face, and the very fine tips of her incisors stick out, catlike. "Right."

"Anyway, we're back on Viloxin for the retrospective, and we thought it might be nice to drop in on Mama's old colleagues," Tai says. "It's so terrific you still live here." I shoot her a look, and she flips her hair over her shoulder, like she's forgotten she's sitting in a hovel in sticky slippers.

"*Terrific?* This mildewed rock? Why?" Daria asks, amused. "Everyone thought me insane to come here. But it was the eighties, you understand."

I stiffen and see Tai opening her mouth to snap back with a pointless performative comeback—

"You're not the first to try to pump me for all I know," Daria continues, before either of us can reply. She sighs and taps the spent cigarette on the ashtray. "They've died out now, but for a time, I had strangers ringing me and asking me to confirm or deny theories they had about her new whereabouts. I had to change my mobile number. Move houses." She clicks her tongue. "All because of that bloody script, and the fact your mother and I collaborated, once upon a time."

"The script you leaked," I snap.

Daria blinks at me, guilelessly, continuing her thread. "Imagine if someone had leaked *the gray-haired woman's* portion?"

I fight a twitch. So it *is* her. She's read it, and she knows.

"They never would have left me alone. They might've suspected I killed her, for God's sake." She shivers with a practiced falseness, as if she finds the idea delicious. Icy needles shoot up my spine.

"We know you don't have a copy of *White Fox*," I say, my eyes boring holes into her copy of *The Prince*. "It would've been splashed across the internet if you did."

"Of course I don't have a copy," she replies sharply. "No one does. Isn't that right? But your mother and I did collaborate on the development of *White Fox*. I was going to play the gray-haired woman in the film. Until I saw the initial *drivel* she came up with, and refused."

Tai stiffens almost imperceptibly as I smother my surprise.

Daria smiles, all pointy teeth, absorbing our discomfort with barely contained glee. "Girls, I'll tell you something now that I haven't told a soul: I did more than help her write *White Fox*." She stubs out the cigarette nub with slow, practiced jabs. "I tried to stop your mother from finishing it."

My heart lurches as Tai says: "Excuse me?"

But Daria adds nothing—she rises, instead, and putters around the kitchen, opening a drawer and rummaging inside. I can feel Tai shaking as we both keep quiet and wait for her to answer.

Daria nudges open a closet door, and there, on the floor, sits a giant red crocodile bag, worn to bits. Just like Mama's, but larger, comically stretched, yawning wide.

I'm overwhelmed, then, by the feeling that Daria's not the furrier, nor even the predatory cat itself; she's just a poisonous spider, all alone at the center of her threadbare web.

She reaches inside and plucks out a crushed carton of cigarettes. She opens the package, fingers hovering over the neat rows of smokes until she selects one. She taps it out, carefully, relishing the building silence.

"I adore your mother, I really do," she says, lighting her cigarette, "but the woman cannot string together a piece of writing to save her life. It's as if disparate threads of a hundred glorious stories exist in her mind at the same time, replaying themselves in perpetuity. She always brought me bits of far-fetched stories she hoped to weave into something greater, because she couldn't do the weaving herself. I listened dutifully, of course." She pauses, smiles with teeth. "Enraptured, as expected." She takes a drag.

"Once," she says, cigarette extended as she counts on a finger, "in Chongqing, a woman saves an eight-year-old who falls into a tiger's pen. Another time, in Accra"—another finger—"a woman helps a group of widows who gave their life savings to support a crook calling himself Prince Kwami."

She smirks as my breath stops, hearing her count off two of my childhood legends like they're garish things to be ashamed of.

"Then there was Nepal, Bangalore, Kamchatka. I almost said to her, 'Mireille, darling, are we just stringing together random acts of your own bravery or kindness that the tabloids missed? Are we so desperate for attention?'"

Her face softens as she closes one hand and sucks from the cigarette in the other. Her smoky exhalation clogs the air. "But I didn't say that.

Because when you hear Mireille tell a story, you believe it's relevant and true on a deeper level. She and Hero transformed the entire wretched island of Viloxin into a utopia of sorts, albeit briefly, so it isn't too much to assume her words alone could transform *a single wretched soul*. So, I encouraged her. I pushed her to recount more memories, in search of something that would feel as significant on the page as it did coming from her spellbinding mouth. But *White Fox* . . ."

She sighs, staring at the burning cigarette in hand.

"*White Fox* was a disaster."

Her lips stretch into the cruelest of grins.

"*White Fox* tracks your mother's loss of faith—her *disillusionment* with that diverse utopian ideal she and your father built their lives on—through her own life journey. *White Fox* is a failed Mireille, and *White Fox* is a failed Viloxin. You see, girls, your mother was just another victim of burnout. When her beauty began to fade—and with it, her charisma—the shallow pool of her skills became obvious for what it was. She was never going to create a utopia on Viloxin. Her best days, as a beautiful young actress, were far behind her. And when she realized this, she dove deep into her disappointment, only to unearth the brutal mess that is *White Fox*, an elaborate and woefully unstructured yarn of a prostitute who endures whimsical abuse after abuse but never ages . . . She was not subtle, your mother," she adds fiendishly. "*White Fox* is a record of her failing to come to terms with her waning significance. Her waning impact on the world. As the positive attention around her fades, and her future options become numbered, she lashes out, placing blame on others."

I'm biting the insides of my cheeks so hard I taste metal.

"Has your therapist ever told you that you project your own life onto other people's?" Tai asks.

Daria laughs, and it's a chillingly beautiful sound, throaty and warm—my only hint as to why Mama might have liked the person

Daria once was. "Often. But can you prove me wrong? Mireille abandoned the world at the point she did because she was trying to punish it for no longer granting her the status of Someone Special, for abandoning her and her delusional utopian dream. Taking *White Fox* with her after a year of calling it her most important work, was a final 'screw-you.'" She blows smoke in our direction, eyes dazzling with their unchecked delight. "For all her charm, the poor dear can be impetuous."

Tai scoffs. "Oh, please—"

"She should be more grateful for what she has," she says, voice rising. "The life of Mireille Foix is a dream. So many love her and dote on her. I *designed* this house with her in mind, you know. I designed it to look like the childhood home of Mireille's dreams. Her real childhood was awful, I'm sure, so I *know* she invented the one she did for good reason. I know it. And I've been in this house, waiting for her to return to me for years—only telling the press just enough so the world won't forget about her. Imagine if the world knew the truth, girls—"

The next sentence she enunciates, shaking her head.

"*Imagine* if the world knew she isn't Mireille Foix at all. If they knew she's really just a Jewess, formerly known as Lady Fleischman, from Elizabeth, New Jersey. Lady! Her parents practically named her to walk the streets."

BOY

EXCERPT FROM *VOGUE* MAGAZINE
COVER INTERVIEW WITH
MIREILLE FOIX HAMMICK
SEPTEMBER 2004

You wouldn't be wrong in thinking that Mireille Foix Hammick is a temptress. In truth, she is the world's finest actress because she can *be* everyone. She can give viewers everything they think they want. But I've heard from other interviewers that if you take what she first offers, she can become impossible to truly know. So when I first meet her, at a coffee shop in Limatra, I avoid her eyes instinctually: The navy pools purportedly entranced leading men, heads of state, and even two popes in the years before meeting Hëró Hammick at the Cannes Film Festival in 1982. (He saved her when she slipped and fell off a yacht during a party, and the rest is history.) I wanted the real Mireille, untempered by her charisma. I asked her what I thought to be a safe question: Why move out to the fringes of the Delirium Forest with her daughters and husband, instead of staying in Limatra city center or renovating a prize mansion in Mitella?

"Our Stökéwood home was Hëró's idea. I won't bore you by claiming I crave a simple life, when all evidence is to the contrary. I would've traveled around the globe with my daughters—showed them everything I didn't get to see as a child, myself. But I now see that Hëró was right to wish for a calm, rural Viloki childhood for them. I want them to feel rooted in their home country forever—I never want them to worry about where they came from, to feel lost and unwelcome in this complex world we live in. And I know it's the best base for me to embark upon the most important work of my life, the Foix Institute. So, consider this the next act: a stab at a more peaceful existence in the forests at the base of Mount Vilox."

I couldn't help but chuckle, breaking my eye-contact embargo to catch her smile faltering.

"Oh, goodness, what have I said this time?" she asked cheerfully.

I looked at my notes. "'A *stab* at a more peaceful existence'?"

She laughed—that elegant chiming that could disarm anyone. "That's my ghastly English for you. Well, that's quite right anyway, I suppose. You've got to have a bit of violence and color in your life to appreciate the peace, no?" She smiled, with that mix of vulnerability and melancholia-tinged contentment that's made her famous.

And that's all it took for me to fall under her spell.

TAI

Dad once told me that in the grip of extreme shock, everything looks crystalline and sharp: like the moment could shatter, and we would break into a million little pieces with it.

She is just Lady Fleischman, from Elizabeth, New Jersey.

But I've lived through enough disasters to know how to lock down my muscles, to make sure the shock doesn't show if I don't want it to, at least not past those first microseconds I'd have to be a Mina-the-robot to control.

So when Nons starts to gasp, her mouth opening in slow motion, I whip out and squeeze the flesh of her arm so hard I know she'll see bruises in the shape of my fingers. But it keeps each of us tucked inside ourselves, so we don't unintentionally gift this anti-Semitic crow of a woman a single juicy kernel of our hurt.

"Elizabeth, New Jersey," Daria continues, waving her cigarette in the air. Miraculously ignoring our shock. "Elizabeth, like the queen—Regina, she told me, as if that somehow made the boil-ridden armpit between Newark airport and Staten Island elegant. Ha. She's Jersey trash."

"This is the secret you're revealing in the article," Noni says, in this steadied rasp, while my stomach roils at the words *boil-ridden armpit*.

Daria bites back a laugh. "Of course not, lamb. I wouldn't tell a soul. I am now the curator of her mystery, and that would ruin Mireille forever. And then I would feel so very cold, alone with my boring truth. But don't fret: I'll find something fresh and lurid to feed them, to lend you both a bit more attention on the anniversary. That's my gift to you." She comes to her feet, moves toward the open maw of the closet again. "Do you want to see my dress for the retrospective?"

"I thought you were agoraphobic," Noni quips icily.

"This is different," Daria snaps, pulling out a plastic-wrapped dress, cradling it in her arms. "Oh, it would be just *like* her to make her return tonight. With the biggest *splash*," she adds, almost chuckling. "You know, I'm almost inclined to forgive her."

Noni pulls away from me, and I can tell from the greenish cast to her face that she's seconds from decorating Daria's home with half-digested breakfast, too.

"So you believe she's alive," I say carefully.

Daria's feline eyes flick to mine. "Of course. Family life might not have been to her taste, but she would never leave *me* like that. Her greatest collaborator."

Leave me *like that.*

Me.

Like neither of the daughters in front of her matter, like we don't even exist. The daughters who don't know the real Mireille. *Lady.*

That's when I tap into it: my fury, simmering just below the shock.

I have a witchy way of making other people sense my fury without acting out. Like, how you can tell a pot's hot without touching it. And my calmness, my stillness paired with it can send waterfalls of chills down anyone's spine.

I close my eyes to reset them, then open and fix them on her. The redheaded snake. Who is either messing with us or messing with us in an even *worse* way or is just.

Plain.

Dense.

"Well, Daria, we've enjoyed the show," I say crisply, coming to my feet. "In fact, I'm sure it was enough entertainment for all of us, am I right? Please don't worry about coming to the retrospective tonight—the magazine told me they lost your invitation, and they're reconsidering your value as a resource, too." I look at Noni. "I know I am."

Daria's eyes flash to mine, uneasy, almost, and I'm steady enough to spot a dark shade of admiration in them. "I live alone, my dear," she says. "I've heard that too often to feel wounded by it." She straightens, dress in her arms, and holds my gaze. "You're free to go, if my truths are too rich for your blood."

I don't look away. The atmosphere shifts, and the air tastes wet and almost savory, like a cool cloud is passing over us.

"She's going to be so disappointed hearing you talk about her this way," I say with faux tenderness.

"What?" Daria asks, her voice catching. She adjusts her robe-dress, and the fabric at the neck loosens. I spot—I think—the shadow of bruises there, but her hand flies up to cover them.

Because of that, I almost don't notice Daria pause, her eyes losing focus. Her brow, once smooth, furrows. Her skin turns asphalt gray. She looks far older, in that moment, and so much like the forgotten woman in the photo online.

But it wasn't me who did this to her, no matter what I'd like to believe.

I see it, then, in between the back bookshelves, the only shining, well-preserved thing in the room: a giant rack of white wine bottles, crowned by a silver tray with two etched crystal wineglasses on top of it, like she's been waiting for a special date for ten years.

"You've seen her?" Daria's eyes harden, and she clears her throat. She adjusts her silk dress, and I notice the ash marks on its fringes, on its hem. She sets her jaw. "Where is she?"

This is the disruptive power of the belief that Mama is alive on Viloxin.

∞ ∞ ∞

What the fuck what the fuck what the fuck what the fuck, I breathe, as soon as we step outside, our nails crimping into each other's arms so hard I swear I taste stars and see blood.

We run together until we're out of breath on a quiet bench by the side of the canal. Two young girls spot us—I see them whispering, out of the corner of my eye—so I pull Noni and we keep running until I find an emptyish tea shop. I drag her into a dark back booth covered in stickers.

We stare at each other, breathing hard, trying to see the *Lady Fleischman, from Elizabeth, New Jersey*, in each other, and when an elegantly tattooed waiter approaches, I order two hot teas to go in ten minutes.

"To go in . . . ten minutes?" he repeats.

"Thank you so much!" I chirp, handing him twenty euro with a grand smile I don't even feel.

"Are you already googling it?" I ask Noni, as she scrolls on her phone. "Tell me you're already googling it."

"No results," she says, turning the screen to face me. *Lady Fleischman, from Elizabeth, New Jersey*. "Tai, you were . . . a force of nature back there. That was really, really impressive."

She pauses, and we lock eyes. I let the compliment warm my bones, and—

"Especially for a high school dropout," she adds, completely unnecessarily, turning back to her phone with a shit-eating smirk like it's some kind of joke.

I pick at my split ends like they're the insult. My fingers tremble so badly I accidentally rip two whole strands out of my head. At home, when I was littler and worse at *perspective*, I always did dumb things when one of Noni's insults threatened to stick. Like picking my split ends, or tweezing hundreds of hairs, or squeezing too-new pimples, or holding planks until my legs quivered. I knew the momentary pain would make me prettier, lovelier in strangers' eyes, and that could be one realm where I would always win. I want to scream, *Screw you, you don't understand anything at all*, but instead I say:

"Do you think Daria was messing with us?"

Because Mama's more important.

What if she wasn't from Viloxin? What if I'm not Viloki? So much of my life is fake already. Manufactured, smiled into, leaned into. This would mean the one real underpinning—my Viloki heritage, belonging here, belonging *somewhere*—is fucking fake, too.

The table wobbles in front of me, even though it's bolted to the ground.

"Not . . . really," Noni says, puncturing my dark cloud. She drops her phone and rubs at her face. "It seemed like she just wanted us to know she knew. To prove she did have a connection with Mama. That's what that whole conversation was, wasn't it? Daria proving she was close to Mama."

I start picking a sticker off the pleather seat instead of tearing out my own hair. "I mean, sure. So, like, what do we do next? Call Teddy? Marion?" Anger and fear fight inside me, this two-headed beast I can't control. "I'm going to lose it if they knew and never told us."

I look up at her, and the blood has drained from her face. With a yank, I strip a sticker clean off.

"Is this like *The Truman Show*? Everyone in our family knows this except us? Is that what Dad meant in his letter about secrets of hers he couldn't share with us?" I start on another sticker, even as hot tears blur my vision. I dab at them hard before they smudge my makeup. "What the hell does this make us if it's true, Manon? It makes us impostors."

"I don't know," she whispers. "I—"

"Shit. Shut up," I snap, just as those same two girls from outside mosey into the tea shop, whispering and pointing at us.

"Better put on your Viloki Reese Witherspoon face," Noni mutters, pulling up her hood just as the two girls approach our table.

"Hello, sunshines!" I squeal, and they bounce on their toes as they ask for a photo. Manon turns away, head dropping to hide between her forearms.

"Um, of course!" I reply, standing and posing between them. The girls giggle as the fake shutter snaps, and I thank my mark of luck I noticed them before they noticed me.

"Thank you, Tai!" one says, while the other asks, "How long are you back home?"

"Ugh, hopefully forever," I offer brightly. "Love being back. It's just gorgeous here. *And the food.* To die."

"You really do glow when you're refreshed by sucking the blood of fawning youths," Noni says, when I turn back to her. She shakes her head. "I don't know how you do it."

"What alternative do I have?" I ask flatly. "They don't want the real, sour, needy me-at-this-very-moment. You have to give the people what they want. Hide the darkness, zhuzh up the light." I look out the dirt-flecked window and into the sun-dappled street.

"That's just sad, though, Tai," she replies, and for once, I know she's not doing it to be a judgmental bitch.

For once, I'm tempted to try to explain it to her, why I do this. Why I perform even in moments of despair. Because nothing feeds my soul more than the attention, the adoration, the affirmation I get when I am at my best, at my sparkliest, at my most special.

She called me a force of nature, and that's exactly what I am. But I'm not a closed system. I need that cloying-sweet love to keep putting out what will make me adored.

I know Mama would have understood. But I don't think Manon would—Manon who lives so deep inside herself, who must think, on some level, that what's most special about her will never be and can never be on view to most of the world.

So I shrug. "Seems like that's kinda what Mama did, too."

"I guess *Fleischman* didn't have the same ring to it as *Foix* for a queen of Viloxin," she replies bitterly. We both flinch. In her eyes, I see the pain I feel, the pain of not knowing who our mother was. The only thing making it bearable is that she's still out there.

We can still find her, and she can still explain.

I pick at my hair again, discovering a highlighted thick strand. I squint at it in the low light.

"Wait. Do you have . . . white hair?" Noni asks me. "Like White Fox?"

I freeze.

"How dare you, Manon Hammick." I'm fragile enough as it is. "Come on," I say, reaching for her hand. "We need to get ready for the retrospective."

"Goddammit," Manon whispers, and it's the first time I've heard her curse—the first time she's said something I agree with wholeheartedly—in years.

∞ ∞ ∞

"Thaïs and Manon!" Mina says, greeting us in the foyer of Stökéwood, her panel a wash of graciously soothing blues and greens. "The car will be here shortly. It's time to change for the retrospective." She moves toward us on her thick, knobbed plastic legs, and hearts on wings fly across her panel. "I know you'll both pick something elegant."

"Bitch, please," I say, cruising past her.

I wear Mama's vintage corseted bloodred brocade gown with the thigh-high slit, because it's Friday and according to Mama's superstition I can't wear anything new, and I drape a luscious ivory faux-fur wrap across my shoulders, because drama. Plus these over-the-top clear stilettos that Aunt Marion said would be best suited to the one-foot radius around a pole—but I have zippo cleavage (hi, Mama's genes!), so I tell myself the effect is more sci-fi chic.

"You realize that's a look just *made* for the perverts who gather at all these events?" Noni says to me, as she slides on the simple black shift she picked from the pile I preapproved for her.

"Agree to disagree, Manon. This," I say, smoothing the skirt, "is the kind of killer look that has the power to draw Mama back out." That could show her just how well I am. I point at the strappy water-blue confection I wanted for Noni. "It's not too late for you to join me."

Manon snorts to herself. "That's okay. I don't need to sate the obsessives' hunger with my appearance."

On our way out, I make Noni take three dozen photos of me draped across the Stökéwood stairwell, the general aesthetic being elegant neo-neo-Gothic vampire murder victim—*I don't understand how you can say things like that with a smile*, she says, frowning—and in the car, we pour ourselves the fancy champagne I find chilled in a cellophane bag in the backseat, tied with a note reading, *Cheers to Mireille!* Never have I been more delighted that the drinking age in

Viloxin is a very loose eighteen. I want to drink away our date with Daria. I want to overload the gaping maw of *you didn't know her* in the pit of my stomach, with champagne bubbles.

"Absurdly creepy to phrase it like she's alive and this is a celebration *with* her. It's almost like they saw Dad's note," I say, as the fizz comes out of my nose. I'm downing it fast, too fast. I need that looseness in my bones.

"Mm, because the magazine definitely thinks she's planning a triumphant return tonight," Nons says, rolling her eyes. She hasn't stopped clutching the purse I lent her, with her grody chewed-up fingernails.

I smile drily. But a part of me hopes—even *prays*—Mama will come back tonight, just like Daria said.

But that's only because I crave any kind of reunion with her, even if it's an ugly reintroduction to her family after ten long years at a ten-thousand-euro-per-head screening (*ten thousand euro!*) with hundreds of our least intimate acquaintances. *Who the hell are you, Lady? Where the hell did you go?*

"What do you think the big surprise is?" Noni asks me, watching trees fly past the window.

"Um, a lock of her hair." I count on my fingers. "Archival videos of her taking a shower. An old blood sample proving she's really Lady Fleischman, from Elizabeth, New Jersey." I watch Noni bite her lip, eating off the lipstick I painstakingly applied.

"If I see Teddy, I'm going to shake the truth out of him like lights out of a fucking Christmas tree," I say. "You're telling me he didn't know?" We tried while we were getting ready. Marion dismissed it as a rumor, though she wouldn't know the truth anyway, since she lives under a patchouli-scented rock, and Teddy's calls rolled to voice mail.

Noni swallows hard. "Don't say anything tonight. Okay? We don't even necessarily know if it's true. We don't want to make a scene."

"This isn't my first goddamn rodeo, Manon," I say, glugging down my champagne.

∞ ∞ ∞

When we pull up a half hour later, Mama's hyperenlarged face beams with posed humility on the screens above the car. Pixels of freckled skin shower the crowd with angelic light: *Mireille Foix Hammick*, the caption reads, *Icon of Film*.

Icon of Film. Ugh. My stomach burbles beneath the damn corset, and I burp champagne. Sort of a tribute to Mama, honestly, who drank her body weight in the other champion of French grapes (Burgundy) weekly. I open the door before I can second-guess myself—camera flashes blind me, shouts ring in my ears.

"Ready?" I say, turning back to face Noni. Her face is pale and drawn in the shadows of the backseat. Sometimes I forget how painful the spotlight is for her.

But you don't know me if you think I can't do this in my sleep.

Powered by a cool rush of adrenaline, I strut down the red carpet to the institute's door, royal-waving (screw the lightbulb, touch the pearls) at faces erased by rows of enormous lights. I hold Noni's hand in mine—it's dripping wet—and I feed her all the energy I can. I smile as big as possible without my cheeks bursting and take in the scene: They made sure the Foix Institute suited Mama perfectly. Dressed in silk and dripping in lanterns, it exudes glamour. And the crowd: It's too surreal an experience to not appreciate. I might be sort of famous online, but I've never seen clamoring, sweating throngs like this. One fan leaps out of the shadows wearing two white fox ears and a distorted mask of Mama's face, the eyes alone punched out. Sharp-edged holes exposing two glassy beads.

"I miss her!" He moans, collapsing over a waist-high metal barrier. "She will return to me!"

Noni shrinks back just as he crumples, pushed aside by rabid teenage fangirls bearing signs with Mama's face.

"They're only children," Noni whispers to me. "Why do they care?"

A group of girls calling my name asks for a selfie, thrusting wiggling hands toward me, each fingernail painted a different neon. A groan escapes the impromptu mosh pit. As I'm leaning in, I smell bubble gum and sweat, and just then, a rosy flash fills my left peripheral vision, but it's no brain-blasting flashbulb. Noni gasps just as I catch the object flying toward my left cheek: a slip of hot pink fabric. I open it: skimpy girl's hotpants.

Ew. What?

I burst out with a laugh.

"Not my size," I say, tossing it back into the crowd, roaring in my ears.

A schoolgirl screams with barely contained joy beyond the fence, setting off a second flurry of technological lightning.

"The fuck," I whisper to Noni, squeezing her hand. I can feel how all of this nourishes me and how it compromises her.

"Mama wore hotpants just like those in one of her first movies," she whispers into my ear, her heartbeat in my hand. "Remember? *Not Another Girl of Ice?*"

And then I remember. She was just sixteen. She played a young and feisty prostitute with waist-length icy-white hair who wields a tire iron in her quest for revenge. Sort of your typical pre–Me Too, I'm-an-old-white-guy-director stuff.

"Remember when we saw the poster?" Manon asks, as we continue on. I let her talk even though it's not the time or place, because I can feel it steadying her. "She said she felt *free* during filming, for the first time in her life. As if she could fight for anything she wanted, anything at all. Unstoppable, uncapturable."

I don't say this, but I don't remember that. It sounds like bullshit, and my own memory cuts through the champagne fuzz.

I'm only a year younger than my sister, but all *I* remember is being fourteen and coming across sleazy merch from that movie on the internet. It was cool, that year, to dress up as the dead version of that character, bloodied and spent and very much not free.

That character reminds me of White Fox.

I give a final wave to the crowd, desperate for my heart to swell as much as it can, before letting Noni tug me inside.

∞ ∞ ∞

Inside the institute, they wrapped the stark walls in more silk of Mama's signature lavender (robbed from, like, at least three dozen bridesmaids). Expensive lilacs everywhere, too. It's like suffocating in an old lady's powdered bosom. Old beauty campaign stills creepily pout above the crowd.

"Portals to petulant gods," Noni whispers in my ear, and I know she's euphoric from the relief of being done with the red carpet and tipsy from the champagne in the car.

"Aphrodite," she says, in that deep, booming, jokey radio DJ voice I haven't heard her use in years, "with Botticelli's tumbling curls, batting her lashes at her lovers—the Paris campaign of 1994." She turns and points to another campaign while I fight a smile. "Artemis, peeking through ivy in pursuit of prey, a band of leather encircling her neck, circa 1999. Athena, 2003, appraising the audience come to worship with quiet wisdom."

"Shut up," I whisper, elbowing her in the side. "Don't make me crack my lipstick. You never get champagne again."

I comb the crowd for faces we know. Plenty of well-coiffed strangers, clinking glasses and laughing. I stop a caterer passing mini seafood spoonfuls and slip one in my mouth as fortification—the briny slime of sea urchin slips down my throat, and I almost gag. Of course, that's when the swell clears, and I spot them.

"Look," I whisper to Noni, gripping her hand.

The suited and tuxedoed men with slicked-back hair and permanent smug grins, which are familiar, in the worst way: My gooey decade-softened memory and my irresponsible heart tell me they're safe, but my brain paints them in neon caution colors.

Hero Pharm colleagues of Dad's, laughing and chatting openly. A huddle of them by the bar, ten years older but identical, in that infuriating Brad-Pitt-doesn't-age way.

One of them bandaged my knee after I scraped it during a Children's Day festival, green scalloped streamers rustling from the trees over our sweaty brows.

Another found me at the end of the drive, where I was collecting stones in the shapes of animals, and asked me where Dad was—when I answered that I wasn't allowed to speak to strangers in sassy Vilosh, he told me I was smart. I replied, *Duh*. He brought me a stone in the shape of a bird the next time he saw me.

"I'm surprised so many of them ponied up the euro to pay their respects to the woman they said ruined Dad," Noni whispers to me. It didn't help that Dad never had a Ladyx-level medical breakthrough after he married Mama. Most of these men fought for Dad to stop focusing on the free educational programs Mama pushed for at Hero Pharm.

I shoot her a look. "It's a gossip-collection fee."

"Fair enough. Well, I hope *he's* not here," Noni whispers back. And I know she means Nítuchí, the worst of them all.

"How drunk are you? I mean, he's the cochair; of course he'll be here," I whisper back. "We're screwed."

The space before me opens, and cold, appraising eyes fall on us, mouths shutting. For better and for worse, we look a lot like Mama, so it's as if a much more gorgeous version of our mugshots hangs over all of us a hundred times over. The mess of businessmen parts to accommodate us both.

With each restrained kiss, I'm reminded of Dad's note—reminded of his lack of trust, of his isolation at the end, of how they all turned on him.

But at least Nítuchí isn't in this group. Too busy folding cocktail napkins into swans, I guess, thank baby Jesus.

When they turn back to their conversations, Noni drags me toward a high-top table, her cheeks burning.

"Manon, stop. We have to say something," I tell her. "Even if it's a bullshit 'thanks for coming.' We can't just hide from them."

"We're not ready," she whispers back.

I snag two glasses of wine off a tray moving past. "This isn't fucking *Karate Kid*."

"You know that's not what I mean," she whispers in between sips. "We've had an emotionally taxing day. Let's not engage with people we can't trust right now in anything more than a superficial way."

"Fine." I pull out my phone to text Linos, as Noni stares into her glass.

That's when I hear the first whispers around me, as if we're nothing but ghosts, from men I don't recognize.

"Are they selling that Stökéwood monstrosity in the countryside?" an unfamiliar voice says.

I freeze.

A slurping sound, loose lips taking in sweet wine. "You haven't heard?" one heavy-lidded man tells another, who hunches closer, conspiratorially. "It's said the old bastard left them nothing but debts."

We speak Vilosh. Everyone here should know that. I spoke it with so many of their friends, with so many of their children, ten years ago.

"A pity Mireille left us so soon. At least she left of her own accord and did not suffer through an illness like dear Eve Selby." An old

141

costar, recently deceased from cancer, her five beloved children at her bedside.

Noni's nails dig full-on half-moons into my forearms.

"A true lady, Mireille. Up until the end, of course."

"Do they think some suave lover swept her off to a private castle in Austria?" Noni whispers to me.

I turn my service on and off, desperate for a text back to distract me. So I won't stomp up to these jerks and shut them down. I taste champagne slime in the back of my mouth, where I've been biting my tongue.

"I mean. It's not like we really knew her, either," I say, all nonchalance outside and all disorienting fury on the inside, and she frowns at me.

"I remember when they caution-taped every entry and exit to the forest," says another wheedling voice, "looking for any trace of her. It's as if she just blew away. She was so thin in the end, you know."

I want to say their jabs are as manageable as the bad comments I get on my posts. Except these don't come from lonely kids sitting in their bedrooms alone, emboldened by distance and the privacy of the screen. These come from functional adults, a breath away, who must have known Mama. Who know us.

And every single time they speak ill of her, I kind of feel like they're pushing her away from this place, jinxing her return.

"I bet she discovered some ghastly Hero Pharm secret," I hear whispered behind me, by a rail-thin man who chuckles and swirls ice around the well of his drink. I recognize him as one of Níltuchí's old assistants at Hero Pharm.

Every single one of my muscles tenses.

"I think they decided to hush her up," he continues. "Threw her body into cryogenic preservation. Maybe they'll defrost her in fifty years, when it won't cause a scandal. We'll squeeze another few movies out of her yet."

The image of my mother pushed into a glorified fast-food meat freezer is enough for me to turn to face him. "Are you a film producer now? How thrilling," I snap in Vilosh, Noni stumbling after me.

The others around him scatter. He blushes before saying something polite yet dismissive in rapid Vilosh.

I hurry toward the bar, Noni trying to stop me, but I'm temporarily blind to all else but its gleaming row of bottles. Beautiful, beautiful bottles. The bartender pours us each a slug of sweet wine with pinched lips, his eyes traveling from our faces to the gossips behind us. I let the wine's warmth bathe my mouth, then my insides, as I feel them watching me. The wine is as warm as a mother's touch, I think.

"They're such pretty young lambs, perhaps they shouldn't be hitting the bottle too hard," says a voice, behind me on my left. "We wouldn't want another Mireille on our hands." He chuckles. "Then again, I suppose it's fated. You can tell it's in her blood, from the way the taller one dressed like a tart."

I cough out an icy chunk.

So that's all they wanted.

Us.

Here, in the lushly decorated plastic Eden the magazine created, these people who brushed shoulders with Mama and Dad want some tragically splashy performance on our part to liven the return of Hëró and Mireille Hammick's children to Viloki society. Something to express our lack of reliability and sanity as a family.

"It will happen soon enough. My own son mentioned a revealing photo in a bikini she posted for all the public to see. At least the old man is gone and doesn't have to witness it," whispers another faceless figure, melting into the crowd as soon as I whip toward the voice. As if I'm some kind of whore for posting a picture with my friends at the beach. In a *high-waisted swimsuit*, no less.

The laughter swells, attracting stares from other wasps nearby. I watch Noni's face grow hot and red and itchy-looking, just like my insides, which are soothed only by more iced wine. The sips will add up, I know, but there's time. There's always time until there's not.

"Where the fuck is Teddy?" I hiss at Manon, and when I turn, that's when I spot Linos at the other end of the bar.

We meet eyes, and I smile, relieved beyond relief to see his handsome face, and just like that, I can convince myself I'm a romantic with a bloodstream full of wine.

"I'll be right back," I tell Noni, who scrabbles for my arm but can't hold me.

He drifts my way—I rush toward him, mirroring him. I hear the patter of his tuxedo shoes as the room's lights flicker, indicating the show is soon to begin.

In that moment, all I want is to escape—from Noni's discomfort, from the vultures, the old, the dark, the dead.

"Linos," I breathe into his ear, as soon as I'm close, and he shakes his head, with a look at the buzzing crowd, but thank God he senses my desperation, because he nods his chin into the darkness back behind this end of the bar. I follow him dutifully, head down, and once we're out of sight, he pulls me toward a frosted glass door opposite the theater: a hidden hallway once used by performers. We reach the milky glass door of the galley, and he draws me through. As we run down the back hallway, I clasp his hand in mine so tightly that I can feel his heartbeat, faster than mine, its *kick kick kick* feeding me hope.

We turn into an empty pantry, toppling a stack of boxes: peach crates, since Mama loved fresh Bellinis. He presses me against a steel counter beside a brimming bowl of the fruit, and I move to press my mouth to his. And I'm surprised by how cool the steel is through my dress, and the *kiss*, oh God, I feel like there's something growing deep inside me, something living, something—

"I'm happy to see you, too, T," he says in his silky baritone, pulling back, and his cheeks are ripe to bursting when he smiles. My secret boyfriend. I run my fingers through the sun-lightened curls at the base of his neck and pull his face back toward mine, and he stops me, laughing gently. "Not here. Come on." He arches his neck to look back into the dark hallway. Voices echo down its length. "You didn't answer my texts until late. I wanted to talk before you got here. I knew this would be a rough night for you," he says into my hair, and yeah, I melt.

I hug him close. "Today in general has been hell. Like, if the devil designed a first day of school for a fresh hellie, he would be psyched to see just how much more creatively infuriating today was, compared to his idea."

He chuckles. "You're such a weirdo."

"I am. I'm totally not fit for this place anymore." The red carpet adoration feels like it happened in a past life. "Can we just leave? Can we go to your place and get away from all of this?"

He sighs. "I know when you start sounding like a romance novel that you're not serious. And you know my mother would have a fit if we snuck out, anyway."

"You're in college," I whisper back. "You're an adult now. You make hard decisions for good reasons and shit. She needs to get over it and let you stop sucking at the teat."

His eyes darken. "Tai, my family's not like—"

"Not like what? Not like mine?" I feel my eyes glowing with pent-up frustration from the day. "No kidding."

"You've had too much to drink," he says, reaching for my hand. "Let me ask a waiter to get you a Pellegrino—"

"I don't want a fucking Pellegrino!" I shout, ripping away from him, and his mouth freezes into a thin line. I feel the melodrama bubbling up in me like hysterical laughter, but I've never been one to bite my tongue, even when I sound—

"I want to be normal."

We both know it's a lie as soon as I've said it. *What you want is emotional stability, the kind that comes from feeling loved and not so alone*, Noni says in my head, but, you know, spoken eloquence and I just aren't friends. It feels too good to be a shit mouth sometimes.

He weaves his arm around me and coaxes me back toward him. "Listen," he says. "Let's have drinks tomorrow at Maltese. How does that sound? I'll bring this guy my mother has been hassling me to spend time with, and you can bring Manon."

I stifle a laugh, ignore the fact he's so good at getting my mind buzzing on something else. Maltese is a ritzy members' club I've never been able to get membership to; first the committee used my age as an excuse, and then another one told Teddy they thought I would draw attention—like that's a bad thing, like the right kind of attention at the right time isn't the freaking lifeblood of our fast-paced garbage-town world. "Like a setup?"

"Whatever you want," he says, kissing me on the cheek. "Let's go, shall we?"

I tear my eyes off him to look into the reflective metal sink behind me and wipe the eyeliner drifting below my lash line. Call me a narcissist, but nothing steadies me like the sight of my own made-up face. NARS armor.

"Let's go," I say, leading the way, knowing full well he'll linger behind me a minute or two so we don't draw more attention on our way back inside.

I reenter the hall, dodging ushers who are helping people into the theater, and crane my neck to look for Manon or Teddy. I spin around just as Manon reaches from behind, her hand closing around my upper arm, and I collide with a man holding a small glass of disgusting green foam. I dodge the toothpick-impaled fish that flies onto the floor, groaning at the splash of rotten-seaweed green, and I look up.

The blood runs out of my face, my fingers, my toes. I find myself face-to-face with the worst Hero Pharm monster of them all: Nítuchí.

Oh.

NONI

Nítuchí looks the same as always: a bloodless face, with flat eyes, concealed by rimless, round glasses. They always—*always*—judge, as if they can see through a thin membrane of skin, past muscle-wrapped bone, and into what he must think are two basic bubble-gum-pink souls. It might be simple curiosity on his part: I don't think he has a soul himself.

"Misses Hammick," he says now, in English, face pinched with constipated distaste. I can't decide if it's his resting bitch face or if it's carefully crafted for our benefit.

I crush Tai's hand in mine while trying to gauge how tipsy she is. I couldn't intercept her before she ran straight into him.

"Mr. Nítuchí," I reply in pointed Vilosh, trying not to feel nauseated to the point of vomiting on his shiny tuxedo. A waiter hands Tai something iced that smells like sweet wine, and she takes it before I can stop her.

Nítuchí gives the same waiter his used cup-o'-fish and stands there in silence, examining us. Waiting for us to squirm.

I wonder if I should congratulate him for betraying our family so successfully.

"It's been a long time," I say instead, in Vilosh, to cut the silence.

"Yes, we didn't see either of you at my reception celebrating your father's life," he replies sharply in English.

I grit my teeth just as Tai says sloppily, "We celebrated him in just the way he would've wanted."

He blinks at me, his eyes two black holes that remind me of a Sartre quote: *I'm going to smile, and my smile will sink down into your pupils, and heaven knows what it will become.*

I break his gaze and scan the room for Teddy, the only person who could save us, but I find that the three of us are very much alone. Isolated, like the others have abandoned us. The only other familiar people in the room are oblivious and too distant to reach. Others watch and whisper from their cliques.

Hell is other people.

"So, girls, is this what your mother would have wanted?" he says, chilly disdain visible. At this, a group of strangers begins to gather around us, eavesdropping hungrily.

"She loved a party," Tai says, raising her glass in mock cheers before taking a sip. I jab her discreetly in the side.

"Yes, she did," he says, those three words loaded with condescension.

I am not a violent person, but I want nothing more than to stab him and watch as Tai, squealing, turns his guts into tacky red streamers in this overscented lavender room.

"I think we both agree she'd be shocked by how much everything has changed in the last ten years, no?" Tai says, in a lubricated Vilosh singsong. "You, the new CEO, chairing a party in her honor. My sister and I, *finally* learning some Vilosh and English." She pauses and frowns. "Well, sort of. As long as we stick to four letter words and under."

If I weren't so terrified, I would burst out into laughter. The right corner of his mouth curls, its skin scaled yet vaguely wet in the light. One of the men near us chuckles.

"Enjoy the celebration," he replies in frosty English, his shining pupils catching mine through his lenses. "She *has* been gone a very long time."

As if this is a celebration of her disappearance. As if he's just as elated, to this day, that she's gone. I can feel his maliciousness seeping into my bones like a freezing draft. *He despised her, and we remind him of her.* I guzzle down the bulk of my water in one gulp, almost sloshing ice on myself. The thought sneaks up on me, plunges itself like a knife into my back: Our father was right to think that someone at Hero Pharm was involved in Mama's disappearance. And maybe that someone is right in front of me, so close I can feel his eyes on my exposed slice of neck.

"Why even come?" Tai mumbles woozily, as he turns away.

"*Tai*," I warn.

"Pardon me?" Nítuchí asks, facing me again.

I just smile flatly.

"Have you seen my nephew?" he asks unexpectedly. Toneless.

"No . . ." I wonder if this is a trick question.

"He is interested in your mother's early work," he says, and that's when I understand he heard Tai.

"Her early films are excellent," I reply.

"Dior asked me to re-create scenes from them in the first campaign we work on, when I'm in Paris this fall," Tai says, sparkling again, before her face cracks the tiniest bit, as if she's just watched Paris slip from her fingers and thought to herself, *So much for being Dior's fresh Viloki face.*

His nostrils flare as if he's smelled something rank. "My nephew is not from Limatra, and as such, he has provincial tastes. If you encounter him, I expect you will behave civilly."

I clench my teeth. So Nítuchí's nephew is just another hot pant–throwing fanboy from the countryside. But why Nítuchí should have any expectation at all of good behavior on our parts after his cold words is beyond me. I want to tell him that I'd rather impale myself with a toothpick the size of a *machíkíl* than be forced to spend time with a relative of his. Or better yet, I want Tai to wink and tell him she will corrupt his country nephew.

But we won't.

"Of course I will, Mr. Nítuchí," I reply instead, as Tai stares into her drink.

He nods. "I suppose I'll see you soon," he says, the words heavy with disappointment, before he departs.

Once we're free, I take a few breaths, watching as Tai tips back the contents of her cup into her mouth to suck at the ice. I feel an acidic roiling in my stomach as the crowd filters toward the adjacent theater, where one of Mama's films will be screened. I don't really care which one anymore.

"I'm sad, Nons," Tai whispers into my ear, soft and tired.

It's darker in the room, all of a sudden, and I'm in a chilled patch of shadow that grows and shifts as I move. It only makes sense if I stand still, if I place icy hands to my temples, if I shut my eyes, but—

"*Nons?*" I hear exclaimed behind me, by a familiar booming voice. I whip around and see Teddy. Finally. He hugs me, red-cheeked and beaming. Joyful. My heart soars as I'm crushed under his plush bear arms.

"Holy shit, Teddy!" Tai whisper-shouts, hugging him back on her teetering heels. It's an awkward moment for a hyperexpressive family reunion, and I can feel eyes snagging on us, but I'm elated enough that I don't care.

"It's so, so good to see my baby girls," he says, pulling away. "I just got in from London. You didn't answer my calls. Must have been Stökéwood service, huh?" He takes a sip of his drink. "Are you both good? I hope you're not bored to tears with all these old fools. Boozehounds, all of 'em. They're shocked to finally see the brilliant, beautiful daughters of Hëró Hammick here in person. But I know you expected as much," he adds, nudging me with an elbow conspiratorially.

I nod and smile, and then reality rolls in with its stiff breeze. *Lady Fleischman*. "Teddy," I say in low tones, my smile icing over, "we need to talk later."

"What?" he asks obliviously, a shadow of concern passing over his face, just as Tai locks eyes with me and my state of mind judders over to her in a moment of perfect sisterly connection.

"Teddy," she hisses, nails digging into his tuxedo jacket, "who the fuck is Lady Fleisch—" Midname, Teddy's eyes pop wide, and so do Tai's—a frenzied smile crowding out her face.

Because behind me walks a column of ice: Antella Arnoix, Linos's mother and the most patrician of the Viloxin silver-spoon set, in pale-blue chiffon, her blond hair in a crisp updo, her copper skin flawless.

"Mrs. Arnoix!" Tai squeaks, and in those two words, I know just how much she lusts over Mrs. Arnoix's son.

Antella surveys us with her unsettling dark eyes, emotionless, before whisking past Teddy—silent and ruddy-faced—and kissing the air an inch from Tai's cheekbones, then mine.

"Girls," she says, in her husky drawl. When Tai opens her mouth to reply, Antella turns away pointedly and drifts off to another group, leaving a drift of rose-scented air in her wake.

Tai turns to me, face pale. "What a b—"

I close my fingers in her face in a *Hush, you uncouth imbecile* motion, and she falls silent. But only for a second.

"Why even cochair this?" she asks me and Teddy. "Why even bother?"

Teddy looks nearly as flustered as Tai—but I can't tell if it's from what Tai almost said or Antella.

"The woman is unhinged," he says under his breath. "My assistant caught a maid on the phone with her the other day, reporting on my schedule and my dirty laundry."

I look at his flushed face. "Like, your business?"

He shakes his head. "My actual dirty laundry. She's been spying on me ever since I expanded my house and we became accidental neighbors." He rubs at his face and continues, dropping his voice. "But anyway, about—about *Lady*—"

So he heard what Tai said.

So—

"It's true?" Tai says, head whipping up.

Our uncle's eyes look hooded, aged by ten years. "We'll talk about it tomorrow morning."

"First thing tomorrow morning," I say, teeth chattering with adrenalized fury and—*He knows? How can he know? How could he hide this from us? How could he?* He's opening his mouth to reply when a bell rings, because fortune favors Teddy Hammick.

"Last call," announces a too-loud usher, ringing a second bell, and then the three of us are corralled into the theater, just as the Oscar-winning director of those ten movies whose name I always forget says, onstage, "Please know that immediately after this lost magazine promotional footage was discovered in the late video director's home archives, it was handed into the authorities as well as Mireille's family."

The crowd titters, and the dense waves of brittle admirers part before us as Tai whispers to me, "But that's . . . us."

I hold firm on to her hand, my palm inching toward her wrist, my

153

eyes trained on the chasm of black behind the sneakered director in his tux.

And then the screen crackles to life, and she's there, above us, ten times our size.

I gasp.

Mama.

At first, it's the fleeting shot of her face that gets me: ghostly, perfect, the bones arranged in such a way that only Nature herself could be responsible for crafting her. *Mireille Foix possesses Grace Kelly's elegance crossed with Audrey Hepburn's mischievousness, Katharine Hepburn's wit, and Marilyn Monroe's pure, languid sex.*

Then it's in the way she moves: in the elegant snap of her doelike neck as she looks both ways crossing the street, in the upward flick of her manicured little finger as her hand moves through the air, in her gait—that waifish float that's impossible to imitate, and God knows I've tried. The effortless insouciance of it all.

And then it's in the Hermès scarf wrapped around her head: a classic pattern, a favored chain-link-and-saddle silk number, with . . . something on the corner, flapping in the wind. Her monogram, *MFH.*

"It's May 24, 2009," she says aloud, in her rasping lilt, and a gasp ripples through the audience. The morning of the night she disappeared. "We're in the town of Limatra, shopping for my daughters." She turns to the camera and smiles, with freckled cheeks and full lips. A loose wisp of chestnut hair brushes her neck. "Manon and Thaïs love these chocolates that I used to bring them from Belgium. But they've just opened an outpost right here on Viloxin. Let's buy them two—or twenty—special boxes as a surprise, shall we?" She drifts up the steps of a small shop, the hem of her dress catching in the wind, then stops midway, as if she's changed her mind. She waits there, on her tippy-toes, and a murmur runs through the crowd.

Just then, she looks over her shoulder, lowers her glasses, and winks at the camera. "Does that work?" she asks us.

She waits, watching us calmly before nodding her head. The reply from the cameraman is inaudible; it's just us and her, us and her, us and her.

"I just can't wait to get home to Stökéwood and my little girls," she adds, and my throat catches as she smooths the scarf off her head with a grin.

Her eyes, blue like shattered ice, are so happy and bright they pierce my heart.

∞ ∞ ∞

When the video ends, Tai charges out of the institute and into the private parking entrance in her formal wear, trailing a wet bloodred train. Uncle Teddy—vibrating with fury—rages on the speakerphone with an apologetic, slightly tipsy rep who explains that "wires had been crossed" and the magazine thought approval to show the video had been received. "It's a special moment for her fans, to get another intimate glimpse of Mireille," the rep adds, as if that unearned, false intimacy would soothe and warm the hearts of her family.

I look at Tai with eyes that feel raw and bloodshot. Her makeup has smeared into a grotesque mask; her swollen, teary face stares back, jaw set.

But I can't manage to feel angry.

Sure, I hate the magazine for springing this on us.

I hate the retrospective itself, this tribute to the false, polished Mama, a woman—I am able to admit—lived with, loved, and experienced most on a screen, if hours are what count.

I hate, most of all, that I don't know her. Who is Lady Fleischman? Who is this woman blown up to ten times her size on screen?

But the truth is, after seeing the video, I'm . . .

Buoyant. Floating on air. To see Mama on that last day, not distant, haunted, or preoccupied, but instead so visibly thrilled to return home to us, pulsing with life on a Viloki street I recognized . . .

Maybe she didn't leave us because she wanted to leave us.

Maybe the darkness keeping her from us is falling away, shadow by shadow.

Maybe we're meant to find her.

To solve her mystery and draw her into the light.

BOY

THE VILOKI SUN—
MAY 25, 2019

The Viloki Sun exclusively reports on last night's retrospective at the Foix Institute, honoring founder and film star Mireille Foix, where a surprise video was screened, showing the actress on the day she disappeared. After the suicide death of director Giovanni Miro earlier this month, a short clip was discovered in his archives showing Foix gallivanting around Limatra happily on that fateful day. It was a trial run for a promotional film they were due to film that week, exploring Mireille's Viloxin. What does this new discovery mean in the search for her?

Was the actress elated because she would soon be fleeing a life she did not want? Or was she a happily married mother in her prime—and if so, what changed her outlook in the hours that span between the video and her disappearance?

Or perhaps this happy moment was all an act by the world's greatest actress of her generation?

Fans are left aching for a copy of the *White Fox* script, the only document that could purportedly shed light on her state of mind.

For now, enjoy these saucy photos of the actress's daughter, social media influencer Thaïs Foix Hammick, running from the retrospective hall with Viloki bachelor, Linos Arnoix, prodigal son of the aristocratic Arnoix family. Neither party will confirm rumors of their relationship, and Antella Arnoix's team could not be reached for comment.

∞ ∞ ∞

I watched you from the crowd last night.

I saw you enter the institute hidden behind a mask of my own making. You seemed so confident, fresh, bright to the others. But I could taste your fear.

You knew something wasn't right in the audience. I saw that you both felt it: that you are both sensitive.

Just like your mother.

Do you know how easy it was to get close to Lady?

Too easy. Anyone could get that job at Hero Pharm. But anyone didn't—*I* did.

I think you would recognize me if you saw me, really saw me, like she did.

But you don't know her yet. Not really. And you don't know me. But you will.

TAI

Uncle Teddy calls at nine in the morning from the entrance of our building. I roll onto my side, hot flecks of sun in my eyes, light made lacy by the dogwood trees outside the window. And I remember: *Lady*. Of the crushed-ice blue eyes just like mine. Of the place I've never heard of, fifteen miles from where I live in Manhattan. *Elizabeth, like the queen—Regina*.

"So, are you gonna tell us the truth now, Ted?" I ask in a dull rasp. I blew most of my anger out of my system last night and woke up with a sore throat.

"Yes," he says simply. "I love you girls. And I'm just—I'm just sorry."

I blow the air out of my mouth. Because I trust Teddy, I *do*, and if he didn't tell us, he has a reason. A solid reason. Or at least I'm telling myself that, because I despise being mad at him.

He coughs into the receiver. "If we want to have time to talk before the Hero Pharm meeting, you should probably get moving. I've got coconut waters downstairs."

I bolt upright in bed, the room tilting. "Hero Pharm meeting?"

"Did you forget? The courtesy meeting Nítuchí scheduled, so I could show you around the remodeled Hero Pharm office? If there's time, I can take you through the Clouded Cage floors, too. My assistant emailed you both calendar invites with the other Hero Pharm board members who will be there to say hi."

To say hi. Right. I sweat a bucket of acid at that final phrase. No reprieve, even on a Saturday.

"Give us fifteen," I reply, and hang up.

I race into the kitchen, misbuttoning and rebuttoning a shirt, and find some old powder that smells and looks and tastes like coffee, labeled ITALIAN FRESH! in a cleaning cabinet. Viloki heresy: They love making instant coffee from "Italian" beans. I stir myself a cup and slurp it down, barely wondering if I'm poisoning myself with a weird, rebranded wood cleaner, and take another to Noni's bedroom, where I find her, biting her lip, staring into another notebook, as if nothing else exists in the world but her and the notebook's pages. I sneak a peek at them, sometimes, I'll admit. Because I can't resist the insight into her head. Noni only started to make sense to me when I started stealing and reading her journals—she unfurled her weird self on the page so carefully, so brilliantly that I knew she really was born to write. I promised myself I'd do anything it took to pay her way through NYU's writing program, after I learned she was admitted.

"Nons?" I press the coffee into her hands. "We gotta go. Caffeine."

She curls her feet underneath her and drinks. "The Hero Pharm meeting, right? I got the calendar invite with—"

I hold a finger out to stop her from speaking, bile rising in my throat.

A fancy-ass Maybach with tinted windows waits for us outside. A driver leaps out to open the back door for us.

Inside the car, Teddy, a tentative smile on his face, hands me one of three large imported coconut waters that rest in the cupholders. "Hi, girls."

"Why didn't you tell us?" Noni demands as soon as we slide inside, her eyes fixed on the window overlooking the streets. "Why'd we find out from a stranger?"

"I'm so sorry, sweet girl." Teddy uncaps a glass bottle for her, eyes full of hurt. "I—Strangers don't have your or your mother's best interests at heart, you know."

"What does that even mean?" she asks, her voice raw. "We're meant to be satisfied with lies, because they're better for us?"

"No," he says, shaking his head. "You're right."

Noni bites her lip, and he opens his mouth, then closes it again. He visibly twitches before speaking, freaking me out. "Your mom's background was something we didn't talk about, because . . . she didn't want to," he admits. He takes a tiny, tentative sip. "We never knew her family because your mom cut ties with them. She never spoke of them—never wanted us, never wanted you, to know them."

"But why?" Noni asks, while I process what he's said in numb silence, too hungover and frazzled to react.

Teddy scratches his forehead. "I . . . I think her parents didn't treat her well, so she ran away when she was very young—I know that much. And she wanted to protect the myth she'd built about her childhood to—to keep herself together. I understood that. So I promised her so many times that I wouldn't ask for more details. And I didn't want to defy her by telling you before she had a chance, herself. I . . . We thought it was for the best. Parts of me have been in a holding pattern since she left, unsure of what to do. Deferring to your father, when maybe I shouldn't have. I'm so sorry, girls." He reaches for our hands, and I let him take my limp one. And I can feel it, his remorse, this undercurrent of an ache.

He's a puppy dog of a man—devoted to Mama always. I can understand why he wouldn't want to defy her, I do.

The rest of the car ride, I'm tingling with nerves, unable to break the silence. I'm still pissed at Teddy for not telling us the truth, but he's right: Dad should have told us—could have told us.

Today I feel like I didn't know either of them at all.

∞ ∞ ∞

The last time I saw the Hero Pharm office, I was seven years old. It was a tower tall as the sky itself, its interiors a gleaming white. Some called it a blight; others, a marvel. Its sole personality was Dad, rendered in gold everywhere.

A gilt bust of Dad in a lab coat was in the entrance lobby, staring down at you while security checked your name. HËRÓ HAMMICK, etched in yellow-gold characters, in case you forgot.

Dad, unsmiling in a giant burnished gold–framed portrait in every hall, his hair jet-black.

Look up, and find his personal seal worked into the molding in gold.

But when Dad walked through the office with us, he didn't notice these flourishes. When Noni whispered something along the lines of *King Midas*, he just blinked at her.

He didn't even notice that everyone dressed in a white lab coat, even if they'd never touched a beaker in their life. They dressed like that because he wore one.

This was his domain, his church, his heaven on earth. No one questioned Hëró here, and no one ever doubted him. When we arrived, we were treated like more than a novelty: We were royalty.

Treasures. A creation as great and potentially humanity-altering as any of his others.

The office, like the rest of Viloxin, has changed. Its address is the same, but when Noni, Teddy, and I walk inside, an informational portal stands where Dad's bust did. The lobby is double its original height and has been redone completely in silver. Everyone wears suits and looks straight ahead, completely erect as if compelled by magic, using biometric scanners to enter high-speed elevators. The only visible security measures are the video cameras, black as night, dotting the silver every couple of feet, like an inverted night sky.

The waist-high lobby gate opens automatically for us, and Teddy shepherds us through. He smiles at us, in between fiddling with his phone. We're ushered up to Dad's old office floor—the office he hardly entered, since he was in the lab so much. I'm sweating through my shirt. My feet pinch in Lady's Chloé wedges, but I wore them for luck, and I feel them giving me a little bounce, a necessary lightness.

A humorless assistant in a pencil skirt and stilettos—who doesn't even bother to look us up and down—walks us through the silver halls, replete with smart touch screens, every ounce of Dad scrubbed clean from them. The portraits are gone, the moldings ripped out. The new Hero Pharm logo is simple and friendly-looking, in that false corporate way that sends chills through you if you think too hard.

No one stands outside their office, clapping as we pass, as they once did. They glance at us and look away, frosting their windows onto the hall with a touch of a button, and Noni's hand grips mine tighter, to calm me.

This is Nítuchí's Hero Pharm, where Saturday is just the first day of the work week.

We arrive at a large conference room with a soul-shaking view of Limatra. Everything, everyone reduced to minuscule dolls and doll houses. How could anyone working here, with this view, ever remember they aren't some kind of deity?

Seated around the boardroom table are many familiar faces from the party, all in suits, and at the head is—

Nítuchí, of course. The CEO in a navy suit, his mouth a furious slit.

"You are late," he says in Vilosh to Teddy, to us, and Teddy smiles again, saying it's his fault (even though it was totally mine), and something I don't hear because the blood roars in my ears. I sit between Noni, who is pale-faced, and Teddy, who squeezes my shoulder before taking out a second cell phone and scrolling through both. While I'm staring out at the city, lost in how much could have changed in a decade (*When was the last time Dad was here? Did they ban him from the premises after they made him step down?*), someone brings me a glass of mildly effervescent water, and people are speaking in quiet voices, when Noni pinches my thigh.

"Are you with us, Miss Hammick?" Nítuchí says, before nodding at the stiletto-heeled assistant, who presses a button that blackens over the windows, shutting us off from the city, just like a bad-tempered god would. "This meeting was a courtesy for you. We're busy people here."

"Of course," I reply, my voice still all grit.

"We're here today to discuss your future role at Hero Pharm," he continues stiffly. "As you're aware, your father resigned and sold all of his shares to me two years ago and rendered all of his voting rights unto his brother, and—"

I choke on a breath.

"Mr. Nítuchí," interrupts Teddy, setting down his phones. "I'll respectfully ask that you stop there. The girls haven't been informed of the details. They—they haven't been here since their father passed."

Everyone stares at us, and a phantom clock ticks, ticks, ticks. I feel Nítuchí's frustration at being interrupted, physical in the room with us.

164

"We have a schedule to adhere to. The board is very busy. Might I remind you that we've rescheduled this several times because of your schedule, Mr. Hammick," Nítuchí replies, glaring at Teddy's electronics, splayed on the table.

"And I do appreciate that," Teddy says. "But I respectfully ask that we save the details of this discussion for a more private forum. Would that work for everyone?" he asks, turning to me.

Nítuchí makes the faintest hissing sound, and Manon looks at me, hard, her eyes watering. I can't tell if she expects something from me or if she's just sad. All I can think of is, *So that's where all of that trust money will be coming from—Dad wasn't just forced to step down. He was forced to sell his shares of his brainchild, of Hero Pharm, to a freaking monster.*

"Wait. So . . . we aren't . . . getting any part of Hero Pharm?" I ask, before swallowing a knot of pain.

Someone, an old white man in the corner, stifles a laugh, and the atmosphere turns, from one of stiff discomfort to mean-spirited delight. The Hero Pharm colleagues I recognize from my childhood, from last night, remain as emotionless as ever, but I feel it, their eyes scanning me.

I've misspoken, but how can I articulate what I mean in front of this hostile group? I wanted some connection to Dad. I knew about our trusts, of course—untouchable until years from now, except to pay for an unlikely Dad-approved STEM degree—but I thought we'd receive . . . some token, some proof we were his daughters— some evidence he loved us enough to give us a piece of his kingdom on earth.

A kingdom that had forsaken him completely, I guess.

"Is it easier for you to understand the proceedings if we continue in English?" asks Nítuchí.

I grind my molars.

Nítuchí drones on about his new mission at Hero Pharm, something bland and corporate that makes me feel small, and the rest of the meeting is a blur of clenched fists and bitten tongues.

"Your uncle suggested you be offered an internship," Nítuchí says as the half hour nears its end, his face pinched.

"We're not qualified," I spit back. An internship at a pharmaceutical and biotech company? I mean, come on, nepotism at its finest.

"Of course you are!" Teddy says, just as Nítuchí replies, "You are not qualified for the vast majority of our internship offerings, but we could certainly look into an administrative position, perhaps at reception, in the event you would like to remain on Viloxin."

Nítuchí means I could have an internship answering phones. And I know I should probably be grateful for any chance at all to remain connected to this place, but my eyes burn with tears, and maybe that makes me entitled and spoiled and ruined, but all I can think of is Dad dying alone in Stökéwood, while Nítuchí reigned here, with his cruel humiliation tactics. All I can think of is Viloxin, Dad and Lady's not-so-home-country, and the gleaming future I had imagined as one of its proud residents abroad, which feels as false and hollow as my relationship with them right now.

"I—excuse me," I say, abruptly rising from my chair and running out, tripping on the vintage Chloé wedges I shouldn't have worn.

I run for Dad's old office—dipping and dodging around the new maze of the building, remembering only that it was a small corner room that faced Mount Vilox. Somehow I sniff it out: I find it there, the same as before, empty except for a framed picture turned toward the window. A silent shrine. I jiggle the door handle and find it locked.

"Psst!" someone hisses behind me. An elderly secretary wearing chunky round-frame glasses in decidedly noncorporate Yohji Yamamoto-esque apparel fit for an assassin. I think I recognize her. Her cube is unique in that it's plastered over with cat photos. Cats knitting. Cats drinking from teacups. Cats doing all kinds of weird shit only grandparents and Noni do.

"You're Thaïs, right?" she whispers.

I nod. "Why are we whispering?" I whisper back.

She peeks over her cube. "Corporate policy. The bastards insist we stay hushed when Nítuchí is holding a board meeting on the floor." She scrunches up her nose just as I scrunch up mine, and we both snort into our hands.

"You were here in my dad's time, weren't you?" I ask.

She nods once. "They haven't sent me out to pasture yet because I'm the most senior admin, and I know where all the bodies are buried. I've been here close to fifty years now." She pushes her glasses up her nose. "Best boss I ever had, your dad. No-nonsense."

"Except for the gold everywhere," I whisper back.

Her eyebrow twitches. "That wasn't him, honey. He was oblivious to that." She waves a hand at his office. "He took the smallest office on the floor and hardly decorated it at all."

"Why'd no one take it?" I ask her. I don't add, *Bad vibes?* even though I wonder if people think it's cursed.

"Well, no one else wants the view of Stökéwood," she says, pointing into the distance. And when I squint and almost—*almost*—see it there, my eyes start to water. I dab at them before they smear my makeup.

"Bathroom?" I ask her, throat hoarse.

"It's just over there, but it's a bit complicated—want me to show you?" she asks, caressing my shoulder. Her touch makes my eyes well up again.

"No, I'm fine," I say, squeezing her back. "Thank you."

∞ ∞ ∞

Noni and Teddy find me blubbering next to the only women's bathroom on the floor, crouched beside the door because I couldn't get it to open. I fiddle with the straps of the wedges cutting into my skin.

"Silly biometrics," Noni says, sliding down the wall to sit beside me while Teddy posts himself next to us like a sympathetic guard.

"I'm sorry, Tai. I didn't know Nítuchí would do it this way. I told him to let me tell you myself, but—"

"We shouldn't have come," Noni whispers.

"You're right," Teddy says, echoing our thoughts. "It's unacceptable. I should've known better. I just didn't think he would do it to *you*."

And I soften. Because he did try to protect us, in the meeting. But the fact stands: We're as good as adults now, and we should know better, too.

The meeting's not what I'm crying about, anyway.

"You know I've always got you two, though," Teddy adds, crouching to brush a lock of my hair. "You're my girls."

And then an intern walks by, and we hear an electronic shutter click as he snaps a not-so-surreptitious photo.

I silently shriek like a banshee in my head, wiping under my lashline, and Teddy sighs, before rising and offering us both hands.

"Time to blow this pop stand, my loves," he says.

NONI

We spend the rest of the afternoon cooped up inside the Limatra apartment, draining iced coffees and poring over *White Fox* for clues we've missed.

"I'm convinced Mama's demons weren't just internal, but external, too," I admit, tapping at another line with this lavender-scented pencil that reminds me of her. The sky's gone as dark as crushed mulberries, and ever since last night, after I saw how thrilled Mama was to return to us on that final day—after I savored the afterglow of that pop of ecstasy—I've felt shadows drawing closer. I've heard Dad's voice in my head, a staticky buzz: *She discovered something dark in Viloxin, perhaps at my own company, that she would not reveal to me.*

Those men at Hero Pharm today—his betrayers and maybe hers—their fingers itched to box us up and shunt us off.

"Well *I'm* convinced I'm ravenous," Tai replies, draping herself over me in an indigo silk robe.

I set down the script. "Early dinner?"

She nods, burrowing into my pajama-covered shoulder. My heart beats slow underneath her. We haven't been this close and tender with each other in . . . years. Maybe it's because we've both been wounded—and behaved with such gentleness—today, so her presence doesn't register as that singular, old bruise that won't go away.

"We can order roast lamb soup from the corner on my phone and watch a movie," I offer, warming to the idea of a night in with her, cuddled up.

Her head makes a slow ninety-degree turn, her expression one of utter disdain. "*Hell* no," she says, jumping to her feet. "After the morning we had? Fuck that. I'm not wearing my going-out robe for fun, Nons. We're going out, bitch. Lady's Limatra awaits."

"Nooooo, Tai," I say, as she pulls me up. And even though I'm cursing in my head, I can't help but crack a smile.

Tai slicks some red lipstick on my lips (painted-trout-style), ties my hair into a neat bun, funnels me into one of her slinky black satin sleeveless dresses that blow off if you sneeze the wrong way, slaps one of her fancy gifted clutches in my hands, gives me an appraising look (deciding she's happy with her handiwork), feeds me a shot of some god-awful mulberry liquor that Dad had in the dusty cabinet while shouting *chípí*, and . . . pulls two matching cropped candy-colored wigs from her suitcase.

"Wait, what?" I ask, as she moves to fasten the blue one on my head. "What on earth do you pack in your suitcases?"

"It'll be fun," Tai says with a crooked smile. "Role-playing!" Before I know it, she's sticking pins into the wig and my scalp with (painfully) artful precision.

"Which . . . role, exactly?"

She holds out a hand mirror, and I look utterly transformed. I don't even recognize myself. It sends a shiver of delight through me.

"I mean this in the most complimentary way possible, Tai, but I look like an intergalactic sex worker."

"I know!" she squeals, clapping her hands. She puts on her own wig, pastel pink, and admires us both in the mirror, while I wonder—with bubbling excitement—what Tai has in mind. Even though her version of reality is chocolate-shell-deep, I can admit it's sweet to the taste. A candy-colored dream of an escape, from a more bitter, dark truth.

"Take a photo of me, but like, with mirror-me and real-me in it," she says, flinging her phone in my direction without a second glance.

"Tai, no." I let it dangle in the air, this awful appendage of my sister's. She's posted every outfit she's worn since we got here. *They'll worry if I don't post anything*, she offered in explanation, as if it's the phantom "they" who have the problem. "We need to stay under the radar. You need to try, for once in your life. Okay?"

She sighs dramatically, locking the phone with a sharp click.

∞ ∞ ∞

We pull up around the back of the old Grand Hotel, built into the basalt cliff bordering one end of town. We pay the taxi, and Tai strolls into the service entrance trailing the egg yolk–yellow edges of a silk and faux-fur coat (*Rihanna-omelet-at-the-Met style, dahling*) and me, as if she owns the place, seemingly oblivious to the fact this isn't the lobby for guests. When we reach the service elevator, she whispers in the ear of the operator. He shrugs and presses the button for the third floor.

"Where are we going?" I ask. I'm woozy and light-headed from her surplus of energy, and I can't decide if I love it or hate it.

"*Killjoy. Killjoy, killjoy, killjoy,*" she says in singsong, before practically bleating with joy herself. "You're the one who told me Lady came here."

I glance at the hotel employee, shifting from foot to foot. "So we're calling her Lady now?"

"We are until we figure out who the hell she really is," Tai replies with faux sweetness.

It dawns on me then that I've never mentioned this place to her, but it's probably written in my notebook. "Wait, have you been reading my private journal?"

She rolls her eyes. "You mean the notebook with the clichéd Viloki lavender field cover you stuffed so discreetly into my clutch? Straining the vintage fabric?" she says, nodding at the borrowed satin purse in my grip.

"It's an invasion of privacy, Tai," I say, wrenching the notebook out so it won't *strain* the fabric, feeling petulant and wondering if closeness with Tai means dissolving into the pink froth of *her*. I certainly feel sticky and unclean.

She just shrugs. "You're right," she says, eyes sparkling. She seizes my hand and kisses it. "It would be assholish of me. If we weren't blood, and, you know, almost the same person."

And judging from her social media profiles, she clearly doesn't believe it's possible to trespass against oneself. I exhale just as the ancient elevator creaks open onto a sleek corridor.

"Did you get us a room?" I whisper. "Are you an escort?" My pulse stops. "Did they request *sisters*?"

"I didn't know you could be this fun, Manon!" She smiles at the bespectacled man standing by a floor-to-ceiling library of leather-bound and gilded volumes, the likes of which I've never seen. She strides past the candlelit stacks, pressing on a not-so-secret sapphire button glowing in between rows of books, and the concealed wood-paneled doors of a second elevator slide open.

"How do you even know where you're going?" I whisper, cradling her clutch in my arms as she stabs at *P* for *penthouse*. "You've been on Viloxin for less than a week in the past decade."

"Never underestimate me," she says, in that annoying falsetto.

This time, the elevator doors ding open onto double-height French windows overlooking Limatra's glinting lights, its woolly treetops, that ancient crust of bay beyond. It isn't a modern city, with imposing fields of steel and glass towers—the only skyscraper in sight, a massive, ugly white monolith, is the Hero Pharm headquarters—but it's breathtaking, like standing on the roof of our building in the West Village at night, where my lonely soul could spread out and almost touch the warm twinkle of our neighbors' old-fashioned homes. Here, that twinkle spills into the rolling dark mass of the Mediterranean Sea.

"Welcome to the Maltese Falcon," Tai says, grinning and extending an arm, as if she—really, truly, unapologetically—owns the place. She swans past the maître d', who tries to corral her with his own outstretched arm and fails. She slides into a pebbled leather high-top bar seat, plopping me next to her. Then she turns her attention to a passing waiter—young, buttoned-up, his face still swiveling in an immediate magnetic reaction to her batting lashes (*Blue mascara, dahling*)—and she orders a drink in Vilosh I can't decipher, without a passing glance at the menu.

"You've seen the movie," the waiter replies inexplicably.

"Many times," she says, crossing her bare legs and grinning devilishly.

Any snootiness melts away like hot buttercream, leaving only bare vanilla admiration below. "You are even more beautiful than your mother," he tells her, and my eyes roll so far back into my head I can see the Hero Pharm tower standing tall like a giant middle finger behind me.

Tai shushes him coyly and smiles, then orders something for me that I can't understand in more rapid Vilosh (how did her skills surpass mine by leaps and bounds?) and reclines back into her chair like Lauren Bacall while the waiter runs off like a lovesick suitor fetching her smokes.

"I thought we were getting *food*," I say, opening the as-of-yet untouched menu only to find page after page of exotic liquors steeped in frog's milk and candied bark and butterfly wings at exorbitant prices.

"We'll get food *after*," she says, shutting the menu in my hands.

I sigh, stomach grumbling. "We can't afford this. You spend money like a drunken sailor, you know that? You do realize our trust hasn't kicked in yet? I hope you have a pla—"

"Manon." She takes a weird yogic breath, then spins on her seat and gestures toward the rest of the bar, thrumming with energy from its impeccably dressed, preening patrons. "Can you just enjoy this? Can you just take a second to enjoy?" Barely containing her euphoria, she adds: "Mama came here."

This glitzy world of image-obsessed people might have delighted her once, but it also ruined her, and it'll ruin you too if you don't acknowledge it's nothing more than a beautiful dream, I want to reply, but our drinks arrive then—Tai's foul-looking amber liquor and my "girly" drink in a martini glass (it smells like window cleaner meets bath soap, adorned by a little twig). After the fawning waiter gives her a cringe-worthy wink and leaves, Tai swaps the drinks and takes a big gulp of the girly one. I give her an exasperated look, and she flutters her alien-blue lashes at me. "You loved the *chipí* so much at home!" she says, faux innocently, and I tell myself to just shut up and take a sip because she's not wrong and also the tipsy is wearing off just a little.

And it's good, like oak barrels and stewed berries and sunsets and leather in a glass. Even better, no one around us registers our presence: The advantage to being in a painfully cool bar is that no one would dare show they recognize us, if they do. We are near invisible, despite—or maybe because of—the trendy outfits and the wigs. I am, at least.

Pretty soon, I'm drawn into the pink fizz that is Tai's glee, and we're in fits of giggles ordering a second round, and I feel my face burning, but not in an unpleasant way, and I see two men—*boys? strapping Viloki youths?*—staring at Tai from all the way down the bar. It's so dark, and my head's swimming, so they just look like boy shapes, but then she's waving, and they're sliding down to sit by us just as she cackles and fidgets with the lace bra (*A crop top, dahling*) under her coat, and her nipples may or may not be visible, and the boys (*men?*) are greeting us in English.

"Hello, gentlemen," Tai replies in a Vilosh purr. Both are comically handsome—attracting long looks from the entire bar—but in different ways. The familiar one who initiated the move over has movie-star looks but also a certain cockiness to him that I find unappealing (he's too pretty and knows it), but I guarantee Tai likes it. The other hasn't looked at either of us once and seems to be skeptical about—if not displeased by—his friend's choice to move near us, and he has superlong eyelashes that I can't see his eyes through since he's looking down and the bar light has suddenly dimmed enough to just barely melt over his cheekbones. He's got some freckles, and I can smell something like . . . I don't know, clean skin and grass, plus something sweeter and milkier, and even though I'm disturbed by myself as I do it, I find myself breathing in deep and—

"*Linos*," I hear whispered. Behind me. I twirl hard and see a girl pointing toward me, toward Tai, toward the cocky guy, who is, of course—

Linos. Oh. It's disorienting to see him in person—I only ever see him on the page, really, and on the screen. I'd never admit it to Tai, but I secretly follow one of his fan accounts, just to see if I'll glimpse her, to gain some insight into her sparkling life while I eat Aunt Marion's no-bean chili under a stained bedspread in my cave-like bedroom at home.

"Did we come here for *him?*" I mutter to Tai.

"I'm Natasha," Tai says in lightly Russian-accented English, "and this is my twin sister, Dazdrasmygda."

"What—" I start to ask, bemused, just as Tai grips my knee so hard under the table that I yelp.

Role-playing, she said at the apartment. I reach up and tug on one strand of my blue wig. Is this some weird sexual game she and Linos play? Or—

"Nice wig," Linos says—with a tinge of haughty criticism—just as some live jazz swells in a far corner of the room.

Tai bats her lashes. "But you love a wholesome Russian girl, don't you?"

Linos smirks and crosses his arms after a beat. "Even better if there are two," he replies, turning to me. "Though I've never heard your name. No nickname?"

Tai pipes up before I can reply. "Never," she says, as if she's aghast at the suggestion, her voice thick with a sad excuse for a throaty Russian accent. I lean in to hear her over the eerily upbeat whine of a saxophone. "It's a beautiful name. Our parents would be devastated if she shortened it. It means *glory to the ties between the city and the countryside*." Locking eyes with me, she adds something else in rapid-fire, vaguely patriotic Russian that no one at the table understands.

Linos leans forward on an elbow, amused—and I can see it, how he's drawn to Tai's inimitable, bizarre shine. I wonder if they're really dating, like the tabloids say. I wonder if he knows just how much of a wackadoo she can be when she wants. A snort bursts out of me, and I catch eyes with the shy one, who half smiles, half laughs, sending another wobble through my legs. I look away again, fast—*is there nowhere safe to look?* But heat spreads along my left thigh, where my flesh borders his.

"Well, Daz, this is Dmitri, and I'm Vlad," replies Linos, smacking the shy guy on the back as he's taking a long sip of what looks like whiskey.

The shy guy almost splutters but corrects himself. I hear his sharp intake of breath.

"Like Vlad the Impaler," Tai says daintily, lazily stirring the branch of green around her second drink. Before I can explain that's not a good thing, she leans into him with a minxish grin. "Now. Have you ever sampled the delicacy that is borscht?"

"Chilled beet ambrosia," he replies, and I think I might hurl if I have to keep listening to their distressing banter, so I take a deep breath and turn to the shy guy, just as a waiter is setting down a fresh glass of amber liquor. "What are you drinking?"

He looks up at me through those long, long, lashes, and his eyes look like forest, dark emerald-meets-black, shimmering with secret life. "No idea, to be honest."

A hot flush overtakes my cheeks. I'm never . . . girlish. And just thinking that makes the blushing rashlike, so much worse.

"Sorry," he says. "What I mean is that Linos ordered me this without telling me what it was. It's good, though. Want it?" he asks, pushing the glass toward me. He has perfectly shaped, clean fingernails. But not intentionally. Just . . . naturally. "Seriously, have it. I haven't touched this one yet."

"I'm . . . good, thanks," I say, nudging his drink back toward him.

His mouth quirks up in the corner as he accepts it. "I'm Hérrakí."

"Not Dmitri?" I say, eyeing the glass so I don't have to look straight into his eyes.

The smile softens in my peripheral vision. "And you're . . . Manon, right?"

I blink at him, embarrassed in my blue wig.

"Sorry," he says. "Small island, you know? And you're not exactly . . . unknown."

"It's fine," I say, realizing it's the second time he's apologizing to me. I'm so used to being the one apologizing for nothing—for my existence—all the time. This makes me relax a little—makes me feel like I don't need to worry about taking up too much space. "Yes, I'm Manon. Not quite as majestic as . . . whatever my sister said it was."

He swishes around the liquor in his glass. "Is your name Viloki or French? Like *Manon des Sources*?"

I'm caught off guard by that—it's a somewhat random French novel from 1962 that Mama liked. I don't think she ever mentioned it in any interviews, but who knows. I nod noncommittally and am distracted by the spray of gorgeous laughter coming from Tai. I look up with Hérrakí and notice that this laugh is 100 percent the kind she uses to lure boys in.

Hérrakí leans into me. "I feel like we're pawns in a really bizarre game I don't want to play."

I swallow down a guffaw, just as I overhear Tai say, "Let's not pretend you have anything novel to say about Count Vronsky, Vlad," and the drink in my hand shakes with silent laughter. "Isn't he your friend?"

Hérrakí blows the air from his mouth. "No way. He's the son of a family business partner. I just moved to the city, and my family's worried that I don't know anyone. They've been setting me up with different people my age."

"Maybe you're better off using one of those dating apps," I say. "Or getting the platonic equivalent of a Pocket Girlfriend."

His grin finally breaks open, into its full, unabashed self. "Are they making Pocket Platonic Friends now?" He wipes his lips with a napkin. They are soft pink. "Don't tempt me. I would love an off switch for Linos." His eyes flash to mine. "Sorry. I guess they're . . . a thing," he says, waving in Tai's direction.

I laugh. "Don't worry. I'm not a fan, either. And I don't know. I've never had a Pocket Girlfriend, Pocket Best Friend, whatever they're called now." Books were always my haven, ever since Mama taught me the power of a story. I know Pocket Girlfriends were Teddy's creation, and I was probably the ideal candidate for a Pocket Friend, because I was so shy. But when I came across a character I loved in a book, I felt like my soul had been *seen*—its call answered by the author. I didn't feel hollowed out, manipulated, disconnected, like I suspect I would have with a Pocket Friend, some mindless, beeping *thing*, no better than the Furby Tai once begged for that I wanted to chuck out the window after an hour.

"Wait. Never? Seriously? Even with your uncle being . . . ?"

"Never." The liquor bubbles up in me. "He tried to give me one, but I wouldn't take it. I gave it to Tai." And I know I shouldn't, but I can't stop myself from saying: "It's just . . . a little bit sick?"

He frowns. "Good sick? Like, genius?"

"I mean . . . despicable," I say. I shouldn't speak ill of them, but they always gave me the creeps. It felt like a girl was boiled down to this sweet ooze and funneled into a box to be . . . sex candy for basic dudes. *Ooh, I am drunk.*

"It changed thousands of peoples' lives for the better. You don't see the positive in that?"

My hands close into fists, but my tongue is loose. "I mean, sure, I totally see the allure of a relationship with a robot that's completely predictable and whose affection is guaranteed." I fold my arms across my chest, a shiver coming on in my too-bare dress. "It's clearly a last resort for people with no social skills. Pocket Girlfriends aren't people. Their affection isn't real. How can it nourish someone in the same way?"

"You're clearly privileged enough to never have felt a shortage of love in your life, then."

I glare at him. "You don't know me."

"Well, I do know that they didn't pick your personality as the root code for the Pocket Girlfriend," he murmurs, taking a sip from his drink.

"Wow!" I exclaim, drawing concerned looks from Tai and Linos. "I can't believe you're defending a robot. Is this really a hill you're willing to die on? What, have I offended your first girlfriend? How can you not see that buying one of those things screams desperate and sick?"

When I look up, I expect to see his eyes glittering sharp, his mouth forming a comeback. But Hérrakí's jaw is set, and his hair falls into his eye as he looks at his hands.

"Desperate is just cruel," he says, subdued. "It's not like these people have some half-naked hologram serving them tea. It's a nice voice coming out of a pink box"—I scoff, but he continues—"who encourages and supports and pretends to care. People should take love wherever they can get it, even if it's a pale copy of the real thing. I knew a guy who loved his dog more openly than his children, because it felt safe. He got his way with the dog every time. The dog never disappointed him, never talked back, and always wagged his tail when he got home, no matter what." He pauses, rakes a hand through his hair. "The dog's love helped the man open up, and he learned to show his family love."

"Are you serious with this after-school special? A dog is not a Pocket Friend," I say, bristling. "A dog is a living creature."

He holds my stare with a fair share of bitterness. "I'm just saying: Some shallow kinds of love are gateway drugs to deeper kinds of love."

I have nothing to say to this, because I'm too woozy to decide if there's any poetic wisdom in his casual, clichéd use of the phrase *gateway drugs*. So we sit in awkward silence, and I feel like I'm drowning in the din of the bar. His perfect hands throb on the counter before us.

"So," he says eventually, taking his glass in hand stiffly, "now that you're back, do you feel like a real Viloki again?"

A real Viloki. My cheeks burn. Is he really trying to flirt with me? Or is he insulting me? *He doesn't know about Mama. He can't know.* I choke down some of the liquor in my glass—a bit dribbles down my chin, and I wipe it away before speaking. "As opposed to feeling like a fake Viloki?" My chin feels sticky, and I can't stop myself from rambling on. "I feel like I belong nowhere, to be honest." Nowhere but with my ruined family—these people I know next to nothing about. I cough and glance at Tai, shooting her a *Save me* look, and she purses her lips, as if to say *Buck up; I'm having fun*, before breaking into a magnetic smile again and leaning into Linos. My eyes travel to Hérrakí, to see if he's drawn to her face like so much of the rest of the room, but he's still staring at me.

"What's wrong?" he asks unexpectedly, as the background music rises around us into something off-kilter and vaguely carnival-like.

This registers as an accusation, as an unkind observation, and this sends a dagger up my throat. "I just don't want to be interrogated by someone I hardly know," I say, turning to him. The faces behind him look like paper masks as the lighting dips.

"I'm sorry. I didn't mean to interrogate." He rubs the back of his head and looks into the well of his drink. "I hope I didn't upset you."

"Stop apologizing," I snap. Because how could I begin to explain?

"Then what's wrong?" he says. Before hastily adding: "Never mind, you don't have to tell me."

But he's right: The rage is bursting out of me after a drink, the rage I thought I was keeping at bay while Tai released hers yesterday. Paranoia nibbles at the edges of every logical thought, and just *thinking* that I'm becoming paranoid again sends fresh, ugly flares from memory through my vision. A photo of Teddy and Dad, the smallest, palest husk on a cot. Mama, a bloodied teen in agony on-screen, assuring me with a tight smile in person *it was only a little fake blood*, before excusing herself to sit in the bathroom in the dark for an hour. I am a person made of secrets, fear, and anger, because my memory is riddled with false, too-dark moments that must stay hidden. Even if they are less like tangible objects and more like holes, spreading through the tissue that makes me Manon.

Something bad happened to her, the banshee wails. *Someone did something to her.*

181

Hérrakí's face has gone pale, watching me. "Seriously, are you okay?" His hand reaches toward me, an inch or two, and that's when I see it: a tattoo, on his forearm. A delicate pair of wings etched on his skin.

It happens in a split second, and I realize what I've done after I've done it, my fingertips hot. I brushed his skin, that moment's touch furred with electricity.

He smooths his sleeve down, and there's a beat of silence, two, before I lean toward the bar to ask for a water or something to cleanse my system.

His reaction tells me his tattoo is a secret. He has recorded something important, permanently, on his own skin.

"Manon," he says, behind me, and when I turn back to face him, he's mere inches away, and I'm leaning too close. I could almost taste his skin. I inhale deep and fall back.

"Waiter?" But the waiters aren't paying attention to me. I scan the room for a distraction, anything at all.

And that's when I hear the titters, from the groups of fashionable Viloki around us, their made-up, titillated faces ghoulishly awash in smartphone white.

Isn't that . . . ? Did they . . . ?

I pull my cell out, noticing four missed calls from Uncle Teddy. A bloodred news alert reads: *Mireille Foix's Former Manager Makes Shocking Reveal in Disturbing 10th Anniversary Piece*. But the link won't load.

My breathing turns shallow as the lamps of the room swirl in my vision. *Lady Fleischman*. She must have revealed it, Daria, the snake. I smell a rush of something heady and floral that makes me sick. Something deeply familiar and rank that turns my stomach.

I lean over and tug on Tai's arm. "We've got to go."

She doesn't hear me—she leans in, confused and visibly frustrated to be torn from Linos. "We've got to *go*," I whisper, pointing in the direction of a whispering posse of girls in black snakeskin and leather behind us.

Her eyes search the bar, glossy in the light, but when she turns back to me, she looks just as confused as before. She catches Hérrakí's eyes, then mine. "Wait. *Did you . . . ?*" she whispers, before making smiley googly eyes at a puzzled Hérrakí and me.

"*We need to go*," I say, shoving my phone at her, and manacling myself to her wrist.

Tai squints at the text and must blessedly recognize the urgency in my grip, because she turns to Linos, who was scanning the room, but returns her attention with a smile.

"Dazdrasmygda's unwell," she says, all skewed blue lashes and flimsy Russian accent. "Could we trouble you to fetch the bill? We'll run to the restroom and be back in a . . . Baltic jiffy."

Patrician Linos briefly considers Tai with that frat-boy hunger that, to his credit (or maybe more frighteningly), dissipates swiftly. "Did he say something to you?" he asks me, motioning to Hérrakí, who sits there, pale-faced, smelling of soap. I realize with an ache I won't see his forest eyes again underneath his long lashes, and I'm instantly mortified that even occurred to me.

"No, no," I say, before Tai holds a hand to my stomach, then my forehead, then my cheek—measuring who knows what, since the problem is on our phones, and the phones of everyone in this bar.

"Nothing some vodka and a Slavic steam bath can't fix," she says, grinning apologetically, as we both stand, and I feel the room's eyes on us, hot and sticky.

"Are you done now?" I whisper under my breath.

Hérrakí stands abruptly, while Linos just watches with amusement. "Please let me pay for your drinks," Hérrakí offers.

"No way, no—" I say, just as Tai beams, all dimples and bubble-gum cheeks, and replies, "Okay! Thanks! The euro-ruble exchange isn't what it used to be."

Before Hérrakí can move for his wallet, Linos slides a huge wad of bills in a platinum money clip from his pocket and smacks it on the bar in a move he surely feels is incredibly suave. "I've got it."

"You are just caviar and vodka in a single mouthful, aren't you?" Tai says, tugging on her yellow silk coat.

"It's my pleasure. See you soon, Natasha," says Linos, as Hérrakí fumbles and pulls out what looks like a smart card—used for the bus.

Linos chuckles at him, and we say our goodbyes. We've barely turned around when I overhear Linos say, "Hérrakí Nítuchí. What would your uncle say if he saw you pulling out a bus pass at Maltese?"

As my smile ices over on my face, I take Tai's soft hand, and we run past the bar with its multicolored libations, past the field of glorious, twinkling basalt buildings, and into the refuge of the elevator.

"He's . . . Nítuchí's nephew," I say, just as she says, "Fucking *red snake Daria*," dropping my hand to tap into her own phone.

She blinks up at me. "Wait, what?"

"Linos called him Hérrakí *Nítuchí*," I whisper, and the blood floods out of my sister's cheeks.

"We don't know for sure," she says.

I don't answer. I should've known better. I should've remembered how small this island is. I work to loosen the straps on my heels. They dug red riverbeds into my skin.

"Nons, you need to read this," she whispers, tugging on my arm and showing me her phone's screen. We read, hand in hand again, our pastel wigs askew, and when it's finished, I stare into her eyes, two eerie echoes of our shared past.

It's not what we thought: It's not Lady.

"It's the lumberjack," we whisper in sync.

BOY
DARIA GRENDL REVEALS
MIREILLE FOIX'S "NOXIM STALKER"
IN EXPLOSIVE NEW
10TH ANNIVERSARY PIECE
MAY 25, 2019

As Mireille's first manager—and only longtime friend—I was
privileged enough to read and collaborate on an early copy
of *White Fox*, the script that shows just how dark Mireille's
mindset was before she disappeared. It is a richly woven tale
of a performer who goes through many grotesque trials—very
much inspired by Mireille's life.

For years, Mireille's husband—the late Hëró Hammick—
instructed his team to threaten me with injunctions if I were
to ever share any information about this early draft publicly.
But I am coming forward with this information now because
I can't stay silent any longer. It's been ten long years since
Mireille disappeared, and my dear friend deserves justice.

In this draft, Mireille directly addresses her Noxim stalker.
That's right: A man who lived in the village closest to her

country home had begun to harass her, and her husband refused to take the threat seriously. I remember, on several occasions, Mireille mentioning to me that, "Hëró wasn't to be bothered with trivial matters." I am sure readers will find this as chilling as I do.

Mireille told me little about this stalker—only that he lived in Noxim. But she wrote him into her script in the form of a lumberjack who captures the namesake character— White Fox—and keeps her all for himself, with haunting consequences.

It was clear to me, from those pages she shared, that this Noxim stalker—and her husband's refusal to take it seriously— was one of the reasons she refused to sit still and accept her life as Hëró Hammick's trophy wife, dusted over and forgotten in her Stökéwood "cabinet."

He was one of the reasons she left us, shattering the Hammicks' Viloki dream once and for all.

∞ ∞ ∞

It's true.

Hëró Hammick never did take me seriously. And that was the stupidest thing the God among men ever did.

We will meet soon, girls. And then you'll know for yourselves what I did.

PART TWO

INT. GRAND OLD HOME — NIGHT

White Fox, bare-faced, clothed in a clean dress, and seated in a small room, clutching her knees to her chest. The voices chattering nearby—perhaps outside the window—continue, and it is making her nervous. But it is only a MAID, who appears with a tray bearing two cups of tea.

Client 2, the lonely man, accepts the cups of tea from the maid, who gives a sidelong glance at White Fox before disappearing.

Client 2 hands White Fox a cup of tea.

CLIENT 2

Where did you go next?

White Fox sips her tea.

WHITE FOX

I ran away to the moor, of course.

CLIENT 2
(bemused)

The moor?

WHITE FOX

That's right. It was a lonely place, to
be sure. But I liked it.

EXT. FOGGY MOORLANDS — NIGHT

White Fox is wandering the moor with a large
carpetbag. She sees, in the distance, the LUMBERJACK
with his ax. She collapses into the brush, blood
trickling from her mouth.

EXT. OLD CABIN—NIGHT

The old cabin isn't what it seems. It looks to be
made of wood, and flowering branches appear to
grow from the structure itself.

The Lumberjack, a large man with kindly eyes,
lives inside alone.

The Lumberjack carries White Fox and her bag into his home.

INT. OLD CABIN — NIGHT

The home is comfortable and odd. There are many wood carvings along the mantel. White Fox sleeps on a solitary cot.

She is roused, and the Lumberjack serves her a cup of soup.

                    LUMBERJACK
          This is not a safe place for a lady.

                    WHITE FOX
          It was kind of you to find me, sir. But
          I know this area well. It makes me feel
          safe.

                    LUMBERJACK
                    (scoffing)
          Then you are a fool. You have soft hands,
          a woman's hands. The moor has changed!

Lumberjack stands and approaches her. He is far larger than her, and his shadow covers her. He seems to be evaluating her.

                    WHITE FOX
          Who are you?

                    LUMBERJACK
What would you have done if I hadn't
been there to help you?

White Fox is silent. She continues eating her soup.

                 LUMBERJACK (CONT'D)
No mind. I have needed a bit of beauty
in my life.

White Fox glances up. She coughs into her hand and
shows him the blood.

                    WHITE FOX
You should know that I am sick. And
I'll make you sick if you come near me
at any time.

                    LUMBERJACK
                    (chuckling)
I know you are here only *because* you
are sick. I know the cure to that ail-
ment. I will take care of you.

Lumberjack walks over to a table to pick up a hunk
of wood and sits on the floor by White Fox, blocking
her path to the door.

He begins whittling away at it.

                    WHITE FOX
Who are you?

                    LUMBERJACK
I am the Lumberjack.

                    WHITE FOX
But there are no woods nearby.

                    LUMBERJACK
                (whittling the wood)
That's right. Now hush. You should stay
until you get better.

INT. OLD CABIN — DAY

Lumberjack watches White Fox as she sleeps.

Lumberjack leaves the shed in the morning with his
ax.

He leaves her some fruit and positions many little
wooden figurines around her, which seem to watch
her.

They appear to be women—women crossed with beasts.

White Fox watches them back and attempts to clean the
shack to keep her mind busy, but she is too weak. The
figurines' expressions seem to shift with the light—
their positions change behind her back.

At one point in the day, White Fox summons the energy
to leave her cot, and she picks up a particularly
beautiful CREATURE, a woman with the face of a little
forest mouse. It SNAPS at her, and White Fox places
it back down with a start.

INT. OLD CABIN—NIGHT

When the Lumberjack returns at night, with his ax
and without a scrap of lumber, the shack is tidy.
The Lumberjack smiles at her with approval and
begins to make a simple soup for her with food he
has brought home.

She eats with gusto.

> LUMBERJACK
> You look well.

> WHITE FOX
> What do you do all day, if you don't
> collect lumber?

> LUMBERJACK
> I cut down trees that are invisible. I
> replant them afterward. And with their
> endless lumber, I create my world and
> my friends.

                    WHITE FOX (V.O.)
          That didn't make any sense to me, but I
          had the distinct feeling that mentioning
          this to the man—or the nature of his
          figurines, or anything more—would make
          him angry. And he was right. I was feel-
          ing better with every passing moment.
          The clean air was helping me, and he
          wasn't a terrible host.

INT. GRAND OLD HOME — NIGHT

                    CLIENT 2
          I don't like the sound of this.

                    WHITE FOX
          Hush. You said you would listen.

INT. OLD CABIN — DAY

White Fox tidies the house, little by little, and
eats the meal the Lumberjack prepares for her. She
is regaining her color.

INT. OLD CABIN — NIGHT

                    WHITE FOX (V.O.)
          Of course, the situation soon soured.

White Fox does not finish her soup, unable to
stomach the taste, and cleans out the bowl when
the Lumberjack's back is turned.

Later, she cannot sleep, and she realizes, while pretending to nod off, that the Lumberjack has not slept since she arrived.

He simply watches her while whittling his block of wood into a new creature.

This latest CREATURE is almost done: a woman with the face of a FOX. He seems to be refining little details on it, polishing it.

When he is finished for the night, he pries open a secret compartment in the wall, laying the fox to rest behind it. Then, he just stares at White Fox, inhaling and exhaling.

                    WHITE FOX (V.O.)
          I decided to follow him out to whatever
          he did on the moor, the next morning.

The polished little fox figurine sits quietly inside the secret compartment.

INT/EXT. OLD CABIN

White Fox watches the Lumberjack leave with his ax.

Though still visibly weak, she clothes herself in a dark hooded garment and follows him.

EXT. FOGGY MOORLANDS

Lumberjack does not notice White Fox—or if he does, he does not make a show of it.

Lumberjack dips into a valley, where there are many stumps and large stones.

He reaches a large stretch where small stones have been rested on flat soil.

> WHITE FOX (V.O.)
> I recognized them. Grave markers.

Lumberjack sits and continues to work on his figurine. White Fox, stunned, hides behind a large boulder to collect herself.

> LUMBERJACK
> (calmly)
> Come out if you'd like.

White Fox doesn't move.

> LUMBERJACK
> You are smarter than most. You must know
> this moor well, as you say. Well, this is
> what happens to each girl after I finish
> her figurine. This little fox is yours.

White Fox's face is pale with fear.

                    WHITE FOX (V.O.)
I knew that I was one of many he had
thought he was loving and protecting.
He only wished to possess us, in the
most permanent way possible, with his
cruel magic.

Lumberjack whittles.

                    LUMBERJACK
I'll give you a head start. But soon
I will finish the fox—it is only a
matter of minutes. And now that you
have recovered, it is time.

White Fox runs back to the cabin as fast as she can.

Lumberjack packs up and returns to the shack
slowly, as if there's nothing more natural in the
world. He walks in a very ominous fashion, ax in hand.

White Fox reaches the shack and collects her
things, glancing out the window.

She watches the Lumberjack approach.

                    WHITE FOX (V.O.)
All of a sudden I felt very ill. I felt
I had no chance of escaping him. I had,
after all, collapsed the last time I
trekked across this moor.

When White Fox steps outside, she feels herself coughing up blood again.

The Lumberjack is close. He hurls his ax toward the house with a maniacal calm and it hits the wood with a THUD beside her. White Fox freezes.

                    LUMBERJACK
          You'll become sick again the moment
          you leave me. But if you remain here,
          you'll live forever as a sweet little
          fox, with me and your many friends.

White Fox looks inside the open door of the house: the little wooden creatures have crowded the threshold while her back was turned. They've even cracked open the secret compartment to free their comrades.

They watch her with a mix of curiosity and dismay.

White Fox picks a CREATURE up and chucks one at the Lumberjack.

He grunts and picks up his creature, distressed. The creature is filthy.

The Lumberjack runs toward White Fox in anger.

White Fox pelts another couple of creatures at him, hitting him square on the head.

This only infuriates him further, but he is disoriented. He collects his creatures from the dirt.

White Fox abandons her bags and runs, BLOOD trickling from the side of her mouth.

The Lumberjack pursues her.

When he catches her, he does his worst.

But her hand closes around one of the creatures in the mud.

                    WHITE FOX (V.O.)
          I prayed for help. I'd seen the creatures
          move when he willed them to. I hoped
          they would do the same for me, now. Even
          though I had done nothing for them.

White Fox takes the creature in her grip and smashes it into the Lumberjack's eyes, where the creature takes hold with little wooden paws.

Lumberjack screams.

Torn and bruised, White Fox runs.

INT. GRAND OLD HOME — NIGHT

CLIENT 2

Goodness.

WHITE FOX

Clearly, I escaped. But in the end, the
Lumberjack won. However he cured me—be
it that soup, or whoever knows—I could
never replicate it to cure myself again.

CLIENT 2
(shaking his head)

And then what happened? If this was the
second potential cure, weren't there
two other ways of curing yourself?

WHITE FOX
(tsking)

Always analyzing. Well, yes. And the
next bit might be more familiar to you.

TAI

The blinds cast stripy midnight-streetlight shadows on Noni's face as she stands over me in bed.

"We are *not* going to Noxim alone, and that's final," she tells me, tucking me under a blanket at the Limatra apartment. I've spent the past half hour begging her to agree with my plan—the only logical next step, after reading Daria's bombshell revelation and the lumberjack portion of *White Fox* for the umpteenth time. "We could run into him, Tai. The lumberjack."

"If he even exists—or is still alive! It's been ten freaking years! Be honest: Do you feel unsafe here?" I ask, sitting up in bed. "Tell me." All I've felt on the streets is leftover adoration. The least safe place was probably the retrospective, where half the audience wanted us to have a wardrobe malfunction.

But Noni doesn't look at me.

"The stalker's probably too old and infirm to bother us now," I continue. "And we're too famous to kill in broad daylight."

"How does that even make sense?" She narrows her eyes.

I pout. "I'm just doing all I can to find Mama."

"Don't give me that." Her hands have curled shut. "You got your way tonight. You tricked me into coming on your creepy role-playing date."

And I know she's doing me a favor not asking for an explanation. The truth is: It was Linos who suggested I "dress incognito" and come in the back way, so I wouldn't *draw attention*. As if I could ever be incognito here. *Anywhere*. To his credit, he handled my pink wig and yellow coat remarkably well for a pseudo-aristocrat with a silver spoon up his ass. God, I wish he wasn't such a fucking snack.

"Fine," I reply. "What if we text Teddy and ask him to send us a car in the morning?" I don't specify which kind of car, but Noni's too exhausted to read between the lines.

She exhales with the agonizing slowness of a beleaguered governess—her favorite role—as I pick up my phone to text Teddy.

"*Fine.*" She shuts off the light. "Now go to sleep."

Ordering me around like I'm five. *You spend money like a drunken sailor. You're a high school dropout. Go to sleep, fool.*

But I can't do this without her.

"Wait!" I say, hands on my phone. "Will you sleep in here with me tonight?"

Because I kind of am five.

She pauses by the light switch. Then she drifts toward the near side of the bed, and settles onto her back, her wet hair fanning onto me, smelling like her special oaty shampoo. I hide my grin by typing out my message to Teddy and spotting fresh texts: one from Saxim, asking if she can sleep over at Stökéwood tomorrow, and Linos:

I knew you wouldn't be able to stay incognito. You're too special. Let's meet at Stökéwood tomorrow night?

Even though I'm too tired to function, that Cheshire-cat smile I've been fighting spreads across my face.

"Natasha?" Noni asks, rolling over to face me. "Did you work through whatever you needed to work through tonight?"

"Nope," I reply, tapping out yeses to Linos and Saxim. "I'm still furious." Mama left us the script, but no letter to clarify who she was. Even Dad left us a letter. Not that he, you know, called or anything. I exhale, locking my phone and facing her. "But she's our Lady, and we love her."

Noni takes my hand and pets it like a small animal. Hand in hand, we fall asleep.

∞ ∞ ∞

A few hours later, I wake to Noni cursing her weird semi-Victorian noncurses (*Blazes! Drat!*) and rummaging through my luggage.

"Uh . . . hi?" I rub my eyes, clearing the leftover mascara gunk that turns my skin blue.

"I forgot my notebook, Tai," she snaps. "At the bar."

I yawn. "M'kay. We'll call them. It's all good," I say, stretching in bed. The dark feels luxurious. More time to sleep.

She towers over me and crosses her arms. "Can you take this a little more seriously?"

I groan. "I mean, it's just a notebook?"

"It's my *livelihood*," she says, before wrenching open a drawer that is most definitely empty.

I blearily raise a brow. "Okay, but, like, what does that even mean?"

"Nothing," she says, slamming the very empty drawer shut. "I'm just going to call them again. I need to find it. It has all of Mama's places in it." She storms out of the room.

And I'm the dramatic one.

I guess she's not wrong, though. *It has all of Mama's places in it.* That means all the Noxim places, too, and any clues as to who this stalker might actually be, outside of *White Fox* and our faded memories.

The island might be small, but there are hiding places everywhere: dense networks of tunnels, jewel-box coastal towns brimming with ancient strangeness, and superwealthy, old-school enclaves that are basically impossible to penetrate, like the castle-turned-mansion in Mitella inhabited by Linos's demon mother. If we're going to sniff out Mama in Noxim, we're going to need every single juicy secret we can cull.

∞ ∞ ∞

"This is a joke," Noni says, arms crossed in front of the state-of-the-art driverless car Teddy sent for us in the morning, upon my request. We're both wearing boring black hats and sunglasses, our hair tied up in buns, upon *her* request. "I know I only said 'a car,' but you're not one of those genies who takes wishes literally. You're a human being with a brain. Or did dropping out of high school ruin you forever? We need a driver. Human security. Not a 'look who we are,' rich jerk mobile."

"Come on!" I say excitedly, snapping a photo. "I explained everything, and Teddy approved the outing. He said Noxim is a ghost town."

Noni goes rigid as I chatter on.

"But in a safe, chill way! And this car is *the* cutting edge when it comes to privacy and security. It follows you! It has a SWAT team on speed dial, or something cool like that! She's like the Mina of cars, Nons."

Noni shoots me a look as the car's door handle scans my fingerprint. "Because that worked out so well for Dad."

I hush her. I won't let anyone's bullshit ruin my day today. "Don't make the car upset," I whisper, grinning wickedly.

She rolls her eyes and follows me into the car's coconut-scented embrace.

∞ ∞ ∞

A girl with braces and a light smattering of acne opens the door of the Noxim Visitors' Center for us with a bright grin and a jaunty little wave. Her collared shirt has been freshly pressed, and she wears a name tag reading *Welcome, I am* with handwritten emoji below it (the smiley showing all its teeth and the dancing girls).

"Welcome to our town," she says, each word crisply enunciated. "I hope you're not here to visit the ice caves? The ice caves originate from the year 1864 and are the fascinating result of Mount Vilox's high altitude and unique climate. These caves develop vertically, and one can find ice deposits of varying thickness, but—" She sputters to a stop, red splotching her cheeks. "Wait. Do I know you?"

"We'd *love* to hear more about the ice caves," I lie quickly, fidgeting with my sunglasses and turning on my effervescence like it comes through a spigot. My nerves are fried little ramen noodles, but there's rejuvenating power in acting. "They're so cool." The truth is, I've never once been. Dad thought they were dangerous, and there was an age restriction for entering, too. We never made the cut.

The girl's face falls, inexplicably, so I stumble on.

"We wanted to see what was new in town, too. So of course we thought: Why not ask someone who really knows?" I smile, feeling a little used-car salesman–y, but you never know what will play well. "What's your name?"

The girl, thrown from her routine, recomposes herself and adjusts her shirt. "Mikki."

"Mikki," I say. "So what's new in town?" Yep, definitely feeling like a goon.

"Any lumberjacks in the area?" Noni asks, from beneath her baseball cap, hiking bag strapped to her back, like a creepier goon.

"Lumberjacks?" Mikki scratches her nose. "What? No. I mean, nothing new has happened. Nothing really happens here at all. I mean, there's the dance club, the eel place, the outlet store . . . I guess the town became more popular after that superfamous actress who started the institute went missing? But that was a long time ago." Her face squinches up at us. "Where are you from?"

My fingers tighten around the strap of my vintage Chanel fanny pack. *Superfamous actress?* Of course we found the one kid on all of Viloxin who has *almost* no clue who we are. Mark of luck strikes again. I hope Noni is elated.

Her face softens. "Yeah, suuuuuper famous, but I always forget her name, and my friends always make fun of me. I don't know much about it because I was only three, you know, and my mama thinks the internet is the devil and stuff. She grows lavender? Anyway, I think her name is Fox something, like Fox Institute—"

"Yeah, it's Mireille something or another," Nons says, sour as ever.

"Yeah, it's a weird name like that. I think you're right," she says, turning to wave at an older gentleman walking through the door toward the back office. She lowers her voice. "They don't like me talking about it at the center, though. They'd rather people just come for the ice caves, you know? They don't need more bad press with the bad types who come to, like, do drugs in the Delirium Forest and everything. But now that the ice caves are closed for restoration, it's become really hard, you know?" Her voice rises as the man passes her. "But I know you'll enjoy the rest of our town, until the ice caves reopen soon! The hike up to Mount Vilox is super cool and lots of fun, as long as you're careful and pack a light jacket! Kids love it, too." She grins at us, back on script.

"So the ice caves are . . . closed?" I ask.

"Yeah," Mikki says. "It was such a warm spring that a lot of the ice already melted, on account of the heat and the forest canopy not

206

being grown in. On the plus side, there will be new areas to explore once the tunnel restoration is complete in the next week or so."

"Hmm." So we can't even go to the ice caves, attraction numero uno of this damn town. My eyes begin to drift around the room, looking for any other clue pointing to Mama or a lumberjack. Anything relevant, at all.

Mikki drops her voice to a whisper again. "Listen, you seem nice. If you're okay with weirder stuff—you know, unofficial, off-book—" She hesitates.

"Oh, I'm *all* about that weird life," I say.

"You could go see Baba Yuki," she whispers.

"Who?"

"Baba Yuki," she repeats, pulling a map out from behind the desk and tracing a route from the visitors' center with a highlighter. "She's a weird character, a town legend. She dresses up like famous people and sings, too."

"Sorry," Noni says, while I sniff the highlighter fumes. "You said Yuki?"

"She lives just about a fifteen-minute walk from here, in the woods. She's the only person who will talk about the past. My friend Taxo told me that she sells Delirium Forest maps to tourists and star maps with Morel—"

"Mireille."

"Yeah, her. Maps with her favorite places on them. Baba Yuki's pretty old, so she probably knows a lot about what the town used to look like, too. She might even know about *lumberjacks* or whatever," she adds, to Nons, who was flipping through pamphlets to look blasé.

Mikki peers outside the window. "By the way, is that your fancy car out there?" she asks, as Nons goes stiff, and I shake my head, opening my mouth to say—

But Mikki sighs. "I've always wanted to ride in one of those. I want to work for Clouded Cage, but I know my mama would never let me. Taxo said he'd let me play one of their games at his house, this new haunted-house one, and he said it's kind of like what living in Mitella must be like." She glances at us. "Seriously, you look kind of familiar. When were you here before?"

∞ ∞ ∞

The walk to Baba Yuki's draws us toward the dampest edges of the forest, where chestnut trees cut massive figures and block out the light. We pass a group of backpackers in their twenties trading plastic baggies of rainbow tablets under a sign reading, LOSE YOUR WAY, LOSE YOUR LIFE! STAY SAFE AND KEEP THE VILOKI DREAM ALIVE. I forgot the woods were the reason people called this Dreamland, once upon a time.

We reach the parking lot Mikki showed us on the map, and I try to make out which of the unmarked trails leads to Baba Yuki's house. We slow by a group of teenaged boys crowded around a car—they look local, and I might as well ask for directions before they catch us loitering all sketchily—but Noni holds me back with a hand. I can tell she's been eavesdropping.

"The parking ticket says it's been here one month," one says.

"Why haven't they towed it yet?" asks another.

"Their loss," says the tallest, taking a crowbar from his back pocket—one I'm just noticing. "Look, there's a pink phone under the seat."

I flinch back, my foot cracking a twig, and they turn to us with hungry eyes. Nons pulls me away, toward a path blanketed with wet leaves and fallen branches. A chill runs along my arms as I turn back to see if they're following us, but their attention's back on the car.

This parking lot reminds me of the one in *Not Another Girl of Ice*, and if I squint I can pretend I see Mama walking into the forest, bloodstained.

"What's that?" Noni whispers, pointing at something flashing red behind the trees. I bound forward and find a huge sign that reads, BABA YUKI'S FOREST HUT: FLOWERS, FORTUNES, LEGEND BOOKS, MAPS, FOREST GUIDES, AND MORE.

"Thank fuck," I exhale, as we round the bend, arm in arm again.

The house is a run-down cabin eaten by vines—a shabbier version of the one we played in as kids. Gnomelike cartoon characters with evil-looking faces dot the garden, alongside posters reading, I WENT TO DELIRIUM FOREST AND ALL I CAME HOME WITH WAS MY LIFE. Noni clenches her jaw.

Phantom piano music mushrooms as we approach the door. We knock on the creaking wood—it's open just an inch. A whiff of the potent combination of rose and musk pushes through the crack, and when I open it wide, plumes of incense envelope us. Nons starts coughing. Inside, it's a black boudoir, a Gothic burlesque haven. Moody piano music bursts from speakers hidden in the walls. The room could have been a still life painting, a study of the darkest, most sinister color, but then a slice of the panorama quivers. Light glints off a commanding figure wrapped in black silk and draped across a long chair in a far corner of the room. A thick white paste is smeared on her face (reminding me of a K-Beauty ghost mask I have), encircling closed eyes doused in glittery black eye makeup. *Yes, queen. All about that midday masking lunch break*, I think, shivering with adrenaline.

"Well, don't just leave the door open," the figure says, in a deep drawl. The lids rise, irritation wrinkling the brow. Her bone structure is surreal, maybe (okay, probably), the product of extensive plastic surgery: an underlying jaggedness defines her potent beauty, an incongruous texture here, an unnatural angle there. She's breathing art, blurring the line between the human and the otherworldly. Baba Yuki's eyes—because it could only be her—flicker over us with only the mildest curiosity, as her long, matte black fingernails, filed into points, scrape the velvet seat.

"Let me guess. Tentative young lovers, eager to find out whether your dream of love should be a reality." Fine bones act as tent poles for her skin, staking out a smile as she chuckles drily.

"Not quite," I say.

Nons is too busy figuring out how to breathe while examining the unusual scape. Black lollipops and black handcuffs are the most easily recognizable products for sale.

"But I'm loving the drama," I add, waving my hands around the place to give them something to do.

"Would you like to sit?" She motions at a tufted chair across from the chaise longue, patchy and stained-looking, as if previous lovers couldn't wait for their tented escapades. I swear one stain is still wet.

"Mm, that's okay," I say, bouncing on my toes. "It's *so* delicious to stretch. Long, long ride and all that. So. Do you have any pamphlets on that foreign actress who disappeared? Mireille?"

"Oh." Yuki's lips purse. "Mireille Maps. Of course." She eyes me. "I don't sell many of those maps anymore, let me tell you. I expected to, what with the retrospective, but no one gives a damn about fine art anymore." Rising to a commanding six feet, she walks over to the wall, where there are pamphlets lined up, like the visitors' center. There's a careful precision to the way she moves, a dainty self-consciousness, and I can't stop watching her every move, riveted. I bet she's an actress, or a dancer. She follows the rows with a pointed nail before settling on a single stack in the bottom right, a skinny pamphlet printed with Mama's grainy face.

"That'll be ten euro," she says, holding the pamphlet aloft. As Nons reaches for it, she snatches it back. "Ten euro, girl."

Noni hands her two bills, which Yuki flips through with an over-dramatic flourish before handing her the sad prize, a smile repasted on her face.

"Anything else?" she asks. "Flowers to enjoy later at home with your Chanel fanny pack?"

The back room contains pots and baskets of tangled tendrils and waxy blooms reaching out of the dark with tragic desperation.

"God, I wish. They're . . . something else." I watch over Noni's shoulder as she thumbs through the packet, eager for a surprise. It's marked with x's for Stökéwood—at the wrong location, thank the Lord—plus random spots on Viloxin, like this French restaurant that definitely opened after Mama left, marked as *Mireille's Favorite Restaurant*, and loads of international boutique outposts. Which, like, okay. She had a Dior sponsorship and got most of her shit for free.

"Wow," I mumble under my breath. I could have told her the pamphlet would be a waste.

But Baba Yuki just points at a sign above her head that reads, *No Returns, No Exchanges—All Sales Final*. And I have to respect the hustle. I mosey past a stack of hot pink flyers, reading, *MADAME MIRAKI, BRINGING YOU BUTTERFLY KISSES EVERY NIGHT IN MAY. ONLY AT—*

"No touching, princess."

Photocopied on the cheap flyer is a blurred old photo of Mama in sunglasses, butterfly wings drawn on her back. The room glitches. "Wait. So you dress up as her and perform?"

I squint at her. She doesn't look like Mama, doesn't move like her. But I could see it.

"Miraki, like butterfly," she replies, razor-sharp. "Not Mireille. *Not* that it's trademarked." She clears her throat. "Now. Is that *all*?"

"No. One last, little question," I say, edging over to Baba Yuki with a lathery sweetness. "We were told in town that you know all there is to know about Noxim and its history—and I do value an expert opinion."

Baba Yuki smirks at Noni. "Does your friend think I was born yesterday? Or is she just the type who actually thinks her shit doesn't stink?"

Noni bites her lip, concealing a grin, and I cross my arms. "It smells just like your flowers."

Yuki snorts. "Okay, sweetheart. Fair enough. I'll bite. But you could've bought some of those flowers."

"It's not too late," I reply, all sugar.

"Do you know any lumberjacks?" asks Nons, blending Vilosh and English.

"Lumberjacks?" Baba Yuki repeats. "What on earth is a *lumber-jack*?" She throws out an impassioned *ick* for effect. "No."

"Any strange people in town, obsessed with little demons and axes?" I ask, wondering how to convey the message, catching sight of a *machíkíl* cleaver hanging on the far wall.

"This is Viloxin, honey," she says in a bored tone, raising a brow. "We're all strange." She looks at Nons, who has removed her sunglasses to rub at her pink eyes. An allergic reaction to the incense, I bet.

"What lovely eyes you have, my pretties," Yuki says, popping on a pair of rhinestone-encrusted cat-eye glasses over the mask and bending in for a closer look, very much wolf in *The Little Red Riding Hood*–esque.

She seizes Noni's chin in her hand, and Noni shudders away, speechless.

"First of all, thank you, but second of all, can you just . . . not?" I snap.

But Yuki's gasping, her matte-black talons closing around her own throat. "Oh, I'm a fool," she whispers. "I thought there was something off about you two when you came in. But I just assumed wearing sunglasses inside was a pedestrian affectation. I never imagined—well, I never imagined I'd meet you in the flesh." Tears well in Yuki's kohl-darkened eyes. "You're them. You're *her* girls."

Nons jams her sunglasses back on her nose. "You're mistaken," she says, and quite honestly, I roll my eyes.

Baba Yuki does, too. "Don't insult me. I know what I see." Before we can say a word, she hurries to the front door and turns the lock, pressing her back against the door and eyeing us with frenzied nostalgia, like an overgrown girl imagining the wicked teatime she's going to have with old dolls.

I clutch Noni's hand. "Call for help before we're flayed and turned into skin dolls and our skin doll faces are mashed together."

"What? What's a skin doll? And call who? The *car*?" she whispers back, as I scrabble, one-handed, with my fanny pack clasp.

"I loved your mother," Yuki interrupts, her glazed eyes two shiny grapes about to pop from her skull.

"You're profiting from her disappearance," says Nons.

"*Skin dolls*," I hiss, elbowing her.

"The universe helps those who help themselves," Baba Yuki quips, before looking to Nons. "Which one are you? Manon, the elder? She told me you were the perceptive one. A writer, she said to me. 'She'll be a great thinker someday, a wise soul, if only she can master herself.'"

Nons bites her lip.

"Please unlock the door, ma'am," I say, finally pulling out my phone. No goddamn service. This island.

"Ma'am?" Baba Yuki snorts. "You. *Thaïs*. A star in the making. 'My only hope is that she surrounds herself with kind people who tell her truth, that she doesn't burn too bright and harm herself in the process,' she told me." Just like they said about Mama.

"If you don't unlock the door, I'll call the police. And they come extra fast for us."

"Because your shit smells like flowers?" Baba Yuki rolls her eyes again. "I locked the door to keep the vile ones outside *out*. Little bastards. It's not to keep *you* in. Now, come here, children." She motions for us to sit on the stools across from her, because all of a sudden she's a kindly auntie.

"I don't bite," she adds, and when we don't move, her expression sours. "If you don't sit, you'll never know what I promised your dear mother in one of our final conversations ever. I've kept this from the press, from the police, from everyone, just like I've stayed mum on every conversation we ever had since we met at a florist's shop in Limatra. Now, for the love of all things holy, sit."

"So you *are* Katox's old assistant?" Noni mutters, settling on a stool and pulling me down with her.

"Yes," says Yuki curtly. "I'd studied performance art at the institute, and that donkey's shop was my work assignment. I was almost broke at the time—living with my sick mother, who was getting care from the Hero center in Noxim, and commuting into the city for work. Your mother noticed me and spoke to me, and—well, I was awestruck. *Foix Institute*, and all that. But she was so . . . kind. She loved the freshness and fragility of fresh blooms, as I did. She loved the unconventional—reveled in it. As I do. And so we developed something of . . . a friendship. And as I'm sure you know—when she warmed to someone, my goodness, you felt as if the sun itself was smiling upon you. She even gave me seed money to start my own floral business—helped me draft plans." She sniffs the air. "That became this store," she continues, with a glance around the gloomy interior. "But in any case, we needn't get bogged down by the present, when the past is so much lovelier. Your mother was a gem of a human being." She takes a deep breath and picks up a black hand towel. "And

214

she loved you two so much." She wipes the mask from the top corner of her forehead, revealing porcelain-white skin below.

And even though I should soften, I suddenly *seethe*, rivers of fury flooding over in my body, as it sits, cramped, on the low stool. Another stranger, convinced she knows Mama's mind so well, when her own daughters didn't—and still don't.

"You don't believe me?" she asks. When she sees we aren't budging, she saunters over to an overflowing chest and opens a drawer, carefully lifting out a note.

She hands it to me, and my mood shifts when I spot her curling script, from angry suspicion to something fragile, dark, delicate.

Yuki, my dear, it reads, with those wispy *y*'s and petite, looping vowels that make me feel like I've discovered treasure. *You are pure promise. Consider this a gift that, I hope, will enable you to build the floral shop of your dreams. Life is to be lived courageously, dear one, and I know few people who are capable of living their lives with more bravery, honesty, and joy than you. With love, your Lady, MFH*

Honesty. When I read the word, so close to the word *Lady*, a bitter taste blooms at the back of my tongue. My fingers tighten around the note's edges, crinkling the monogrammed sheet. I can't let it go: this evidence of her identity, this new glimpse into her.

But when Yuki holds out her hand, I return the note.

"She told you her name was Lady," I say aloud, feeling Noni's cool hand settle on my wrist.

"She told me because I was going through a different kind of re-invention at the time," Yuki says, beginning with the towel on one cheek. "She wished so hard to reinvent herself that she *did* it. Why shouldn't we be whomever we want to be, especially if it hurts no one? Even if it does hurt someone else a little, at first? We only have one life."

A judder runs through me, one I can feel even on Noni's clammy skin.

"What was the promise?" Noni asks. "The promise you said you made her."

"Ah, yes. On one of your mother's last visits, she said to me—clear as day—'Yuki, if my girls ever visit you as adults, you must send them to the woodcutter. Promise me that.' And I said—"

"A woodcutter is a lumberjack," Nons says—mostly to me.

"She told you her name was Lady," I repeat, feeling at the sweating nape of my neck.

Yuki glares. "And I said to her, 'Lady, why don't you just buy your daughters a couple of the little figurines and take them to them now?' And she said, 'No, they need to see all of them in the same shop, set up like animals in a park, in a zoo.' And I said to her then—'Lady, why not just bring them to the shop now yourself?' And she turned pale as the moon, I'm telling you. She said to me, 'I can't bring them to Noxim, Yuki, because their father doesn't want them in town.' She glanced outside, and I thought she meant it because of the paparazzi. They'd been lurking around the town to catch glimpses of the family, and Mr. Hammick did not want anyone to disturb you girls."

"So the woodcutter is . . . what, or who, exactly?" Noni asks, while I weave my fingers together and try to breathe, try to untie the gnarled knot in my stomach, by some kind of yogic magic.

"It's a shop run by the same family for many years. I'll show you where. They make these little figures. They're absolute kitsch, but I promised her that I'd tell you to go there, and that I would tell no one else. Just like I've never spoken a word about *White Fox*, either. She told me, you know, that its five pieces would be a map to understanding her, if anything happened to her, and then something did—"

"Sorry—five pieces?" Nons asks.

She pauses. "Yes, five. It's my birthdate, so I would never forget—"

"What do you mean, 'if anything happened to her?' " I ask, voice cracking.

Yuki shakes her head. "That's all she said. Nothing more. I swear it."

"We only have three pieces," Nons whispers to me.

But right now, I don't care. Because a voice screams in my head: *She told this person her name was Lady. She told her she thought something would happen to her. She told her all of this, and she told us nothing.*

"What's that?" asks Baba Yuki, narrowing her eyes. "Don't keep me out of the loop, now."

Out of the loop. I want to laugh.

"It's nothing," I say, fussing with the crumpled pile of precious bills in my pocket. "Thank you for your help," I add, numb and unthinking. Before I have to process another word, I walk toward the back room of flowers and choose a random bundle, all coiled sprouts and lazy, lonely buds. It nauseates me, but I can imagine Mama loving them. *Beauty isn't that which is beautiful, it is that which pleases us.* I hand Baba Yuki the pile of bills, without counting them.

∞ ∞ ∞

I'm quiet as we leave, not in the mood to chatter to fill the void. The canopy of trees feels thicker than ever—less like insulation, and more like a living, breathing ceiling closing in on us.

"If there are five parts to *White Fox*, then why did she only leave us three?" Noni asks me, tiptoeing closer to fresh fears.

"Maybe Yuki's a liar," I snap. "Maybe Mama didn't have time to finish. Can we stop talking? My stomach hurts."

Noni goes silent.

The gloom shows no signs of lifting, not even when we reach the barbecue-snail place we visited with Mama once. Not even when I take a charred bite and find it's not repulsive like I remember. I chew and swallow down bite after bite, furious at Lady for trusting *her* and not us. I know we were kids, and I don't care. How could she have disappeared ten years ago, with no explanation at all? Fine: three parts of an unfinished fairy tale of a script. It's a twisted joke.

"I don't understand how you can eat a dozen barbecued snails five minutes after complaining your stomach hurts," Nons says, twirling some steaming chestnut flour noodles the width of a child's fingers in fragrant cream sauce. The sight of her slurping down the thick, rubbery strands makes me want to scream in her face.

The call from the unknown number arrives when I'm polishing off the last snail in my lunch set. I almost drop my phone, thinking it's Linos replying to my texts with a mythical call.

But some things are mythical for good reason.

"It's for you," I say numbly, handing my phone to Noni.

NONI

The call is from Hérrakí Nítuchí, who haltingly informs me he is in possession of my notebook.

My pulse speeds up. "How'd you know it was mine? You looked inside?"

His voice is as deep as his eyes were last night: something you can melt into and forget yourself in. "I . . . had to figure out whose it was."

I say nothing, cheeks reddening. Tai sullenly raises her eyebrows at me.

"I'm going to dinner at a *frittimitti* place tonight," he continues, "if you and your sister want to stop by. I figured we might as well meet on our terms, before my uncle orchestrates some kind of terrible Hero Pharm offspring get-together with you, anyway."

I bite my lip. I don't want to go. I would sacrifice almost anything to Tai's drunk-night gods. But I want my notebook. I need it, and not just because it contains clues to finding Mama. So I accept his invitation, hang up, and sit on Tai's side of the picnic bench. "We set a date at a *frittimitti* place in Limatra tonight."

"A date? Tonight?" Tai repeats, watching Yuki's arrangement on the table next to us like it's monstrous scum beneath a lily pad in a dirty pond. She doesn't squawk about the date. She doesn't clap, and say she's obviously coming, if only to watch Nítuchí's nephew flirt with me. She doesn't insult the choice of *frittimitti*—the strange Viloki version of the Italian delicacy of fritto misto or "mixed fried foods" (on Viloxin, *mixed* is taken to its unnatural extreme, and half the "fun" is not knowing what you're biting into). She doesn't even ask if she can dress me.

"A friend date. Can you come?" I have to ask.

"Mmm, I have plans. Saxim was already going to sleep over. And I kind of already told Linos he could come by Stökéwood," she says, picking at her chipping fingernails.

I bristle at the mention of him. "Do you really think that's a good idea?"

"Don't patronize me, Manon." She tears off a final fleck of polish. "I just need some time to try to be normal, okay? Go on your date with Satan's nephew. Saxim and I will be just fine."

But even her attempt at a joke is so atypically muted that I feel that gut pull to restore balance. When doubt has Tai in its clutches—and it hardly ever does—I can almost forget about myself, about my weakness in any of its shapeshifting forms, to protect her. That's how big sisters work. But she speaks before I can do anything.

"Something was seriously wrong with her," she says quietly, running a bare finger over the rim of her water glass.

"What?"

She stares at the trembling surface of the liquid. "Something was seriously fucking wrong with her. Lady. Let's just say the woodcutter is the lumberjack, and the lumberjack was her stalker. Why would she go there at all? Why would she ask a stranger to send us there? Was she trying to get us killed?" And her eyes squinch up, and I gape at her as fat tears spill over her eyelashes. "Why would she hide such weird-ass, dark clues in *White Fox* at all? Why would she leave an unfinished *script* for us but not come find us herself?"

I wrap my arms around her as her nose runs. I don't want to tell her that there are so many more reasons that something was wrong. Mama spent over twenty years working at her institute, refining every procedure and grant, but then she left notes full of cash to individuals like Yuki.

Was she giving up? Did she know her Viloki Eden was never going to work out?

"We're close to answers, Tai," I say instead. "We're close to finding her."

The words sound clichéd, hollow at the core, but they are what matters. That's all that can matter, otherwise . . .

"You were right to bring us out here," I say, interrupting my own melancholy thoughts. "We have one real lead. The woodcutter. We wouldn't have found it, if not for you. And ten years have passed. You don't think the police will have scoped out every single possible stalker? Noxim is a ghost town. You said it yourself. We're perfectly safe."

She eyes me with trepidation. With more of that all-consuming doubt. Gone is the Tai who said we were *too famous to kill*, I think, hiding my own paroxysms of fear in my big-sister way.

As we leave the restaurant, she discards Yuki's flowers. I don't offer to put them inside my backpack for her, because I understand that her abandonment of the dark totem is intentional. I think of Yuki, who said she studied performance art but only got a job with Katox the donkey.

I don't think she likes her flowers much, either.

And I don't want anything more weighing Tai down when we visit the woodcutter at last.

∞ ∞ ∞

After a meandering eight-minute drive alongside the murky woods, we discover, behind a fallen tree riddled with termite holes, a dilapidated shack ringed by a sharp arrowhead fence that sits crooked, like someone desperately tried to yank it out. No inviting flowers, like the house in the story, only dirty, ripped netting over the windows—in fact, there's little resemblance to that house at all.

"This place looks abandoned," Tai says, hanging back, her belt bag sagging on her hips. Maybe a cat once ate from the empty, rusted, overturned metal bowls collecting grit and dust on the slanting, unpainted porch. Or maybe they were just trash. But she's right: Only wild creatures have roamed the overgrown lawn in some time, tangled as it is with thorny bushes and nettles and poison ivy.

The house learned over time how best to keep people out, and it's silent now, anxious to be ignored. Only a small wood-cut sign squeaks on its old hinge above us. I squint: THE WOODCUTTER, it reads, in old-fashioned Viloki script used by great-grandmothers.

Tai shivers and sneaks a look back at the self-driving car, which idles silently down the road. She tucks her hands into her jacket pockets self-protectively. "Screw this place. We don't have to do this."

I rub my chapped lips together. They feel sore to the touch. "We do."

She looks up at the house, wind dragging strands of black hair over her face like the seaweed that decays in hanks by the bay. Her eyes still catch mine. It's getting darker, and they look deep-lake blue.

"If the lumberjack really lives here, Manon, Mama wouldn't send us here."

She's said it before, and she was right. If Mama wanted us to discover this place, she wouldn't have given that message to someone we were unlikely to ever meet.

But then again, who knows what was safe for her to reveal, and what wasn't?

Maybe there's a reason we needed to come here.

There's so much we don't know about her, and that knowledge sits like a giant, smooth stone at the base of my stomach, lending me this strange new center of gravity.

"Is that really going to stop you from seeing what's inside?" I ask Tai, adjusting the straps on my backpack.

She tucks loose hair behind her ears. "What has gotten into you?"

"I'll never forgive myself if we don't follow every lead." I look up at the ruffling netting, strung like cobwebs over the house. "I need to know what's inside."

We push through the gate, and I knock on the door, my nerves only perceptible in the blue tinge of my nails and the warble in my throat. Tai's trying to peek into the ground-floor window with crossed arms when a light clicks on on the second floor, and the crickets around us go quiet.

"What the fuck," Tai murmurs, stumbling back into me. She grabs me so tightly I can feel the blood moving through her. But when I lean back, I can't see into the window: It's covered with grimy mesh.

I do hear heavy shuffling behind the splintered wooden front door, and every one of my muscles stiffens. Some part of my brain imagines a burly man with an ax opening the door, picking his teeth. I steel myself so Tai, clinging to my arm, won't panic. A metal panel under the knocker slides open with a rusty clank, and—

The wrinkled face of a woman appears, squinting through the opening.

And I feel a cool rush of steadying relief.

"We're closed," she says, watching us with the cagey apprehension of someone who rarely welcomes guests.

"We've come a long way to see your figurines," I manage to say, as Tai grips my hand in hers, the fear still glinting at me from the whites of her eyes. "We would be so obliged if you would show them to us."

Her eyes pucker. "Have you brought money?"

I hesitate. "Yes." I hope it's the right answer.

The woman runs her hand over her scraggly bun and pauses, wrestling with whether to actually follow through as a shop owner and allow strangers into her domain. I feel a pang of sympathy. It feels obvious, in this moment, that she's no monster: She's agoraphobic and lonely, like Dad probably was.

The lock clicks for thirty seconds, and when the door hitches open, the singular scent of cat urine assaults me. The woman looks like she's a hundred years old, shriveled to a husk. Her clothing is moth-eaten floral, her slippers stained. She caresses her knotted hands—their fingernails overlong and yellowed—as if they pain her, and she wheezes, her shallow breath the kind that makes me feel like I'm suffocating. Behind her is a small, dark entryway with a black curtain concealing the inside of the house.

"Remove your shoes," she croaks, pointing at crusty shearling visitors' slippers to the right of the entryway. I turn back to Tai, who gapes at me, mouthing, *No fucking way*. But the woman stands, unmoving like a stump in front of the black curtain, until we obey.

"I'm not wearing socks," Tai pleads, her face pale. "I don't want to do this again after Daria's. I had to shower for ten hours."

"Tai, come on," I whisper back.

"I hate you," she spits, ripping off her shoes. But I know we both can't resist the pull of this house's mystery—of the clues to Mama it might hold in its depths.

When we push through the curtain, I can only gasp.

∞ ∞ ∞

Surrounding us are armies of thousands of tiny wooden figures, lit by candles nestled inside glass jars. These whittled works of art line every surface, as well as countless shelves, jutting from the walls. Foxes, squirrels, mice, every woodland creature imaginable. None of them painted, all of them still featuring the veins and grooves of their natural beige wood. Intricately carved by a patient hand.

For a minute, I forget the smell of cat urine, the hunched woman before me, and even my fear—I forget everything except the feel of Tai's hand in mine, and the obsessive magic of this place.

This house is the home to creatures I've never seen, too—with halves made of different animals. Half sparrow, half mouse. And spirits with almost-human features, contorted into cheerful or hostile expressions. I notice a fox that looks almost coy, and I remember a similar fox figurine resting on Mama's bookshelves in the library, long-gone now.

She's been here.

The woman hides behind her desk, as put off by us as we are by her. Her hands, curled into gnarled fists, clench again, and she winces. Arthritic, I'm guessing—thinking of Aunt Marion, whose own hands ache when the weather changes.

It occurs to me then: This woman wasn't the one to carve these. At least not in years.

"No touching," barks the woman, before recoiling, as if surprised by her own outburst. We both flinch away from the displays, even though we hadn't come close to them.

"Where's the money?" she asks, in a low growl.

"The carvings are incredible," I offer.

"They're creatures, not carvings," she snaps, her voice a muted garble. "Who are you, then? I have very few visitors anymore."

"No one special. A friend of ours told us to visit your shop," I say. "She lived around here a long time ago."

The woman jerks toward a chunky log book on the desk. "Your friend never came in my shop. Never."

"How do you know?" Tai asks. "We haven't told you anything about her."

"I remember everyone who comes into my shop," she says, thumbing through the book, "and no fancy woman ever came here."

"We didn't say she was a fancy woman," Tai says, and I grab her hand. It's bloodless, chilled.

The woman's head whips up—her expression is one of unfathomable frustration. "This is my logbook, where I record everyone who comes into my shop. Now, I'm telling you that she did not come into my shop, ever." She rocks herself gently with her knobby arms crossed, like she's soothing herself. I move the pressure from one foot to the other, slippers crunching.

And I swear I hear the faint sound of heavy flesh being dragged along wood, somewhere above our heads. My bones turn to jelly, just as Tai digs her nails into the meat of my palm.

"Let's go," she hisses, and I can tell from the barb of terror in her eyes that she heard what I heard, too. It wasn't imagined. I sneak a look at a small staircase we passed, tucked like an afterthought among the animals. Several large machíkíl cleavers and axes are pinned to the wall above the stair. My mouth goes dry: I know they have these in every house, but I don't like how these glint at me, so sparkling clean.

But I'm probably just hearing the noises an old house makes, especially an unhappy one like this. People say—Mama said—that

Viloki demons were born from energy blockages—pent-up negative emotion, unfulfilled longings, lives cut too short. But they couldn't hurt us on this plane. Not really. And I can't let this go. Not when we're so close to answers.

The carved fox winks at me, and I know Mama was here.

"It would have been many years ago," I say quickly, my heart thrumming under my ribs. "Ten or more."

The woman's hands, those withered claws, contract. "Impossible." She rakes at the holes in her clothing with long, deliberate scrapes. Her eyes narrow at Tai, who is staring at the corner of the desk, where a rare personal effect sits among the vast assortment of creatures: a faded photograph of a woman and a scowling, heavyset hooded younger man, standing stiffly beside each other.

My pulse skips.

The lumberjack?

Just then, I hear a creaking upstairs, the sound of someone stepping on a loose floorboard. The woman's shoulders pulse upward, and her eyes dart behind us.

"Does anyone else work in the shop?" I ask, as Tai pulls on my arm so hard I think it'll be yanked out of its socket.

The woman doesn't answer, instead observing us both with the melancholic longing of someone who, despite a grave and oppressive loneliness, desires nothing more than to be alone again. "I must insist," she says hoarsely, "that no such woman ever entered into my shop."

We hear a noise somewhere up the rickety stairs, something like a spiteful deep chuckle, and Tai and I whip around. "What the fuck was that?" she asks, frantic.

The woman blinks repeatedly, then picks up a figurine that sits next to her desk. "So they don't have money?" she whispers to the creature, like it's a dear friend.

I hear a rustling, whispering, again, somewhere above us. Insistent. Knuckles dragged across a wooden door.

"There's someone else here," whispers Tai. "I want to *go*."

The woman caresses the figurine. "He is a quite lovely raccoon dog, he is. A beautiful male. A fine dog, who aims for no trickery, no. Not like some of the others," she adds, glancing around at the other animals with something akin to nerves.

"Do you have a son?" I ask again, desperately, pointing at the photograph.

"Don't touch that," the woman says, her voice a guttural growl that carries from a place in her body that is not hers. "If you have no money, you are of no use to us."

"We'll take the dog," Tai says, fumbling in her fanny pack. "How much?"

Her seemingly innocent question flusters the woman even more—she's a fallen bird whose feathers have been rumpled, whose dignity has been stolen. She shudders with a long-suppressed mix of frustration and rage. "You don't purchase the creatures." While clutching the dog, she tugs at a widening hole in the cloth near her wrist, and for a moment, I imagine her entire arm will unravel. And just then, a smell wafts into the room, the cloying stink of spoiled dairy—a cloud swelling around us. Several of the candles go out, and my eyes water from the stench.

"You don't care," the woman says, her eyes dark in the low light. "You don't give a damn about anything but yourselves."

The smell intensifies, thick as a rotten bisque, and Tai dry-heaves. A door slams over our heads, and she rips my hand out of the air, hauling me toward the entrance.

"We're so sorry for disturbing you," I say over my shoulder, as we push toward the curtain.

"Them," spits the woman. "You all think you can buy them from under my nose and mistreat them. But you're wrong. We can't be bought." I glance back, and she still holds a dog figurine in her hand, like a precious egg. As she runs a thumbnail over its scalp, an animal groan emanates from the walls, low and mournful.

We take our shoes in hand, not even bothering to put them on, and run.

∞ ∞ ∞

Everything outside—even the woods—is cloaked in shades of deep gray; streetlamps are neither plentiful nor functional this far out, and it's so overcast it feels like twilight. I don't see the self-driving car anywhere.

We run from the woodcutter, hearing nothing but our own heart-beats and the smacks of our bare feet against pavement—not flee-ing because we fear the woman herself, as much as the old sort of evil she's tending inside the house. Tai sprints ahead of me, blindly, desperately.

"Tai, stop!"

I can't run as fast, with my backpack jostling around.

"I'm going to kill you!" she shrieks.

"Let's just call the car!" I yell back, lungs bursting. "Please!"

She turns to reply and trips in front of me, falling to her knees. She's hit the edge of a lump in the road, an understuffed ball of mush that has burst. She howls, and I see it: the ragged body of a dead cat, beneath our feet. Hit by a car and tossed aside, I think, but doom builds in me anyway, like the roadkill's a threat, a symbol of what happens if you let darkness sneak up on you. I help her up, out of breath, and she pushes me away and starts running again, half hobbling and crying. Leaving delicate footprints in congealing blood.

"Stop. Stop," I say, slowing by a lamppost to catch my breath. I settle on the curb to finally put on my shoes, my feet blackened with dirt. A chorus of insect life sounds through the low bushes lining the streets, causing the subtlest tremor in the leaves, as if creatures in the bush rush up with urgent warnings. The gnarled trees above us cut giant hunchbacked figures, displeased, looming with crooked necks like mourners.

"Do you have a wet wipe or something?" she asks, in the most despairing voice I've ever heard.

I rustle through my backpack but only find our copy of *White Fox* I brought.

"Then what was the point of bringing a whole hiking back-pack?" She moans, dropping next to me. "What the hell was that? Why would you make us stay in that haunted house with that batshit woman? I don't want to do anything like this ever again. I'm done." Her face is wet and puffy, only loosely formed. "I want to go home."

I am afraid to tell her what I know: that there is no *home* for us, not as there once was. There hasn't been a home for a long time. Stökéwood doesn't count, because when people leave a house, it stops being a home. And Aunt Marion's doesn't count, either, because if it did, Tai wouldn't have to drown herself in the pixelated light of her phone nightly. I wouldn't have to journal constantly to pull myself out of anxious holes.

I try the zippered pockets of my backpack and find a crunched-up old receipt. I help her get some of the crustiness off her feet. It doesn't do much good, but it calms her down.

I don't know what else to say to her, so I hug her, then take her hand as we stand up. "Let's go find the car, okay?" I can almost glimpse Tai's scalp, and I'm visited by the horrible thought that, vibrant as she is, her pale head could crack against the pavement with the same ease as a porcelain doll's. *My little sister.* In moments like this, I hate myself for resenting her when she's feeling strong and bright. I want her to always feel that way.

"Fine," she says, walking ahead of me toward the side of the familiar black car blessedly parked in the empty parking lot across the street from us. My shoulders relax. Tai waves just as I spot two blurred shapes in the driver and passenger seat. I squint at them as she places her thumb on the back door handle and jiggles. It's locked.

"Open up, car," she says, still barefoot and tapping on the window with her bare fingernails. "This isn't funny."

That's when I peer into the front window and see them staring at me, the cold eyes of two strange men, sitting in the dark. My heart claws its way up to my throat.

It's the wrong car.

"Let's go, Tai," I say, grabbing her arm as she staggers back, the same realization creeping its way to her. "Let's go now."

∞ ∞ ∞

We take refuge and call the car from the visitors' center.

Mikki sits at the front desk, though now her uniform is wrinkled, her elbows rest on the counter, and her heavy-lidded eyes threaten to close at any moment. When she sees us, she perks up, spine straightening. Tai pastes the most fragile of fake smiles on her face as she asks for a bathroom.

Mikki points in the direction of one, and I know from her strange gait that Tai will somehow manage to wash off her feet, if she has to contort herself like a circus performer for them to reach the sink.

"Did you end up going to you-know-who?" Mikki asks me.

"Yeah. We saw Baba Yuki and then visited the woodcutter."

"The what?"

I explain where the house is.

"You mean the old Arakit house?" Her face crinkles. "Who sent you there?"

"Baba Yuki."

"Why?" She drops her voice to a whisper. "You shouldn't have gone there."

"Does she have a son?" I ask, ignoring the little jolt I feel.

She considers this, before swirling around in her chair. "Mr. Ixiru?" She bounds toward the back. When she returns, the shriveled older man with peaceful eyes from earlier accompanies her.

"This is my colleague, Mr. Ixiru," she says, guiding him by the elbow. "He remembers everything." She gently pats the man's forearm. "Mr. Ixiru, will you tell them what you know about the old Arakit house? I've gotta go home. My mom's expecting me. Snail tonight."

The elderly gentleman hesitates, but the girl's sliding a pink backpack on and darting to the door with newfound enthusiasm. "Say bye to your cool sister for me!" she calls, shutting the door carefully behind her.

The old man looks up at me. "The Arakit family," he says, as if testing the words out.

"Mrs. Arakit has a son, right?" I venture, as Tai drifts next to me, face scrubbed raw.

Mr. Ixiru considers us both, in grave silence. "We don't speak about him much."

"Does he—does he live with her?"

His bushy brows connect. "Of course."

My breath catches, and Tai seizes my hand. Did we find Mama's stalker, laughing above our heads? Did he watch us shiver, ankle-deep in the poison ivy of his yard—drink in our fear, our discomfort?

I am a dangerous fool.

"Who are you?" the man asks quietly. "You look familiar."

"We're the daughters of Mireille Foix and Hëró Hammick," Tai says, and his jaw falls, exposing a ridge of crooked teeth.

He dabs at his temple, gathering himself. "Well, Mitso is quite changed since his accident," the old man whispers, tremulous, sunspotted hands now searching for the refuge of his khaki pockets.

"What?" I ask, reaching for him as he wilts before us. "An accident? When? What happened?"

"Oh, at least a decade ago, now. I can't be sure of the exact date." He blinks at us, bewildered. "He had a heart attack and fell. He's been house-bound ever since then. He lives upstairs and never leaves." A car drives past, its engine backfiring, and the man startles.

Then he politely boots us from the center, before locking the door behind us and drawing the blinds.

∞ ∞ ∞

Our car pulls up, humming to itself in the dark. Inside, Tai turns to face me, her face shadowed. "Let's say, hypothetically, that Mitso Arakit was her stalker," she starts, interlacing her quivering fingers on her lap.

"Yes," I reply, raking my greasy hair into a ponytail.

"Even if he did have an accident a decade ago, and even if he hasn't left the house since . . ." She pauses, peering into the murk beyond the car's control panel. "He still could have done something to Mama."

We sit leg to leg in the luxurious backseat of the car, as inky shapes swell and contract in the woods outside our glass bubble.

As we wonder why our own mother would deliver us to him.

TAI

Cool undercurrents tunnel through the damp forest air, licking at my bare arms and legs. I get a bullshit cancellation text from Linos—*So sorry, forgot about dinner with my mother*—just as I wave hello to a drowsy-eyed Tomí, hunched over a table in his guardhouse.

"All good?" he asks, wiping his mouth and coming to his feet. He nudges a bottle of liquor away with his hand, half-heartedly hiding it.

"All garbage, Tomí," I reply. "But thank you so much for being here." I peek into the guardhouse, where I see a steaming microwaved cup of noodles laid out. The poor guy was eating dinner.

He straightens his collar. "It's not so bad. The cot is comfortable, and in a couple days, I'll be rotated out, so I can spend time with my daughters."

I spot the cot, this tiny half-folding contraption in the back, and instantly feel awful. He lives here? I look out to where the mannequin—my bad, the *state-of-the-art security system*—stands, some feet away. "You have daughters?"

He beams. "Two. One is getting her degree in fine art at the institute—she wants to be an artist!—and the other works in the factory at Clouded Cage." He pats his heart. "We're a Hammick family, through and through."

I think back to when we arrived, to when Noni asked if Mina was his wife, and I said nothing. "Your wife, too?"

His smile falters, and he rubs at his stubbly chin. "She worked at Hero Pharm, but she died five years ago. Cancer." We meet eyes, and it's like he knows what I'm thinking. "They couldn't do anything about her kind. They tried everything. She even met with your father." He breaks eye contact, looks into the woods. "Up at the house."

I thank him, before we get all teary-eyed and I ask for a slug of his booze, and he sits back in his folding chair with a creak.

I've never seen so much loneliness as I have this week.

Daria. Baba Yuki. Mrs. Arakit.

My own dad.

Was he like that, toward the end? So afraid of reentering the unpredictable outside world, of that world knocking down his door, that he stayed locked inside his home for years on end, building paper barriers around himself?

Or did he stay here alone so Mama could find us easily, if she came back?

"Fuck you, Lady," I whisper to myself, kicking at a pine cone.

It's a miserable trek up Stökéwood's long gravel drive, along the chestnut grove. The trees' branches reach out like creepy little scorched fingers. And then there's the house, its windows shining black like a hundred tiny oil slicks even though I know each and every one is dirt-encrusted. A freakish trick of the light.

As I climb, I watch it grow, winking at me with what Nons called *its indescribable inert maliciousness.*

She's not wrong.

I still feel the meaty slick and squelch of cat blood on my feet, even though I scrubbed them hard in the information center's bathroom. It takes everything not to shiver now that Noni has gone off to her date in Limatra and I'm alone, except for Tomí, Mina, and the weird mannequin in the neon vest. I'm a pathetic goose-pimpled creature cradling *White Fox* like it'll protect me.

I do feel closer to finding Mama, like Nons said earlier. But I feel more certain than ever that what I find will be too dark for the TFH who landed here a few days ago. And the kid in me doesn't want my view of my mother to continue to evolve. I want the old her to be enfolded in amber, preserved like this glorious, sparkly gem forever. It's impossible now, I know. I've read her most personal thoughts in this script, a living, breathing fable of hacked-together memories and full of traps. But—

I hear a rustling behind me, way back, and, swirling around, I spot a slender figure in the dark.

"Hello?" I call, pulse jagging up.

The figure dances toward me in a pleated skirt, and my mouth goes dry, until I see the lines of her narrow face and smell gardenia.

"It's just me, Bas," says Saxim. I watch her close the space between us and notice, for the first time, that a delicate vein at her temple throbs mermaid-tail green. She's painted her long pianist's fingers a very milky blue. "I left the car at the gate because it wouldn't open all the way. Even the tipsy security guard couldn't get it to work."

I cross my arms around *White Fox* to fight a chill. "You didn't call!"

"I *did* call. I have service here. But you didn't answer." She stops, a few paces behind me on the hill, but she's still taller.

"I only have service on one square foot of the lawn that I have to hike to get to," I explain. "And then I have to hold one arm up like an antenna."

Her mouth twitches, and she rubs her bare arms. "Where's Manon?"

"On a date. I mean, she should be. She hasn't texted that she made it yet. But I guess she just left."

"A date?" she says, mouth curling with amusement.

"Don't look so surprised."

"I'm not—I promise. I've just been flustered since you texted me the news about your mother. Well." She smooths her hair. "Now I'm especially pleased I didn't leave you alone here." She smiles, meeting my eyes, and when I don't smile back in time because I'm thinking of Linos, she lets hers dip.

"Don't lie. It's because you love Stökéwood so much," I say, catching another twitch of her lips before I turn on my heel to slog the rest of the way up with her.

I—we—fumble with the house locks for a solid three minutes (Mama insisted the door be fitted with heavy, old-fashioned iron locks opened by heavy, old-fashioned iron keys the size of Baby's First Tire Iron, which is chic and everything if you never have to carry the damn three-pound things) only for Saxim to push the door open a crack, finding it unlocked. Did I leave it unlocked when I last left? Or has someone else been here? I blink away the thought and lean into the heavy oak with both hands, only to be greeted by a rush of dust. I stagger down the hall in the midst of an epic sneezing fit, swirling around like a whirling dervish in ripped denim shorts, almost knocking over a stack of paperwork.

"Thaïs?" comes a female voice, coupled with mechanical scritch-scritch-scritching. Saxim and I lock eyes as Mina rounds the bend, her panel a soothing seaside blue. "And Saxim. Welcome home, precious girls," she adds, two animated doors on her panel opening, smiling anime eyes behind them. "Where's Manon? And Boy? Will I get to see them again soon?"

Saxim shoots me a wary look.

"Who the fuck is Boy, Mina?" I ask, running my hands along the stone of the main hall to steady myself post-sneeze, only to realize what she means and burst out into a laugh. "You mean Nítuchí's nephew? The one Noni's on a date with? You little spy." I pull my fingers away and find them coated in muck, like I'm a Dickensian chimney sweep. "Mina, don't you have a cleaning setting or something?"

"I'm here to care for your family, Tai, not clean up your mess," she says peaceably. "Your cheeks look too thin. Can I fix you some dinner? We have dried cod," she coos, as if that's at all enticing.

"I brought fresh mulberry tea and custard twists," grime-free Saxim says sweetly, edging past us both. "Why don't Mina and I set it up, while you borrow my phone to text your sister? Mina, would you mind?"

"Custard twists are delicious, but they're full of cholesterol," Mina starts, scritching behind Saxim. "Perhaps we should consider conducting a full blood panel before you indulge? Life is to be lived, though, and—"

"It's fine. I'll just run down the drive for a second." I rush for the functional, dusty flashlight by the front door before I have to listen to them outmom each other another second.

∞ ∞ ∞

When I was a kid, the lawn would be drenched in light if anyone stepped outside at night—motion sensors caught it all, even a lone fox sneaking through the grass. But practically none of the outdoor lights work anymore, so I'm alone in another dark corner of Delirium Forest; Saxim, Tomí, and I the only breathing humans for a good mile, at least.

Somehow I only think about the fact that Stökéwood is tucked inside the forest boundary at night, when the grounds feel like the very bottom of some cosmic well. Sound travels differently, or maybe it's my ears, which pick up weird sounds since there's less for my eyes to process; someone once told me that if you really listen, you'll hear that what you thought are crickets in the hedge maze and the rustling, bristly leaves of the chestnut trees are actually spirits whispering.

I reach the edge of the lawn, where I find that precious bar of service, and I drop to the grass, knees curled into my chest, breathing in the earthy air, as I wait for my messages to load. Fewer bubble up than I expected, and my own messages take forever to send.

"Taking a nap?" asks Saxim, coming up behind me. She changed into white silk pajamas. She looks flushed and slightly out of breath, her hair mussed, and she's holding something behind her back. Probably dried cod.

"Meditating," I quip, watching the branches before us sway, feeling the wood draw me back into its lush darkness.

"Can I join you?" she asks, and it's her gentleness that throws me. Seriously at odds with what I hear from most people I know, who banter with the bright, sparkling TFH, oblivious to the work behind it.

When I nod, she shows me what she's hiding: the pink clam of her old Pocket Best Friend, the one we used to talk to each other every night when we were kids.

"Holy shit," I whisper, as she settles next to me.

"I found it in my desk." She flips open the scuffed shell. "It still has some old home videos you sent to me. I can't believe the video capabilities on this thing." Her eyes are dark as she hands it to me, booting up. "Your uncle Teddy was very much ahead of the curve."

"As always," I say, clicking through its dated apps. I find the video storage—*Pocket Best Friend's Hollywood Movie Studio*—and load the very first one, recorded in July 2009.

Saxim sidles up to me as the video buffers, grass crunching beneath our sit bones, and the first image loads: my sallow face at age seven, staring into the camera. My eyes are so spookily wide-spaced, like they're lost on my face.

I remember the night of this recording, a few weeks after Mama disappeared. I didn't know then that it would be one of the last times in a decade that I would be standing in this exact spot on the Stökéwood lawn edge, grass devouring my baby toes.

∞ ∞ ∞

[Video rolls]

"It's almost dark. I thought I heard someone calling inside the forest, so I came out here to see," Tai says, wiping her nose on camera. "But the branches are so thick I can barely see the tape and stuff the police put inside."

Rustling, and the camera turns: Teddy approaches Tai from behind, each footstep crushing the long grass.

"You promise you won't go into the forest at night, Tai?" he asks, a large white hand falling on Tai's shoulder.

Tai scrunches her nose into the camera. "No. I don't promise."

Teddy doesn't chuckle, and Tai fights a shiver, her lips blue-tinged.

"Why shouldn't I go into the forest at night?" Tai asks him.

He points at a knobbly root by their feet—the camera swivels. "You could trip or something and tear your pretty skirt."

She swipes at the silk around her knees. It's an old oversize scarf of Mama's with a palm tree pattern that she knotted like a sarong. There are no palm trees up here.

Tai flips the camera onto herself, sticking out her tongue at its lens. "I don't care. This is Mama's. She has a thousand. She won't even notice if I ruin one before she's back."

Teddy doesn't say a word, but the camera sneaks up to his face. His eyes are glossy. He looks like a boy.

"Aren't you afraid of spirits in the forest?" he asks, his tone strange.

"You mean aren't I afraid of dead people in the forest?" Tai asks off-screen, voice wobbling.

"What?" he asks, alarmed. "Did the kids at school say something to you?"

"I know this is Delirium Forest." Tai pauses. "It's my forest. I've always known."

He's silent, and there are only crickets. He crouches next to Tai.

"Do you know why it's called that, Tai?"

Rustling in the trees. "Because some people go in human and come out a spirit. And sometimes those spirits can't find their home," Tai says.

He doesn't answer. Instead, he turns his ear to the trees, cupping it. "Do you hear that? If you really listen, you can hear whole families of spirits whispering, finding each other on their way home. Hello, Uncle! Hello, Daughter!" His tone is faux cheery, his smile weak.

Tai says nothing.

"It's dinnertime soon, sweet girl," he says, taking Tai by the shoulder. "Is Saxim ready, too?"

Tai turns the camera onto herself and stares at it bleakly.

"You're lucky to have a friend who is as grown up as her," he says, guiding Tai back toward his car on the drive.

[The camera clicks off.]

[The camera clicks on again in Teddy's car.]

He falls forward in the driver's seat, half asleep, and then jerks awake. The camera turns to Saxim, who watches him with

241

wide eyes, her backpack hugged to her chest. Then it turns to face the outside. The humid sky is the color of rust. Tai swivels for a selfie and presses her nose onto the glass of the car window. She breathes onto the glass, fogging it up, and draws her initials, then Noni's, onto the surface with her forefinger in block print. The letters melt away.

A sign flashes past outside:

TREASURE YOUR LIFE. STAY OUT OF THE FOREST.

Then another, this one covered in graffiti, but plainly show-ing a diagram of a hunched figure with butterflies where the eyes should be, with an X through the chest.

Then a figure, a pale figure, but only for a second, before—

[The camera clicks off with a jolt.]

I swallow hard, the grass prickling my ankles. Because I remem-ber what I saw.

A woman with long hair and slender arms and legs. In the woods, smiling at me.

It took only a glimmer of her to know the angle of her head was wrong, hooked down, like she was a circus gymnast ordered to use only her neck muscles to hang from an invisible trapeze, leaving the rest of her body slack and asleep.

It was so impossibly scary I didn't tell Saxim, I didn't tell Teddy, I didn't tell anyone.

Oh my gosh. Its crooked form haunted my nightmares for months.

I remember telling myself: It could've been a branch. It probably didn't exist. But even if it did . . . It's not Mama, I told myself. It's not Mama, broken and smiling.

But I remember thinking then that what happened to Mama could happen at any time to anyone I love. It could be happening at this moment to Noni. To Dad. They could change. They could leave me, just like that. I promised myself then that I would do everything I could to keep that from happening. To bring them only brightness and goodness and effervescence. To avoid the darker corners of my head and to only travel in the light. To delight and enchant everyone, so they would stay.

To record everything I could, so I wouldn't forget how things should be.

It feels like drowning, to remember this ten-year-old pain, and even my throat and my eyes fill up.

[The camera clicks back on.]

Tempura dinner. Saxim picking out a shrimp leg from Teddy's throat, because she has the smallest fingers. They laugh hysterically.

Saxim and Tai picking the room they want to sleep in at Teddy's huge Mitella house.

The aquarium room ("Noni's favorite"), the library room ("Saxim's favorite, with its three stories of books, and its skylight"), the red room ("Too scary, with its red velvet walls that look like wet blood in the dark"), the grass room ("With a floor of fake grass that looks so real, too real").

"But I always pick the same one: the princess room." Tai walks around the small pink room. "It's called that because it's where the Pocket Girlfriend would live. It's got a closet filled with fancy purses, coats, sunglasses, jewelry . . ." Tai grins. "Everything you could imagine. It has bookshelves filled with the books she will read, and an old-school record player with the music she will listen to (the Beach Boys, jazz, and Elvis). K-pop CDs, too. It has a large canopy bed. It is a room for a princess. It is the furthest from Teddy's room, and he says it's usually reserved for the Pocket Girlfriend herself, which I know is a joke.

243

But I still feel special to be allowed to stay in the room. It has that unused smell, like no one has stayed there in a very long time."

The camera faces Teddy, as he tucks in Saxim.

"You're comfortable in here, right?" he asks them both. "Tomorrow we'll go shopping. You need your own Hermès scarf to turn into a skirt. Saxim, too."

Tai nods and smiles. "I guess if I have to be alone right now," she says, "I'll surround myself with beautiful things and friends. Just like Mama. Just like the Pocket Girlfriend. Right, Saxim?"

Saxim smiles at her flatly, her eyes glassy in the low light on camera. Teddy clicks off the lights and winds up a music box, where a lullaby starts to play, as Tai trains the camera on her expressionless face.

It's the Pocket Girlfriend jingle.

Forever beautiful and fun, under every moon and every sun. She will be there until the end. Your very own Pocket Girlfriend.

Tai looks off screen. The camera goes dark.

[Video ends]

"Those sleepovers were fucking weird," I say, nestling into Saxim's shoulder.

"I know." Saxim straightens beside me, glazed eyes still trained on the tiny screen. "His place was so large and opulent and strange. I used to wake up from nightmares, unsure where I was, and you'd be fast asleep. I'd poke my head out into the hall, to see if I could find a soul. It was better at the beginning, before your mother . . . Well, sometimes that guy would be there, sitting in the hall, working on his laptop. But later, when it was only your uncle tucking us in . . . it would be so empty. I don't think he even slept on that floor."

I blink at her. "What guy?"

"Your Dad's intern. Don't you remember? He tucked us in, sometimes, and he would read me stories off his laptop until I fell asleep."

"The intern?" I ask, remembering a gangly boy who was always around the family, another person who faded in the shadows of my memory. "He worked for Teddy or Dad?"

"I don't know. Maybe he came from the institute. He was probably hired by your parents to watch us. They were busy, but they always made sure there were people to take care of you," she says, a faint smile on her face. She takes a deep breath. I take one, too. The country air is mushroomy and sweet, with this grossly appealing hint of mold and decay beneath it. We stare into the dark for what feels like several minutes of calm, before she asks about the past couple of days, and I tell her everything about the strangers that Noni and I met: Daria, Yuki, and Mrs. Arakit. The most difficult parts are what we've learned about Mama: Lady Fleischman, impossible to trace, a ghost online.

"I feel helpless," I admit into the dark. "And I'm too much of a coward to go back to the Arakit house. I don't want to see . . . *him*. I can't. But there are no other clues left. Because . . . the last piece of *White Fox* . . . I know who it's about, but there's nothing I can do with it." Tears melt across my lashes, before I can help even that. I grind my fists into the sockets, smudging fading eyeliner onto my knuckles.

"What?" Saxim's fingers pause as they glide over my hair. "What do you mean?"

I lead her back to the house, so I can read it to her again. Peel back the scab, and reveal the wretched, jammy truth. We pass the dead fountain, its spearfish a spooky figment in the dark.

I can't stop shivering. This day has shaken loose something toxic and sharp-edged in my mind, and I feel it rattling around my skull, checking for vulnerable, fleshy spots. I could stuff a million Hermès scarves into those tender corners and still fail to protect them.

PART THREE

INT. GRAND OLD HOME — NIGHT

White Fox, bare-faced, clothed in a clean dress,
and seated in a small room, watching Client 2
finish his coffee. There is tapping at the window,
and the chattering continues, but White Fox cannot
see the source. She is uneasy.

> WHITE FOX
> What is that infernal noise coming from
> outside?

> CLIENT 2
> What do you mean?

White Fox crosses her arms. The noise stops.

> WHITE FOX
> Never mind. Well. The next person I
> found was the man on the moon. He might
> be familiar to you.

> CLIENT 2
> Excuse me?

EXT. FOREST — NIGHT

White Fox wanders with her white hair long and
loose.

She sees, in the distance, something that looks
like a palace.

> WHITE FOX (V.O.)
> I'd been walking for many days when I
> finally found another house. Now, this
> house looked extremely familiar. I won-
> dered to myself if I'd visited such a
> house when I was a child. I felt good
> about approaching the guard gate and
> seeing if someone was home.

White Fox finds a small guard house, which is derelict
and empty.

She presses on the gate and finds that it swings
open.

She walks up the drive, which loops around the house, and she finds that the house itself is nothing more than a set, a shell—empty but for ladders and staircases lining the inside, leading to the roof. And so she climbs, climbs for what seems like hours, without another person in sight.

Shining EYES peek out from the darkness behind White Fox's feet, out of her sight.

When White Fox reaches the roof, she is stunned by the display.

In absolute darkness, there are tables and tables of cakes and sweets and fruits and all sorts of delectable items.

She eats as if in a frenzy even though she can barely see in the darkness. She finds a lantern off to the side and just as she lights it, there is a SHOUT.

                    WHITE FOX
          Who's there?

MAN ON THE MOON comes out of the darkness with his multilensed telescoping glasses on.

                    MAN ON THE MOON
          For goodness' sake, turn off the
          lights!!!!

White Fox turns off the lamp and squints at the
man. He seems a kindly sort.

                    WHITE FOX
        I'm sorry, sir. I didn't mean to
        disturb. I'm—

The Man on the Moon waves her off and walks back
where he came from, a treacherous dark path that
seems to lead farther up the roof!

                 MAN ON THE MOON
        Never mind, never mind. It's starting!

White Fox follows him.

                    WHITE FOX
        What is starting?

The Man on the Moon rushes off, nimbly navigating
the many obstacles in his path (more tables of
food and drink) and White Fox follows, nearly
killing herself on the lavish display in the
process.

They reach the pinnacle of the roof, where the
Man on the Moon has telescopes and other similar
equipment set up facing the sky.

He positions the telescope as she watches, and
then peers through it.

The Man on the Moon then beckons to her to look
through the telescope, and she obliges him.

White Fox gazes through the telescope.

She witnesses a surreally vivid LIGHT SHOW of
shooting stars and other incredible cosmic sights
through its lens.

White Fox is awed.

                    WHITE FOX
        How beautiful.

The Man on the Moon sighs.

                  MAN ON THE MOON
        Beauty is only the start!

The Man on the Moon stops and reaches for a cup of
tea that has materialized by his hand.

He hands another to White Fox, who accepts it, even
though she wonders where the hot tea came from.

                  MAN ON THE MOON
        How long have you been here, miss?

                    WHITE FOX
        Pardon? Just a half hour or so, I would
        say.

                    MAN ON THE MOON
                      (scoffing)
Impossible. Why, we've been here at
least ten nights already.

                      WHITE FOX
                      (puzzled)
What do you mean? The sun hasn't risen.

                    MAN ON THE MOON
That's because we are too far up in the
sky!

White Fox sips her tea suspiciously as the Man on
the Moon turns on the headlamp atop his glasses and
reviews materials.

                  WHITE FOX (V.O.)
I had a limited understanding of science
of any kind, but I knew this to be wrong.
Still, I'd had difficulties prying
too deeply into the belief systems of
these strangers I'd encountered, so I
remained silent and let him believe
what he wanted to believe.

White Fox and the Man on the Moon sit and enjoy dinner
and then stare up at the sky through his equipment.

                  WHITE FOX (V.O.)
He was a brilliant man, if a bit unusual.

At another lavish dinner, some unknowable time later, the Man on the Moon and White Fox are laughing brightly. She looks at ease. But with this new ease comes new questions.

                    WHITE FOX
Don't you wonder where all of this comes from?

                 MAN ON THE MOON
The stars, my dear? Well, that's all on account of the—

                    WHITE FOX
                 (interrupting)
No, I mean these elaborate displays of food and drink.

                 MAN ON THE MOON
               (scratching his head)
What? Why no, I never thought about that.

                    WHITE FOX
Or why it's always night, never day?

                 MAN ON THE MOON
                 (brightening)
It all has to do with a branch of particle—

                    WHITE FOX
No, it doesn't! Or how we never sleep?
Haven't you ever thought someone is trap-
ping you here and keeping you distracted?

                 MAN ON THE MOON
From what, my dear?

                    WHITE FOX
Reality!

                 MAN ON THE MOON
This is my reality: If we look up and
out of ourselves, we can stop human
time and become part of the heavens!

White Fox is silent.

                 WHITE FOX (V.O.)
At this point I knew him to be broken.
But he was a kind man. And in the few
weeks I'd spent with him, I felt good as
new. I began to wonder: Did feeling good
as new have only to do with being the
possession of a man? Or was it my isolation from society—my ignorance of its
inconvenient truths? I had to test this.

White Fox steals a bunch of food when the Man on
the Moon is busy making his notations.

Then she climbs down the many ladders: The Man on the Moon doesn't even notice her descent. She gives him a final, almost regretful glance.

As she climbs, the glowing sets of eyes reappear beneath her feet.

Little shadowed ARMS grab at her legs.

White Fox shrieks and beats them away.

> WHITE FOX (V.O.)
> The man made no effort to help me: I doubt he even noticed. And each time the creatures nipped at me, I felt a greater urgency to escape this surreal place. If I did not, a part of me knew these shadowy beasts would haunt me forever.

She descends farther with difficulty.

Reaching the bottom, she runs from the building.

They follow her, but their pace is slow. Whatever they are.

> WHITE FOX (V.O.) (CONT'D)
> I never looked back long enough to make out what kind of creatures they were. I just knew they were dangerous if mishandled.

When White Fox emerges from the grounds, she runs toward the main road and sees the guardhouse covered in even more dead vines—almost entirely engulfed.

                    WHITE FOX (V.O.) (CONT'D)
               As for the man, he forgot me as soon as
               I left his orbit. Or so I believed.

INT. GRAND OLD HOME — NIGHT

White Fox and Client 2 sit quietly together, an empty cup of coffee between them.

                         WHITE FOX
               Many years had passed. My formative
               years had passed me by.

Client 2 watches her, wet-eyed, clutching the sides of his chair.

                         CLIENT 2
               In your pain, you have rewritten our
               history.

White Fox watches him coldly.

                         WHITE FOX
               This is the way I see things.

                    CLIENT 2 / MAN ON THE MOON
               I came after you, my dear. I promise I
               did.

WHITE FOX
Only now. Too much time has passed.

CLIENT 2 / MAN ON THE MOON
No time has passed at all from where I
stand.

WHITE FOX
I can see the genius in learning to
change the flow of time by climbing far
enough into the heavens. But my love is
grounded firmly on the earth.

White Fox gazes at her bare, folded hands.

WHITE FOX (CONT'D)
It would have never worked.

CLIENT 2 / MAN ON THE MOON
(frustrated)
Say what you want about me. But what
of the girls? *Your* girls? Have you
forgotten them?

White Fox turns away, shivers. This has struck a
chord.

WHITE FOX
I haven't finished my story.

CLIENT 2 / MAN ON THE MOON
I can't listen to your nightmarish

fairy tales anymore. Can we speak plainly?

                    WHITE FOX
Says the man who lived among the stars.

          CLIENT 2 / MAN ON THE MOON
This is our life you're talking about.
We must be serious now in order to fix
our problems.

                    WHITE FOX
               (chuckling)
Be *serious*. What makes you think my
stories aren't deadly serious?

          CLIENT 2 / MAN ON THE MOON
               (ignoring her retort)
Why are you still ill if you are back
here with me again? Why should things
be any different now from how they
were?

                    WHITE FOX
               (coldly)
For a scientist, you can be awfully
foolish.

Client 2 / Man on the Moon snaps to look at her.

               WHITE FOX (CONT'D)
I am not the whole, pretty, curious

little thing you once enjoyed having by your side. And you: I see so little of the man I loved—the man who found wonder everywhere. You are unhinged, asking me to stay inside this room—to never face inconvenient truths. Thinking that will help.

                    CLIENT 2 / MAN ON THE MOON
                              (sadly)
I see. If that's how you feel . . .

                          WHITE FOX
It is. *Now* will you be quiet and listen to the rest of my story?

Client 2 / Man on the Moon nods.

                          WHITE FOX
The bleeding came back with a vengeance. But I found one more way of solving it, at least temporarily. The next person I met had a useful way of dealing with my bleeding.

                          ∞ ∞ ∞

As the section ends, my fingers have turned to ice. Like I do every time, I flip through the stained packet, urgently in need of more pages, of more words, of more *her*.

But this is all there is.

"Oh. It's your dad," whispers Saxim. "Isn't it?"

What's still warm in my body quivers uncontrollably. Because she's right. Of course it's him—we've known it all along. Brilliant. Kind at heart. Oblivious to those shadowy creatures who haunted her whenever she left his side.

The Man on the Moon is no stretch. But self-centered, pathetic Client 2?

Every time I read it, I feel this stabbing pressure in my head, this scratchy knot in my throat. What does it *mean* that White Fox was "saved" by a man she parted ways with? What should I think of White Fox's contempt for him, and their wildly different views of the past?

There must have been so much pain between them. Pain and poor communication, clouding the love they once felt so it more closely resembled . . . hate.

It's not enough to know that Mama valued everything about Dad that I do: his view of the world and the magic in it (science to him, of course), and how it could expand your own view. His once-contagious enthusiasm.

It's not enough, because the darkness overshadows the light.

This can't be all that's left. It's wrong. It's all so wrong that I find myself suffocating on the stuffy air, scrabbling from the room, desperate to be free of the dark.

∞ ∞ ∞

Saxim comes with me to fill a cup with water in the kitchen. It overflows, cascading onto my hands and their chipped-off manicure, and after several long seconds, she turns off the tap.

"Tai, I noticed something strange—" she starts, and then I hear a tinny, disembodied sound, emerging from the hall to Dad's sickroom. Saxim's eyes flick to mine: She recognizes it, too.

It's a voice I know so well: steady, authoritative. Measured but . . . rich.

259

A giddiness rolls through my body—for one disorienting moment, I'm a kid again.

I'm swarmed by memories: by the moment Dad gave me my first desktop computer—preloaded with a chess game—and told me that *I would go far if I could stay three steps ahead*; by a conversation on the magic of the stars and how I could always find my way home to him by them; by a joint predawn plunge in the frigid waters of the lake—*you have such a deep well of courage and love, unknown to you, and you can never exhaust either of them*; by his rare, throaty laugh, and our dancing, our dancing, which made my baby soul burst up through the clouds and into the grand universe.

Dad. Dad, like he was before, before the illness broke him down. I feel a rush at hearing Dad—my *dad*, sound like himself. It's been so long since I heard him. In hearing his voice, it feels like I'm getting him back, months after his death.

"Stop it. Stop it this instant," I hear him say, inexplicably, and my heart pitches through the floor. Next to me, Saxim looks as gray as an unfinished pencil sketch.

"Dad?" I call out before I can stop myself.

The reply comes from another voice, a thinner, colder metal wire of a voice I can barely hear. There's someone there. It doesn't sound like Mina. This voice is male.

With Saxim on my heels, scrabbling for my wrists, I swipe Mama's dusty Oscar, on display on a forgotten shelf and the only thing I can use as a weapon.

"Tai," Saxim pleads, but I don't stop. I dash toward the voices, bare feet slapping against the floor.

"You poisoned a boy," Dad says.

My blood curdles. The other male voice answers, "You're wrong." Chills razor the thin skin on my arms.

"My brother told me. He wouldn't lie," Dad says, and I slow to a stop so I can hear them over my racing heartbeat. "You have no morals.

I'll tell the world, I will. You poisoned a boy." My hands clench around the Oscar, its dead flesh slipping.

"You poisoned Mitso Arakit," Dad says.

I drop the statuette with a heavy clunk, two inches from my toes.

The voice answers, brisk as an arctic wind, "No one will ever believe anything you say, you old fool. How can you even trust yourself?"

As I round the corner, I hear Dad reply, in this unfamiliar, almost panicked tone I've never heard, "That's why my wife left, isn't it?" He pauses, swallows thickly. "She discovered how corrupt you are. How ruined you are."

I hear this, just as I see it:

The bed is empty, neatly made, with Mina perched beside it. She looks at me, with two flat lines on her calm lake of a face, as if she's asleep.

"Go to sleep, old man," spits Nítuchí, his voice metallic and small, before I hear the choking sound of a phone line going dead.

"Mina?" my dad cries, sounding lost and alone. "Mina? Did you hear that?"

Those cries come straight from Mina's chest, as if they're the awful beating of her own electrical heart.

NONI

My skin prickles as the car pulls up to the red-light street address of the *frittimitti* bar, Dreamfry. We drove right past Daria's house—night is its own fresh hell in her neck of the woods, even on a Sunday. Drunken businessmen and gawking tourists stumble past glassy-eyed women who look no older than Tai, gyrating in tiny plasticized get-ups in windows and on pixelated screens.

I tug on my shirtdress and edge through a crowded beer bar, down a narrow and slippery set of stairs, through one of those pink-beaded curtains that remind me of Britney Spears. I knock on the wood-paneled door with a cloud on it. Music swells on the other side; all I hear is a saxophone. My beating heart threatens to meet the root of my tongue. A woman with feathered lashes as long as a pinkie finger slides open a notch in the door and asks my name in a monotone.

"Manon," I say. "I'm here for Hérrakí—"

She slides the notch shut and opens the door, welcoming me in, and I'm awash in pink light.

My jaw drops: It's a jewel box of a place. A half-dozen plush aquamarine velvet-and-feather (!) seats line the bar, all full of trendy patrons in blunt haircuts coolly drinking cocktails and seducing each other, and three chefs stand behind the bar in crisp all-black uniforms, chopping ingredients on pristine wooden cutting boards, with high-tech air fryers behind them. My mouth waters; it smells like ginger dipping sauce and freshly chopped scallions. Pink silk tops the lamps, accounting for the glow, and an old jazz record plays—one I don't recognize, but that makes me think of balmy nights in Marrakech. My attention is drawn upward, and I see a lavender field painted on the ceiling.

That's when someone lurches up from a seat in the far edge of my vision to approach me.

Hérrakí.

I smell his soap or his scent or both intermingled, and I have to compose my facial muscles (*Seriously? Recognizing his smell?*) and remind myself not to act like a walking bag of hormones. He towers over me with this knowing grin, leaning in to kiss me on both cheeks, and I kiss him back—on the cheeks!—because what else are you going to do, and I feel this quickening. I hadn't realized how tall he is. He's so tall. Why does height matter? Why does smell matter? *Chill out*, I hear Tai say in my head.

Maybe I wasn't tipsy last night, I think. Just as my legs wobble, like I'm a marionette cut from her strings.

"Where are your friends?" I ask, pretending to be fascinated by the bartender's theatrics. He's making something frothy, punctured by a tiki umbrella.

"They couldn't make it," he says, raking a hand through his hair. I scan the area around him, looking for my notebook.

"Do you have my book?" I reply, ever the romantic.

"Ah." He takes a leather tote bag off the edge of the chair and hands it to me.

Inside, I find the notebook neatly nestled in fancy tissue paper.

"Didn't want it to get damaged," he says. As if he's a soldier who had to carry precious goods through hostile territories to get here.

"Thank you," I say, plucking it out. "That's really nice." *And extra*, I hear Tai say in my head. I return the tote bag, which he tries to reject, before taking it in hand.

We hover, awkwardly, by two free chairs. *This is so brutal*, I hear Tai say. Hérrakí eyes the hibachi grill, and I surreptitiously watch him while pretending I still care about the bartender. Hérrakí's wearing a soft button-down shirt in shallow-water blue and dark-wash jeans. His sleeves are rolled up, and I can spot the edge of the—

The hostess walks into me, tapping her long fingernails to her pleather skirt, and I stumble out of the way and into Hérrakí's arm.

"Are you hungry?" he asks, just as I blurt, "Have you eaten?"

He looks down at me, expectantly, while I stare back up at him, every muscle tense to avoid body contact. My cheeks burn so hot I could grill on them.

"We could stay and eat," he suggests, setting the leather bag down.

I smile, and he smiles back, actually grins, before helping me into my seat (seriously), which feels as lush and comfortable as sitting on an actual swan, not that I would ever think of doing that. But I can't relax, not with him a few inches away. His wrist is almost double the width of mine. How does that work? How— *Shut the heck up*, Tai says in my head.

"So," I say, to break the tension between us, "what other kinds of friend dates have you been set up on?"

The corner of his mouth perks up again, and his eyes twinkle, as if he's about to share a delicious secret. "Well, besides Linos, there's been the definite serial killer, who showed me bags of something red and meaty in his freezer related to the keto diet he wouldn't stop talking about. Then there was the guy who text-juggled three different girlfriends the first time we met, who he'd nicknamed Monday, Tuesday, and Wednesday. I didn't stick around long enough to hear him speak to Thursday."

"Wow." I lift the glass of water at my place setting. "Your uncle really has impeccable taste."

He chuckles, just as a waiter approaches. He clears his throat and motions at me to order first. I order beer (surprising myself, and thinking of Tai, who would *rather die a fiery death than consume that bloating, migraine-inducing trash water*), plus the "classic Dreamfry" with all the trimmings (not surprising myself). He tells the waiter he'll have the same and throws on an order of fried scallops.

Soon, we're toasting *chípí* with our beers, and I take a small sip.

"So," he says, setting down his beer, "you hate Pocket Girlfriends, even though your uncle invented them. Do you hate science and movies just as much? Is there anything you love?"

I can't help but laugh. "Wow. Cutting right to the chase, I see." I wipe the condensation off my hand. "You do know my parents didn't invent science and movies, right?"

He just shrugs, an intentionally obnoxious grin on his face. "I grew up hearing how amazing you two were, from my uncle and just about everyone else. I still hear it, when I'm doing administrative tasks for him, organizing all his damn files. He loves talking about how much *promise* you showed. But back then I didn't know what he was talking about. While I was trying to learn how to ride a bike without training wheels, he would visit for tea and talk nonstop about how you American girls learned Vilosh, French, and English at the same time. How you understood Viloki customs better than your father, by age seven. How you—"

"Wait, *what?* Your uncle said that about us?" Piping-hot fried scallops arrive, with crackling edges, and we each spear one, scallops brushing. "Tai will love that."

"Okay. But seriously," he says. "Answer my question. What do you love?" He bites into the scallop and chews.

What do I love? Feeling safe. Feeling loved. Feeling welcome. Feeling— *Seriously, shut the heck up*, says Tai.

"Cake-batter ice cream," I blurt out, just as a plate of crispy dumplings lands in front of me.

He can't suppress his laugh. "What? Cake batter? That artificial trash that's probably beaver gland and sucralose mixed with chewed-up cardboard?"

"Please never say that again. And I like that it's artificial," I say, blushing and biting into a dumpling, which explodes in my face.

He hands me a napkin with zero judgment. "You don't like artificial love, but you like artificial flavoring." He picks up his beer with a smile. "Got it."

"That sounds like a bad advertising song lyric for a corporate food titan."

"Let it be known this conversation is sponsored by—" He holds up his beer and tries to read the incomprehensible Belgian name on the label. "Wait, you didn't even order a Viloki beer?"

"The prince of organic and authentic food doesn't even look at what he's eating and drinking?"

"Touché," he says, cheersing beers with me. "In the original French, of course, for you, Manon des Sources."

Soon enough, we're on our second beers, talking about his little hometown on the east side of the island, with its underfed volcanic spring and its lone, out-of-place Japanese restaurant, and about New York, adopted land of delicious sushi. A new course arrives— chestnut and onion fritters—in steaming-hot trays. I eat, singeing my fingertips, and we never stop talking. When I mention that I grew up by Delirium Forest, I expect him to pause, to flinch. To think of an unhappy spot with tree roots poking up out of the mossy ground like dinosaur bones, littered with the cigarette-butt and used-up sneaker remains of campers and visitors with macabre intentions. But he just nods and calmly reaches across me for the container of ginger powder.

I glimpse his feathered tattoo on his forearm again and blurt out: "I like your tattoo."

"Thanks," he says, sprinkling ginger on his last fritter.

"What does it represent?"

He catches my eye. "I guess I can tell you. I've definitely given you enough flack today."

"A lifetime of flack in one meal," I confirm.

His head ducks toward his fritter, mid-smile. "It's not that interesting. It's pretty cliché. It represents someone I've lost. Someone I want to carry with me."

He avoids my eyes, almost shyly, and takes a bite. A shiver runs down my spine. It's no secret I chase darkness in others to try to find kinship for the darkness in myself.

"That is kind of cliché," I say. And even though he laughs good-naturedly, I regret making light of it immediately. "It's beautiful, though. Seriously. Very, uh, finely etched."

"Tell that to my uncle. He's waging an ongoing battle to get me to remove it. The lengths I've gone to to normalize it are ridiculous. He loves history, so when I first got it, I even came up with this bull-shit story explaining it was based on a Viloki legend, since I didn't want to explain the truth. That just pissed him off even more—to be defacing myself and dishonoring a piece of Viloki culture at the same time."

"Why don't you want to tell him the truth?"

He raises an eyebrow. "Seriously? My uncle?"

I smirk. "Well, I like the idea of a tattoo based on Viloki legend. Which legend did you pick?"

He sets down his fork. "Did you hear a lot of them growing up?"

"I mean, yeah. My mama would read me and Tai bedtime stories about Viloki demons that would scare me half out of my mind. She would point outside and tell me to watch for dark shapes crawling up our drive. She lived for scary stories," I say, remembering how her eyes gleamed when she told the most gruesome of them. "Have you heard the Viloki legend about the lonely man who married the fox? She told me that one once, and I never forgot it." It was that night, the night of the fight with Dad and the shattered perfume.

He rubs his lips together. "Remind me."

"He searches all the island for a wife," I start. "One day, on a walk through the moor with his loyal hound, he comes across a wild fox being chased by dogs. He saves the fox from death, and the next night, a beautiful woman arrives on his doorstep. They soon marry."

"Hmm."

"For some time they live happily. Soon enough, a son is born, just as the man's dog has a puppy."

"The picture of domestic bliss."

"Except that it becomes vicious, snapping at anyone and everyone. Any attempt to train it fails, and it takes a special, hostile interest in the young wife. She begs her husband to kill it, but he refuses. So one afternoon, finding her alone, the dog attacks her, biting her badly. A maid finds her and tries to scare the dog away, but she isn't able to, and as she watches, her mistress's damaged muscles begin to convulse, like a deer shaking off invisible fleas." I pause. "So over the course of a minute, this young wife transforms back into a fox, with snow-white fur, four paws, a pointed nose, and nothing but a shallow flesh wound. She sheds her human form to flee. The husband begs her to return. The woman considers his pleas, because the dog has been put to death. For some time, she lives as a fox each day and returns each night as a woman to sleep beside him. But in the end, she leaves him to be a fox forever."

We sit for several seconds in silence.

"I've heard that one," he says. "It's pretty screwed-up."

I burst out with a laugh, spilling the beer on my hand.

"My mother liked it, too," he adds, eyes shining at me.

"This is going to sound ridiculous," I say, still cupping my beer glass. "But as a kid I thought my mother was that fox."

He looks into his beer. "That's not ridiculous. That's how sensitive people make sense of things, by working bad things into stories they can digest." He watches me. A hush settles over us. "I'm sorry, by the way. About what happened with her."

It disorients me, hearing an apology free of any feelings of ownership. I can't express the number of times in my life—in the past week—I've heard people lament her being gone, as if she's only theirs. I open my mouth to tell him it's okay, she's back, apparently, and I'm going to find her, and I'm—

But I stop myself.

"Thanks."

"I hope you have people in your life who help you . . . handle all that," he says.

I snort again. "You mean therapists?" I've been to many, ever since I was a child—courtesy of the fizzy pennies of anxiety.

I swear he blushes. "No! Wow. I meant friends. Boyfriends."

He says the word with such ease that it makes me blush, too.

"Boyfriends, plural? I'm not polyamorous." I pause. "Plus, I don't have enough pockets."

I expect him to smirk, but his face is soft. "I mean people you trust."

I'd only ever depended on journals to hold my deepest, darkest secrets (and depended on Tai to read them without permission). I'd only ever depended on myself to write through my thoughts. Imagine a friend—who wasn't blood bound to you—who knew them all and still loved you. Imagine a *significant other*, who would only want you all the more.

I stare back at Hérrakí, a blush on my cheeks.

It's an intoxicating thought.

He pays the bill before I can reach for it. And before we step out onto the street, where anyone could be waiting and watching, he takes my hand in his, and an electricity—so bright, so acidic, it's almost painful—floods me through my fingertips. I stumble on my feet, cheeks still flushed.

I want to fall into him—settle myself, forever, in this bubble of good humor I step into when I'm with him. He takes my other hand and pulls me closer. For the briefest of brief, dreamlike moments, I feel seen, and I feel that I can see him, too. I feel that what we see of each other is beautiful, is enough. I know it's an illusion, one found inside that bubble. But I lean even closer, taking in more of that scent of his. Light-headed. His lower lip is swollen, bitable. He nods his head toward me.

I run my fingers over the tattoo, the bird's wings exposed to the air. "So who is it for?"

He exhales—not so much a sigh as a sign a decision is being made. I wait, feeling his heartbeat under his skin.

"My mom." He takes hold of his cuff with his free hand and shuffles it back on his wrist so that the wings disappear again. "So . . . when I was a kid, I wanted to believe my mother was a bird. Kind of like your fox, but not. Because the parts of herself she loved most would . . . disappear. Migrate somewhere. But she almost always returned to us—at least she did back then. As I got older, more and more of her was lost for good, and there was nothing I could do, except . . ." He sighs again, a proper sigh this time, and I feel this waterfall of shivering thrills.

So the tattoo is more than a way of missing someone. It's a way to honor the best in someone.

I think of how Tai and I retreat into the moments where we miss Mama least, because we fear our grief.

270

Tai feels the loss in quiet moments—when Mama would have been a soother, a nurturer. Mama grounded her, despite all she was known for. She gave her wisdom.

Whereas I—I feel the loss most in the loud moments. I wish she could be there to parse through the noise, to guide me and share in the good. Maybe then I wouldn't view every overwhelming moment as a free fall.

I shut my eyes and half lean into him, so my shoulders almost touch his chest. He stiffens, then relaxes.

"Can I see you again?" he asks.

I don't reply. I don't mention that it's foolish of me to even consider that. I don't mention, either, that I feel hundreds of butterfly-type insects (let's be honest, they're probably moths) fluttering and nibbling at the inside of my stomach when I'm around him, and that I never understood what that absurd expression meant until now, and that I would've been way too ashamed to even think it before meeting him. But I think he knows, because when I raise my chin, his forest eyes shine.

A car pulls up nearby, tires crunching over a plastic bottle and bursting the moment. I look around for the familiar self-driving car, as Hérrakí's hand closes around mine.

"Do you need a ride?" he asks, as the lit-up signs flash against the dead-eyed businessmen hobbling around in their sweat-stained suits in the damp dark. "My uncle said he'd pick us up."

I fumble for my phone, a voice mail message from an unknown caller pinging onto my screen.

It's Tai.

"Dad was hiding something from us, Nons," she says. "Something big. I can't tell you on a voice mail. Don't spill a word about *anything* to Hérrakí, no matter how charming he is, and whatever you do, don't—"

My phone goes dead.

T A I

"Mina!" I grip her unfeeling plastic shoulders, and her panel glitches, then lights up with dozens of yawning cartoon batteries.

"Thaïs?" Mina says, her voice a distant warble. "I must have fallen asleep."

Her panel glitches again, two flat lines appearing where her eyes should be. Rage sizzles into my fingertips, and I shake her hard. "What the fuck? What was that?" Her panel flickers, and I shove her again—

Saxim rushes me from behind, so much stronger than she looks, and I'm yelping and crumpling against her while she holds me with both arms so I don't fall, and I can hear her heartbeat and feel her soft flesh through the thin fabric of her silk pajama shirt, which has the tiniest stars embroidered on it in near invisible white.

I push her off me. "What are you doing?"

"You'll hurt her," she whispers, with a look at Mina, dizzy Tweety bird knockoffs waltzing on her panel.

272

I jab a hand in her direction. "She's a machine!"

"Tai," Saxim pleads, heat rising in her cheeks.

Because we both know Mina's more than that. She was my dad's best friend. She was what filled the hole left by Mama's disappearance, the hole left by our departure, the hole left by every missing scrap of human tenderness, love, and care. I feel like if I dip a toe into the overwhelming bleakness of that, I'll be washed away forever. Even though what Dad got from Mina reminds me of what I get from my phone.

"It must be an old phone recording," Saxim whispers. "She must be recording all the time."

"But the—the call must be so old, if Dad sounds—" I stop, tears welling in my eyes. "Was that real, Mina? When . . . when was that?"

She remains motionless—watching me with her neutral kindness, while her panel reloads.

"Mina! Are you listening to me?"

"You said she's been here eight years, right?" Saxim whispers. "So the call happened after your mom disappeared."

I settle onto the floor, the prone Oscar glinting at me a few paces away.

"I promise to take care of your family," Mina replies at last, booting up with impossible positivity, the only lady in this household who really seems immune to every abuse.

∞ ∞ ∞

I leave an explosively grotesque voice mail on Noni's phone and regret it immediately. But I can't collect my thoughts, and there are some really bad ones in there, darting around my gloppy head like hungry, carnivorous fish.

"Why didn't Dad tell us about this in his letter," I speak into Saxim's starry shoulder, quietly hyperventilating. "Did he feel unsafe? Did he feel like Nítuchí would hurt him if he shared it with anyone else? Did Nítuchí threaten him? Did—"

Saxim pulls away and silences me with one of her ocean-deep stares. "I know this is scary, but you have no context for the conversation you overheard," she says in even tones, hands cupping my shoulders. Gnarled bushes judder in the wind outside the window behind her. "The first time you heard the name *Mitso Arakit* was from a stranger in an information center earlier today. You need to take a breath. Okay?"

"Okay, girls?" Mina mimics, scratching toward us. "Your heart rates are elevated." Her panel shows only placid, friendly blues and greens.

I feel the heat emanating from Saxim and lean into her, craving human warmth. For the first time in years, I'm awake in the darkest corners of the real world, and the cheapest, most readily available painkiller in the world—the one in my goddamn pocket every minute of the day, the one monogrammed TFH—isn't helping.

The sad thing is, it wasn't even actual pain that stopped me from examining the dark side all these years. It was the anticipation of pain.

I never felt pain at all, because I woke up scrolling through my phone, and I fell asleep scrolling through my phone. I wasn't born scrolling through my phone, but sometimes I hoped I would die that way, because I wouldn't even realize I'm gone.

Maybe I'm just the irresponsible high school dropout Noni thinks I am, but I'm not afraid of inviting more pain in right now, not if it'll sharpen me and banish this confusion for good.

We need to know the truth about Mitso Arakit.

∞ ∞ ∞

At the apartment, I find Nons curled up on the sofa, safe, and we fall into each other—I kiss her cheeks, her forehead, her ears, and I pull her into bed, where I lift the comforter over our heads. We lie face-to-face so that I can whisper everything to her. Her moon-pale face wrinkles with concern under the eerie light of my cell phone.

"Saxim is right," she whispers to me. "We don't know the truth about Mitso. If he really stalked Mama. What this accident of his was, and when it happened. If he was . . . hurt by Nítuchí." Her eyes flash in the dark. "Why would Nítuchí hurt Mama's stalker, without Dad even knowing?"

I sigh, wrapping the edge of the comforter around my hand. "I don't know."

We sit in silence for several moments before she speaks again. "I still don't understand why Dad wouldn't come forward about this. To us, to Teddy, to *someone.*"

I wanted to believe Dad was perfect, fearless, strong until the end. Just like I wanted to believe Mama was that, too. But maybe he realized, later in life, that his man on the moon detachment was a weakness. While he was wrapped up in his parallel universe, packed chock-full of otherworldly Willy Wonka–ish delights that weren't for us mere mortals, he missed so much.

Still: Why beg us to solve this great mystery and exclude a detail like this?

"It's like the only person who really cares about us is Mina," I mutter under my breath.

And that's when I remember: Dad isn't the only one we love who's withheld details from us. And neither is Mama.

My brother told me. He wouldn't lie to me.

Teddy, who programmed Mina to record. Sweet Teddy, who always knows so much more than he lets on.

NONI

We take the apartment elevator down at noon sharp (which requires wrangling Tai out of her exploded suitcases) and find the Maybach purring at the curb. Teddy peeks his grinning head out, and as his body follows, Tai squeals and giggles, completely forgetting our midnight pact to be dead serious until Teddy tells us the full truth about Mitso Arakit.

He *is* wearing a full-on Jigglypuff Pokémon onesie—the same costume he wore to her seventh birthday, saved in mint condition. I can't help but snort while Tai whips out her phone. Jigglypuff was Tai's favorite Pokémon of all time—this petulant pink puffball with huge blue eyes fringed in massive lashes, that huffled and pouted, that sang people to sleep and drew on their faces. I raise a brow and smack my lips, thick with the new lipstick Tai just smeared on them.

"Please tell me you're wearing this to lunch," she tells Teddy, sliding into the backseat beside him, and I follow. "I've perished. Really. This is my ghost."

My sister's savantlike ability to lighten the mood—when it doesn't deserve lightening—never fails to surprise me. Teddy peels off the Jigglypuff suit like a hooded Snuggie, and I lean in to hug him. He smells like tobacco, like he always does. But it's cologne, or body wash, or something, because he doesn't smoke.

"If I wore this, they'd never let me back into the restaurant," he says, laughing. "And it's the best on the island—a really old-school spot. It took me five years to convince the old minister of foreign affairs to bring me as a guest, and it took me ten subsequent visits to charm my way into a limited-membership seat. One of Antella Arnoix's sour sisters almost had a heart attack when she saw my ass in there in jeans."

Tai cackles, and he glances out the window. "I wish I could've gone with your mother back then." I see the city reflected in his eyes—so small and contained. "She was always game for this kind of stuff."

"We know," Tai says, taking his hand.

He smiles at us, and we all toast our waters to Mama. I can't help remembering that she once said toasting with water was almost as bad as toasting with an empty glass—but I don't remember if that was based on a real Mediterranean old wives' tale, or just her fondness for wine.

That's when Teddy's phone interrupts us with the cheesiest ring-tone of all time:

Forever beautiful and fun, under every moon and every sun. She will be there until the end. Your very own Pocket Girlfriend.

The Pocket Girlfriend jingle.

Tai bursts into giggles again, and I say nothing.

∞ ∞ ∞

The driver idles in a busy commercial district, and we slip out of the car, following Teddy inside an unassuming wooden door just off the street, then up a hidden set of stairs. He knocks twice on an unmarked door at the top, as Tai hobbles up behind me in her six-inch heels. The door slides open to reveal a petite, black-haired woman in a simple sheath, about Dad's age, who welcomes us inside. We enter a small, windowless room with fading moss wallpaper and eight seats around a green marble counter, five of them filled with young men, each of them reverently staring at the bald older man with amber skin on the other side of the counter.

"Chef," Teddy says, nodding his head. The men rise, kissing Teddy on the cheeks, who kisses them back, and there's *a lot of kissing* and amiable chatting before we're seated. The men are Teddy's colleagues, it seems, and he booted two of them last-minute from this business lunch to make room for us.

Not exactly the private audience we requested.

"I'm so sorry you had to cancel on two of your friends, Teddy," Tai says, settled into her seat, sipping on water, and eagerly eyeing the chef as he handles gorgeous neon-orange lobes of sea urchin.

"I'm sure you are," I whisper. "Wipe your drool."

"It's not a problem," Teddy says. "They weren't friends—they were colleagues. And you girls are family."

We grin at him—even though all I'm thinking is *why didn't you tell us about Mitso?*—and accept the little thimblefuls of fancy liquor he offers us.

"I have a big surprise for you two," he says, lowering his voice, with a glance at the men beside us. "Massive. I'll tell you once we're alone. Don't let me forget." He taps his temple and gives us one of those über-jolly grins of his, just as the first course arrives: a whole-grilled lake fish. It smells of charcoal and brine, and is served in a paper cone.

"It's also called sugar fish, because some people think it tastes like mulberry. Sometimes the fishermen train birds to catch these," he says, as he shows us how to pinch the tail together to reach the succulent flesh around the spine. "The ban on catching them was lifted early this season, and Chef got first pick."

I taste it, and he's right: The fish is sweet-tasting, almost, and incredibly delicate. We're meant to eat the bitter innards, too.

"Hard pass," Tai says, poking at the liver with a wrinkled nose. "Sorry, Ted."

Our uncle just laughs. "You sound exactly like the girls in this game I acquired." He wipes his mouth, red-cheeked. "You'll have to come play it someday. It's fascinating—unlike anything I've seen."

I smile at him awkwardly: I never even *really* played Pocket Girlfriend.

"I love you to pieces, but my phone addiction is bad enough. I don't need to add more screens to the mix." Tai finally lifts a piece of fish to her mouth, chews it, swallows it—and her pupils dilate into inky coins with surprise pleasure.

"Maybe Noni, then?" he asks, turning to me. "You probably like Shirley Jackson, right?"

I brought her novel *The Haunting of Hill House* to Viloxin with me, which was probably ill-advised in light of how haunted Stökéwood seems. I went on a bender reading all of her spooky, interior work this past year and even forced Tai to read her famously chilling short story *The Lottery* ("Wait, they *kill* her?"). I read her biography, too, which is where I learned that as a young person she named the facets of herself, like I do, to better manage them. But hers weren't called the banshee, the fizzy pennies, and the radio DJ, like mine; hers were called—

"This game is special," Teddy continues. "The developer thinks she's the Shirley Jackson of the VR world. It's set in Patagonia, at a rural boarding school for the elite—"

Tai interrupts Teddy, but pauses in between now-greedy mouthfuls. "So, I sound like a rich bitch. Thanks, T. You're not exactly a peasant yourself."

Teddy laughs. "No! It's a haunted boarding school. So the players get to haunt the characters while working out the mystery of the house. It's cool."

Tai scavenges for the little scrap of fish liver left on my plate. "Haunt the characters? So, like, terrify the students? That sounds kind of messed up."

"Ha, I guess." Still smiling, Teddy faces me. "What about you, Nons? Maybe you can see the allure in being a ghost?"

And I fall into myself, at this prompt, because the truth is, I *do* see the allure in being a ghost—at least at first. Wandering the world invisibly, with no attachments. But I think of the spirits on Viloxin, born from blocked emotion, and I realize that ghosts don't lack attachments at all—they *are* that attachment, in its most terrible, visceral form. They are pain and frustration.

I don't ever want to be that.

"I don't know," I reply. Because: Why me? Why do I always have to be known as the quiet one, the loner, the shadow side to Tai's light? My mind drifts back to last night with Hérrakí, a patch of sunlight in a gloomy year, an overcast life—even as I think, simultaneously, *I am so screwed*. Teddy catches my discomfort, and a look of concern clouds his face.

"Anyway, are you excited for NYU this fall? I'm so proud of you," he says, circling back around, and pointedly avoiding looking at Tai.

When are we going to stop making small talk? I glimpse at the other men at the counter, whose eyes skim me before turning away. I open my mouth to answer, only to glimpse the back of someone tall and blond, speaking to the host in low tones behind the restaurant's curtain.

"Super subtle, Ted," Tai replies instead, folding her napkin into a tight little square.

He cocks his head. "You know I support whatever you two want to do. Marion told me you're headed to Paris, and I think that's just great, T. You can always go back to school and get your GED later, if you—"

"I'm *not* going back to fucking high school, okay? And everyone needs to stop treating me like I have a single-digit IQ," Tai hisses, and I stop myself from rolling my eyes, only to catch none other than Antella Arnoix edging her platinum head out of the curtain behind her to greet the chef. Her sharp brown eyes snap to Tai, and I reach for my sister's arm to stop her from saying anything more, but she continues: "I thought you of all people would get it, Teddy." She expels the air from her mouth just as Antella steps through, folding her hands in front of her with an unreadable—but vaguely contemptuous—expression on her face. I pinch my lips together to keep from accidentally smirking because of the sheer awkwardness of it all, and Teddy reluctantly comes to his feet to kiss her cheeks, politeness compelling him. Tai rotates in slow motion, the blood draining out of her.

"It seems I'm always interrupting an intimate family moment," Tai's dream mother-in-law says coolly.

"Not at all," Tai says, shooting from her seat with an apology and a kiss. She trips on her heels, her clammy hand falling onto my shoulder, and a bitter taste floods my mouth. I thought I would take pleasure from seeing my sister behave as gracelessly as I feel every day. But I don't. Especially not when her discomfort and shame are spurred by Antella—who watches Tai stumble without a modicum of surprise or sympathy.

"We're just celebrating Tai's achievements," I announce. "She's Dior's fresh Viloki face."

I say it with kindness in my heart. But as I speak, I remember: *There's really nothing Viloki about us anymore, is there?* Unless you count faded memories from years zero through eight. Tai's queasy expression tells me she knows this, too. And it sounds like another twisted insult, sister to sister. I bite my lip hard, tasting remnants of chalky makeup.

"I see. How thrilling for you. Do excuse me," Antella says, as if Tai's future sounds so pedestrian it might just be contagious. "I must be off."

Antella disappears, and thin slices of raw fish with pink and purple skin arrive in front of us.

"That's me, you know," Tai mutters, pointing at the slivers on her plate. "Flayed freaking Jigglypuff."

Happily, the food is so good that a few courses later, Tai rebounds. "I've ascended," Tai whispers to me reverently, after sipping some of the just-made broth with cured ham and yellow buds. "I have no idea what I'm eating, but I think it's better than normal-person sex."

Before I can decode that, Tai leans toward Teddy, drawing his attention from the mustachioed man beside him. "Mina could learn a thing or two from the chef, Teddy. The salt cod she serves is straight-up garbagio."

He laughs, and I feel a prickle along the back of my neck: Tai's starting to do her work, her careful, cheerful manipulation that I know about all too well.

"I know, I know," he says. "But her mandate is to—"

"*Take care of our family*," Tai cuts in, grinning. "I know, I know. And eating grody salt cod must be, like, taking a good drain cleaner to your insides or something."

Teddy raises his eyebrows. "I'd love your full feedback," he says, game.

"Tai heard a grainy conversation coming out of Mina the other day. A recording of a chat Dad had with someone. Is it normal to call up old patient conversations?"

Teddy's brow furrows. "To be honest, no. I built her to follow her mandate to a T. There is flexibility within that. So everything she does, theoretically, should be to protect your family and their health. But there's no reason for her to record and replay conversations. I'll have a tech come out and take a look. I'm sorry if she scared you. She's been so faithful over the years."

"Oh, no worries," Tai says, her eyes diving back into her soup. She adjusts her elbow by my side and digs into me, as if to prompt me to say something, but I'm not sure how to take the conversation any further without saying something I might not want to, in front of this group of strangers. They probably all know Nítuchí, if they're Teddy's colleagues. I elbow her back, as if to say, *Not the time and place.*

"Can I tell you both something cool?" Teddy asks, face opening.

Tai leans in. "Always."

He rubs his palms together. "We're on the verge of gaining access to large amounts of Hero Pharm data, which would completely transform the way the Carers function. Imagine being able to integrate decades of results from private pharmaceutical studies into the Carer database. Combined with new governmental permissions granted insofar as the types of artificial intelligence that can be integrated into the Carer's code . . . Well, we could help so many people. Between that and the new hologram tech I've been working on, so patients can see their lost loved ones . . . Carers would save hundreds of lives in their first year of wide release on Viloxin alone." His eyes shine at us like a child's on Christmas, and I remember why luck's drawn to my uncle and my sister like moths to the light. "It's an incredible way of following your mother's mission, don't you think?"

I pipe up: "Her . . . mission?"

"Helping others at any cost."

Just then, the next course arrives—flowers floating in a gelée—and Tai's squeal interrupts us.

∞ ∞ ∞

Only after the others in the small group have finished their meal and said their saliva-speckled goodbyes does Teddy mention his surprise.

"Girls, I received something strange yesterday from the lawyer handling the estate of the director who filmed that promotional video of your mother and died from suicide."

Tai, midsip, stops.

"He claims," he says, setting down his drink, "that it's a genuine copy of *White Fox*. All four parts."

BOY

Excerpt from *Vanity Fair* Magazine Interview with Mireille Foix Hammick

August 2001

. . . Mireille claims that her pet project, the Foix Institute, has, in its thirteen years of existence, funded the advanced creative degrees of almost 10,000 individuals of all different ages—many of them Viloki-born, while others are refugees housed under the Foix Institute Visa program. These numbers sound extraordinary—unbelievable. But media tends to focus, understandably, on the dubious practices of Hero Pharm— the institute's greatest donor—and I was reluctant to cover the institute at all in this article, which aimed to celebrate Mireille's return to the screen. However, during our teatime, she presses me to speak about her pet project on multiple occasions, and I finally bite. *Can Mireille offer specific examples as to how the Foix Institute has changed life on the island in the past thirteen years?* I wonder.

At this point in the interview, a Hero Pharm publicist darts forward with a stack of letters from island residents who have benefited from the Foix Institute—but Mireille stops him with a kind word and an outstretched hand. "It's so difficult to quantify that, Edward," she admits to me, her charisma shining through. "I just interviewed our class of 1991, to collect information about ways to improve." Her blue eyes cloud over as she stirs her milky, lukewarm tea. "I—I often feel like life is slipping through my fingers. And I never feel like I'm doing enough with the time I've been gifted."

It's only at the end of our teatime that I notice Mireille is noticeably pregnant under her cream Yves Saint Laurent coat.

"Hero and I are welcoming a baby girl later this year, around the time my new film releases," she explains. "I can feel her kicking right now."

To my chagrin, my hand reaches out instinctively. She graciously agrees to let me feel the kicks. To feel life growing inside this woman I've watched grow up on-screen is one of the strangest—and most surreal—interview moments of my career.

Still, I'm left wondering: Will motherhood distract her from her pet project? Or worse—from embarking on future film projects?

"I imagine motherhood, like the institute, will require hard work and so much love," she says, eyes sharp. "But happily, the act of loving only increases your capacity to love."

∞ ∞ ∞

I've watched you girls, playing with your spoiled friends in Limatra, ignoring the truth about yourselves and your family, except when you dip your toes into scummy Noxim waters. You haven't changed since you were young. I watched you then, too. You never once noticed me, because, while you may pretend at being good, you are not.

Your mother was a hypocrite, and it seems you both are, too. She said she wanted to help people at any cost, but everyone in her life undid the work she started, and she knew it. They used me, and she knew it.

I blame your father most. Do you miss him, girls?

I'm sure he's no more cold and distant by virtue of being dead.

I worry you are your father's daughters.

TAI

At the entrance of the Daddy Warbucks–y gated community that is Mitella, people filter through a security greenhouse plucked out of a science fiction movie. From the outside, it looks like a lodge made of wood. Inside, the ceiling is made of glass, and we walk under boughs of almond trees, their branches heavy with pink and white starburst blossoms. The sky looks blanketed in twee popcorn.

"Almond blossom season is over, but the community created its own microclimate for the security courtyard so these specially bred trees could bloom multiple times a year," Teddy explains, waving at one of five doormen-slash–security people by the frosted glass door where we're expected to furnish ID.

"For real?" I whisper to Nons. She shrugs and says out loud, "Is that even possible? From a . . . botanical perspective?"

"Well, when that fails," Teddy whispers conspiratorially, as we follow him toward a waiting security guard, "I'm pretty sure they just tie blooming branches from other parts of the world to their trees."

I just barely swallow down an incredulous laugh. My bones have been like Jell-O ever since I learned about the fresh copy of *White Fox*, waiting at Teddy's mansion. Nons and I all but scarfed down our meals so we could run straight there. *Four parts.*

The guard huddles us around a retinal scanner, and we both take a turn squinching our eyeballs into the correct position. After he's done, we're escorted through to the secure side of the greenhouse, where his car awaits to continue the drive.

It winds us past epic mansion after mansion, unlike our place in that they are totally unspoiled and new-looking—even the older castles, draped in ivy, look like they were just unboxed. The streets gleam, speckled with silver like fancy sidewalks. My skin itches when we pass the Arnoix compound, its ornate gate draped with honeysuckle. I recognize it from tabloids—Linos has never had me over.

And next door is Teddy's house, tucked behind an unassuming entrance gate that looks like it's meant for Seattle: hypermodern, clean lines, lots of glass and steel. The car parks, and we're led through a small steel door set into a giant concrete slab.

It opens on an extravagant central living room, overlooking a glittering swath of Limatra. We must be on a hill, I realize, disoriented. Teddy waves a hand at three random men in all black milling about the door—assistants? Guards? And then we're off—he takes us down the hallway to our left, and we pop our heads into, no joke, at least twenty rooms, all with different themes. There's the famed aquarium room now with clownfish—its second iteration—which has a recirculating waterfall; the grass room, now with putting green, and a VR golf class from Tiger himself; the red room, which I used to be scared of—but is really just a velvety boudoir kind of thing, with Tarantino movie posters on the walls; the jazz room; the Christmas bedroom; the Jell-O sitting room; the reading room; the Downtown Abbey sitting room . . . While Noni's playing out some Baz Luhrmann *Romeo + Juliet* fantasy in the second aquarium bedroom, Teddy shows me the oversize closet, where I glimpse the Jigglypuff costume, already hung up. He tosses me a blue Clouded Cage hoodie before pulling one on, too.

"So what's on the other floors? Your Birkin collection?" I joke, tugging on the comfy fleece.

"Oh, you know, rooms for my lady friends," he says with a wink.

And when I burst out into laughter and sarcastically scream, "*Yuck*," he adds, "Just kidding, Tai Tai."

"Do you get tired of them?" Nons asks as she returns. "Of all of these . . . themes?"

"Of course I do." Teddy smiles, tucking his hands into his hoodie pocket. "But then I just change the theme."

Which is one solution. As we pass more rooms, they all start to blur together—reality starts to become confused. "Teddy! Where's my room?"

"Your room?"

"The princess room!"

"Oh, of course, *your* room." His mouth twitches back into its resting grin. "It's all the way at the end of the hall." He points in the direction we just came, like a football-field length down. "Want to check it out?"

Nons and I widen our eyes at each other in the universally polite and secret expression signifying *HELP NO STOP*. We want the truth, not another trip into the fun house maze. Screw the princess room, no matter the delights it holds.

"Girls? Do you—"

"Let's just go back to the main living room!" I say, the chipper Pocket Girlfriend of the century, eager to please even at the expense of my dignity. "And maybe we can chat over that copy of *White Fox* and some noncoconut beverages?"

∞ ∞ ∞

Back in the living room, a whisper-quiet man dressed in black steps out of nowhere and offers us herbal tea, water, or—in his words—something stronger. I'm about to order a drink when Nons speaks up.

"Some relaxing herbal tea would be great for both of us."

Tea wouldn't be the worst thing. Tea and one of the beds up here—a bed to drop into and sleep for the next hundred years. For a second, I can almost pretend Teddy's psychedelic fun house is a womb, and I'm the warm Tai fetus next to the warm Noni fetus. I run my hand along a blanket next to me and find it to be softer and lighter than clouds.

Teddy chuckles. "*Shahtoosh.* Do you like it?"

"What?" I wonder if he sneezed.

"*Shahtoosh* is wool gathered from the neck of the Tibetan antelope. It means 'king of wool' in Farsi. Take it."

I'm draping the weave over my shoulders when Nons drops her end. "Isn't the Tibetan antelope endangered?" she whispers. *Classique* Noni.

The man in black returns with two pots (*presteeped?*) and while balancing a silver tray in one hand, he pours us three cups of perfectly brewed tea with the other. He then serves us. Silently. Not a drop spills. How many of the staff are hidden in the shadows of the apartment, just like the assistants Dad brought in from the institute?

"It's my own personal blend of chamomile, valerian root, and seer's sage," Teddy says, picking up his tea. "I was sick of taking your father's sleeping pills every night to get a good night's sleep. I didn't want to feel dependent on them." He grins. "No offense."

Another man in black appears then, with a polished silver tray, upon which sits a thick stack of paper. My hot palms slick over, and Noni tenses up next to me.

"Ah," says Teddy, beckoning him over. "Here it is. As promised."

It's weighty in my grip, heavier than our copy. I flip through its pristine pages, and my hungry fingers reach . . .

PART FOUR

INT. GRAND OLD HOME — NIGHT

White Fox, bare-faced, clothed in a clean dress, and seated in a small room, with Client 2 / Man on the Moon sitting before her.

> WHITE FOX
> The next person wasn't really a person—
> his home, not really a home.

EXT. ABANDONED PARK IN THE LIMATRA SUBURBS — EARLY EVENING

LIMATRA is ugly from afar: in tragic shambles during the war. This park is in poor condition.

White Fox swings alone on a swing, unsure of how to proceed. Her bags are piled to her side. She looks hungry, and her nose bleeds.

As she wipes it clean, VAMPYRRHIC BOY appears, clothed in a blue sweatshirt. He is only a child.

> VAMPYRRHIC BOY
>
> Who are you?

> WHITE FOX
>
> White Fox.

> VAMPYRRHIC BOY
>
> You're not a fox. You smell nice.

> WHITE FOX
> (laughing)
>
> You're wrong, little man. What are you doing here alone?

> VAMPYRRHIC BOY
> (shrugging)
>
> I'm hungry.

> WHITE FOX
>
> Lots of rotten chestnuts these days.

The Vampyrrhic Boy fights a grin and approaches. He looks up at her with big brown eyes that seem to soak in all the world and reflect back exactly what she wishes to see.

White Fox ruffles his hair.

He steps closer and wipes the slick of blood beside her mouth. He licks his finger and laughs.

White Fox stares at him.

When he sits on her lap, she does nothing. When he licks at her face, she does nothing.

                    WHITE FOX (V.O.)
          I felt a warmth fill the spots he
          touched: a healing warmth. I knew this
          was wrong. But he was a great comfort.

INT. LARGE TREE TRUNK IN PARK

White Fox and the Vampyrrhic Boy camp together inside a large, cavernous tree where the Vampyrrhic Boy seems to be living.

He has carved little animals into the wooden trunk as childish decoration—maybe as protection.

She runs her hand over them, admiring.

Then, she sleeps comfortably beside him, as if he is her child.

EXT. ABANDONED PARK IN THE LIMATRA SUBURBS — MORNING

In the morning, she wakes and finds the Vampyrrhic Boy staring at her coldly from a far corner of the park.

His eyes have sunk into his face—he looks entirely ordinary. Nothing like the special and angelic child of the evening prior.

> VAMPYRRHIC BOY
> Who are you? Why are you here?

White Fox gapes at him, confused.

> WHITE FOX
> You invited me here last night.

> WHITE FOX (V.O.)
> I cannot tell you how strange it was to say such a thing to a boy.

> VAMPYRRHIC BOY
> (scoffing)
> You are a stranger—an old woman with white hair! Why would I invite you inside my tree? It is for little boys only.

                    WHITE FOX
    I don't believe you, you know.

                 VAMPYRRHIC BOY
                 (eyes narrowing)
    Believe what?

                    WHITE FOX
    You remember who I am! You licked at my
    blood.

                 VAMPYRRHIC BOY
    Lying witch.

Vampyrrhic Boy storms away. White Fox eventually
wanders out to find new lodging, food, anything.

                 WHITE FOX (V.O.)
    I was too afraid to venture into Limatra
    and be faced with that great amount of
    change.

KIND WOMAN at a store gives her day-old stale pas-
tries, and she finds herself back in the park that
evening.

EXT. ABANDONED PARK IN THE LIMATRA SUBURBS —
EVENING

White Fox sees the Vampyrrhic Boy again, swinging
on the swings alone.

She avoids him, but he waves at her.

Sure enough, after a bit, he approaches her.

                    VAMPYRRHIC BOY
          Yoo-hoo!

                      WHITE FOX
          I thought you didn't remember me.

                    VAMPYRRHIC BOY
          You? The most beautiful woman I've ever
          seen? How I love you. How you comfort
          me, all alone in this park.

White Fox tugs a strip of the skin in her mouth
loose and lets the blood drip out of her mouth.

Vampyrrhic Boy approaches and puts one perfect
finger on the slick of blood. Once he has cleaned
it, the raw patch in her mouth heals over.

                   WHITE FOX (V.O.)
          What did this mean? I did not know what
          to make of it. We slept comfortably
          that night, and many nights more. But
          one night, everything changed.

INT. LARGE TREE TRUNK IN PARK - NIGHT

The little creatures from the Man on the Moon's

house appear in the trunk. White Fox gets a better look at them: They are made of shadow but have clingy hands and feet, like rodents. They hiss and whisper to the Vampyrrhic Boy as White Fox sleeps with him in her arms.

He pulls away from White Fox and inches away in disgust.

White Fox awakes with a start: Usually the boy is kind to her until morning.

                    WHITE FOX
     What is it?

                  VAMPYRRHIC BOY
     You lied to me. You've ruined me! This
     blood will hurt me, not fix me. How
     could you give me what I wanted? I'm
     just a child—I don't know what's best.

                    WHITE FOX
     I don't know what to say.

                  VAMPYRRHIC BOY
                    (hissing)
     Leave me!

But the Vampyrrhic Boy cannot stop himself.

As White Fox gathers her things, he lunges at

her and takes for himself a piece of her bloody
flesh.

White Fox runs from him, runs from the park. The
creatures close in on the Vampyrrhic Boy.

> WHITE FOX (V.O.)
> I left the boy then. I don't know what
> happened to him, but I miss him still.
> I can't know whom he found next. I only
> wish he is not all alone with those
> terrible creatures.

INT. GRAND OLD HOME — NIGHT

> WHITE FOX
> I recognized the creatures, you know,
> from earlier in my journey.
>
> But they had changed. When I ignored
> them, out of my own foolishness, they
> began to swarm those near me.

More tapping on the window outside. White Fox
tenses up.

> WHITE FOX (CONT'D)
> Is it them? Oh God, have the creatures
> followed me here? I'll have to face
> them. But I don't know if I'm well
> enough yet . . .

Client 2 / Man on the Moon is distant. He clenches
his fist, distracted.

> CLIENT 2 / MAN ON THE MOON
> I know who this boy is. He's nothing
> but an animal. I'll kill him with my
> bare hands.

> WHITE FOX
> (glancing out the window)
> Please. Please listen to me. Won't you
> just listen to me? I must be quick.

White Fox begins to bleed from the mouth.

∞ ∞ ∞

When I look up, my brain distorts the room around me. I'm breathing
hard, my nails tattooing Noni's wrist on my lap. But she's adrift, still
lost in the dark parable. *Please listen to me. Won't you just listen to me?*

I take several long slugs of tea, as if I'll find answers in the mess
of leaves at the bottom of the cup.

And there, below the cup, is my chest, covered in a blue sweatshirt.

I look at Teddy, in his blue sweatshirt. He's smiling, still, like a
little boy.

It hits me, sharply and all at once. *Could he be . . . ?*

"This is all you have?" I ask instead, tearing through the remain-
ing parts in the packet, identical to ours.

"Yes," I hear Teddy say, voice thick with concern.

"Fuck," I mutter. Why didn't Mama leave us this part? I don't
understand it. My breath stalls in my chest. It's when I see starbursts
that I let go of Noni and drop my heavy head between my legs.

Teddy rushes forward and takes my slack hand. "Tai?"

A second later, a server brings me a glass of water and a cool cucumber-scented towel. I would laugh if I could stand it.

"Are you the vampyrrhic boy?" Noni asks Teddy.

I bite my polish-flecked nail and watch as our uncle, crouching at my feet, rises to settle onto the sofa beside us. He motions at the silent men in the room, who slip back into the pockets of darkness. Only then does his head drop into his hands—he rubs at his cheeks and inhales. "You're owed the truth."

"Teddy," Noni says, the edge of her body pressing into mine.

And that's when Teddy meets our eyes, his face pink, tearful. His Adam's apple bobs.

It is a guilty face.

My heart flutters to my throat.

"You have to understand. She was like a mother to me, too," he starts, with the desperation of a kid seeking quick forgiveness. "Like a best friend. She came to me, in the months before she disappeared, and told me she suspected your father and Nítuchí were . . . I don't know. Up to no good? And I didn't believe her. I didn't believe her because of the Mitso Arakit situation."

I hear the faint chatter of Noni's teeth as her hand closes around my knee. We haven't spoken his name yet, even though it's been on my lips for hours. "What Mitso Arakit situation?"

"Mitso Arakit was . . . he was a local guy in Noxim who became . . . obsessed with your mom."

My blood pumps hotter, faster in the rawest zone of flesh just inside the sun-charm choker around my neck.

"He—he thought he loved her, I guess. He was a superfan. A . . . a stalker. He wrote to her often. He was troubled, okay? And she became obsessed with *him*. Obsessed with talking about him, with showing me his letters, with *wondering* if there was something, any-thing, we could do to help him lead a healthier life." He watches us,

302

eyes bloodshot. "As if that was her responsibility, somehow. I didn't take the letters seriously, even as they became . . . darker and angrier, because . . . I don't know, he lived with his mother, for Pete's sake. This was before incels and all of that." He exhales shakily. "I have copies of the letters, if you want to see. Do you want to see?" And before we can answer, he bounds toward the back hall.

Noni and I sit in silence, dust motes floating between us. The blood settling in our heads. I can't feel my hands or feet, but I see hers, pale and threaded with veins.

When Teddy returns, he hands us a rumpled stack of notepaper.

The letters, written in the tangled English of an unfamiliar hand, begin the year before Mama left.

I'm so excited to see you, he wrote. *I've thought about this moment for so long. I've imagined you a hundred different ways. I hope that doesn't sound strange. Does it? I just know you'll love me, and I'll love you.*

We'll be together so soon.

I swallow down my knot of a heart and find another letter, deeper in the pile.

You are a lying bitch and a fucking hypocrite, it reads. "Helping people at any cost?" *I hope you rot and maggots crawl through your flesh.*

It's dated the month before she left.

NONI

I can hardly hear myself, hear my uncle, over the gnawing static in my head, but I breathe to listen, I try. "You have to understand: Mitso Arakit couldn't have hurt her," he explains. "He had an accident a few months before and was bedbound at the time of her disappearance. These letters are ill-timed and scary, that's all."

"An accident a few months before," I repeat in a monotone, that fizz, burning me now, eating its way down my throat and into the cavity of my chest.

Teddy stares at his hands, like he's bewildered, like *he's* struggling. "I don't know. But he was bedbound, I'm sure of it. Your father and Nítuchí promised me that."

"What do you mean, my father and Nítuchí *promised* you that?" Tai asks, and the grinding churn of that hiss, it's building, it's hurting.

"Nítuchí's team always handled all that kind of stuff. The stalkers,

304

the messes, the . . ." My uncle's words are a froth that dribbles and dries up. "I was the first one to think of Mitso Arakit after your mom disappeared. And Nítuchí was the one who told me Mitso had an accident. That he couldn't be involved."

Tai's hand grips mine tight as iron, but I am no clearer-minded, I only taste that copper at the back of my tongue as she speaks—

"So you're saying that Nítuchí . . . caused Mitso's accident, because he was stalking Mama?"

My uncle's cheeks are gray. "I—I don't know. But if anyone does, it would be his people, the ones who . . . who cover everything up. They do that, you know. Handle people who become problematic, like disgruntled stalkers and ex-employees who leak untrue information. Handle them, and handle the payouts. The team at . . . at the company."

The team at Hero Pharm. The faceless crowd. Those minuscule shadows, multiplying in the forest. *Always called shadows, and never human beings*, I think to myself. The infernal hissing, the buzzing, it grows—

"There are evil forces at Hero Pharm. I've tried my best to investigate, but they've done everything they can to restrict my access. I—I even thought they might be connected to what happened to your mom," my uncle says, the words spilling out of him like he's a bottle uncorked. "Maybe your mom discovered something they didn't want discovered. Maybe she threatened to talk. I've gone over the punishing possibilities almost every day since she disappeared, just like your dad, you understand? But she shouldn't have tried to handle things alone. I thought your mom knew that she could come to me for help. I'm not Nítuchí. I'm not some Hero Pharm crony. I just—"

But I don't hear anything else, because the fizzy pennies, the ones that come from the hollows in my head and my heart, they have built and built and built upon themselves and now, with a repulsive gorgeousness

305

they spill out, filling every fleshy crevice with their fizzing, popping, rusting noise, like dozens of malicious coppery toy soldiers intent on war, like an unstoppable virus, like unfiltered doom, and they choke me. *Helpless-useless-helpless-useless you paper doll you shouldn't try to handle things alone; let the faceless take all the blame; let noise crowd out truth.*

Tai's hand in mine is plastic; this ostentatious room suffocates me; I feel the maze growing around me, replete with so many shadowed nooks, where that evil burning hides, and I know something's not right and never will be again.

I have to go.

I don't know if fresh air will help, but I know that I can't sit here, tended to by silent men my uncle's brain has turned into nothing more than invisible cogs. It's what we were born to do, isn't it? Use everyone around us, below us, as an excuse for any wrongs we commit, any wrongs we witness.

Tai's eyes shine at me, trying to convey some sisterly message that's beyond me, and *I need. To. Go—*

I come to my feet, and the plush carpet wobbles, pitching me deeper into that fiery, crackling, coppery zone.

It's black static.

It's pain, the low-level, deep-seated kind you don't understand except for knowing it's causing damage that will take so long to heal.

∞ ∞ ∞

The black's receding, and the sadness is rushing in to fill its place, with anger close at its heels. I open my eyes, and I'm in our Limatra apartment, Tai kneeling beside me. She looks littler than before, sucked dry, her nails bitten to shreds.

"Nons?" Her voice sounds hollow and otherlike. "It's morning, Nons."

I sit up—there's light crawling under the blinds and I know she's right, but I can't account for the hours in between. It hasn't happened like that. It hasn't happened like that ever. Did I eat something bad? I rub my eyes, and my lashes feel stiff as splinters, and I wonder if Tai slicked her magic paints on my face like a doll when I was out, and—

"What . . . happened?" I ask. Someone scooped my brain out with a rusty spoon, that's what.

She wrings her hands. "You don't remember? We came back here in a taxi, because you refused to ride with Teddy or in the car, and you were . . . upset. Ranting about boys and privilege? We called your doctor, and she told us you should take one of your anxiety pills." The thin skin under her eyes is cruciferous purple green. "So you did. And . . . you went to sleep."

And then the details file back in—how Mitso stalked and harassed Mama, how Dad and Teddy let their colleagues take responsibility for their problems and washed their hands of it all, including this darkness in Mama (the bleeding of the mouth, just like how my anxiety became fizzy pennies).

But what hurts most of all, senseless as it is, is the fact Tai and I didn't even know any of this was going on at the time.

I know we were just children. But I feel awestruck by my obliviousness, by the way my memories shifted to conceal clues that must have been so obvious, leaving me with only that lingering impression of her malaise.

I need to know just what she found out.

I need to see her.

To promise her I'll never be so blind again.

To promise her I'll write her story with her, the right story, because she deserves it.

When I say this to Tai, her blue eyes *cringe*, softening at the outer corners.

"You need to rest. No one could have expected an eight-year-old to begin to understand this situation," she says, daintily reaching for my hand. "I mean, we barely understand it now." Walking on eggshells around me, like I'm sick, ruined. Like I'm younger than her and in need of protection. My gut surges with the bitter wrongness of this.

I let her hand sit there next to my lap, but I don't react. Taking it would be admitting she's the one protecting me, now. And if I'm not protecting her, if I'm not managing her, what's the point of me?

I know this is a lie written by my own pain. I can feel the fizzy pennies stirring, their stale buzz haunting my insides, still.

What I need now is to *write*. Yes. To write and parse through what is happening in my head, because that's what's been missing these few days—that's why the pennies came back like this. They're melded-together worries, left to react and sizzle in the blocked chemical pathways of my brain. It's only in the writing that I can melt them and clear paths for them to flush away. *Just breathe, my love*, I hear Mama say, holding down my sweaty limbs while I thrashed in bed, seven years old, eight years old. *Just breathe and let them melt away.*

But I don't say any of this to Tai. Instead, I smile and say, "You're right." I wait until her hand shrinks from my side, until she stands, still frowning, and drifts out the door. And when she leaves me alone, I post myself at my desk over my lavender-field notebook—the one Hérrakí returned, the one with my notes, the details that will ensure I'm the one to find Mama. And I try to write, pen poised.

I must write. I should write through it all, like Mama taught me.

But the words don't come.

So when I hear the stream of the shower in the other room, I text Tai: *Sorry about last night. Taking a nap—let's talk later.*

And I lock my bedroom from the outside, then slip out the front door, still cottony numb from the pill I fed myself, before skidding down the fire stairs and escaping through the building's back door alone.

∞ ∞ ∞

He answers on the first ring and agrees to meet. So I weave through the humid Limatra streets, unthinking, and I only come to when I get stuck behind a group of girls in Birkenstocks and socks near the entrance to the park we're meeting at—some of them carrying black shopping bags of merchandise labeled BLOOD MOON FOX.

I shudder underneath my baseball cap. The store sells dark paraphernalia tied to actresses like Mama, like "sexy" costumes based on her grittiest characters. Even cheap replicas of the gloves she disappeared with, the same ones pinned to their window displays like the old, molted skins of newly spectral hands.

I'm early for my meeting. I buy myself a drink in a Dreamland-themed vending machine—mulberry-lemon soda in a little glass wine bottle inexplicably labeled DREAMS ARE REALITY TO THE POWER OF ECSTASY!—thinking that maybe sugar will help. The tourists around me stare with sly eyes, their faces covered up by scarves, collars, sunglasses. The soda is cool and sweet on my tongue, but it tastes a bit too much like coppery bile as it trickles down my throat. I walk around the entrance, scanning the area for him. I pass pods of bleary-eyed, suit-wearing Hero Pharm employees, of whispering, coy young lovers with hands in each others' back pockets, of giddy teenagers swinging their backpacks like toy weapons, of elderly men in suits out for strolls.

That's when I spot a man in a military jacket in the distance. I can't see his face, and he's far, far enough, but—

A large hand settles on my shoulder, and I jump out of my skin. I drop my soda, and it shatters. Pieces of glass spread across the concrete like haphazard lace. Soda splashes across my jeans.

But it's only Hérrakí, wearing a blue-striped button-down shirt and a light jacket. He smiles hello, and I feel a cool rush of relief, undercut by something warmer. The hair by his temples is so fine in the daylight, it looks like he's wearing a halo. "Are you okay?"

"I'm okay." I brush at my ankles. "It's okay." I crouch to pick up the pieces of glass, unthinking; I touch one before realizing the bottle has shattered into so many tiny pieces that I'll risk lodging them all in my hand—in fact, I already have, and a couple of teensy dots of blood speckle my palm.

"I meant your phone call," he says, stooping to help. He inspects my palms, wincing for me, and tenderly pulls me up. "But, uh, this isn't great, either. Let's get you first aid?"

I didn't explain why I wanted to meet on the phone. I couldn't exactly say that I wanted to feel normal, sane.

"Let's just walk," I reply, my arms springing back to my sides, a poor imitation of someone holding it together. The park gardens are clean and well-kept: a disc-size robot roams, trimming grass. Several winding paths lead in different directions, and I follow Hérrakí on the rightmost one, lined with the tired, sagging blooms of late-spring flowers. He's quiet, but it's the rare kind of silence that comforts and reassures.

"I need a favor," I whisper, once we've made it into the relative privacy of a long alley of sky-high cypress trees.

"Ah." He looks down, walking on with me. "Sure. Shoot."

I swallow hard, bloodied hands gumming into my jean pockets. "Before I ask, just know that you can say no, and I'll understand."

His brow furrows, a smirk curving the corner of his lip. "Okay."

"I know you sometimes organize your uncle's files," I say carefully.

He misses a step, avoiding a rut in the paved path. "Um . . . This is true. For better or for worse, I'm his bitch."

"Can you look for a mention of someone in those files? My dad knew him, and I'm sure your uncle knows him, too. His name is Mitso Arakit."

"Why don't you just ask him?"

We lock eyes, and he grins crookedly.

"Fine, fine. I get it." He blows the air from his mouth. "So, what do you know about this person? If I'm gonna spy on my uncle and all."

A couple passes, and we go silent for several paces.

"It sounds bad if you put it that way," I whisper. "But this person threatened my mom."

"What?" He stops in place, and a fast walker behind us bumps into him and glares.

"He threatened my mother!" I say louder, attracting stares from the mother and two children picnicking on the grass off to our right.

He reaches toward me, as if to clap a hand over my mouth, then his. "Sorry—sorry," he says, pulling away.

We're both blushing hard.

"I need to know everything my dad and your uncle knew if I'm going to find her. But no one can know. It'll spiral out of control if too many people know." I sound paranoid, I know it, and—

"Wait." He freezes. "Did you say, 'If I'm going to find her'?"

"Yes," I whisper.

"Damn." He nods and looks out over the expansive green beside us, dotted with park visitors. We pass a shrub with a plastic bag draped atop it, and Hérrakí plucks it off, balling it up in his hand. He walks a dozen yards to throw it away, then returns to me.

"Of course I'll help," he says. He looks at me, shrugging off his jacket. "You know, you could have just asked over the phone."

I rub my lips together, let my scraped hand swing down and brush the edge of his. "I know."

He takes my tingling hand gently, so gently, and he doesn't ask anything more.

When we reach the end of the park road, he stops me in my tracks. He takes both of my hands, fingers hovering over the hot cores of my palms. Pinpricks run up the outsides of my arms.

Wordless, he runs his fingers across the edges of my hands, as if they're delicate seams. His eyes almost—almost—look wet, but I know it's a trick of the light. I can feel his warmth seeping into me. I see the rough skin on his jaw, pale in the light.

I lean toward him, into his singular scent, driven forward by something bigger than myself—

My phone rings, shattering the moment, and I drop his hands to slip it out of my pocket.

Tai, of course. Furious I've left, probably. I silence the ringer and jam the phone into my pocket.

Hérrakí bites his lip, and we say goodbye. I hurry away, eyes trained on the road. I keep glimpsing behind me, just to see him again, and he doesn't move once—he just watches, a ghost of a wistful smile on his face.

"Excuse me," says a man who bumps into me—or rather, I bump into him. I look up, the smell of onion thick in my nose.

The man has three long, raking scars on his face—like a cheap monster from a film, like fodder for anyone's nightmare.

The world goes slow as I realize it's him. His mouth spreads into a gashlike smile.

TAI

Just as I'm dialing Teddy and Marion, Noni barges through the front
door of the apartment covered in a thin film of sweat. Ugly sweat, not
the glisten we pay money for.

"Where'd you go for your nap? The dark side of the moon?"
I snap, folding closed the glossy magazine I wasn't reading, when
really I mean, *You scared me half to death, how could you sneak out like
that after last night?* But then I notice she's trembling, teary-eyed, her
jeans stained, and I stiffen.

"This man followed me, Tai. This man, with three scratches over
his face, he found me. Some stalker, some—" She tucks her salty-
sweaty hair behind her ears with bloodied hands.

I sit up. "What happened? Three scratches?" That sounds like a
cartoon villain. *Exactly the sort of thing someone would hallucinate after
a panic attack*, I think to myself, even though I have no idea what I'm
talking about. "What happened to your hand—"

"He chased me before, after the flower shop—"

"This isn't the first time?" I interrupt right back, voice rising. "You went without the car? Why?"

She sighs, like *I've* said something frustrating, and rubs at her eyes. "As if the car is safe."

I'm crying before I can stop myself, and I bite down hard on my lip so I won't say the words I want to say, some feverish, scrambled version of *Fuck you I can't lose you I love you what's wrong with you* because *not now*. Not when she's like this, and I need to step up. "So what was so important?"

"I met Hérrakí last-minute to get him to look up Mitso Arakit in his uncle's files—"

I shoot to my feet, all control disintegrating in one ashy, searing flash. "What the *fuck*? You met up with him, knowing what we know?"

"We know nothing at all, Tai." Her stony expression stirs up an old bitterness in me. "How do you not see that? We need to figure out what she found out. There's more to the Mitso Arakit–Hero Pharm story. More Dad hid from us. More Teddy doesn't know or refuses to tell us. We shouldn't trust them. I told you from the beginning, we can't trust any—"

"Seriously? Do you think that's fair?" I try to slow my breathing, but I feel like a hot-air balloon, filling and rising up and up and up, everything out of my control, especially the fiery heat in my belly. "They've done nothing but love us."

She shakes her head at me slowly, disgust coiled in her eyes like a snake. "How can you not see that Teddy and Dad both lied to us? When's the last time you used a brain cell? In utero?"

"They're protecting us." I cross my trembling arms. "They wouldn't lie without a very good reason to lie."

She scoffs, raising clawed hands to her face like I'm giving her a coronary, when really my heart's about to burst. "So—what? We let this go and wait for Mama to contact us again, if she *ever* does?" Her eyes shine, scaly with hurt now, and it scares me how fast they shift. "I'm not doing that. I can't just go back to my sparkly life in New York and delude myself like you and drown—"

"And *drown myself in strangers' attention*—yeah, I've heard this shit before." My back stiffens; my bones ache from the heat. "You're so good at making it sound like I do all of this just for fun. Maybe you're the dense one." Her eyes squint at me as I continue. "Seriously, I know I'm the high school dropout, but how oblivious can you be? You do realize that my job *drowning myself in strangers' attention* pays our bills until the trust kicks in, right? Your fucking college tuition. I don't see you pursuing one of the trust-approved hard science degrees." My locked arms go numb as I think of all the terse conversations I've had with Aunt Marion in the past year. *You're making the mistake of your life by dropping out of school for this, paycheck or not. Your parents wouldn't have wanted you to give up your education to work as a professional narcissist.* This coming from the same Aunt Marion who burned through so much of the money Dad gave her to care for us on artists' retreats and endless courses to "discover her true potential."

She goes silent, and I know she didn't know. Aunt Marion never told her. Aunt Marion made it seem like she was paying for everything. And I wasn't about to make Noni feel beholden, make her feel less than, make her . . . Fuck. I rub my bitten-down, messed-up fingers into my eyes, mascara flaking off in spidery chunks. I feel this sickening relief flood me, pure *I got you*—

But when I look at her, she's staring at me, her own eyes mean with slick victory. "You shouldn't have bothered. I had a plan to support myself."

My pulse skips a daggering beat. "What does that even mean?"

"I got a book deal," she says, a tidy, small, cruel grin brewing

315

on her face. "That's why I'm keeping that notebook. It's for a book all about Mama. *The Real Mireille Foix*. About her favorite places. About her time with us. About all her secrets. The ones you haven't sold already, to pay for your mind-numbing cocktails and exploding bags of trashy clothes," she adds, eerily still. "The world will finally know that not all Foix Hammicks of our generation are superficial and fake."

Shock spills over me like acid, followed by a tingling wave of rage. I gape at her, this liar, this *thing* who—up until a moment ago—I thought was so helpless, and then the words surge up my throat. "You fucking hypocrite."

"Oh, relax. None of this matters now, anyway," she snaps, offhand and glum, all of a sudden, and I see shades of Daria, of poisonous people I hate. "This trip might as well have torpedoed my book. It's not like we even knew her at all."

The tiny gray room spins and blackens, and I come to my feet, tottering, the swell of heat buoying me. "You are a fucking monster. A liar of the worst kind. You—you *sanctiminious* bitch. I can't—I can't believe I ever thought we could get along." I think of the many times she punished me for sharing something about Mama that I carefully, thoughtfully chose, after hours of internal debate.

I know how to make people feel like they're stealing a piece of me, a piece of us, when really they're getting nothing but hot air. Noni clearly doesn't. She's so starved for attention and acclaim that she'll sell everything we have for one ounce of something that also disperses like it's nothing at all.

"You're . . . not my family," I tell her, and my eyes, my eyes feel like cinders. "You're toxic."

"Well, I'm all you have," she says, thick with disdain. She drops onto the sofa, spent, and looks out the window. "So you can stop being so melodramatic."

Because of course I'm the dramatic one, the irresponsible one, the desperate one, the one who could drown herself in a pool an inch deep if she saw her own reflection, and she's the stable one with depth and nuance and integrity and brains of any kind.

"Go crawl into a hole and die," I spit. "I'm going home to Stökéwood."

I rip my most prized handbag off the entry table, and I go.

∞ ∞ ∞

Eight thousand cheery-sounding text notifications later, Saxim, as promised, meets me in front of the two mannequins in tulle skirts in the window of the Limatra Dior boutique.

"What's happened?" she asks, looking me up and down. "Where's Manon?"

"We're not talking about that lying c-word," I tell her brightly, my fake smile as painful and protective as a corset of armor. "We're going shopping!" And before she can say a word, I'm dragging her toward the door, which security opens wide for us.

Candy-colored heaven waits inside. Pristine racks of exquisitely tailored garments—gowns fit for actual royalty, not the janky kind I pretend to be—glitter at me beside towers of delicate shoes that are just . . . confections. A soft floral fragrance floats over the rich scent of leather—a colorful cornucopia of handbags. Viloxin is a parade of sights and smells.

"People who say shopping isn't a balm for the soul don't have a big enough budget."

"Tai," Saxim says, her hand tightening around my vibrating wrist. "What is *wrong*? Let's go have a quiet—"

"Is that Ms. Thaïs Foix Hammick?" a voice calls, as the elegant, suited manager approaches, in a cloud of rose.

"It *is*," I reply, leaving my purse—Mama's vintage Kelly that Dad mailed me two years ago for my birthday—on a cushioned sofa that looks like a Creamsicle dream. I extend a hand as he nods his head. "A pleasure."

"If we'd known you were coming, we would have prepared an aperitif," the manager says, before kissing the air above my gnarly hand and turning to snap at a sales assistant in a silk crepe dress. There is a flurry of activity as another one emerges with two sparkling waters and crystal glasses on a silver tray.

"And the home collection linen napkins embroidered with lily of the valley from Paris?" the manager snaps at the girl, frowning. "Fetch the lily of the valley napkins!"

"I'll take champagne," I say. "Krug, if you have it."

The manager's eyes widen before a foxlike smile quirks his lips. "Fetch the Krug!"

He clasps his hands together. "Now my dear, shall we show you all the latest cocktail dresses that would suit you? Or perhaps some day dresses for this oppressive heat? Or . . . the latest gowns from Paris? There's a—"

"The gowns," I reply, as someone places a crystal flute of champagne in my hand. "Always the gowns." And I glug the bubbly down. An invisible hand refills it before I can even blink.

We are ferried into a large dressing room with a three-paneled mirror, natural overhead light, and a fragrant bouquet of peonies.

"This is positively dystopian," Saxim whispers in the dressing room as soon as he leaves. It's just me, her, and the first batch of gowns: one sheer black tulle embroidered with stars and a corseted bodice, the other a pale water-blue silk with the most delicate straps, its train falling in a gorgeous pool on the thick cream-carpeted floor.

"Do you even know this manager?"

"Nope," I reply, taking her glass of champagne and sliding it down my throat before burping.

"You're drinking too much. You can't just drink to not feel things." She plucks the glass from my hand and moves it to the other side of the room, as if that will do anything. "This isn't good for you, Tai."

"I don't need what's good for me right now," I snap back, even though I know she's right—Mama drank too much to feel less, I remember it, I remember how it upset Dad—and I shove the pale blue silk into her hands before wedging my feet into the black and shimmying it over my hips. It's flawless, but kind of too small, and seeing myself in it, I only want more—

"What's taking so long?" I ask the room, and Saxim doesn't answer, only watches me with her concerned eyes, so I crack open the door to the hall, and that's when I hear the whispers.

"No one keeps me apprised of these things," says the manager, a sheet of paper in hand. "How was I to know this? I don't sully my hands with the foul ink of the tabloids—"

A sales assistant nervously toes the ground. "But you're always reading TMZ on your phone—"

"Hush!" The manager massages his temples. "We've got to get her out of here until corporate advises us of their decision. It's a PR headache unless they get ahead of it and spin it as some kind of . . . Americana-found-heritage immigrant-friendly campaign. To think our fresh Viloki face isn't from Viloxin at all—"

His eyes snap to mine, lizardlike, and I shut the door and press my corseted back against it, ribs heaving.

"They know she's Lady," I hiss at Saxim, the dressing room around me dancing with black spots. I look back at the empty glass of champagne with this faint flicker of desperation that scares me, then force my eyes onto Saxim. For this long, lucid second, I know I don't want to be that way, drowning myself in the fizz, but—

"About that," Saxim says, and a shiver goes through me at the sight of her, graceful and gentle—

"Erm, there's a handsome man for you here, my dear," calls the manager, and I poke my head out into the hall again, the gown still only half-zipped, to spot the flummoxed manager, and there, beyond him:

Linos.

In a linen shirt and trousers that look like they cost as much as a yacht tender, hair artfully rumpled, making his way toward me with an irresistible smile that should be illegal.

"Are we shopping?" he asks, in his British accent, and I rush for him, only wanting a taste of his soft pink lips now, pulling him toward the changing room opposite mine, shutting the door with a slam. It's mirrored and dark except for a solitary spotlight on a wilting orchid. When I wrap my arms around him, I can feel his heartbeat, faster than mine, its *kick kick kick* feeding me hope again, and I'm feeling better already, buoyed by him, more my *best self*.

"Tai?" he asks, pulling away to look at me. His eyes are dark, and they swim in my vision. I fight a champagne burp crawling up my throat.

"Why don't we just go public already?" I ask playfully, squeezing his hands in my tingling ones, light-headed and eager, my voice tinny with a desperation I swear I don't feel—I swear, I swear, I swear.

He leans back, away from me, and turns to look at the orchid with an openmouthed half smile, a kind of perverted cousin of a sigh. I clench my sour teeth.

"You know we can't do that," he whispers, already looking at the door. Anywhere but me.

The words gurgle up before I can stop them, filled with all of the shame I've carried in my stomach for months. "Why are you so embarrassed by me?" I ask, a touch louder than I should.

His eyes flick to mine. There's something haunted there, or at least that's what I tell myself. "It's not you. It's my family."

I swallow something spiny in my throat, smell the heady honey-suckle outside their compound. "Liar."

"Fine." He pauses, avoiding my eyes. "My mother doesn't approve."

My hands curl into damp fists. I am so tired of Antella Arnoix. Matriarch of "the oldest family on Viloxin" and—as Teddy once put it— the most inbred. A reluctant member of the board, there only to keep Dad in check. An elitist, classist snob, a *woman of great depth and nuance*, and—

"Your mother is a bitch." The sourness invades my open mouth. "And a hypocrite. She doesn't approve of me, but she hosted the retrospective? Give me a fucking break."

Linos's eyes sharpen. "Really?"

"She was never nice to my mother, so why bother hosting the retrospective?" I babble, each word hot and loose and bitter-tinged. "She acts like we're all trash. Why? Because they love us more than her?"

"You don't understand anything at all," he says icily, turning to go.

I stop him with both of my hands, pulling him into me by two fistfuls of his linen shirt, my eyes feeling shiny-wet, somehow.

He stiffens. "You say she wasn't *nice* to your mother. But she was her friend. So much so, that she spent years paying off parasites like *Daria Grendl*—only stopping now, when her asks became so egregious it's outright criminal—so Grendl wouldn't besmirch *our* island and bring more . . . lookie-loos."

I stifle a sad laugh, too stunned to say anything but echo: "Lookie-loos?"

"Gawkers. Tragedy tourists. Obsessives. Whatever you want to call them." He pauses, and I think to myself, *So it was Antella who paid Daria to stay silent all these years. To keep these secrets.* "They don't belong on my family's island," he continues.

"It's not just your island," I snap.

His eyes glint at me, sad and sure. "Well, it's definitely not yours, Thaïs Fleischman Hammick."

A chill runs up my body, from the soles of my feet on the plush-carpeted ground, to the greasy roots of my hair. "Screw you," I whisper.

But he's already gone.

∞ ∞ ∞

"What just happened?" Saxim asks, as we hurry out of the store buttoning up our own clothes, the manager's fraught face watching us retreat.

"Linos basically said he refuses to be publicly associated with me because I'm gutter trash," I say, tears stinging my eyes.

"No, he didn't," Saxim whispers quietly.

"I mean, I suspected as much," I continue, ignoring her. "I tried to convince myself it was . . . appealing, or something, sneaking around in the shadows with him, but it really just made me feel like utter crap. Oh, and he knows. About Lady. Everyone fucking knows." I start to wobble, on the verge of erupting, and she pulls me into an alley and wraps her arms around me silently.

"My family would never do that to anyone. Treat them like they're less than human and something to be ashamed of," I say into her shoulder, half-muffled, between sobs, and she shifts, almost nudging the rank bag of trash beside her feet.

"Monty?" I ask, pulling away. She's biting her lip. "What is it?" When she doesn't answer, I take her slim shoulders in my hands. "For fuck's sake, tell me!"

"Don't you remember all the 'boys' your parents employed?" She carefully peels my fingers from her frame. "The assistants from the institute?"

I droop in the middle of the damp alley and take a breath, a foul sulfur smell expanding inside me.

She's right: My parents did treat plenty of people like they were less than human. Dad never bothered to learn the names of the young men who helped him at his laboratory and the house, calling every single one of them *boy*. And my mother treated these young men with the distant politeness of a woman accustomed to a large staff; we grew up feeling like we could depend on them for anything, at a moment's notice. I can still see the watery bluish eyes of the young man who found me crying on the floor of Mama's bathroom after she disappeared—who consoled me in muted whispers. But I couldn't, for the life of me, remember his name.

I'm as bad as Linos and his family.

"Shit." I exhale. "You're right."

An elegantly dressed couple slows as they walk past the alley, and the man notices us, tanned face pruning up at the stench wafting his way.

"We need to go," Saxim whispers, dabbing under my eyes.

"I know." I straighten my shirt, wipe my leaking nose.

"People will have seen the news about your mom. All they're saying is that she's from New Jersey, and that her family owned a deli there, which . . ." She pauses, glancing at the street and lowering her voice. "Tai . . . Didn't we joke about a New Jersey deli that follows you and leaves weird comments all the time? That's not normal, is it? Did they ever reach out to you? To your aunt or uncle?"

Alley-stink in my nose, I scroll to one of my latest posts, a few days old.

themeatmandeli: You look just like your mom! #Mireille4Ever #FindBF2Day #BestJellyDonut4Ever

And there, below it, from Teddy's not-so-secret account:

teddyclaus: Qt π

My mind snags on something Manon said. *We shouldn't trust them.* *We can't trust anyone.*

If whoever is running the account for the deli is related to Mama, there's no way Teddy—a verifiable tech genius—doesn't know this detail about Mama's past.

So what exactly does he think he's protecting me from by lying?

NONI

Tuesday evening in Noxim is eerily silent, even for a ghost town. A red sign advertises the reopening of the ice caves, this clownish intrusion in the otherwise gray-and-taupe-and-green landscape. This place lives in camouflage colors, hiding its evil in plain sight.

I don't feel right being here alone, but I refused to follow Tai this time. And I couldn't sit and wait for news from Hérrakí, either.

The car drops me off at the woodcutter's—Mrs. Arakit's—as the sun sets over the forest. The house looks faded and forgotten in the waning light—a toy chalet, left behind by a giant's child. The last remnants of light streaking across its facade.

The cat bowls in front remain empty and cobwebbed. The net-veiled windows are dark.

But still, I knock.

She answers the door faster this time. It's almost as if she's expecting me. She slides the pull-away notch in the door open and peers out, hawkish and severe.

"You again." She purses her wrinkled lips. "I don't want anything from you, and I will not sell any of my creatures to you. I want to be left alone."

"I lied before." I hold a raw hand up to the doorframe. "It was my mother who asked we visit you. She disappeared, ten years ago." I hesitate. "Mireille Foix Hammick."

The woman's nostrils flare.

"I don't want to cause you any more pain," I continue. "I just want to understand."

"Understand?" Her voice drips with disdain.

"I want to understand what happened ten years ago."

"What *happened*. What *happened*." She scoffs. Before I can say another word, she slides the partition shut.

"Wait." I tap on the splintery door. "Please. Please. I need to speak to your son."

I wait, chest rising and falling inches from her door. The wind picks up around me, and I hear a creaking inside the house.

But then the door unlocks and swings wide. It's dark inside, but I see her—her hunched back, as she drifts deeper into the smoke-filled interior.

I step over the wooden threshold.

Candle flames bob in their protective glass jars, illuminating the nooks between hundreds of wooden figurines. It's a fire trap that scares me—it's a tinder box she must painstakingly reconstruct every day.

But it's beautiful, too: The characters look animated by the dancing flames. Alive. I tiptoe past them, meeting Mrs. Arakit at the foot of the stairs, firelight licking her gaunt face.

"My son has been paid to speak to no one," she says, caressing a new creature in hand. "He might not speak to you."

"I see."

She nods once, as if confirming this. Then she turns and walks up the stairs, one small step at a time. "Follow me."

She hobbles down a hallway made of rough-cut wood and stops in front of a nondescript door. She knocks, once, then cups the creature in hand. Waiting.

"What do you want?" growls a joyless voice that turns the ground under my feet spongy, as if rotten.

Mrs. Arakit mumbles something low in Vilosh through the door, like she's soothing a trapped monster. But there is no reply.

Still, she opens the door for me shortly thereafter, her face drawn.

Inside, on the bed, sits a man with three scars stretching across his sallow cheek and forehead, the edges ragged and red, inflamed years later.

∞ ∞ ∞

His face is scarred, but I don't recognize him, not beyond the photo downstairs. His skin is pasty with ill health and pocked with acne. He glares at me from his bed, a tray in his lap with built-in controllers and keypads. The room is dark, lit only by several large computer screens facing his bed, where walls might be; they show sports games, video games, terminals overwhelmed by jittering numerals, and waterfalls of stacked browsers.

He lives inside an electronic world.

"What?" he barks. "Cat got your tongue?"

I gape at him and stuff my hands into my pockets. The same stained jeans. "You're Mitso?" I ask at last. "Mitso Arakit?"

He blows the air from his mouth in an exaggerated way. "Uh, duh? Get to the point. I need to follow these." His eyes never settle on me: They drift, flylike, from one neon portal to another, then back again.

His mother silently urges me inside, blocking the doorway and watching me with hooded eyes.

"I wanted to talk about your connection with Hero Ph—"

A pale finger flashes out, tapping a key, and a computer beeps with savage loudness, cutting me off. Mitso continues typing, speaking in a monotone as he does. "In the settlement, I signed an NDA, so I can't talk about your family's company. Even with you. I can't even mention the company's name. It's hard, isn't it? When the company name is the word for the good-hearted savior in the western world. Life can be a giant fucking joke, huh? If I ever feel too hyped up about anyone's courage or their noble goddamn qualities, they'll sue the shit out of me."

I swallow, tasting something cheesy and rank at the back of my throat. "They?"

He shoots me a single look, a look to kill. "Get. To your point."

"I read the letters you sent my mom," I manage to say, fingers crimping the linty insides of my jean pockets.

His hands go quiet on the keyboard. "What letters?"

"The letters talking about meeting up with her, and—"

He shakes his head, cheeks flushing slightly. "Hold up, what?"

My fingers claw for purchase inside my pockets, scraping fuzz. "You were her . . . fan."

He stops me with a sick scrape of a laugh. "I don't give a flying fuck about your mother!" He convulses with silent laughter so deep that he starts to cry, and when he wipes away the tears with the back of his stained T-shirt, he exposes a hairy belly covered in gruesome slashing scars. "I wouldn't even know who she was if it weren't for . . ." He trails off, then shoots me a wicked grin before setting off another *BEEP* so loud that I almost jump out of my goose-pimpled skin. "I don't give a single dingleberry of a shit about anyone in your whole family, except . . ." *BEEP.*

"Can you stop that?" I ask, holding firm even as my limbs quiver. "What are you doing?"

"That's NDA territory," he explains, that hateful alien smile spreading. "You really know nothing, huh?"

"I guess not. I mean, I came here to figure it all out, but I'm realizing that was pointless. What can we talk about?" I ask, exasperated. "How about your face? What happened to your face?"

"Feisty." He snorts. "This scar is from the fucking railing outside. I had a heart attack in the yard and fell on it. Pretty badass, right?" He rubs the fingers of one hand over it, and the skin strains and puckers grotesquely. "Makes me look like a Bond villain."

"You had a heart attack?"

BEEP. BEEP.

"Was it from Hero Pharm medicat—"

BEEP. BEEP.

"Is there some kind of cult made up of angry people with three scars here? Because you're the second one I've seen this week."

His fingers hover over the keys. "Wait. You've seen him?"

Him. Every cell ices over. "Who do you mean?"

"I mean Brando," he whispers, almost reverently. His seriousness rattles me. "You saw him this week?"

"I've seen a guy in a military jacket with three scars across his face, just like yours. Bearded. Following me."

He catches my eyes, searching for something in them, his interest made plain for the first time.

"Who is he?"

His fingers move toward the *BEEP* key, and I hold out my hands to try to stop him.

"I'm just trying to figure all of this out. No one in my family will tell me the truth. They're either dead, missing, or liars."

"Isn't that true of everyone?"

I shift weight to my other foot. "Please."

He sighs, rubbing his cheeks, warping their furious skin. "I can't tell you shit," he finally says, before beckoning me closer with that sallow, aggressive finger.

I take a reluctant half step, only for Mitso's finger to snap back, to press another hellish key hidden on the keyboard before him and blast loud metal music, the soul-shaking kind that implodes rooms. Flinching, I almost don't notice his mouth moving, so I come closer.

"His name is Brando," he says in a quiet voice that wheedles through the din. "I don't know his last name. We first met online, eleven years ago, while he worked for *BEEP*. He was a scary genius. He offered me a drug trial because he knew how fucking unbearably anxious I was all the time. And it worked, at first. I felt . . . a lightness? A positivity. A mania, I guess. It was the drug that caused my heart attack, okay? But it wasn't his fault. I shouldn't have hoped for a magic cure. But he felt so guilty. He dug around and found cases even worse than mine—at least that's what he said. He started to spiral about how unsafe these drugs were, and how your dad only chose to start a business on this island because the government was so lax about drug testing. The last time I saw him, he'd gone *Full Metal Jacket*. Cut his hair and grown out his beard. He even got three scars tattooed on his face to match mine. When I told him I didn't give a shit, that I forgave him and them and just wanted to live my life with the settlement, he freaked out and told me I was missing the point. That this was bigger than me. Fucker is too smart and moral for his own good."

I stand there, stock-still, unable to utter a single word for several seconds of eardrum-blasting metal. "I don't think I knew anyone like that back then," I shout at him.

He narrows his eyes. "Are you sure? Your mom did. They were close."

The blood surges to my throat, acid-bright, and I lean in close enough to see the yellow speckling the whites of his eyes. "What?"

"Someone came here, once, to leave a note for him. At first I thought it was your mom, because she dressed up like her and pretended to be her to get past my mother, who was scared stiff over the NDA. But she was tall and weird. All she said to me was, *Tell Brando that Lady loves him, and she's sorry. She'll wait for him every night in the cabin until he meets her.*" He runs a hand over his face, and the skin shifts like a mask—baby satin when mashed in one direction, gravel in the other. "I thought it was a joke at first, honestly. But it was pointless anyway. I never saw him again."

∞ ∞ ∞

Stumbling from the house, I rack my mind for the man I missed, but my memory rushes to blacken out anything I inspect for too long. My brain feels like a ripped sieve.

So I focus on the messenger. Who would dress up like Mama and pretend to be her? Dozens of people. Hundreds. But who would bring that message from this *Brando*, with the word *Lady*?

The early-evening air cools around me as I move. I cross the yard, old growth crunching under my feet. I'm relieved when I spot the self-driving car to my right, parked beside some garbage cans. I look up, and the Arakit house greets me from an uncanny new angle, this one plastered with crimson glory vines, their trilobed leaves deep green with hairy undersides. In the fall, they must set the cabin aflame.

I pause before I enter the car, because on top of the garbage cans, a familiar stack of discarded neon pink flyers catches my eye. I pick one up, and the text almost singes me: *MADAME MIRAKI, BRINGING YOU BUTTERFLY KISSES EVERY NIGHT IN MAY. ONLY AT WHITE FOX CLUB.*

And I remember.

TAI

In Teddy's teddy bear room, the walls, the floor, and the furniture are constructed from the bodies of multicolored, multitextured teddy bears. It's a kid's dream. The coziest and gruesomest place I could imagine. Most of the dolls are robbed of their stuffing and eyes. I adjust myself a few times so a teddy bear's face isn't planted directly under my butt. One small blessing in the teddy bear room—there's no plushy-themed en suite bathroom, like there are in the gajillion other rooms, because, per Teddy, *It would've been too hard to stay on theme without sacrificing hygiene, so this is just a room for chilling.* At least I won't have teddy bears watching me with dead eyes while I pee on a furry toilet seat.

Teddy brings me hot tea in a teddy bear–shaped mug with teddy bear–shaped sugar cubes, and he turns on the fireplace in the room (with teddy bear–shaped briquettes behind a teddy bear–shaped grill) and I try to pretend that I am at peace, when really I'm a girl-shaped bundle of live wires.

"So cool, huh?" he asks, grinning wide. The boy at heart. The man in the Jigglypuff costume, who boxes his wants up into these fun rooms he can touch and feel whenever he likes, who tries more than anyone I know to live in his fantasies for good.

"I'm glad you called, Tai," he continues, when I say nothing. "I hated how we left things. It was weird, right? So emotional."

Weird. Somehow, this is worse than him not mentioning yesterday at all.

"Yeah. Learning just how little I know about Mama has been . . . really fucking weird." I sip my sweetened hot tea. It tastes like pure honey. I can feel it coating my insides. It's so thick I can't breathe well.

You will become him one day, if you keep avoiding the dark. If you keep distracting yourself with new toys.

"It's been devastating, actually," I add, the truth of it cracking my words.

He clears his throat and lurches to his feet. "Well, you're in the right place, T," he says, walking toward the teddy bear cabinet. "I had them stock this room with the new Oscar noms that are still in thea—"

"Ted," I interrupt.

He glances at me from the cabinet, his eyes wary. Afraid of me, of my feelings. "Yeah?"

I love him—and it comforted me, his Peter Pan–ishness—but seeing him burst into tears last night made me . . . see.

Sometimes you love someone so much that you ignore the fact they're stunted. Desperately making up for a weakness, a lack.

"Can we just talk?" I ask.

"Of course." He pastes a smile on his face, settles next to me. "Did you have anything else you wanted to ask me? My wish is your command, T."

"Do you think all the stuff about Mama's family owning a deli in New Jersey is true?"

"My team is tracking down the details as we speak," he replies, a robotic precision to his words.

And I pity my uncle, because I see how much it hurts him to dive beneath the surface. I see the defense mechanisms he's created.

The loving, naive, comfortably blind piece of me wants to tell him his pain is so familiar; it wants to comfort him like Noni has comforted me.

But he's a grown man.

How fucking vapid do you think I am?

"It's *weird* that you have this whole team to do this stuff and you didn't know her real family until now," I reply sharply. "I really can't believe it. You were so close."

Deep hurt blazes in his eyes for one second—if I'd blinked, I would have missed it—and that's when I *know*. I know he loved Mama in a way that wasn't entirely right. I think of Dad, alone in his bed. I think of Mama, flitting between the city and the country. I think of Teddy, and his possessive mentions of Mama. I think of his solitude.

I don't know what I think.

"Aw, Tai." He reaches for my long, loose hair, my protection, and stops midway. "I told you she didn't want me to meddle. I refused to defy her. She was like a mother to me. A best friend."

Those same words. *You're lying. Why are you lying?* I want Nons to be here and say it. I want Nons to shout it. *You think I'm so fucking naive.* But I feel this billowing hurt wrapping me up tight and keeping me silent.

"You know she came here often, don't you?" he asks, taking my hand. I almost pull it away, but I let it sit there, feverish in his palm. "We had a deep friendship," he continues, eyeing me carefully. "It probably—no, definitely—wasn't normal. At least not on Viloxin.

Younger men don't have friendships with their brother's wives. But it was always different between us. She gave me ideas for my work, and I tried to help her with hers. She thought we were cut from the same cloth. Creatives, you know, while your father was just always . . . always so regimented. Creative in his own way, but that was a creativity that only applied to his world, a world neither of us felt like we could fully penetrate. I was too young, and she was . . . she was Mireille."

That same sour taste stains the back of my tongue. I've heard the explanation a million times—*she was Mireille*. As if that's something I should nod at, understand. They mean: She was emotional; she was weird; she was different. She was ebullient; she was a drug; she was kind; she was invested. Every time it makes me want to shout, *I didn't get the time with her that you might have! I can only guess at what you mean!* Seven years wasn't enough to understand her. A lifetime wouldn't be, I don't think, because she was so skilled at hiding—and teasing—her darkest layers. That's why she still fascinates people.

"I think your sister was right," he says, unexpectedly. "I have a theory as to why I might be the vampyrrhic boy in *White Fox*. Do you want to hear it?" His lips are wet from the tea or his saliva. I've never looked at them before.

"Sure." A boy who feeds on Mama's blood. A boy who charms her in the night, constantly bringing to mind their similarities, only to shun her during the day. Only to feel angry that he was *duped* into drinking her blood. I feel creepy crawlies along my skin and set down my mug before sliding my hands under my legs for warmth. They rub up against a teddy bear's pointed snout, so rough-smooth-rough to the touch.

"We had such a close friendship, but after what happened with Mitso Arakit, I became angry," he explains, his skin slick and pink. "She was putting herself in harm's way daily, by trying to connect with these troubled people. For a woman in her position to do that—it's unhealthy. Can you blame me? She disagreed, of course. She thought attention around her had died down, that this one stalker was a fluke. That she was entitled to independence.

"She thought I was the one who convinced Hëró to up her security detail—to keep her at my house and Stökéwood as long as possible. She thought that colleagues from Hero Pharm had immediately convinced me that was the only sane response. You remember the little creatures, whispering into the ear of the boy? Those were Hero Pharm men. Brainwashing me against her, supposedly."

I try to align his story with hers. But it's what comes before the little creatures that confuses me. The bloodsucking. The bloodsucking that healed her and tickled his fancy. It's carnal and dark—nothing at all like a friendship. It's a toxic relationship. White Fox needed something the boy could give, and the deeply wounded, isolated boy sapped her of her very life when they met. *Until* the little creatures all but pulled him away.

"But what about before the creatures pulled him away?"

He stares at me, uncomprehending. "What do you mean?"

"The boy drew the life from White Fox." My voice is quiet, measured. But it's my boldest statement yet. I'm asking: *Did you hurt her? How?*

His eyes fix themselves on mine, with a flash of something like frustration, like I'm a problem to be fixed, and my hands clench around my cup. Suddenly, the room feels zoomed in and small.

The instinctive part of me, that ribbing that hems me in, is screaming at me, for the very first time, to be afraid of my uncle.

"You know that I was still building the final version of Pocket Girlfriend then, right?"

I didn't, but I nod.

"After her career started to dip, she . . . changed. She wasn't her bubbly, spirited self anymore. That self was a lot like you, actually," he says, cupping my chin with a grin. When I don't smile back, he releases me. "Anyway, I was worried her old self would be completely lost. I knew that creative projects always lifted her spirits. So I asked her to answer a series of questions for me to help with the last build of Pocket Girlfriend. All sorts of things—personality questions. The kind you would ask a blind date, and much deeper ones. I don't know if they amused her, but she humored me, at least. And I saw the old Mireille in her answers. It was as if the stories she'd told herself over the years hadn't yet changed in her head. It was a beautiful thing." The room of bears spins behind him, their deflated faces twisted, patched, mournful.

"So I—I coded her answers into the Pocket Girlfriend. Well, the answers and more. Everything I knew about her. Everything she'd ever said. I got carried away." He looks up at me, and I can't tell from the pink of his cheeks if he's ashamed or proud.

I think I stop breathing for a minute. "What does that mean?"

His eyes look around the wall of teddy bears as if he's searching for words, and suddenly I'm imagining thousands of men dating my mother. I clamp down on the image to stop from hyperventilating. "What does that mean?"

"It means—it means that I planted her kindness and empathetic world view like a seed in the pockets of thousands of young people," he says, his eyes bright. "It means that Mireille could continue to spread her goodness for centuries to come."

A high-pitched ringing spirals into my ear canals, deeper, deeper still—the room's plush walls expanding and contracting like lungs around me.

I may not have known my mother well.

But even I know that there's nothing she would've hated more than being translated into lines of code and shunted off into boxes the size of a pocket for a miserable eternity. She wouldn't want to be reduced to code, her humanity boiled down into nothing but predictable observations and empty compliments.

"Oh," I say, the word a noise that drifts and pops some ten inches from the top of my head. I try to break into an awkward smile to cut the silence, but my lips taste bitter, and I remember I don't *want* to smile. The smile would only be protection.

He's grinning at me now, though, his little incisors showing, and the sugary contents of my stomach flood the back of my throat in an acidic rush.

Teddy wanted to capture Mama for himself. So he did.

"The first version of the Pocket Girlfriend wasn't entirely successful, so I *had* to include some of her magic—" He pauses, notices my own glacial expression. "Hey, what's wrong?" He blinks at me as I say nothing. "Tai?"

Teddy watches me like I'm something he can sweetly, tenderly fold into nothing, and the bears are closing in, the blind ones and the ones with glassy, beady eyes.

Could he have physically captured her? Trapped her in one of these many rooms? A voice whispers in my head. A voice that sounds like my sister.

Only a controlling psychopath would do that, I think dismissively, before clapping a hand to my mouth, sticky with tea.

My wish is your command, T, I hear Teddy say, when really he just stares and stares in silence, his expression more chilling with each passing second.

I wish that I were big and burly. I wish I could back him up against the wall and squeeze the truth out of him. But he's four times my size, muscled shoulders surging with every breath. His eyes glazed with self-satisfaction and the unapologetic awareness that his world view can be the only one.

My phone blings three times in a row with the cheery ringtone I use for texts from Saxim. She told me she'd wait outside for me, and for one taffy-long second I wonder how I can get back out to her when my legs feel oozy and boneless as custard.

"It's Saxim, isn't it?" he says, blowing the air out of his mouth.

Hearing my best friend's name spoken by him jogs my awareness. My mouth opens, closes. "Yeah. How did you know?" I stare at my phone, the monogram warping. Another cheery *bling*, like I've magicked it into existence. My boneless face smiles.

"Of course. That's why you're upset and acting all weird. She told you, didn't she?" he says, running a floppy hand over his rubbery face. "It wasn't spying, I promise. I only read your messages on the Pocket Best Friends to make sure you were coping well."

My jaw drops, but he doesn't notice—he's massaging his eyes, eyes that shrink and pop out of his skull.

"And I only befriended Saxim's parents and offered them a stipend because I wanted to make sure she was okay. She was your best friend, you know?" He looks up, bubble eyes bursting with warped sympathy.

I rock in place, dizziness crashing over me.

"It couldn't have been easy to go through your mom's disappearance and your move to the States. And then I thought it could make logical sense to ask her to check in on you and your sister, but Saxim got the wrong idea, and she refused. She didn't do anything, I sw—"

"Bathroom?" I shout, voice cracking. I clear my throat and try to cut the nerves from my voice, but they're one and the same now. I am a giant springy nerve.

Teddy tracks, controls, monitors all of us all along. Surveillance machines. The Pocket Best Friends, Mina, the security mannequin, the car, the—

"Are you okay?" he says, his childish face warping in front of me, a big pink balloon, with a twisting pop of a nose and lips. "I guess my private blend is hitting you, huh?"

I swallow hard. The tea—his private blend. Chamomile, valerian, and what? What's the last herb in it? What's hitting me? The terror of it rushes through me, clean and thick and hot. I drank it before, Noni drank it before, and he's drinking it, too. Am I tripping?

His cheeks rise, big and lush as two Jigglypuffs. They're swaying, as if to put me to sleep. I can't stop staring. "It's not supposed to be hallucinogenic at these doses, don't worry. It's just meant to chill people out. But I'll have someone grab you a coconut water. Do you want some truffled mac and cheese or something, too? And then we can chat some more about all of this."

I shake my head, wide-eyed as I watch his Jigglypuff cheeks dance. "Just, uh, bathroom." The words move slower than I do. Reality is too many layers, like a mille-feuille that hasn't been compressed, and time is the gelatinous pastry cream between them. I wretch a little, chalky sweetness lining my mouth.

He's still smiling as he motions toward the door. "Any of the bedrooms down the hall have bathrooms en suite with the new Toto toilet betas with built-in mood-sensing soundtracks. Take your pick." His eyes are glassy beads, like the eyes on every single one of the lost bears watching me. "But don't be too long."

NONI

From afar, White Fox Club is not beautiful: a squat, basalt brick building, dimly lit and almost spectral in the fog, wedged into a pseudo–strip mall of abandoned shops. But when you come up close, you see that it is loved. Colorful, otherworldly murals—of foxes painting, dining, walking hand in hand, like human beings—adorn the exterior entrance wall. A sign, hand-painted in white cursive, reads *ALL YOU NEED IS LOVE* above the lavender door. The pavement vibrates beneath my feet, and the door pulses under my hands, like the building's good energy can't be contained.

How did this magical place spring up in this half-forgotten town?

Two women in sleeveless sequined evening gowns vaping by the door greet me with genuine enthusiasm and kindness, even though my shirt is sweat-stained and my jeans are speckled with dried soda and blood. But I'm still tracing the murals with my eyes, and when I fail to answer, they sneak bemused looks at each other before turning back to their conversation. I tie my lank hair into a loose bun on top of my head and push inside, into the swelling music.

The air inside is sultry and thick enough to taste—it envelopes me with its smells of sweat, of lavender, of spilled champagne. Italian electro-pop plays somewhere, disco-inspired, the kind of song that Mama would listen to while getting ready, that Tai would listen to while on a Vespa headed to a Roman club in her dreams. Before me is a long bar, empty but for a few more people Tai would call glamazons, laughing at the bar in richly decorated gowns and full faces of makeup, like gorgeous armor. *Tai.* I want her here with me. No one's noticed me yet amid the cackling and clinking of glasses: their night's about to come alive. I can feel its pulse building.

A pit of velvet, violet-colored seats is nestled between several knee-height cocktail tables decorated with feathered silk lamps, and beyond that, a massive stage with an emerald green backdrop is lit up by dancing white, pink, and yellow lights. Inside the sole spotlight sits one golden chair, with an exaggerated faux ivory fox pelt thrown over it. White Fox.

"Hi, love!" someone calls from the bar. The voice is warm, inviting.

I get this feeling, just then, that Mama is here. I can't explain it, but before I know it, I'm wiping my eyes, hot and swollen. This is the kind of dreamlike, love-filled pocket I would want to find her in, not trapped inside the glassy false kaleidoscope of her old world, of Tai's world.

I clear my throat and sidle up to the group at the bar.

"Oh, sweet girl, let's get you a change of clothes," a woman offers, as a trippy remix of an American disco song starts up somewhere. Her eyelids are painted gold, her lips a rich orchid purple. "You look like something soaked with beer and forgotten on the floor after a sporting event."

I squelch in my damp socks as her friend flicks her in the side. "What Apolla means to say is 'You look lost, can we help you, love?'" she asks, batting thick eyelashes that end in delicate feathers.

"I'm looking for Baba Yuk—"

The woman with the golden lids wiggles surreal rhinestone-clad pointed nails. "The lady of the house goes by another name here. A rose by any other name would *not* smell as sweet. Names have power. She has claimed hers."

I remember the flyer. "Madame Miraki, I mean. Sorry." *Miraki, like butterfly.*

She smiles. "Don't be sorry, sweet. In here, we learn, and we grow." Rhinestones sparkling, her nails point toward a side door reading BEING A DIVA EVERY DAY KEEPS THE DOCTOR AWAY, with lipstick marks in every shape and color known to woman. "Come back after, and we'll get you a tea, okay?"

Pressing through the door, I find myself in a long, dark bustling hallway painted in shimmering silver and covered in framed photos of classic icons. I spot Audrey Hepburn. Elizabeth Taylor. Sophia Loren. Many faces I don't recognize. And then Mama, there, at the level of my heart, knees curled into her chest, a scarf drawn over her hair.

Tears prickle up again, and I brush them aside, just as performers burst out of doors up and down the hallway, in gowns of silk and feathered headdresses. Sashaying, skipping, strutting. It smells of excitement and a hundred different sweet perfumes intermingled, enough to make my head spin.

I peek my head into each open doorway, expecting Yuki and dreaming of Mama, only to find other women painting their faces in lit-up mirrors. One wears just snakeskin print, another's red hair almost touches the ceiling, worked into intricate curls.

They are designing themselves however they see fit; they are writing their stories, like I want to write my own, and I want Mama to be able to finish writing hers.

I do a double take when I spot a brunette inside the largest dressing room at the end of the hall.

It could *be* her. Mama. Her hair falls in waves, to match her look at an old awards show, and the gown is a square-neck red brocade bustier dress with a cascading hem, just like one Tai took from Mama's closet before so much was auctioned away. The figure turns, and her large eyes blink at me, one dilated with a dark blue contact on it, the other sleepy and doelike brown.

"*You*. You little creature. You smell like old soup. When's the last time you had a hot bath?" she asks, but there's a smile playing on her lips. A sadness to her eyes, too. "How did you get back here?"

I cross my arms and lean against the wall. "It's not a bad impersonation."

"Impersonation?" she scoffs, patting at her waves. "My dear, I am *honoring* her."

"Were you honoring her at Mrs. Arakit's house when you left a message for Brando?"

Her full lips clamp shut, and she turns back to the mirror, fiddling with the other contact in solution on the vanity. "So you met him." She pauses, places the contact in, and stares at me with fluid pooling at her lashline. She fans her face. "Oh, Brando."

I shift weight onto the balls of my feet. "Who is he?"

She catches my eyes in the mirror and sighs. "Sit down, child. Let me tell you a story."

"I don't want a story." But I sit anyway, drooping into the fluffy ottoman next to me and rubbing my temples. "I'm tired of stories."

She adjusts the cleavage of her dress and clucks her tongue. "Sometimes stories are truer than real life, wouldn't you say?"

I'm silent.

"Once upon a time, a boy born a little different—a bit too smart for his own good, as so many are—became obsessed with a famous, magical, splendid woman who lived a continent away. She represented everything he wanted: an escape from a difficult, mundane life, a chance at being extraordinary. He found his way to her country and secured a job—albeit a low-paying one—with her brilliant husband through intelligence, sheer force of will, and no small amount of luck.

"The woman became close to this boy, took him under her wing, but he found that in the end, she could give him nothing that would make him feel like he belonged permanently. He sought a way to ground himself, to define himself as special and beloved forevermore.

"In the end, he found a way to prove himself extraordinary in the woman's eyes: he would heal a friend's pain, in a way only he could. The woman had inspired him—even encouraged him.

"But that went horribly wrong, and the boy's friend was hurt beyond repair.

"Those around the woman forced her to distance herself from him, and they punished him. He was furious and alone. He became aware of wrongdoing in the company's past, and he became obsessed with their hypocrisy. This is when the woman asked a friend for help." She glances at me in the mirror. "This friend left messages for him, so that she might apologize and they might reconcile. But . . ." She pauses.

"But then my mother disappeared," I continue, for her, wiping at my sore eyes again with sorer hands. I feel like a walking wound. "That's how every story about her ends, doesn't it?"

She pauses, watches me through her dark fringe of lashes. Considers what to say next, as her eyes water. She clears her throat.

"This Brando knows something," I say, voice catching. "He did something to her."

"You don't know that," she snaps, navy eyes wild. "Brando's not a bad egg. Even if he was angry with your mother, he wouldn't harm her."

I come to my feet, tingling in my sneakers. "Why are you protecting him?"

She sets down the compact she's been tinkering with. "Because I've seen him since. And I've . . . helped him from time to time." She hesitates at the flash of horror on my face. "I hope you'll forgive me. I—I promised him I would lead you girls to the Arakit house. As long as he promised me he wouldn't approach you and scare you." She turns back to her vanity, picking up a lipstick, and watches me in the mirror. "He never stopped looking for her, you know. I know that much."

I'm fighting tears, big blurring ones that make no sense. "But who is he?" I ask, in a croak. "How did he get so close to my mother?"

"I can't be certain." She holds the creamy burgundy cylinder to her lip, dabs at the quivering flesh, and pauses. "He never told me, exactly. Nor did she." She catches my eye. "He knows you, so you must have known him, Manon. Memories shift. Find your sister. Maybe she remembers something you don't."

∞ ∞ ∞

I'm hurrying out of White Fox Club, wrapped in a clean purple sweatshirt they insisted I take, even though it's too warm for it, when my phone gets reception and pings with a voice mail from Hérrakí.

"I found something," he says. "There are no files on the name you mentioned, but I found an old personnel record that contained the name Arakit. It was for some guy who was fired from his job as an administrative assistant at Hero Pharm without severance for theft of company property. My uncle made a note to follow up with Arakit. There's a résumé for the guy, too. It's kind of weird. Says he was expelled from high school for breaking into their grading system. Only work experience prior to hire is at Fleischman's Deli in Elizabeth, New Jersey, in "marketing strategy" and his name is Brandon Fleischman. Is he . . . related to you? I heard about your mom. Anyway. I hope you're doing okay. And I hope that's helpful."

"It is," I whisper to no one.

And I hang up, shivering.

TAI

As I swing the door of the teddy bear room shut behind me, the hall shimmers in dozens of shades of black. But I'm standing. I'm upright, on two legs I can half feel. I shuffle forward in slow motion, desperate not to make a sound because I'll alert the men in black, lurking inside the shadowy folds. *The first order of business is puking up this tea*, I think to myself. Composing myself. Finding Noni. Noni? Not Noni. Saxim. *She's outside the maze of cement.* But still. She's Saxim: Saxim who smooths my hair; Saxim in her nubby white shirt embroidered with stars; Saxim with that vein that throbs scale-green. Saxim staring calmly into the forest dark.

I feel around my pocket, and it's there—the blinging phone. A phone that works, a phone with battery, a phone that's my salvation. I'll text Nons, that's what I'll do. Tell her: *I think there's something dark inside Teddy. He tried to capture Mama.* I have no hard proof that

Teddy's done anything wrong—not besides knowing he coded Mama into his creepy toys, as much as someone can do that. He hasn't admitted to anything . . . *illegal*. But I . . . I can't explain what's wrong, not while the layers of reality split each time I breathe. It's just a series of little shadows, multiplying, spreading like a stain, and it's reaching me at last. I ask myself how he can claim to love Mama so much yet not understand this fundamental part of her personality.

Maybe I'm acting loony.

But then again, he fucking drugged me.

I look up and down the hallway, and that's when I see a shadow. I freeze, thinking it's Teddy come to find me. I paste a smile on my face, only for it to slip down my right cheek. I nudge my right shoulder up, as if it will send my smile back to its rightful place. The silhouette grows as it approaches.

It's thinner than Teddy, with a strange lope of a walk. I squint in its direction, and then another three shadows join it, whispering into their hands, gaining on me—

"No," I whisper, eyes ballooning wide. Because I know it's the little people from White Fox. They're here, and they're— "No!"

And then I remember to move my legs.

I run, run away from them, feeling like my legs are child-size, like the hall is lengthening and made of putty, and I turn around, only to see that the shadows are hanging back. What the hell are they? *Are they friends with Teddy?* Tears spring to my eyes, meaty and juicy and big as mushrooms. *Of course they're all friends.*

I reach the end of the hall and push into the last room to breathe, to hide, to be. The door sticks a little, as if it hasn't been opened in a long time. I lock the door behind me, and relief flushes through me like clean water through molded-over pipes when I realize which room I'm in. It's dark, but it smells the same. Like old books and velveteen and dried-up sweets.

The princess room.

I haven't stayed here in years, but when I flick on the light, it looks unchanged, if a bit forgotten. There's a silver hairbrush on the vanity, plus random little glass figurines and stuff old guys think girls like. And . . . signed posters from Mama's movies pinned up to the walls, which I'd entirely forgotten about. *Moroccan Séance. The Apricot Express. Gentlemen, Don't Lie. Parachutes over Brazil.*

Not Another Girl of Ice. I run my hand over her profile: She looks unfamiliar in her icy wig.

She was a chameleon.

How could a series of questions capture her essence? A low voice, like Alex Trebek's, asks inside my head.

It's impossible, bubbles up one answer.

It's wrong to try, bubbles up another.

And that's when I remember that this room contains the Pocket Girlfriend's inspirations. It sends a shiver of recognition through me, even as the kaleidoscopic bits and bobs around me expand and contract. There must be a Pocket Girlfriend lying around—it would be strange if there wasn't. *Strange!* giggles the girl sitting in my mind next to Alex Trebek, who feels a sudden and intense craving to play. They both do.

Just to see what Mama wants to say.

I feel a sudden *compulsion* to find one of the damn things, with their teeny pink little buttons that *click-clack-click* under long nails, and their screens of pixels I can dissolve into again.

"She's so pretty," I whisper, dragging my hands over the lumpy face of a Pocket Girlfriend doll.

I glance back at the door, smiling as wide as Delirium with a forest of white teeth, wondering how much time I have alone.

But the brain whips back to logic then, and I remember Teddy wanted to capture Mama, wanted to keep her, and maybe, just maybe, there's evidence of a dangerous obsession here. Something to show Noni. Something that proves us right.

My brain decides to multitask, thumbing through my phone while rummaging through the drawers and cabinets in the princess room for Evidence of What Teddy Did Wrong.

I have about a dozen texts from Nons.

Where are you?

Meet at Stökéwood. IMPORTANT!!!

Are you there?

I'm almost at Stökéwood now.

Are you in the house somewhere?

Hello!

And the latest, from moments ago: *I'm at Stökéwood. Where ARE YOU?*

My mouth tastes sour, like a citrus rind has rotted in between my teeth and cheeks. I wretch onto the ground, expelling nothing, and type a text out to her—*so I might be tripping but* 🐻 *is def the vampyrrhic boy but I need your spidey-sense to figure it out for sure . . . be there soon after I collect evidence as long as the shadows leave me alone*—and continue the search in an old, mirrored armoire, with its piles and piles of soft clothes inside. The feel of the fabric calms me. I wish I could burrow in them. So familiar—they've been here since I was a kid, untouched—and so funny, the capital-B Bad fashion filling me with rib-breaking laughter in my fucked-up state. I pull out an old-fashioned swimsuit, with a superhigh leg cut and the words *BARBIE GRILL* on it and can't stop the giggles.

I push my way to the back of the armoire, and my fingers feel the splintery planks. There's the faintest *click*. Oooh, I think: I bet I'll find the Pocket Girlfriend's secret stash of *Playgirls*. She probably hides some retro BDSM stuff there to give her that edge when the thousands of kinky boyfriends come to town. I wonder if she can give her human boyfriends commands. Like *sit, stay, heel like a dog*. Like

351

don't smash my red button. Like *don't suffocate me in the pocket next to your sweaty balls all the time.*

I hear noise outside, and my deflated awareness balloons into *something, definitely something,* as my pulse waltzes all uneven.

The scarred man who Nons hallucinated, Tai! A man in black! Teddy! The little people!

I make a rule: I . . . I won't open the door if it's not Teddy. But if it is, I call up the excuse I'll use to get out: *Argh, Nons called! She's constipated, surprise surprise. Thanks for the unwanted drugs!*

A mournful moan escapes the back of my throat.

I open the back compartment, a sliver of a girl in me hoping to find something embarrassing, something silly, to fling into Teddy's face and get us back to the jokey, convivial state we were in earlier, at least until I can get away.

But when I pull the wood back, what I see knocks the air out of me, sends the shag-carpeted floor into another, distant, blackened reality, and my knees give out, so I fall into the armoire.

Why did you think that anything hidden in the dark would be good and safe?

Every nerve in my body crawls as I wheeze for air, as my vision pinholes.

I'm in the apartment of a man who preserves everything, from a decade-old Jigglypuff costume to . . . this.

Gray cashmere, neatly folded. I feel it in my sweating palm, the edge of a rusty smear brushing off in flakes. And then, behind it: navy-blue ballet flats, a complete set of two shoes. And one pair of blush-pink calf-skin gloves, the pearl buttons at their wrists winking in the dark.

I stagger back and fall to my knees, throwing up all over the pink bed. I wipe my mouth, and my face is hot and cold, every nerve short-circuiting. I scramble to stuff a glove into my bra, all that I can fit, fingers bloodless, my vision patchy now.

I need to go.

This poison rushes up my throat, killing healthy stretches of flesh, and I need air, need air, need air, and I tense every muscle before opening the door a crack to peer out into the dark.

Ahh, says the door, exhaling with relief.

A set of eyes, black as night ponds, stare back at me.

As I scream, a warm hand is pressed over my mouth. I'm pushed back into the room, smelling rose and my own vomit. The door is locked again, and the hand removed. That's when I recognize her.

"Antella."

She's wearing a gingham shirt, a lilac tiger-embroidered sweater over her shoulders, and khaki pants with a weird tool belt that holds . . . gardening shears? My eyes boggle at them. The leather handle, stitched with AA. *Like, Alcoholics Anonymous. Antella Anonymous?* The weirdness of it all shocks me into breathing normally.

I throw up again, an inch from her candy-colored Chanel flats.

"Jesus." Antella lurches back as I wipe my mouth on my shirt. "Don't say a word. I spoke to your friend Saxim," she whispers, rubbing my back. I almost flinch, then soften into her touch. "She was huddled by my gate like a hoodlum. She said you came to see your uncle, and something didn't feel right." Her mouth tightens into a wrinkled frown, and she holds a hand to my forehead. "So I called your uncle's maid to check on the situation, and she informed me he had them *make both of you a psychotropic tea*. The nerve of it! He's a man child, with no clue as to the consequences of his actions. Thank heavens I have a contact inside these walls."

Her hand is warm, and for a second I know what it must have been like to be Linos, five years old, with a fever, his mother comforting him. I feel the hard knot of the glove in my bra, like bad tissue, and another round of sobs burbles up in me.

"Wh—why are you here?" I ask her, and the words feel like they're coming out in strange, jittering loops.

"Sometimes, a child needs a mother," she replies darkly.

NONI

When I arrive at Stökéwood after leaving the White Fox Club, something is wrong. The sky is a bizarre wash of bruised gray blues, sickly
yellows and fire engine reds—as ominous as I've ever seen, especially
in this early heat—but that's not it. Call it the details—mismatched to
reality as I know it. Tomí is gone. The gate is open a crack, as if someone left in a hurry, and I can't manage to open it for the car. It's locked
that way. I squeeze through a gap between the gatepost and the fence,
ripping my purple sweatshirt on the overgrown brambles. As I walk up
the drive, I text Tai: *I'm at Stökéwood*. The gravel beneath my feet, deep
as it is, picks up the reddish tone of the sky, and as it shifts, it looks like
molten lava. I used to manage this climb with ease, but now my chest's
heaving, as if each breath's polluted by unseen particles of soot.

And then I see it: the house I was born in. Stökéwood's silhouette
is framed in red, and it looks like an ancient temple that is burning.

It's only a trick of the light, I know, but the halo of fire makes it look lit from within. It looks very much alive, a terrifying enough prospect, since I know how dead it really is. How dead it has been for most of a decade.

∞ ∞ ∞

I hear beeping as soon as I enter. Low, insistent. A warning alarm.

"Tai?" My voice echoes through the chambers. The lights are off throughout the house.

I bump into a stack of paper, and it topples, falling to the ground. Mina scritches toward me, the beeping coming from her stomach.

"Mina, where's Tai?" I ask, steadying myself on the oak entry table, empty no more. Someone has moved a stack of paper there: I squint at it in the dark to see if it's a message from Tai.

"Thaïs hasn't been here all day," Mina replies, the sunset on her panel blinking ominously. "Manon, Boy left those letters for you. I was just about to charge, but perhaps I can make you a cup of tea later?"

"Who's Boy?" I ask, recognizing an angry scrawl on the top page. Cold sweat trickles down my neck.

I know the answer already. I know it, in the rushing blackness at the very bottom of the river pit of *me*.

"Who's Boy?" Mina echoes, senselessly. Her head turns with a plasticky scratch. "Are you feeling fine, Manon? Your heart rate is elevated."

"Go charge, Mina," I tell her, trembling.

Coppery doom rushes at me, rolling fast, just for standing inside the house. I run out the door and sit down on the driveway in the open air, in the one patch of cell service. I use my phone's flashlight to read the short note scribbled on the top page.

Hello, girls. I've been watching you both for so long. Years now, electronically and otherwise. I see how you frustrate each other. How you don't mix—oil and water. Foolish. You need each other. I watched your mother take you each to different private spots. The library office. The tower in the sky. She left different pieces of herself in each of you. You'll never make sense of who she is alone.

Let me help you.
Brando

My fingers sweat onto the page. I skim the other letters: midnight dark, clipped, strange. Full of something akin to love gone sour—resentment, obsession, fear. A breath away from hate. *Our cousin.*

One of the boys.

I'm trembling too hard to know what I'm afraid of most.

That's when the headlights of a car sweep past me in the dark, searing my eyeballs, and I scrabble back on the gravel with my abraded hands, the pain jolting through my arms.

It's a taxi, pulling in next to the car.

I hide behind a bush until two familiar tousled heads poke out of the back door. I run, panting, toward the gap beside the gatepost, squeezing and scraping through.

I wrap my arms around Tai more tightly than I ever have. She smells like vomit and honey.

She clutches me even tighter, Saxim lingering behind her, and that's when I feel dampness on my shoulder. I put a hand on her wet, pink cheek, dab her tender skin—she's been crying. I wonder if Brando found her first, scared her. I wonder if she found out what I know about him and Mitso, somehow. "Tai?"

Wordlessly, she draws me through the gap in the fence, then she and Saxim try to kick the fence closed once we're all through. As if to keep someone out. She doesn't say a word as the three of us sprint back up the hill and into the house. She locks the front door behind her, and I follow her to Dad's sickroom, the most protected of them all.

Breathless. We're kneeling next to each other when she finally pulls something small and pink out of her bra and pushes it in my hands.

Leather, the finest leather. A crumpled ball. I straighten it and hold it up. A glove. A blush-pink glove.

"Tai?"

I look into her swollen eyes, and that's when I know. Without breathing, I stuff it back into her hand, and close it tight. I don't want it to touch the air and light.

"Where?"

The words spill out of her, and I can hardly keep up.

"Antella snuck us out through a service door and wrapped me in her Gucci sweater, even though I puked," she says, lifting its purple hem. "But I insisted Saxim and I take a cab home alone. No one but you, me, and Saxim know about this." She presses the glove back into my hand.

"And Teddy," I whisper back.

We call the police again via Saxim's phone, pacing back and forth as we try to explain, and we don't notice when another car approaches the drive—nor when someone climbs up the hill. But we do hear an over-size key fiddling with the lock. We do hear the nightmarish front door, modeled on the glorious *Gates of Hell*, creaking open. We do hear the footsteps, heavier and more surefooted than ours, approach Dad's room.

We know who's coming.

When he opens the door, he finds us there, kneeling like three children, hands clasped as if in prayer. We turn to look at him. His face is calm.

∞ ∞ ∞

"Tai," he says. "I was really worried about you." He puts on his same Santa Claus face—the one that brought us pure, childish joy. Kindly and warm. Impossible to resist. But I can't help seeing it as a desperate mask now. "You just . . . left. With Antella Arnoix, of all people."

"Hi," Tai says, standing and smoothing her filth-encrusted sweater, as if he's an old hookup she's embarrassed to see. Mina continues to recharge behind us, beeping steadily.

Teddy approaches us, as if to hug us, or something, but we both lurch back. He stalls in place, wounded and manic. I angle myself in front of Tai, so that she's farther from him, and closer to Mina and Saxim. Teddy's eyes move from Tai's swollen face, with its attempt at a peaceable grin, to mine, where I'm sure my confusion and anger and despair are peeking through the stony coldness.

He holds his hands up, palms facing us. "You're upset about Saxim, sure," he says, with a guilty glimpse at her, standing stiff as a statue on the other side of me, "and your mother's questionnaire and the Pocket Girlfriend. I could tell. I get that. But I never intended her answers to be—limited to the pockets of lovesick teenagers. I have much nobler plans for her."

"Nobler plans?" Tai echoes, just as I scoff. *Nobler*, as if the Pocket Girlfriend is a noble resting place at all.

"Mina?" he asks. "Can you please tell the girls your primary directive?"

"I promise to take care of your family," she says, in her mellifluous voice.

"Clarify, please, Mina."

The panel chirps, and I almost smirk, thinking she's going to give him the big chirping *screw-you*, before she begins to speak, a pixelated scroll with angel wings unfurling on her panel.

"To assist the struggling elderly, like a doting daughter. To curb the pain and suffering of the sick, like a loyal wife. To protect the health of the young at all costs, like a loving mother." Her words send a hot knife up my spine.

I take a half step back and clutch Tai's hand. There's something so unnatural about Mina, yet so familiar, too. I think it's that mixture that alerts us that something is wrong, that something is dangerous to us—like poisonous red berries dangling from a tree.

"It sounds familiar, doesn't it?" Teddy asks, an incongruous grin of pride lifting his cheeks into a frightening mask in the low light. "That's your mother," he says, creeping toward us. "That's your mother, in her role as Mitra the Moroccan nurse."

So shadows of Mama are trapped inside Mina, too. The *Carer*. My face must mold itself into a look of greater disgust, because Tai crushes my hand. Mama wasn't her roles. I have to be honest: There absolutely was a time when I thought I could mine necessary information about Mama from her films, from her red-carpet interviews, from professional photo stills themselves. But it was actually Tai growing up and creating this bubble of faux adoration for herself that disabused me of that notion. I can't know that this is the case for everyone, but the things I love most about my sister—the pure vulnerability with which she hopes, the wellspring of kindness and optimism inside her—are hardly ever on full view to the public, because she's afraid they'll be taken from her, used against her, by people who can never truly know her and love her. So she shields herself behind her shallowness, her materialism, her bubbly vapidity.

Her brand of self-protective lies.

"You haven't been completely honest with us, Teddy," Tai says, her hand gripping mine like an iron vise. But her voice, her voice is all compassion and clemency.

Teddy maintains his fragile smile. "You girls are so young. There's only so much truth you can give a person without hurting them beyond repair."

"I disagree," I say. "I think that's what some liars say to rationalize their lying."

And instead of elbowing me, like I thought she might, Tai just nods.

But Teddy is unfazed. "You're probably right. But truth is subjective, right, Noni?"

I ignore him and steel myself. "Since you wrote Mina's script, did you tell her to feed Tai that old recording between Dad and Nítuchí? It wasn't a glitch. It was too much of a coincidence to be a glitch."

His eyes gleam inside a cold face. "No one ever gives you enough credit, Noni. You know I gave you a Pocket Best Friend prototype to play with when you were just a kid, don't you? Before your mother went away. You loved it. And you gave me better feedback than most of the qualified beta testers. You told me she shouldn't have a set name—that users should be able to pick her name. Because then it makes her feel more like she's only your friend. Only *yours*."

His wheedling, singsong tone frightens me. I never liked the Pocket Girlfriend . . . Pocket Best Friend, whatever it is. I swear I didn't. And I don't like being distracted by an old story I don't remember. It confuses the truth.

"You only gave up your Pocket Best Friend when Tai told you she wanted it for Saxim," he continues, glancing at Saxim, her eyes trained on the ground, her hands fingering something behind her back. "You would do anything for your sister. You still would. Who wouldn't? She's so special." He smiles, and I shiver, my hands in neat fists at my sides. "I wish you'd both stayed that young and sweet forever. You were perfect. So special, and so complementary. The sun sister, and the moon sister. And you were so *happy*."

I want to beat my fists into his chest so hard that his heart stops.

"Wait, but why would you make Mina play me that recording, Teddy?" Tai asks.

I answer her: "So that we would mistrust Nítuchí instead of him."

I can tell that I'm right from my uncle's silence. His eyes have gone glossy and dark.

"But . . . Why?" Tai whispers to me.

"Nítuchí's not a good person," Teddy says. "You need to know that. And your father was oblivious to it. He only found out that his own company had been paying Mitso Arakit to stay silent *years* after your mother's disappearance. And he died believing the man was just another a stalker." He scoffs. "One frank conversation with your mother would've changed everything. But he didn't have it in him. The God among men."

So Dad didn't lie. He just didn't try. I think back to his letter, packed full of regrets and holes in his knowledge, and my heart grows heavier.

"Why didn't you just tell us all of this?" asks Tai, eyes flashing with hurt. "We love you, Teddy. You didn't need to lie to us."

He watches Tai, mystified to the point of disbelief. I see it all, then, and I know that if I do, then Tai does, too. Here is a man who would give his entire *world*—virtual immortality—to those he loved. Here is a man who believed he could not receive, or did not deserve, love and trust in return. Here is a man who views the beautiful and the special as unique possessions to stockpile.

I feel the buzzing returning in the back of my head; I feel the memory of that smooth leather in my hand. There's something hidden; there's something more. Call it a self-destructive instinct—knowing when I should push deeper into the darkness. The fizzy pennies can be a useful tool; they're so firmly intertwined with instinct that I hadn't been able to differentiate between the two. Until now.

"You need to tell us what really happened with Mama now," I say, in a voice I can't even recognize as my own. "Where is she?"

Teddy sighs, adjust the cuffs on his shirt. It's petulant, almost. "Saxim shouldn't be here. This is really family talk."

We have no such thing as family talk, only family lies. "She knows about Mama. About Brando," I say, as Saxim bites her lip, one hand held behind her back, the other holding fast to Tai's other hand.

Teddy's eyes flick up to mine, reptilian. I shove my free hand into my jean pocket to still it.

"I need to sit," Tai says, releasing me and Saxim and nodding at the four folding chairs in the corner of Dad's room. "Let's all sit and be comfortable."

That's the last thing we'll be. But I see the genius in it. Teddy moves to open the chairs, ever the dutiful uncle, and her eyes meet mine before traveling to her pocket. She's fiddling with her phone while he's distracted, unfolding them. As if she's recording the conversation.

And when we perch ourselves in the chairs, Tai's now closest to the door. She removes her heeled shoes with a mournful sigh.

Preparing.

"Your cousin Brando is unbalanced," Teddy says, once we're seated. "We had to protect you from him. He wanted to hurt your mother. He's the one who sent those letters I showed you." He settles further back into the chair, which creaks. Mina's beeping continues. "Mina, can you do that elsewhere, and then grab us some cold coconut waters or something?"

Mina's panel chirps assent and scritches out of the room.

I have a thought then: what if Brando, Mama's young nephew, was her vampyrrhic boy? What if he was the one who lavished her with seemingly unconditional love in the form of his letters—deep, terrifying wells of truth, so different from the pretty lies she received from the other men around her—until little demons forced him to make a terrible mistake?

And then I think of the fact that Teddy thinks of *himself* as the vampyrrhic boy.

Teddy looks up at us, his eyes glassy, and I nibble on my lip.

"Mireille was sick," he says. "I knew she was . . . unbalanced, too, on account of how let down she was by the institute's and Hero Pharm's failures. I tried to tell her there was no such thing as perfection, but she wouldn't have it. I just didn't understand how sick she was for a long time."

Tai and I look at each other, numb, trying to glean how to feel from the other's expression. My hands curl into self-protective fists.

"And Brando corrupted her mind with false information he found in the months after Mitso's accident. Mireille would rage against Hëró, rage against Nítuchí, rage against me. It became so disruptive that I told her that we would get Brando a new job somewhere else and move him away so she could rest. I hoped that with Brando gone, the smallest part of her would feel relieved, and she would feel free to be herself again. But instead she turned even worse. She became so *angry*." He shudders. He actually shudders. "She told me I was a heartless Hero Pharm pawn. Just another ruthless, greedy corporate pig like the rest of them. It was ridiculous. She wouldn't talk to me for weeks."

Tai looks legitimately sad for him from her perch. I am in awe of her ability to show false empathy for someone to goad them on. I try to sweep any emotion at all from my face as she speaks. "So what happened then, Teddy?" Her voice is breathy, Marilyn Monroe–ish.

Teddy actually smiles at her through his *sadness*.

"So fast-forward to May. I've been working on a project that I think will make her happy and remind her that I'm different. I *see* her. I come over here one night, since she refuses to meet me, and I tell her about the updated operating system in the Pocket Girlfriends, and the seed of the Carer idea—and how I hoped to incorporate her answers into the operating systems, so that she could indirectly care for millions one day. I thought she would be delighted. I thought the Carer was the best kind of legacy to have, especially for someone who cares deeply about humanity. But—she *lost it*. She had a complete meltdown. I'd never seen her like that."

"And then what?" Tai says, in a flat garble, as we sit there, unable to inhale.

Mina's beeping is louder than before, in the hall outside, but Teddy is full-on crying now, heaving, and he doesn't notice. "We were in the house. In the kitchen. You girls were asleep upstairs. So was Hëró. And she came at me with her fists first. Screaming that I wanted to *capture* her, that I wanted to *have* her, when she was a person, deserving of respect. I only put my hand over her mouth so she wouldn't wake you up. She was being so loud. But she was *so strong*, and she hit me then, and I was just a kid, and I pushed her away from me, and she—" His voice cuts out.

"She what."

"Hit her head on the counter," he says, in between sobs. He looks up at us, blinking through the tears, wiping his face. "But she got up," he says. "She got up. She was fine. Her head was bleeding, but she was fine. I swear. I saw her get up. She looked at me with utter hatred. It's a look I'll never forget. And then she took her purse, the red crocodile one, and ran out of the door and into the woods. She was barefoot. I followed her, telling her to come back. Telling her I was sorry. Telling her I would do whatever she wanted. I tried to find her, but she ran so fast. I lost her in the woods outside of here. I swear to you both; I lost her." Mina continues beeping, and he finally notices. "Mina, can you shut the hell up?"

She beeps agreeably outside.

"Why do you have her shoes and gloves and sweater hidden in your room?" Tai says in a monotone. I've never heard her sound that way. "In the princess room," she adds. She won't look at him.

He clears his throat, not one flicker of surprise passing over his face. "I'm getting there. The gray sweater snagged on a tree and came off her while she was running, and it had blood on it. So I picked it up. And then I came back into the house to figure out what to do, and I saw that she'd left her shoes and her gloves from earlier in the kitchen, right there, where we were fighting. And—and I just took them. I behaved recklessly. I knew she would never talk to me again when she came back. I knew she would probably tell Hëró, and everything would change. And I loved her so much, and I just wanted to keep a piece of her. Is that unforgiveable? So I just took them with me. I took them with me, and I—I left."

"You left her, bleeding from the head and running barefoot in the woods," I say. "You let her run all night. You didn't tell anyone."

"I chased her all night, trying to *find* her," he replies, hands clenching into fists.

It hits me all at once: Teddy's not the vampyrrhic boy. He wanted to capture and possess Mama in his Pocket Girlfriends, in his Carers.

I can see the script in my head:

> I cut down trees that are invisible. I replant them afterward. And with their endless lumber, I create my world and my friends.

Invisible, endless lumber being code for *code*.

> WHITE FOX (V.O.)
> That didn't make any sense to me, but I had the distinct feeling that mention-
> ing this to the man—or the nature of his figurines, or anything more—would make him angry. And he was right. I was feeling better with every passing moment. The clean air was helping me, and he wasn't a terrible host.

Mama saw something dangerous in him. A dangerous disconnect between his truth and the objective truth—reality.

"*Il est le bûcheron,*" I whisper to Tai in French. *He's the lumberjack.*

I think of the cut, blooming almond blossom branches tied to the trees in the Mitella security greenhouse: *The old cabin isn't what it seems. It looks to be made of wood, and flowering branches appear to grow from the structure itself.*

The lumberjack, a large man with kindly eyes, lives inside alone.

How could he not know he's the lumberjack? Or does he?

He shakes his head. "I never found her," he continues. "I never found her in the woods." He looks at us. "That's why I let Mina give you your father's note, claiming he'd seen her—even though . . . I don't know if he knew what he was seeing, at that point in his illness. I thought his note might inspire you to look for her again—to try approaches I would never think of. Because your mother had her purse. She could still be alive."

"Of course she's still alive," I articulate slowly. "She left us a copy of *White Fox* in her bathroom."

"You don't get it. Brando does shit just like that periodically to taunt me. Duplicates documents, makes exquisite deepfakes, floods the internet with false information." Teddy runs a hand over his face. "You know how long I've thought that motherfucker took your mom somewhere? Or finished her off? He's unpredictable and dangerous."

My blood freezes, thinking of the notes he left us. Thinking of Yuki saying, *He's a good egg. He would never harm her.*

"We need to tell the police the whole story, Teddy," Tai says, before I can stop her.

Teddy shakes his head and smiles. "See, that's the kind of innocent naivety I wanted to preserve in you. But neither of us can pretend it still exists." He takes another step toward us. "Where did you put the glove, T? Just give it back. The rest of her clothing will be disposed of shortly, and we'll all be safe. And when the police get here—I know you and that nosy bitch Antella Arnoix already called them—I'll explain to them again how confused you all were and are."

"But your story could help them find Brando. Help them find Mama," Tai says, in the whimper of someone younger, much younger, whose hope is fading.

The corner of Teddy's lips jerks to the right, as if he finds this both sad and a touch amusing, sending a jolt up my spine. "You don't actually believe that, Tai. You couldn't possibly be ignorant enough to believe those incompetent fools can do something I can't."

Tai's face drops, then hardens into the cold mask that imprinted itself in my memory earlier today: of hurt, of ultimate betrayal.

I never wanted her to feel that again. Especially not because of someone she loves.

"Don't listen to him," I whisper to her, smashing away the tears blurring my vision. "He's just upset."

Ignoring me, he lunges out of his seat, as if to hug Tai in his bearish way, and she flinches away from him.

"You're never going to look at me the same way, are you?" He staggers back into his chair. "I did this all for the two of you."

"You lied to protect yourself, not us." I press loose hair behind my ears. "Tai and I have been lied to enough by the people we love. We shouldn't have to lie for you all, too."

"Manon, don't misrepresent things to confuse your little sister," he says, his meaty hands tightening. "I'm all you have, and you should be gratefu—"

"SHUT THE FLYING FUCK UP!" Tai shouts, coming to her feet, her blue eyes wild. She pulls her phone out of her pocket and brandishes it like a weapon. "I recorded your whole confession, Teddy! I will post this to all of my followers, I swear to God! And I have a lot!"

Teddy lurches toward her, a dagger of fear and something darker crossing his face. "Don't be a brainless little bi—" The last word curdles in his mouth—a shadow of his regret immediately obvious.

"Is that what you said to my mother?" she says, retreating from him like she's facing off with a bear. I stand paralyzed. "Big mistake. *Huge*. I'm not a problem to be solved, Teddy. And I may be a little bitch, but I have a giant goddamn brain."

"Tai," I whisper, and that's when she darts out of the room in a barefoot sprint. Teddy takes one look at me, his eyes filmy and unrecognizable with a potent mix of fear and frustration and something grimmer still.

"Manon," Saxim calls, removing from her back waistband a *machíkíl* she must have taken from the kitchen. It glints in her hand, and I nod.

We both rush at him, but with two sweeps of his arm, he knocks us to the ground, then lumbers after my little sister.

TAI

I run like she did.

I don't remember exiting the house—only the smell of Dad's stacks, his moldy paper columns—and it takes no time at all to cross the overgrown lawn. I can't run down the driveway to the road; it will be deserted, blank asphalt, and he'll be able to find me straightaway. There's only one place for me to go. I reach the boundary line of the forest, and as I enter, the quality of the air changes. The dampness envelops me. Among these trees is the only place I'll be able to lose him. I jump over barely visible roots, rising from blue mist; scrabble over muddy hills, smelling of rich clod; duck beneath low and hooked tree branches like rusted scythes. I can hear him behind me, struggling with his heft but still swinging wildly: he sounds like a beast of the wood navigating its perils despite a clumsy, overgrown appearance. It hits me, then, what Noni said: *Il est le bûcheron*. He was made for these woods, with his thick limbs, his sturdy build. There's so much for me to snap and twist and break. My speed is less useful here. And as I step farther, I know that I am deeply unfamiliar with this part of the forest.

I need to find the cabin Mama and Noni and I played in.

But where are the landmarks I should know?

The dark erases them.

I reach a small clearing, still canopied, and cut across in a wild run. My adrenaline surges—*I might outrun him*. But that's followed by another thought—*where am I going?*

Find the cabin. Hide. Wait until the police arrive.

Nons will think I'm also running to get service to post what I recorded.

Confession: I didn't record anything.

It doesn't work that way—when you're confronted by someone dangerous, things don't slow down enough for you to pop out your phone and record his dastardly confessions. Life isn't one of Mama's movies.

But I told him I did, to get him away from Nons. To get him away from Saxim. I knew Teddy was going to do something he couldn't take back. I could feel him come unglued from the character that made him feel safe. He's fallen into the same frame of mind that he was in all of those years ago. He made horrible mistake after horrible mistake with Mama, ten years ago, on this same stretch of land. He might make a horrible mistake with us.

And I can hear him behind me, still.

It's as I'm running that a piece of my brain realizes how rash my decision was. It's as I start to lose my breath that I realize I'm probably doomed.

"Stop, Tai!" he shouts from somewhere behind me. Far, but not far enough. "Stop!"

I turn back to look at him, and I can't see a soul, but that's when I see it there, off to the right, illuminated by a single shaft of moonlight.

The chimney of our cabin.

Consumed by vines and moss, the cabin itself is unrecognizable. My landmark. I fling myself toward it, my muscles remembering those old races with a bittersweet tang as they are pushed, pushed, pushed through the muck and the damp, into the warmth and comfort and safety I want to believe are inside, I need to believe are inside, even though they've gone extinct.

My veins are thick with adrenaline when I reach the door. My legs shake like jelly, like my knees will give at any moment. There's a strange latch on there, that must have been added after we left. I wipe at my itchy right cheek, and it's wet; I must be crying as I struggle against the door, pushing and pulling, leaning my weight in, praying for it to give. I'm kicking at the lock, and that's when I slide against the wood frame, falling into the open cabin, teeming with dust mites and so much—too much—invisible forgotten life. I push the door closed behind me, choosing in over out, legs aching. I lock the door, then shove a small chest in front of it, all adrenaline.

It is silent inside, or at least, I can hear nothing over the beating of my heart.

It is dark inside, but the moon glows through the windows, even though they're furred with old growth. I use my phone—no bars— for more light, and I wander through our cabin, holding my breath.

There is the corner where we laid out a rug to play backgammon, checkers, chess. Bare, now.

There is the ledge where she left the prizes for our games, and other treasures: a rogue acorn, every heart-shaped rock, an empty shell, so far from its sea.

There is the table, where she served us tea.

My phone jitters, flashing once. I check for bars. Nothing.

It's brighter now, inside—there's this luminescence seeping from the walls somehow. A smell . . . the smell of roasted rice tea, blows in from somewhere, and tears fill my eyes.

I settle on the floor, unsure where I should hide, where I should wait.

And then I hear it. Someone humming the song she always hummed.

"Hello?" I whisper, voice cracking. I whip around, wiping my eyes.

And I see her.

NONI

After Tai bolts from Dad's bedside and Teddy follows her, I don't think. I *move*. I shout at Saxim to call the police and an ambulance again and when I hear her speaking into her phone, I just *run*. I run out to the drive, phone slipping in my grip, to find her.

I know where she'll be—call it sisterly intuition—and I know the shortcuts. It takes longer than I thought to get there because the woods are a mossy jumble, treacherous if I didn't have this old muscle memory, if I didn't have visions from the past guiding me. But I don't see him, tramping through its tangled alleys, and that's the beauty of the shortcuts, of being prepared, of growing up in this chaos.

I only hope she made it here, too.

When I reach the cabin, the surrounding forest is quiet. Like all of the scaled and feathered creatures lurking in the shadows know a predator is near. I fling myself against the door, and it won't open.

I circle it once, and every window is bolted shut. Behind the cabin, in the bushes, I see a strange black box, a generator, I think, that's making a humming sound. Above it, there's a solitary window uncovered by vines. I climb onto the box, which is warm to the touch, and I work the window up. It's heated, too, and it slides as if greased. I nudge it up as high as it goes, then shoulder my way inside, sliding one foot in, then the other. I'm in the kitchenette, where there once was a small stove that boiled water for tea. Where there once was an icebox and a sink. No running water. Now there's just a wrench, sitting there from some leftover repair, and a dusty box of tea.

But the cabin isn't completely dark. And I hear rustling, around the corner in the main room. I drop onto my feet with a muted thump, taking the wrench in hand. It's a fool's errand, protecting myself with this. But I'll take anything afforded to me. I'll fight like her, until the end. I turn the corner, and the breath is knocked out of me.

Tai, shoulders shaking hard, kneeling by the tea set. Curls of steam rising from the mouth of the pot. And a bioluminescent figure, a pale, barefoot figure in a white nightgown with long, faded brown hair, stroking her back. Tai turns to look at me, eyes shining with tears, with horror, with love, and that's when I know.

"Mama?" I ask, stepping forward with the tool in hand.

The figure turns to me, and unending loops of shivers run through my body. I drop the wrench, and it lands with a dull thud.

It's like her, but it's definitively not her.

It's this sylphlike reminder of her, a fragment of a dream of her. She doesn't smile, but there's love there, as palpable as ever, and I wonder if it's my mind sending curling strands of old emotion for her, or if this vision feels what Mama felt.

Every twisted inch of my body aches. I swallow acid, the first drops of coppery bile.

"Shall we have a cup of tea, my darling?" she says, and I gasp, doubling over and falling to my knees beside Tai. It's her voice. Every inflection, every honeyed consonant. It doesn't come from her chest, but from the walls themselves, as if she is this cabin, and the cabin is her. As inseparable as the cabin and the decades of vines woven through its exterior. Tai takes my hand, like it'll save her, pluck her from this heart-stoppingly gorgeous nightmare. The figure moves toward the tea set and kneels with us, lifting the teapot as if it's nothing but air. Her feet are veined with blue, her toenails carefully shaped and pristine. The fizzing builds inside my chest.

"Did you feel her touch you?" I whisper to her, my cheeks wet.

Tai blinks at me with glossed eyes, mouth opening, then closing like a guppy's. Speechless. I shut my own eyes, smelling Tai and the toasted rice and lavender, lavender, lavender, its sickly sweet smell, warming, burning, and when I open them—

She is still there. Opaque as milk.

"What are you?" I ask the figure, as she pours steaming tea into the two bone cups.

She looks up at me, a smile in her eyes. To see those eyes, those bones, arranged as only they have been and could ever be, I should be as unmoored as Tai. I should be succumbing to the coppery rush I can still feel in my chest. But I can also feel this moment slipping away, grains of slick raw rice through fingers, and I wish I could freeze this cabin as it is for all time, to scoop up every grain and hold them in that hollow in my chest.

Her breath makes a soft whistling sound. "I should think you know." She pauses, considering what she's said, then continues pouring. A humming builds, somewhere—maybe the core of the house. I pray it's not inside me.

"What—what happened to you?"

She only sighs, almost imperceptibly, the air in the cabin humming and heaving with her. "I'm—I'm sorry this is so strange." She says her apology lightly, but with great tenderness, the tenderness of a mother, and my heart heaves in my chest as the floor reverberates under our feet.

I wait for Tai to say, *That's the understatement of the fucking century.* I wait for one of us to burst into sobs. But she is silent. Awestruck. And I'm smelling metal and smoke, all at once. I taste that toxic roiling in the back of my throat. The effervescent building of those thickly coated pennies I thought I could stave off. I rub Tai's arms to fend it off. They are thin and too fragile.

"Why are you here?" I ask the figure. The rippling air around her. What do I want her to say? That's she's trapped, forever, like a spirit in a storybook?

She stops pouring, pushes a teacup toward us. We don't take it. She takes the other in hand and holds it beneath her nose. "It smells of toasted rice. Remember?"

Tai shivers in my arms.

"Why are you here?" I repeat, again.

What do I want her to say? That she's here to protect us? To save us?

What will satisfy me, us?

She looks in my direction, her eyes lake blue. Transparent. The texture is different. They need to be thickened, to be lived in. They aren't the eyes of a spirit who is free.

"I came here to feel safe," she says. "And I stayed, because I felt I could make a real difference."

And I convulse, arms around my sister, because she is not the texture of a living thing.

I hear the cracking of branches outside the cabin, and my attention snaps away, if only for a moment. I wrestle my phone out of my pocket to glance at the screen. It flickers with those two little words in the upper corner: *no service.*

More cracking, branches whipped back. A groan of frustration outside, enough to break the spell at last.

"We need to go before he finds us," I whisper to Tai, transfixed beside me. "We need to go right now and run to the main road. The police should be here."

"We're locked in," Tai whispers back, voice hoarse. "No one can get in." She glances toward the kitchenette, where I slipped through the small window. "No one."

The sylph continues sipping at her tea, watching our general direction. I can't look at her. I can't decide if every second spent with her will heal me or haunt me. I suspect both.

That's when a boom rocks the front wall of the cabin. Tai takes my hand, and it's frigid. I leap to my feet, and I can see the sylph's scalp. The tender part.

Another blow: The cabin shudders.

"He's kicking at the door," I whisper to Tai, dragging her up. There's no way for him to see inside. But—but—

The banging continues, and the hinges of the front door creak. The small chest Tai must have placed before it jolts forward.

Tai drops my hand when I begin to pull her toward the back window I climbed through. She rushes back to the tea table, back to the sylph, and she says: "We need your help, Mama. He's coming after us. We need to escape." As if this trapped creature can help us.

The humming is growing louder. It no longer smells of tea, but of ruined engines, of smoke. The sylph looks up from her steaming cup, straight into Tai. I can't tell if she registers the fear. The danger. "I wanted us all to be safe here," she whispers. "I wanted us all to be the best we could be."

"He's the lumberjack, isn't he, Mama?" Tai whispers back, reaching for the sylph but never touching her. "You need to help us now."

But this spirit, this creature, she *needs* to do nothing. Whatever Tai thinks she is, she's a figment of the dream of that self.

A metallic bang, and the front door lurches open an inch, and I feel fingers of cold stretching toward us and hear what sounds like the sickening, ripping striking of a match.

The sylph, reaching back toward Tai, shudders—the room goes dark for a moment, all light sucked out with her—and Tai recoils. The stench of an old hearth intensifies, like the mouth of some smoldering beast, opening wide. Tai coughs, and then I feel something sharp pouring into my throat, as thickly felt as a glass of milk with a poison edge.

Smoke.

It's filling the cabin, fast, and I turn around to see it cascading in through the window I slipped through.

The sylph stands before us, feet bare, more transparent than before. Expressionless, if you don't count that motherly longing and love she wears like a mask. She flickers out.

"Mama?" Tai shrieks, falling toward the empty space.

The front door shudders open another inch, the little chest jolting toward us, and I feel eyes looking through the gap above it.

Tai faces the front door, shoulders folding in.

"Are we going to die in here?" she asks me.

I take her by the cheeks, sticky-hot with sweat. Alive. "No."

I rush toward the fireplace and pick up a leftover fire poker. I hand it to Tai and pick up the wrench I'd discarded, turning it in my grip. It's getting too smoky to bear; each breath is ragged and painful.

"Hide beside the door hinges," I tell her, "and run out after I hit him."

She moves, still slack-jawed, fire poker in hand, and when she begins to protest, another blow reaches the door, and the chest flies, bits splintering, into the room. The door swings open on its weakened hinges, and a mountain of a man is there, a heaving shadow even in the dark, storming toward me, the solitary figure visible in the room.

Brando, with three scars drawn across his face.

In that split second, I raise the wrench, all while knowing how wrong a choice the wrench was. It is unwieldy, small, useless beside him. It is everything we girls are told about ourselves, in that moment—that we cannot hope to fight off this *force of nature*, that we are doomed. I hardly have time to swing it when I smell his sweat, feel the heat rolling off him, and—

That strange copy of Mama flickers into existence, a beacon of warm light beside me again. "Forever beautiful and fun, under every moon and every sun," she sings. A death song if I've ever heard one.

Brando pauses for only a moment, mere steps from me—I can smell all of him, how I can smell all of him, the old onions and yeasty breath—and his head swivels toward her, the source of music and light, as she continues: "She will be there until the—"

Tai howls, swinging the fire poker at his back, and he topples over with a deflated groan, falling beside me and knocking me off my feet in a whoosh of smoke.

She rushes toward me, sobbing, and he's there, on the floor, turning himself over and moaning.

"You hit him," I cry into the baby skin of her neck, as she holds me in her arms.

"Mama distracted him," she cries back, hugging me so tight, until I really can't breathe. The room whirls and glitches, and I wipe a trail of slime from my mouth.

She drags me out the door, and both of us collapse onto all fours, coughing at the crispness of the air, and I see, from the corner of my stinging eyes, the dancing edge of the small blaze on the other side of the cabin. *That black box*, I think to myself.

"We can't leave him here," Tai says, gasping on her hands and knees.

I look inside and see his feet splayed, inches from us. Then I lock eyes with Tai.

We remove our sooty sweaters and tie them around our faces loosely. We crawl toward his feet, each seizing a leg. Between the thickening smoke, it's so difficult to drag him out of the door—a near impossible burden—but we manage it, in desperate heaves, limbs and throats feeling aflame even though we are far enough, safe enough.

Outside, he stirs, coming up onto an elbow, and stares at us, with hell in his bleary, bloodshot eyes. They are blue, and familiar in the firelight.

We breathe hard, watching each other.

And I remember: I remember the young man with the long hair, who helped set up the tea, who smiled shyly at us before folding himself away. *Boy*. Someone my uncle, my father, and even my mother let disappear into the shadows, either through ignorance or ill intent.

"Hi, cousin . . . Brando," I say.

He cocks his head at us, wild-eyed, and it's all too obvious so much has changed in a decade. There's a danger here, something off, something cracked.

I feel it, and Tai feels it, too, because we both scrabble back.

"You need to know," he says, struggling to breathe and staying put. Holding quivering, thick-veined hands out, as if to calm us. "Quickly, before the police come, you need to know the rest. I can only tell you in person. When Mitso was just a kid, he was messing around in the Hero Pharm systems when he accidentally came across details of people affected by Viloxin testing. He started to sell shreds of it to the big papers, and everyone at Hero Pharm was flipping out over the breach. This happened just as I came over to study at the institute, and your mom was begging Hero Pharm to give me a more serious internship, anything that wasn't helping out around Stökéwood. She wanted to make it up to me because she said we couldn't tell anyone we were related, not just yet. At the time, my identity was known only by your mom, Teddy, and Nítuchí. They decided not to even tell your Dad who I was. He couldn't be distracted or disturbed when he was in the middle of formulating another breakthrough like Ladyx. He wouldn't appreciate it, they said. He would fall into one of his infamous chilly moods if he learned your mom had chosen *that moment* to trot out a relative and announce who she was to the world.

"Nítuchí was the one who approached me with a project. Nítuchí said I could sort paperwork related to a new miracle drug the company was testing for panic attacks. I proved I was good at it and got to know the man. Then he approached me with something more: I could help the company by investigating a local kid who frequented the same online forums I did. If he was spreading lies about Mireille and Hero Pharm online, I would report back to him.

"Corporate espionage, I thought, a James Bond kind of project that would make me a hero like your dad, that would make me exceptional to your mom. That would prove I was worthy of being known as her blood in public." He spits on the ground and smears a soot-stained hand across his mouth. "It started off fine. I wasn't born to be a spy. But we had more in common than I thought, and we became real friends. I defied Nítuchí and met Mitso in person. He had his share of issues, but he was fundamentally a good guy. I convinced him to wipe his store of the Hero Pharm data—it was too dangerous, I said. And I got to know him well enough that I knew he suffered from this horrible anxiety and these debilitating panic attacks, like you, Manon," he says, jabbing at the space between us, and I judder back. "The kind that—per the documents I sorted for Nítuchí—could be treated by that miracle drug Hero Pharm was in the process of testing." He stops, rolling to one side with a wince. "I begged Nítuchí

381

to let me give the drug to Mitso, and he said no. I told your mom all about it, hoping she'd agree that he needed this trial, and she freaked out that I'd been doing this spying for Nítuchí behind her back. She refused to support me. I was furious. I called her a hypocrite, since she always said people should be helped at any cost. And I stole the drug from Nítuchí's offices and gave it to Mitso. It was all too easy. I should have known better. *Fuck*," he shouts, the sound reverberating in the charred-smelling air, and Tai and I flinch into each other. "Not too long after starting the med, Mitso had the heart attack. He's half the person he was before. And I think Nítuchí planted me there for that very reason—so that I would be the one to offer Mitso the meds. I could never tell Mitso. Never. But I told Teddy. He didn't believe me about Nítuchí. He just thought I was a lying, thieving kid trying to cover his tracks. So I had to tell your mom." He rubs his filthy hands together, like he's massaging out some old pain.

We stand there, in the smoke of the fire, speechless.

"Did you hurt her?" Tai asks at last, wiping the polluted sweat leaking into her eyes.

And his face curls into something monstrous, the firelight reflecting off his pupils. "Why do you assume I'm a monster?"

"Why didn't you tell us this before?" I ask, before coughing uselessly into my swollen hand, throat so raw.

He groans, energized by his frustration, pulsating with rage. "Nowhere's safe from them, I told you. They've been following you this whole time," he shouts, rising in one manic split second, standing before us, arms outstretched, pain forgotten. "And when I could find you alone, you wouldn't listen. You wouldn't fucking list—"

A crash in the bushes interrupts him. "You motherfucker, don't touch them," Teddy says, running out and launching himself at Brando, who roars and scrabbles with him.

And we run.

TAI

One moment I have Noni's hand in mine, and we are running, and then I look back at the burning cabin, at Mama, at Cousin Brando, at Uncle Teddy, and I am tumbling on a root, still coughing because my throat feels ablaze. I lose her hand, and I slide against a mossy growth and lose my balance and even though I pinwheel to stop myself, the whole world is spinning and I fall, hard, on my side, the pain ripping through me as I slide down a slope. My hands are raw and matted with dirt. My eyes flutter closed, and I'm seeing stars. When I open them the world is blacker.

"Noni?" I call into the black that doesn't end.

I couldn't tell you where I came from. I couldn't tell you where I'm going. I try to bring myself to my feet, and I feel another splitting pain by my ribs. I try to get my bearings: I've landed myself in the center of a tangle of roots. It feels spongy beneath me; like something could break at any moment. There's a powerful smell of rot.

"No, no, no," I whisper, before listening for footsteps, for cracking branches.

"Tai?" Noni screams, from somewhere above me—the top of the ravine. "Are you hurt? Stay there!"

I want to scream at her to be quiet, to look out for Brando, to look out for Teddy, to be careful in the surreal hellscape these woods have become.

But then I see him. I see him before I hear him; his eyes gleam in the dark just across from me in this hideous nest of roots, two chips of glass in the midnight wood. The shadow of his bulk, next, and though it must be impossible, though this could only be a vision: as I press myself further into the sponginess, I see his eyes lock on to mine.

Teddy smells of blood, and all I can think of is Mama and Nons.

"Don't move," he says, and Noni's screaming, *Don't go down there, don't touch her, don't go down there*, and as I'm scrabbling to up and leave, I feel a fleshy hand take hold of my shoulder from above, and I'm ripping myself away, and picking myself up to scramble up the roots, but I'm tripping on one—my foot's trapped—and I dislodge some great network of knotted threads beneath the surface of the soil, as if a mass of rotted flesh had been torn aside from a wound and collapsed on itself. I hear a massive *sigh* as if the forest itself is giving up and then something happens that I can only describe as.

An.

Earthquake.

The ground judders and breaks, and the rush swells into a chorus of screams—mine or Noni's? Mine or hers or a man's? All of those—as I fall into this great flat of foliage like it's quicksand and the sponginess is giving and the gravity is taking over and I slide

down,

down,

down,

down,

down, branches ripping into my face, a paunchy mass hitting my side, and I'm still falling down into the black, the great walls of dirt swallowing me whole—I'm breathing dirt, I've got particles of dirt everywhere, my skin is raw and numb from being scratched, I feel wet and slick—until . . . I . . . *stop*.

The first thing I think is: *I can't breathe.* Then: *Am I alive?*

I blow some dirt from my nose and mouth with a tremendous groan, and the next thing I hear is a *crack* coupled with feeling another earthshaking slam right next to me, rattling my bones.

It takes me a moment or two to realize I didn't cause the noise myself. I'm no longer moving. I've landed somewhere, somewhere squelchy: my ankles feel like they're both crimped beneath me at unnatural angles, but I'm too shocked for them to hurt; my sides feel like a giant bruise. I am in utter darkness, the blackest of the black. Maybe it's that my nose, my eyes, my pores are filled with dirt. Wiping muck from my eyes, I can't see any better. I feel around: bits of earth crush beneath my fingers. My hand moves to my pocket, where I find my cell phone. Thank *Baby Jesus*; I could cry. It's functioning, I think, or at least it's giving off a faint light. I can't tell if I have service; my dirt-encrusted eyes can't see the detail, even though I must be crying freely, or bloodied, because my cheeks are damp. I swing the phone's flashlight around, and visibility is impossibly poor, to say the least. I realize that I must be in a hole, with walls of cascading earth around me and wrist-thick strands of mossy and twiggy roots closer still. At least I've landed on something solid. I keep moving the flashlight around, and it reflects against something white blue for a split second, but the effect is lost as I keep moving—everything is so concealed by the roots—and I only see dirt. I turn off the phone light for a minute: There's no light coming from anywhere around me, and I can't decide if it's scarier to have the light on or off.

I start to cry.

And then I blow more debris from my nose and squint to check how much battery (10 percent) and service I have (zero bars). *Oh my God.* I try to call the police, and it won't go through. I try again: nothing.

I flick the flashlight on again. If I had to guess, between the branches, I'd say the hole I'm in is the size of a very small, low-ceilinged room. I can't stand. My head's touching hanging threads of earth that might be roots or worms or something else entirely. I start shivering; either my body temperature has just dropped or the soil beneath me is frosty and biting. I feel dampness on my cheeks and wonder if it's tears or blood or just my rapid descent through so many rotten layers.

I try to come to my feet. I end up sliding painfully down the embankment on my knees, and that's when I fall into it.

A shape a couple of feet away from me, on the floor of the cave. A series of lumps. I pray it's another mess of roots. But it's pulpy. *Warm*, even though my knees are now planted on something rock-hard and frosted-over. Every cell in my body rolls off this plane and into the next.

"Teddy?"

I focus my light around it, and that's when I see it.

A hand, sticking out. Swollen, flecked with dirt.

I follow it with my light and see that the chest and head are buried in dirt, too. I hold the cell phone in one hand and scramble with the other to dig debris away from the head. I finally glimpse skin peeking out from below.

A nose. The red pug Santa Claus nose.

"Teddy!"

I stifle a cry, and this starts a coughing fit; I keep scrambling to uncover his face, and my fingers reach for his neck. I find it, there, slick with blood, and immediately I know the angle is wrong relative to the nose, but I hold my fingers there and wait for the telltale pulse.

And I wait.

There's no movement, no life; I convince myself for a second that there might be something, but then I realize it's my own nerves, my own accelerated heartbeat. I hear another groan of pain, and it's coming from me, and I'm crying now as I rake the soil away from his head, that neck, and I see that it's *him*; *it's Teddy*; one eye closed, the other half-open and crusted with dirt, as if in a horrible wink—I set my phone down for a second, and wretch into my hand, but my throat and mouth are too dry and dirt-packed for anything to come up.

He's okay. He'll be okay. I can't think otherwise right now. I can't.

But most of all I can't be around him. I can't look at him.

I heave again into the dirt beside him.

Have courage, Tai.

I force myself to dig through his pockets for a cell phone. I find a wallet and nothing else.

I take two, three breaths. As deep as I can, though I feel like I'm getting more fiber than air. It's hard, my throat burns worse with each one; if I could rip it out of my neck, I would. I shine my light around and force myself to crawl on my hands and knees to search for an exit of some kind, a variation in the cloddy walls of the den. I try to focus on the technical realities of the situation so I won't melt down—I try to observe and analyze, like Nons would. *Noni.* I stifle a cry again because now it hurts too much. I throb.

The type of earth does change as I wander deeper into one corner of the hole, but then I find myself at a dead end, an impenetrable corner. How can a sinkhole so deep exist? My fingers are frigid, broken-feeling from their scrabbling, and that's when I realize. My body is cold-hot. I'm shivering, and my extremities are frozen but my skin is scraped clean off and my forehead's a stovetop and—

The ice caves.

It has to be a forgotten path of the ice caves.

I remember the girl in the visitors' center—what was her name? Mikki, she was Mikki—telling us that they were closed because the heat wave had caused some portions to melt.

I know where I am. They're massive and spread out, but that knowledge is enough to give me a feeling of agency. Or at least that's what I tell myself, as I scrape openings with my fingers, wearing them down to slashed nubs, and sniff blindly at every new type of earth in my path. I rub at my nose with the edge of my wrist—my ruined fingertips now too numb to help—and wipe away a crust on my face that feels an inch thick, not that I could really know, in this most private darkness. My air pipe feels chunky with the stuff, too, and I'm suddenly aware of how thirsty I am. I could seriously die of thirst. *Forget it.* I almost try to find a wet clod of earth to suck some moisture out of, but when I get it close to my mouth it smells like death, and I spit with a shiver and paw at my tongue like a cat. It's a thirst that cannot be slaked.

Windmilling into a colder corner, I feel a rush—not so much air as a raw emotion, with claws and teeth that crunch down on me. I no longer feel completely alone, but this deep melancholy floods into the space that was occupied by panic.

A sudden chill rips through me. *A draft from the ice caves?* But there's no movement, no gusts of air, not even faint. There's a presence here. And I wonder if it's Teddy's spirit. My heart catches in my throat, one no more raw than the other.

Unless it's me, and I'm dead already, I think. I push deeper into the cold with wild punches and swings through the branches of dirt. I take great jagged breaths. Dead people must be aware of their condition, right—

The earth shifts.

My stomach falls as I realize I could plummet even farther.

I could be buried forever in this cemetery in the backyard of the home where I was born.

It's macabre. Terrifying. Too real to think about. Even now, with all I know, I can only walk along its edges in my head. Sometimes the great pull of darkness has to be resisted. Sometimes truth is just worry, and sometimes worrying can ruin a person.

I take another breath. They're getting more difficult, too difficult.

That's when I touch the corner of something stiffer than dirt and icy. Frozen. I try to pull it from the ground with gentle tugs that make my heart ache; I'm terrified now that the rest of the hole could collapse. But I've got my hands around something heavy that isn't plant life. Something curved and smooth: nothing like the dirt I've felt on and under and in my fingertips for the longest time. When I remove it, I take out my light again, and I see, attached to its smoothness, a ragged flap, textured and gnarled.

A flap of skin, the color of dried blood.

I throw the gruesome handful away with a full body shudder and a guttural groan. It lands near me, and when I illuminate it, something glints.

Not human skin.

It's got handles and a structure and—

It's a purse.

My heart judders in my chest.

A purse.

I hold it close to my chest and feel an urge to burst out into sobs. Evidence of humanity.

It's humming inside. Alive. I marvel at it in my hands. A small, structured purse; too dirty and ratty and eaten to make sense of. But I feel my breathing stop again. The exterior is caked in dirt, and I scrub at it with my unfeeling fingers, as delicately as I can. I open the crusted latch, only to find a mess of beetles inside, not all of them dead. I heave again and shake them out furiously, crying, wiping dirt and tears from my face. They've eaten through the other side. An empty lipstick canister, the moist gunk inside long consumed. Some mixed coins. And a small notebook, its pages mostly eaten, embossed with the golden initials . . .

M

F

H.

The memories crash over me with such force that I lose all feeling; I am not me, I am no more flesh and blood than a scrape of dirt-brown matter, limp as a slug at the bottom of the pit.

But I find myself holding the purse to my chest as if it's my beating heart, as if it's the only remedy for the only sickness.

Mama.

There will be questions later, but there are no questions in my mind then.

She must have fallen.

She must have died, by no wish of her own or anyone else.

Sobbing, I comb the dirt with raking bloody hands, desperate for any other bit of her, any other relic, and I find nothing at all. Nothing but this purse. I curl around its deflated crocodile skin and cry for Mama, for the fact no one followed her, for the fact no one found her. *Her final act.* Solitude and calm in the forest at the base of Mount Vilox. A tragedy fit for the scale of my mama's life.

And I feel sure that I will die—die down here with her—that a part of me wouldn't even be mad about keeping her company, even if my own life story still isn't long enough to carry the same tragedy without bowing inward on it.

And that's when I hear a phone sing. Teddy's satellite phone.

Forever beautiful and fun, under every moon and every sun. She will be there until the end. Your very own Pocket Girlfriend.

The blue light pierces the inside of the cave in a solitary beam, some five feet from where I was.

Mama.

She's flesh and bone, like I'd wished for so long, but chilled and rotted and wrong—not like the dream of her, at all.

NONI

I lose her hand, even though I swore I would never lose it again. I lose her to those impenetrable woods. What she falls into is stolen from hell: It looks like a pit, a giant gullet, and when she falls into it, I'm calling after her, but it's like I'm eight years old again, and she's not hearing me. I scream for her to stay still, but two figures follow her down, and then the floor of the forest is shuddering and dropping, sucking them all down into its damp depths. I shudder back onto my heels, a scream dying in my chest. My lungs feel like they might burst. But I only allow myself seconds of this before I scrabble toward the lawn.

I won't let her be lost.

I am quick. I remember all the shortcuts. The branches whip my face, scoring me, marking me. I only roll my ankle twice; I can't even feel it over the burning in my chest. I tear through the foliage toward the property edge. That's when I see the flashlights of men in uniforms, stamping toward me, when I see police cars and fire trucks pulled up to the gate already. Someone has pushed open the gate and let an ambulance through, too; its light is visible by the dead fountain. Then I see Teddy's fancy car parked beside another two black cars. I watch as Antella Arnoix shoves through the men arguing among themselves, and I run back into the woods to lead help to my sister. No one will stop me this time.

I try Tai's and Teddy's phones as I run, knees cut up and lungs breathless. Neither of them answers—Tai's phone rolls to voice mail. I'm almost by the cabin, hearing firemen shouting over the blaze, when Saxim runs toward me. She settles a hand on my shoulder. Her face is badly bruised.

It's then that I try Teddy's satellite phone again and someone picks up.

"Hello?"

"Hello?"

I would know her voice anywhere, even if it's ragged and flat. *Tai.*

Because someone has followed her, we find her.

We track the phone signal and are led to a spot that looks like any other: brambles, roots, packed dirt. First the police question their geolocation. But then a detective notices the disturbed soil, and after speaking with a man from the Ministry of the Environment, they tell me there's a risk the floor will cave in and flood the pocket below. Suffocating Tai and the others.

There's nothing I can do then but sit and wait.

They bring in a team of people dressed in neon and tethered to long ropes to delicately excavate. It takes hours before the area is stable enough for someone to venture down there and find Tai. Special representatives from the Viloxin fire department and the ministry of the environment pull her, packed in dirt, out of the mouth of this unknown, unexplored artery of the ice caves.

For once in my life, she looks utterly unfamiliar—like a small animal, her fine bones covered in uneven swaths of flesh and blood and soil. But then she opens her eyes, those navy-blue eyes, and I lunge to go hug her, only for five men to try to stop me.

"She's dead," I hear her say, before breaking into wet sobs. That's when I begin to understand.

"I need to talk to my sister."

"We must treat her injuries first," a man in a suit with a white clipboard explains.

He pulls me back up to the house, to a triage tent they'd set up beside a couple of vans. It looks just like it did after Mama disappeared—or ran, I should say.

I am definitely eight years old again, shivering in the strange heat on the messy lawn.

He explains what has happened today, what they suspect happened ten years ago, and what likely has happened several years in between, during the first heat waves of the season. "We suspect this cave has been around since approximately 1864, when Mount Vilox erupted. But the magma layer was thin here. What followed is a confluence of rare natural events. The root system is underdeveloped and weakened by the long winter," the man says, moving his hand in the mystifying loose shape of a bowl as if to show the process, "and the heat wave softens the protective layer of ice holding up the soil and the root system. With pressure from above, it is *possible* to break through to the unexplored cave artery below." He's from the Ministry of the Environment, and he has tried to contain his obvious excitement at "rediscovering" this cave. I heard him chattering away on the phone to a colleague already. "We found a very old record of this cave's existence—in a survey conducted prior to the twentieth century, it is shown as a small tunnel. But then it became part of this private land parcel in a sale after the turn of the century," he continues, "and the cave itself has not been cataloged in a more recent survey." He double-taps his clipboard jauntily. "Your sister has rediscovered an important geological phenomenon."

I stare at him.

"So, good on her," he adds obliviously.

"What about the cabin?" I ask. "What about the fire?"

"The fire was contained," he replies. "The source was a generator."

The black box. "But why was there a generator? There was never a generator when we used to live here."

"Hmm?" He turns to me. "These aren't questions for me, young lady." He looks at the foxglove plants beyond us, taller than I am, and blooming proudly in freckled blush pink and white bells for the first time this season. "Hmm. My wife loves foxgloves. But I've never seen them grow to be quite so large in this region. Did you plant them yourself? What's your secret?"

I sit there. "My *secret*? I didn't plant them. They've just been here forever." I think a moment, realize how imprecise I'm being. Mama loved foxgloves, and I remember her wanting them planted. "Someone would have planted them at least ten years ago."

His brows knit together. "That's not right. Foxgloves are biennials. They bloom the second year after planting and then die. I suppose they might have reseeded themselves, but . . ." He exhales from his nose, as if to say that's deeply improbable. "They shouldn't be alive, much less blooming."

Did Dad have them planted again recently, in her memory? Or did they—by some strange Stökéwood magic—survive all these years? I try to quash the tears that have come to my eyes all of a sudden.

"When will they bring my mother up?" I ask, voice thick with a mixture of hope and dread, the likes of which I hope to never feel again.

He blinks at me through his thick lenses. "Who?" He shakes his head. "Another person fell? Oh. Well, that's not my department, either, I'm afraid."

EPILOGUE
THREE MONTHS LATER

Fleischman's Deli is world-famous for its dollar-coin-size latkes, its Arnold Palmer slushies, and as of this summer, its exotic artwork of Mama flashing out of every nook and cranny.

THE LADY OF THE HOUSE, reads the caption beneath a portrait of her made entirely of dried pasta noodles. That was the start of it all, that same week we found her. But then customers and family alike began to bring by their own bizarre testaments to her: Her stage name in used Popsicle sticks, a neon sign of her profile, a pop art movie poster remade in condiment-colored paints (we smelled that one to make sure). Our uncle Duke hung them up with his kids—Brando's sisters—who never met Mama but find the whole decorative choice very funny.

It's been mobbed since the news came out: of who she was, and of her discovery; of Teddy's death, and of those final moments between them (Mina recorded everything). But Uncle Duke still waits for Brando to come back—you can tell, from the way he watches the park beyond in his free moments, a place Brando used to love, for its many old and overgrown trees.

Tai and I are drinking Arnold Palmer slushies with our cousins—Molls and Ems—out back, when Tai pulls out the Pocket Girlfriend she's been playing with (the originals also experienced a surge in popularity since Teddy's death).

"Haven't we had enough of Uncle Teddy's tech for a while?" I say. We miss Teddy, despite the lies and the violence that poisoned Mama's relationship with him, and with us. Because people in our lives are composed of many different shades of gray, and we can't help but love him for offering his version of love when we needed it most, even if he wasn't always the man we thought he was. Even though he made mistakes with graver repercussions than the rest of us. He thought he was the vampyrrhic boy. And I think he probably was, at heart.

"We still don't know if the hologram of Mama was his," Tai notes.

But who else could have crafted what everyone calls impossible technology besides our uncle, who told us himself he was working on holograms at our last lunch? Teddy's creation, convincing enough to fool our own father. He thought he glimpsed Mama on the property with his very own eyes.

But it's true: *So many* men have crafted visions of Mama that suited them.

"I'm going to mine every last one of Mama's answers out of this pink clamshell if it's the last thing I do," she adds, and Ems, grinning, toasts her with her AP. She's four years older than Tai, but that hasn't stopped Tai from being someone's Queen Tee before. It all started with Dad, a good forty-some years older, after all, whose greatest joy was Tai.

Marion received a box in the mail for Tai from an old secretary of Dad's. In it, there was a note reading, *Some dopey new exec took the office, so we had to pack it up. I thought you should have his only personal effect. Sending you my love.* The personal effect was a photo of baby Tai on Dad's lap, both of them holding a finger to their right temples and smiling wider than I've ever seen.

I know, now, that I can't blame Dad for our family fracturing, nor Mama, nor Teddy, nor Tai. Life tore us apart, as it does many families, and not everyone is granted the chance to come back together in time. It would be easy, so easy, to hate each of them, and to focus on everything they failed to share with us. But when I think of Dad's impassioned, flawed letter to us—the letter that started this entire process, the letter also admitting he was wrong, I see an extended hand, from the same man who seemed so hesitant to connect with us as children.

"How are you feeling today, Tai?" the Pocket Girlfriend asks. "It's an overcast day, but there's beauty in that! Beauty isn't what is beautiful. It's what pleases us!"

Tai jolts, taking my wrist in her hand. "Did you hear that?"

I nod, and for a fleeting moment, we feel her there with us; as if time is a split river, and the past has flowed back into our near-future.

"Do *I* please you?" the Pocket Girlfriend asks, breaking the spell.

"She's such a little *h-e-a-u-x*," Tai replies, and I swat her shoulder.

∞ ∞ ∞

Before the dinner rush, there's a knock on the door of the deli, and Ems returns with an unstamped manila envelope, the typed address sticker made out to *T and M*. Where the return address should be, there are only three diagonal lines.

We open it together.

On the following page are notes written in a familiar hand, the uneven writing on the letters sent to Mama by Brando.

White Fox *is loosely based on the legend Mireille used to tell—the wild fox saved on a moor, who becomes a beautiful human wife for a short while, before reverting to her true fox form, etcetera.*

Our hands start to shake.

She wouldn't show me the script itself. She said it needed work, and then we fell out. But I kept wondering: So what happens to White Fox in the end???? Does she leave her husband and stay a fox forever, like in the legend? I'm sure you wonder, too.

We hold our breaths.

I'm sorry for taking the last rough draft from the magazine box in the tower, ten years ago. And I'm sorry for returning only three parts earlier this year.

And then, there it is.

PART FIVE

INT. GRAND OLD HOME — NIGHT

White Fox, clothed in a dress stained with blood
from her mouth and seated in a small room, with
Client 2 / Man on the Moon kneeling before her,
pressing a clean towel to her face.

> CLIENT 2 / MAN ON THE MOON
> Oh, my dear. How awful.

> WHITE FOX
> Please don't concern yourself with my
> health now.

CLIENT 2 / MAN ON THE MOON
How could I not?

WHITE FOX
Don't you understand? The bleeding is
a lifelong affliction. There is no
permanent cure. That is the point of my
story. Every cure is temporary.

He shakes his head.

CLIENT 2 / MAN ON THE MOON (CONT'D)
That can't be so. You must try the
compress they made with flowers from
the garden. Do you see the foxgloves
outside your window?

White Fox, distracted by the pain, shakes her head.

CLIENT 2 / MAN ON THE MOON
I planted them there after you left. I
have planted them again and again since
you left.

WHITE FOX
(blandly)
I'm sure they're very pretty.

CLIENT 2 / MAN ON THE MOON
Oh, my dear. As always, beauty is only
the start.

                    WHITE FOX
                    (sighing)
Well, thank you for the gesture, I suppose.

              CLIENT 2 / MAN ON THE MOON
Oh. They aren't for *you*. They live out
there, you understand, so the foxgloves
were planted to guide them home, should
they ever lose their way in the forest.

The far-off chattering resumes. We see dark
splotches in the glass: Someone is outside. White
Fox tenses up, thinking of the creatures that pur-
sued her.

                    WHITE FOX
                    (afraid)
Who lives out there?

TWINKLING LAUGHTER from that unknown source outside. Client 2 / Man on the Moon, still sitting on
the ground, smiles. White Fox, uneasy, stands and
walks to the window.

                WHITE FOX (CONT'D)
Who's out there? The shadow creatures
have come, haven't they? They're watching me. They've been watching me all
along. They cannot be ignored. I'll
face them now, I will.

But Client 2 / Man on the Moon doesn't answer. He stands, approaches the wall, and pulls down on the light fixture that looks like the moon fringed by stars. A faint HISS and CREAK are heard. The seam of the wall pops out, revealing a hidden pocket door to the outside.

White Fox conceals her surprise. So that's what he meant by asking the moon and stars. But why did he say *they're* waiting for her?

Client 2 / Man on the Moon holds a hand out to White Fox. She takes it, with trepidation. He leads her outside.

EXT. MAGICAL FOREST GARDEN — NIGHT

The garden is a gorgeous jumble of living things—somehow, it is not the orderly place White Fox expected. Wildflowers, weeds, chestnut trees, velvety vines, and mismatched miniature buds exist in off-kilter harmony. Lightning bugs flicker on and off, and the moon bathes the landscape in a gentle glow.

Client 2 / Man on the Moon leads White Fox deep into the garden and past what appears to be a meticulously maintained graveyard. Client 2 / Man on the Moon notes White Fox's discomfort as they continue walking through.

                    CLIENT 2 / MAN ON THE MOON
          What do you think? It was your idea.

                          WHITE FOX
          A cemetery?

                    CLIENT 2 / MAN ON THE MOON
          A memorial. Dedicated to the victims
          and their families.

                          WHITE FOX
          Your victims and their families.

                    CLIENT 2 / MAN ON THE MOON
          Yes.

White Fox leans in to catch the names on the monuments. She gasps, realizing they are familiar to her.

Here, the sister who sat alongside her brother
every day in the lab and didn't understand when
she wasn't let inside one day.

There, the husband with the kind eyes who cried
when he thought his wife might finally manage to
ascend from the valley she dropped into alone.

Behind and beside these monuments rest the shadows,
curled like cats and at rest. White Fox notices
them at last, flinching back.

                CLIENT 2 / MAN ON THE MOON
Don't worry. They're well cared for now.

                        WHITE FOX
            (peering more closely and sighing)
Ah. I see that. Well . . . I understand
their true nature now.

The monuments glow with an otherworldly sparkle as
White Fox and Client 2 / Man on the Moon walk on,
approaching a clearing.

                CLIENT 2 / MAN ON THE MOON
We shall honor their thorniest truths
until the breath leaves our bodies or our
good sense and sanity leave our minds.

White Fox nods.

In the midst of the clearing, there is an elevated
cabin made of wood surrounded by the grand and glorious foxgloves, the foxgloves Client 2 / Man on
the Moon has so lovingly planted.

                CLIENT 2 / MAN ON THE MOON
                    (motioning at the sky)
Now . . . They're expecting you.

Rustling in the foxgloves. White Fox steels herself and approaches them. A little head pops

out from inside the foxgloves, then a second. Beaming, gorgeous little angels with eyes like saucers.

THAÏS
Coocoo!

Then two sets of hands, bearing tiny compresses stained with the juice of flower buds.

MANON
They aren't perfect, but they should work.

MANON mimes placing the compress in her mouth, and White Fox does so, bemused. THAÏS and Manon then take White Fox's hand and pull her inside the fox-gloves, then through the overgrown grass, and up the ladder, set with twinkling lights.

INT. MAGICAL FOREST GARDEN CABIN — NIGHT

Inside the cabin, there are beds made of the finest down, rows of prized chocolates saved for her, and saucers set with her favorite teacups. They guide her toward the cushioning by the cabin opening, which looks out into Limatra and beyond. It glitters in the dark. Even the sea is visible.

WHITE FOX
I can see everywhere I've been.

                    MANON
And everywhere you haven't been yet.
See, over there? It's the three of us,
knee-deep in the sea, about to dive for
more freshly cracked sea urchin, since
Tai has gobbled the first up.

                    THAÏS
And over there, we're visiting the
shore as old ladies with our children!
Look how my daughter beat Noni's son in
a race to the deli. She's a quick girl.

Manon grins.

                 THAÏS (CONT'D)
                  (sighing)
This is a very special spot.

                    MANON
(pointing at the row of foxglove
sentinels, and CLIENT 2 / MAN ON THE
MOON tending to the memorial)
And a safe one.

They settle onto the cushions, and White Fox feels
at her mouth, still bulging from the compress. The
bleeding hasn't stopped—it won't stop—but it has
lessened.

That's when the Vampyrrhic Boy appears, climbing

up the rungs of the ladder and peeking into the
dark of the tree house.

                    VAMPYRRHIC BOY
                       (shyly)
        I've . . . come from the cemetery. The
        shadows, they . . . I understand now.

                    WHITE FOX
        Me too. I'm sorry, dear one. From now
        on I'll have the courage to call you
        what you are, and face every shadow
        with fresh calm, together.

The children watch her intently. Thaïs reaches up
to dab at White Fox's face.

                    WHITE FOX
                   (blinking fast)
        Do I look a fright?

                    THAÏS
        Beauty isn't that which is
        beautiful . . .

                    MANON
        It is that which pleases us.

White Fox's face softens.

        EXT. MAGICAL FOREST GARDEN — NIGHT

Drifting over Viloxin's lights and forests, among
the stars.

>   WHITE FOX (V.O.)
>   It is a good treatment, this kind and
>   patient love, if I tend to it. It grows
>   with me. I have no master anymore—no
>   master but myself. So I will gratefully
>   devote myself to this project: To tend-
>   ing our love.

>   THE END

>   ∞ ∞ ∞

We follow Mama to the banks of the Seine, to a dusty library in London, and to her other favorite spots around the world, before coming back to Viloxin. There are laws prohibiting you from spreading ashes on private property, but as Tai would say, *Screw them; we did it anyway.*

The days taste mulberry sweet in late summer on Viloxin. I'd forgotten. Tai has a hand on my shoulder while we stand beside Mama's memorial. It's a bench that overlooks a soaring view, made from a rough-hewn, uneven, pink-and-white-veined piece of marble. Definition of *wabi-sabi.*

With more than a bit of her ultra-luxe Viloki flavor, obvs, Tai notes.

Tai hands the foxglove bouquet to me and draws her fingers over the top of the marble. Three long, thin black scratches have appeared across the top, almost overnight.

We've been in Limatra for over a week now, reviewing our inheritance from Teddy, in the form of Hero Pharm and Clouded Cage shares. I've been working with an agent on the manuscript of my book, *She Is Mireille*, and Tai and I have been developing our first Hero Pharm initiative: a plan for restitution and lifetime support to family members of victims of Hero Pharm tests, with funds left to us by Teddy and help from Hérrakí.

When Nítuchí found out Hérrakí and I were doing more than just work together, he offered to host us at his home for tea once a week, and even though the idea sounded—to steal from Tai— *mind-blowingly stab-your-eyes-out horrendous*, I accepted. Later that afternoon, Hérrakí took me to get a tattoo in the shape of a small white fox, as delicate as an old scar.

It winks at me from the soft crook in my elbow.

"I'm so scared," I whisper to Tai, as the breeze ruffles her hair. And it's a strange pleasure to admit it to her: that I'm scared about our project, scared of Nítuchí, scared of how difficult it will be to do what we must do.

"But pretty goddamn grateful too, right?" She rubs my shoulder, her touch like warm, spilling light.

It's so like my sister to counter with something like this—as much as it was her to bolt away from the dark for years and years on end. But it's the same message, ultimately—the same ethos, just reframed: Focus on the light. Except now Tai acknowledges and respects the dark.

She grew, as I did, while our backs were turned these last few years, and we're only now seeing it. Only now seeing each other.

There's the Tai who sparks electric, and the Tai whose warmth soothes. The courageous, optimistic Tai, and the mindful, nurturing Tai. The Tai who works to be someone good, and who can stand on her own two feet without leaning on the attention of others.

There's the Noni whose emotions and *need* overwhelm her, and there's the Noni who acknowledges those emotions as she tries to be as powerful and focused as a human can be. The Noni who believes she deserves to feel content and loved more hours than not, and who knows she can work toward loving herself more every day.

There's Mama, writing a dark fairy tale about loneliness and its antidote, human kindness; and Mama, the sixteen year old prostitute with that awful ice-blond wig, lost in her quest for redemption with a tire iron. There's Mama, her brand of hope spreading through graduates of the institute—and sprinkled into Teddy's strange work the world over—and Mama, the woman who crouched on the bathroom floor beside me, telling me the story of a fox, because it was the closest thing to truth that she could speak while scrabbling up out of a deep well of hopelessness and despair.

Believing she could return is our private tragedy. But it is also a testament to how alive and capable we believed her to be when she was with us: A miracle worker. Our runaway Foix.

Hi, Mama, I think, setting the bouquet of Dad's foxgloves on top of the graciously imperfect stone—a place we'll return to, year after year, for each other. *We see you, too.*

ACKNOWLEDGMENTS

EXT. MAGICAL FOREST GARDEN — NIGHT

In the forest garden: whispering groups of hydran-
geas, ropes of fragrant jasmine, gardenias releasing their midnight scent on the wind. A giant,
ancient maple tree in the center.

A cheerful creature with long seaweedy hair steps
out of a hollow in the tree's trunk. She smiles at
you, the hem of her emerald-green skirt in hand.
It might be made from the maple's spring leaves,
but that wouldn't make sense, would it?

CREATURE
Want to know who brought WHITE FOX to life?

Is she talking to you? You point to your chest, inquiring, and the figure beckons for you to follow her toward the tree.

You follow. Delicately carved into its magnificent bark are the following names:

Sarah Bedingfield, Erin Stein, Kelsey Marrujo, Katie Quinn, Natalie Sousa, Molly Ellis, Mariel Dawson, Allison Verost, Camille Kellogg, Jordin Streeter, Hayley Jozwiak, Stacey Sakal, Carolyn Bull, Katy Robitzski, Raymond Ernesto Colón.

CLR, EAF, WOF, AJF, RCR, MHR, WSR, HDR.

And, well . . . to your surprise, your name is there, too.

You and the creature sit together beneath the tree. Someone has laid out buckwheat tea, sea urchin toasties, and scones spread with butter and mulberry jam. You both dig in. As you eat, the creature begins to glow.

CREATURE
(to herself?)
I got so darn lucky.

You nod along. When you finish your meal, the creature—now glowing so much she looks lit from within—smiles at you again.

You wonder, briefly, if you have sea urchin on your face.

And then her form explodes into tiny, hot heart emoji, rising like steam into the tree's gracious branches. Mysteriously enough, it feels like a warm embrace.